in the heart of the dark wood

BILLY COFFEY

NASHVILLE MEXICO CITY RIO DE JANEIRO

For Will, who doesn't need a
hat to know he's brave.

Published in Nashville, Tennessee, by Thomas Nelson. Thomas Nelson is a registered trademark of HarperCollins Christian Publishing, Inc.

Published in association with the literary agency of WordServe Literary Group, Ltd., 10152 S. Knoll Circle, Highlands Ranch, Colorado 80130.

Thomas Nelson books may be purchased in bulk for educational, business, fund-raising, or sales promotional use. For information, please e-mail SpecialMarkets@ThomasNelson.com.

Library of Congress Cataloging-in-Publication Data

Coffey, Billy.
In the heart of the dark wood / Billy Coffey.
pages cm
ISBN 978-1-4016-9009-0 (paperback)
1. Teenage girls—Fiction. 2. Mothers—Death—Fiction. 3. Virginia—Fiction.
I. Title.
PS3603.O3165I5 2014
813'.6—dc23 2014018966

Printed in the United States of America

14 15 16 17 18 RRD 5 4 3 2

Publisher's Note

Billy Coffey's novels all take place in Mattingly, Virginia, and can be read in any order. If you've already read *When Mockingbirds Sing* or *The Devil Walks in Mattingly,* it may be helpful to know that this story takes place eighteen months after the Carnival Day storm.

Enjoy!

We are not necessarily doubting that God will do the best for us; we are wondering how painful the best will turn out to be.

—C. S. Lewis

And that, of course, is the message of Christmas. We are never alone.

—Taylor Caldwell

December 19

1

Allie Granderson had not cried once in the five hundred forty-two days since everything ended; even as she sat hunched and dying, she vowed not to cry on the five hundred forty-third.

In her mind she saw the class turning to witness her final moments, mouths ajar and eyes wide. All else—the busywork of their ridiculous project, the joy of the coming holiday, the squeak of the gerbil wheel, and the gurgle of the fish tank—would be set aside. Everyone would stare as Allie sloughed off her mortal coil. Lisa Ann Campbell would sob into her sleeve from across the room. Not because Lisa Ann particularly cared for Allie's well-being (or anyone's, for that matter), but because she'd found cause to bawl at least once a day over *something* since the beginning of the school year. That small eruption would be more than enough to light the larger one in Tommy Robertson's stomach. Tommy sat three seats up from Allie in Miss Howard's classroom and spilled his breakfast nearly as regularly as Lisa Ann spilled her tears. His attacks would commence with a suddenness that defied belief; too often, the only foreshock would be the thrusting up of both hands in a vain attempt to gain the teacher's attention. By then it was too late. "Touchdown Tommy" was what the kids called him. The nickname was neither fair nor entirely accurate, but such things mattered little in sixth grade. This was a fact Little Orphan Allie knew well.

The throbbing again—a thousand angry bees swarming in her stomach.

Allie shut her eyes and reached for the broken compass strapped to her left wrist, rubbing it like a worry stone. She drew her legs up and knocked them against the bottom of her desk, scattering both the bottle of Elmer's and the bits of colored paper on top. Her guts were going to explode. She was going to pop like a bubble and ruin Christmas, get her insides all over the posters of the parts of speech and fractions-to-decimals that covered the walls. Lisa Ann would bawl; Tommy would yark. The only thing that made Allie feel better was knowing she wouldn't be embarrassed because she would be dead.

The pain had arrived without warning just after lunch. The Salisbury steak was the most likely culprit—one hunk of gristly meat carved from some poor malnourished beast and drowned in a soupy brown gravy. Zach had warned her not to eat it, but Allie didn't have a choice. She'd barely had enough time to pack her father's lunch that morning, much less fix one for herself.

She folded her arms and hugged herself. The hurt slammed into her like a cold wind. Allie shut her eyes and bit down on the red-and-white checkered scarf around her neck. She leaned down on her desk, feeling the scarf's prickly wool against her tongue, rubbing the compass again. That helped until a ball of notebook paper smacked her cheek.

Zach stared from his seat across the aisle. At some point between Allie eating the Salisbury steak and the Salisbury steak eating her, he'd put on his daddy's old cowboy hat. The library book he'd checked out in second period (something about prehistoric animals of North America; Zach was always into that stuff, and Allie didn't know why—unless of course it was just to impress their stupid teacher) lay on his desk. Resting atop that was Zach's own ornament, nearly complete—he only had to glue the picture of his face onto the elf's body and affix the three cotton balls down the front. He lifted his chin to the note he'd thrown at her. Allie kept her head in place and unfolded it, reading the words sideways:

R U OK?

No, is what Allie wanted to say. *No, I am most definitely not okay because God's calling in the mark He put on me, and this is good-bye, Zach—Vaya con Dios, baby.*

Allie nodded yes instead. She lifted her face from the desk and peeled off a strip of red construction paper that had stuck to the side of her head. The pain ebbed enough for her to nearly straighten. She tried smiling and thought it came through satisfactory enough.

Zach wasn't swayed. He'd seen Allie's fake smile enough times in the last year and a half; he wasn't fooled now. He raised his ornament and mouthed, *Kindergarten stuff.* Allie nodded and realized the longer she stared at him, the quicker her lie would crumble. She looked to the front of the room instead, where she found a bigger problem.

Miss Howard was staring straight at her from the cluttered desk in front of the room. Looking over those old-lady glasses she liked to wear, thinking they made her look so smart. Allie wondered just how long her teacher had been watching and just how much she'd seen. Probably all dang day. Probably everything.

She slipped Zach's note into her pocket. Miss Howard's chair made a raking sound over the floor as it slid back, breaking the sort of fragile peace that is nearly impossible to maintain the last day before Christmas vacation. Allie refused to watch. She was much more concerned with the invisible fist curling its fingers around her guts.

Zach whispered, "Hey."

Allie looked at him and tried not to see Miss Howard walking past the Christmas tree (the ornaments were molecules fashioned by colored cotton balls and pipe cleaners, the star made of five plastic test tubes glued together) to the far end of the room, where she praised Lisa Ann's ornament enough to stay what tears lay waiting in the little girl's eyes. Zach shifted his ornament to his left hand and pointed to Allie's wrist.

"Gonna lose that."

She turned her hand over. Five hundred and forty-two days of wear had turned the compass's band from bright red to a dull pink. The clasp was nothing more than three raised bumps on one end that inserted into three matching holes on the other. Two of those bumps had been worn away. The last hung only by a thin ridge of plastic. Allie clamped the band down and whispered back, "Thanks." Zach tipped his black hat. He was by far the cutest boy in school, but that didn't stop Allie from thinking that hat looked like a sombrero on anyone but the sheriff. A cough echoed through Zach's smile. The sound came out harsh and scratchy.

Miss Howard had covered the entire first row. She stopped at each desk and pushed her blond hair

(blond from a bottle)

behind her ear, smiling at everyone's stupid decoration, making the girls purr like kittens and the boys coo like babies. It was disgusting. Even more disgusting? It was all for show. Allie knew the only reason Miss Grace Howard had gotten up was so she could make her way to the last desk in the last row—so she could once more stick her nose where it didn't belong.

It would suit things just fine if God killed Allie before Miss Howard got there, even if it meant Zach would have to spend the rest of his life lonesome. Then again, Allie thought that if she really was okay with dying in the next few seconds, it would be just like the Almighty to make her stick around. She reclaimed the bottle of glue and bits of construction paper scattered over her desk and began piecing her project together—green shoes and mittens to red arms and legs, red arms and legs to the green body, the picture of herself on top—just as Her Highness had shown them. As though sixth graders had forgotten how to glue and cut.

Miss Howard reached Zach's desk and pronounced his elf "the cutest thing *ever*." That may or may not have been true; Allie guessed her teacher really had no way of knowing because Miss Howard hadn't looked at Zach's elf at all. Her eyes were square on Allie now, and that only made Allie's stomach swirl more.

She wiped the excess glue from her ornament. *MERRY CHRISTMAS DADDY* went diagonally across the elf's swollen belly in pencil. Beneath it and after careful thought, Allie added *AND MOMMY*. The agony swelled again as she finished the downward stroke of the *Y*, this time worse than all the others strung together. Her body folded in on itself once more, making a ball. The smell of Miss Howard's fancy perfume filled her nose.

"Allie?"

She couldn't turn her head. The pain hammered her, making her grimace.

"Allie, are you okay?"

"Yes, ma'am."

Miss Howard bent low and placed a hand on Allie's desk, too close for comfort. Allie glanced up to see her teacher staring at the ornament. Miss Howard's lips parted, meaning to say "That's really lovely" maybe, or "Allie Granderson, that belongs in some fancy Paris museum." But there was only silence.

It's that last little bit, Allie thought. *The* AND MOMMY. *And I'll count it to my credit if I go to my grave reminding you of that, you old battle-ax.*

"Sweetheart, you don't look well."

Allie felt Zach's eyes—felt everyone's. Tommy Robertson turned around in his seat, hoping it was finally someone else's turn to puke all over everything. A part of Allie, that grown-up part she had yet to realize was there, knew whatever had gone wrong inside her wasn't the Salisbury steak. But it was the little girl she remained that looked into her teacher's eyes just then and wondered why Grace Howard had to be so pretty and so nice, and what Allie had done to warrant the life she'd been handed. No answers came. Allie believed none ever would. That silence filled her with an anger that left her reaching for the compass once more. If God was going to kill her, then she wasn't about to let it happen in front of the boy she didn't want to love but did and the woman she wanted to hate but couldn't. And Allie would. Not. *Cry*.

"I think I'd very much like to be excused to the bathroom," she whispered. "If it's okay, Ma'am."

Allie spent the next panicked moment of her life wondering if Miss Howard would not only grant that request but demand to tag along.

"Certainly."

Allie didn't wait. She stood and took her griping stomach out of the classroom, brushing Zach's elbow as she left. One small squeeze, one last good-bye.

At least the hall was empty. Allie held her stomach and pressed her right shoulder against the wall as she walked, using it to brace her failing body. She passed the two remaining sixth-grade classrooms. Tiny sets of eyes stared back, wondering what had happened to her now. The bathroom door stood just down the hallway to the right. Allie reached the first stall just before a final wave of agony shot through her. It was all she could do to remain upright. She couldn't even lock the door.

She unbuttoned her jeans and sat. Both seemed right, even if whatever alarms were blaring inside her had nothing to do with toilet business. The cool of the porcelain soothed her. That feeling disappeared when Allie looked down.

Centered in the jumble of denim and cotton bunched just above her pink Chucks was a red blotch the size of a quarter. Allie bent forward, needing but not wanting a closer look. Her head shook *no*. Slow at first. Then faster.

Allie Granderson would not cry. That was the promise she'd made nearly a year and a half before, because crying meant it was over, and it was a promise she meant to keep. But crying was not the same as screaming, and scream she did. She screamed loud and long and did not stop even when the teacher across the hall burst into the bathroom, wanting to know who was hurt. Allie screamed at her too. She screamed that she was dying. That she was bleeding to death.

2

She didn't look any different, at least according to the mirror. It was still the same brown hair parted down the middle, still the same two pigtails framing the same narrow face. Her clothes still fit. She certainly didn't feel any wiser than she had that morning and felt no sudden interest in purses or makeup. As far as Allie could tell, the only differences between the girl who'd left her bedroom for school that morning and the woman who'd stumbled back in that afternoon were the two things no one could see: angry bees in her stomach, and a disagreeable hunk of smooth gauze the school nurse had instructed her to put in a place where nothing had any business being. She had no idea getting grown-up meant walking around with a grimace on her face and a hitch in her step.

"Wish somebody'd filled me in on that, Sam."

She turned from the mirror to the beagle attached to the thumping tail on the mattress. Allie thought her dog, much like herself, was caught somewhere in the middle place between pup and adult. But that was where their similarities ended. Sam had no center of reference when it came to female afflictions. He raised his floppy ears and barked.

"Dumb old dog."

Allie stepped away from the mirror, pausing to kiss a forefinger and touch the framed picture on her dresser. Her insides still hurt (as did her throat, what with all the hollering she'd done in the bathroom), but her daddy had given her aspirin when they'd gotten home. She scooted Sam away and sat, staring out the bedroom window. A wind gauge stood on the porch just outside. The contraption wasn't much—a small, pink bucket filled with gravel and sand, and a wooden dowel rising from its innards. Two strips of cardboard a foot long and an inch wide had been tacked to the top, forming an X. Fastened to each end was a plastic cup, three blue and one red. Another of Miss Howard's endless classroom projects, this one much more beneficial than the ornament. Aside from needing the cardboard strips and a few of the cups replaced during the past months, the gauge had held up like a marvel of engineering. Allie watched the cups turn in the building wind. She counted the next minute aloud as her fingers tallied how many times the red cup passed.

"Ten. Ten ain't much, is it, Samwise?"

Sam didn't know.

"Nope. Ten ain't much more'n a puff."

It would be a little while before school and work ended. For the moment, the smattering of ranches and Cape Cods along the street stood quiet. All of them bore signs of the season—candles in the windows, bulbs on the trees, lighted icicles hanging from the gutters. Pretty enough, Allie thought, but nothing more than the same-old.

Still, the neighborhood had turned itself into a veritable winter wonderland compared to the Granderson house. The only sign of Christmas there was the leaning pine Allie's father had brought home the week before and plunked down in front of the living room window. The two of them had decorated it in silence; only Sam had commented on the finished product. It was a horrible thing for Allie to endure, having to put all those memories on the tree. That her daddy had to endure it as well only made Allie feel worse. She kept waiting for him to say maybe they should just skip Christmas again, like the town had the year before. But Marshall Granderson had only sat in front of a pile of knotted lights and tinsel, drowning in all that quiet. There in front of the window, Allie considered for the first time that maybe her daddy had been thinking that very same thing. He'd just been wanting Allie to suggest it first—to say that maybe treating Christmas like any other day would make it not hurt so bad.

The only evidence of peace on earth and goodwill to men outside was the Nativity in the front yard. Marshall had hauled the Mary, Joseph, and Baby Jesus out from the shed the previous Christmas, just before the mayor had announced that everyone's heart was still too heavy for joy. Allie had refused to let him box them up ever since. Her father had bucked about the Nativity still being out there when the new year arrived and the season of the not-Christmas was over. He hollered about it again when the grass turned from brown to green and the church folk went from singing about Jesus being born in a cave to Him walking out of one. But Allie had held fast—the Nativity was going to stay put. The last time Marshall had protested (this the summer just past, right at the time of the first anniversary), Allie told him it wasn't right for a family to be boxed up and separated from each other eleven months of the year. Her father hadn't said much after that.

Sam snorted in her face, wanting to trade melancholy for playtime.

"No, Sam. You just sit."

He did, settling on his haunches beside her. They both stared out at the plastic Mary. Allie felt Sam's tail thump her side. She rubbed his neck, making one of his back paws jitter.

She smiled despite herself and said, "You're a stupid dog, and I don't love you at all."

There came a knock at the door, followed by a tired voice: "Allie, can I come in?"

"Sure, Daddy."

The bedroom door eased open. For a brief moment, Allie thought Marshall Granderson had just woken from a long nap. The front of his work shirt hung free of a waist that had withered to the point where he'd had to poke new holes in his belt. His beard had turned more gray than brown in the past year, but Allie thought her daddy still held the handsome look of a brave man trying to shoulder the burdens upon him. He looked from a pair of red eyes at the picture on her dresser and made his way to the bed.

He sat between Allie and Sam and put a hand to her forehead. Two Life Savers clicked in his mouth. "Don't think you got the fever. You feeling better?"

"Some." Allie tried not to curl her nose at the smell. It was like something had crawled down her daddy's throat and died eating an orange and a cherry. "Stomach's settling a bit. It was Salisbury steak day."

Marshall cringed. "I recall those days myself."

"Sorry you had to leave work and come get me."

"Don't you worry about that," he said. "You getting hungry?"

Allie knew what that meant. She shook her head no but said, "I'm fine to get something up for you, though."

"Only if you're able. Better do it soon, though. Bobby's coming over to help with the car. I do believe we almost got that old heap running."

Allie gazed back out the window. "I don't like Bobby," she said. "He looks at me wrong."

"I wouldn't lay too much on that, Allie. Bobby looks at most everybody that way."

She nodded and kept her eyes to the Nativity. Her father's friends had fallen away in the last five hundred and forty-three days (*five forty-four almost*, Allie thought). For reasons Allie could not understand, the hole left by all that loneliness had been filled by the town drunk. Bobby Barnes was at their home at least twice a week, all in the guise of helping to fix the old Camaro Marshall kept in the shed out back. Allie knew better. Bobby and her daddy did more tearing themselves apart than putting a car back together.

"We gotta be in town before dark," Marshall said.

"I don't really want to go tonight, Daddy. It being so cold out. And me unwell."

"You just said you felt better."

"Comes and goes, I guess." She shrugged, needing to change the subject. "Weatherman says snow tonight. We'll have to keep her warm, Daddy."

Marshall looked outside and crunched down on his Life Savers, letting the juice wash over his gums. He still tasted beer. "We'll keep her plenty warm. Tend to it when we get back from town. I promise."

"Wind's gonna blow."

"It'll be fine."

Marshall craned his neck against the window. Allie followed his gaze. Far down the street, a blue Honda turned onto the block.

"Oh no," she said.

Marshall held his gaze as the car came closer. He crunched Life Savers more and swallowed, gripped by a sudden thirst.

"Now don't be like that," he said. "Miss Grace is just heading home's all."

"Plenty of other ways for her to get there than this'n."

She was right—they both knew it, but it didn't matter. Miss Howard's car slowed and turned into the driveway. Sam barked when the tall woman got out. Marshall swallowed. Allie moaned.

"She just wants to check on you," Marshall said.

"Don't need nobody checking on me, and her especially." Allie took her father's sleeve. When he didn't turn, she pulled his face to hers, taking the full brunt of the dead thing in his throat. "She's got wiles, Daddy."

"What you know about wiles?"

Miss Howard reached the porch. She carried a large plastic bag in her hand.

"Nothing," Allie said. "Only that she's got'm."

"You stay here with Sam. I'll go."

The doorbell rang. Marshall patted Allie's leg as he rose and left the door open. She thought maybe that was her daddy's way of asking her to please come out and give Grace a chance. Really, closing the door had been the furthest thing from Marshall's mind. He'd been too busy trying to figure out how many Life Savers it would take to bury the smell of beer.

3

Allie told Sam to stay and crept into the hall, where she heard Marshall say, "Hello, Grace" and "Come in" and "What brings you by?" and heard Miss Howard say something about Allie maybe needing some supplies. Though no longer a praying girl, Allie sent a silent plea into the ether that *supplies* didn't mean what she feared.

She reached a spot at the end of the hallway close to the living room and sank to her stomach, crawling the rest of the way. Miss Howard was sitting on the sofa much too close to her daddy. The bag lay on the coffee table in front of them. She'd folded her overcoat and placed it in her lap, meaning to stay awhile. And she was smiling. That in itself wasn't so strange—Miss Howard was always doing that, always acting like she was just the happiest person in the whole big world—but it was the *way* she was smiling that struck Allie just then. Maybe it was the way the lights from the Christmas tree bounced off her hair or how she looked so fine in her red skirt and white sweater. Maybe it was just the way she was looking at Marshall just then, and how peaceful she seemed. Whatever it was, in that moment Miss Howard looked like she'd just fallen out of heaven. Allie hated her more than ever.

"Went by the pharmacy," Grace said. "Got Allie some things she's going to need."

Marshall rubbed his beard and said, "Well, I appreciate that, Grace, but Allie's feeling some better. Guess the cafeteria ladies decided to clear out any suspect fare before shuttering up for Christmas. I gave her some aspirin a while ago. She'll be fine come morning."

He cleared his throat and swallowed, tasting more candy than beer. Allie's teacher had been inside the Granderson home often over the years, though each time in the past year and a half had been just as awkward and confusing as the last. Miss Grace couldn't so much as have a glass of tea without leaving Marshall convinced he was doing something wrong. He was often sweating by the time she left. What little bit of Marshall that still pondered the condition of his soul believed that particular sensation was the fires of hell already claiming him. He fingered the wedding band on his left hand, twisting it as a reminder even if one was not needed.

"You gave her aspirin?" Grace asked. "You're not supposed to do that, Marshall. Aspirin's a blood thinner."

"What's that got to do with a stomachache?"

"A stomachache?" Grace looked at the bag and pulled her lips inward. They came back red and full, like a blooming rose.

Claws pattered up the hallway. Allie looked back to see Sam coming toward her. He whined, turning Marshall's eyes toward the hall. Allie pulled her dog close, shushing him.

"You didn't talk to the nurse when you picked Allie up?"

"No. Allie came out soon as I pulled up. I didn't even go in."

Allie eased her head out a little more, wanting to see.

"Marshall, you have to go in and sign her out. It's the law. You didn't know that?"

A long pause, then: "I was never the one who'd pick Allie up from school, Grace."

"Oh. Right." Grace kept her eyes away—to Allie, it was as though she'd gotten turned around in a bad place and couldn't find her way out—and smoothed the hem of her skirt. She reached for the plastic bag and moved it away, then reconsidered and moved it closer. "Marshall, you know I care for Allie."

"I do," he said.

"And"—still looking away—"I believe you to be a good friend, always have. So since the three of us have that familiarity, I'd like to say I'm happy to . . . help. However I can. Times like this, it's really nice to have a woman close."

Marshall shook his head, saying, "I don't . . ." and looked back to the hall just as Allie's head disappeared.

"Allie's changing, Marshall."

Allie peeked again as her daddy's attention turned away.

Grace had found courage enough to raise her chin. That brief meeting of their eyes was enough not only for both of them to look away, but Allie as well.

"I know she is," he said. "'Course she is. You show me one person in town who's the same as they were a year and a half ago."

Grace shook her head. "That's not what I mean. Marshall, Allie got her period today. In school. That's why she had to come home."

Allie uttered a low moan and buried her head into Sam's back. Marshall opened his mouth to speak, closed it, opened it again. He looked like a fish that had been plucked from the water.

"That's crazy," he said. "Allie's only eleven. She's just a little girl."

"Happens more than you think," Grace said. "I go through it every year with at least one of my students. I know it's scary. For you, for her especially. But she's growing up, and that's a fine thing. Allie's becoming a woman."

For a long while there was only silence. Marshall sat there swallowing and getting all sweaty. Then he muttered, "The tree."

Allie's presents had already been wrapped and placed there. Dolls and stuffed animals mostly, along with a scooter she'd coveted since summer—all child's toys. She'd picked them all herself, had even stood with Marshall in line at the Walmart watching them make their way down the conveyer. What last vestiges of faith Allie had placed in Santa or magic or everything working out in the end had fallen away since everything ended. Marshall couldn't blame his daughter for that. One look at the bottles stashed in his bedroom closet was all the proof needed to show that much of what he had once believed was gone now too.

"There was a class back in the fall," Grace said. "Family Life is what they call it. All the female students get together with a guidance counselor to discuss this sort of thing. Allie didn't go?"

Marshall shook his head. "I don't remember nothing of that."

"Allie would've had to get you to sign a form saying it was okay for her to attend."

Marshall looked to the hallway again. This time Allie didn't bother ducking away. He said more to Allie than to Grace, "Didn't get no paper to sign."

"Here," Grace said. She slid the bag toward him. "There's plenty to get Allie through the next few months. They were on sale, and I don't want any money. I have something else too." She slipped a hand into her coat. "We were making these in class when Allie had to leave. Thought she might like to hang it on the tree."

She handed Marshall the ornament. Allie watched as Marshall rubbed her picture. He smiled.

"My little elf. Thank you, Grace. That was kind."

"You're welcome. I'd like to talk about what Allie wrote at the bottom."

Allie shook her head. Leave it to Miss Howard to bring that out, all in the grand cause of Talking Things Over.

"I don't think it's healthy for Allie to be writing such things about her mother," Grace said. "I know it's not my place, Marshall, and forgive me if I've overstepped. But Mary's gone. She's been gone for a while now. Pretending she isn't won't make anything better. Allie has to start healing, and before she can do that, she has to grieve."

"We all grieve in our own way," Marshall said. He swallowed again, gripped by that thirst, and thought of the bedroom closet. "We all tell ourselves truth and call that good, and we say the lies we're tricked into believing are bad. I don't think that's right at all, Grace. Whatever carries us through the day, that's what's right and good."

He rose from the couch and placed the ornament high on

the front of the tree, just beneath the blinking star. Allie knew her teacher wasn't convinced by anything her father just said. Miss Howard could speak of healing up and moving on as much as anyone else in Mattingly, but they'd all been spared much of the hell that God had set upon the Grandersons. Marshall opened the drawer on the end table. He returned to the sofa with a stack of cards held together by a thick, rotting rubber band and handed them to Grace.

"Christmas. Birthdays. Valentine's. Easter. Mother's Day. That one especially."

"Why?" Grace asked.

"Because Allie wants to hold on. It's why she sets an extra place at the table each night and why that Nativity's still out in the front yard. Same reason she won't take that compass off her wrist. That was the last thing her momma gave her before she left, and Allie swears she'll still have it on when her momma comes back. And if that's what it takes to get her through, then I say fine. It's good to have a hope, however false that hope may be." He looked at Allie and gritted his teeth, regretting his choice of words. "And who knows, maybe her momma'll do just that someday. Maybe she'll just come on home."

Allie sank her head back into the hallway and stroked Sam's head.

"I understand," Grace said. "It just breaks my heart to see her like this, Marshall. Allie's broken inside. She never smiles, never speaks. I'm worried about her. I know she loves her mother. I know you do too, Marshall. So did I. Mary was a friend."

Allie saw Miss Howard dip her head.

"Allie's gonna be fine," Marshall said. "It's just been a rough afternoon."

Grace wiped her eyes and said, "If you like, I can stay long enough to whip up some supper."

"I appreciate it. But we got company comin', and we gotta head to town first."

"Could use some things from the grocery," Grace said. "I could ride along."

"Sort of a private thing. Apologies."

Allie let Sam go and pushed herself back down the hallway, stopping when the squeaking sounds her belly made on the floor became too loud. She'd never liked their trips to town (and never would), but this trip was enough to get Miss Howard away. Sam followed her back as Marshall showed Grace out. Allie thought her daddy would probably come back to her bedroom and Talk Things Over, all the time holding that bag in his hand. Then she thought no, he'd go to his bedroom closet first. He'd have to go get himself a bottle of courage. Sometimes life was better faced when you were numb. That way, nothing hurt at all.

4

The ride was quiet and broken only by Sam, who sat in the middle of the truck's bench seat and yipped at what little of the world he saw above the dash. His tail slapped against the plastic wrapping around the flowers between him and Marshall. Sam always enjoyed their rides to town, much more than Allie enjoyed having him along. To her, the spot where her dog sat still belonged to someone else.

She shoved her hands into her coat pockets and shivered as heat from the vent sprouted goose bumps on her legs. The sun disappeared behind a bank of gray clouds easing over the mountains.

"Snow's comin'," she said.

Marshall looked out the side window and nodded.

"We're gonna keep her warm, right?"

"Said we would," he said. "Nothing to worry about."

"It'll blow."

"We'll take care of that too."

Marshall's old Ford crept on. Allie stared at the encroaching sky. She was rarely mistaken in her weather predictions. She pored over the back page of each morning's *Gazette* and never missed an evening forecast on the TV. Even some of the teachers at school would ask her when the next snow day would be, or the last frost. Marshall listened with feigned interest as Allie slipped into a lecture concerning cold fronts and northwesterly winds and low pressures. He would take his eyes off the road and nod, seeing not a pig-tailed little girl

(young woman)

but a grown adult on the Channel 3 news, standing beside a map displaying thick, thick clouds hovering over an outline of Virginia and rubbing her compass. Telling everyone the cold was coming and the snow with it, but neither of those really mattered. *It's the wind y'all need to watch,* Marshall could hear her say, *because it's gonna blow, and you better hold tight to the ones you love.*

Allie finished with a report on the wind gauge outside her bedroom window, telling Marshall she and Sam didn't think a ten was bad at all. She squirmed as another shock of pain rushed through her deep places.

"Tummy okay?" Marshall asked.

"Yessir."

"Did you . . . you know. In the bathroom? Before we left?"

Allie winced at the memory of taking that stupid old bag (which, coincidentally enough, had been delivered by The Stupid Old Bag) into the bathroom and opening one of the packages. Turning the pad over in her hands. Trying to remember which way it went. Having to sit on the toilet and fish the messy one from her underwear before wrapping it up in half a roll of toilet paper so her daddy wouldn't see. "I don't really care to speak on what I did in the bathroom, Daddy. It was bad enough having to do it."

Marshall looked back through the windshield. The silence that followed was broken not by Sam, but by the sound of Life Savers being crunched. Marshall wished for a drink and the dark curtain it turned down over his life, making everything seem smaller and farther away.

Cornfields and woods yielded to the manicured lawns and still-empty homes at the edge of town. Marshall turned left at the sign and eased through the iron gates. Much of Oak Lawn still bore the scars of what had happened. Allie had always considered Oak Lawn a happy cemetery before. Now many of the aged oaks and magnolias that had guarded the gravestones were reduced to splintered stumps. Many more had simply been uprooted and flung away, never to be seen again. Only a few remained, lonely and whole. It was the trees that had gone untouched that angered Allie most. Sometimes she dreamed of cutting those survivors down and using them as kindling for the fireplace. In her darkest heart, Allie thought it would have been better if everything and everybody had been taken. That would have at least been fair.

The truck weaved along the slender lane that snaked its way among rows of the numbered dead and stopped at the foot of a knoll. A sudden wind whipped against the driver's side door, shaking both the truck and Allie. Sam yelped and crowded close.

"Ready?" Marshall asked.

Allie's reply was both immediate and the same as it had been all the times before: "I'd rather not, sir, seeing as how that ain't her over there."

And just as he had all the times before, Marshall smiled and said, "I think you should try. You might find you feel better after."

"You don't ever feel better after."

Marshall looked down, nodding again. Allie shook her head. That was all her daddy ever did nowadays. Nodded. It was like someone he couldn't see kept punching him in the face, and he was just trying to stay upright.

"There's value in getting things off your heart and out in the open," he said.

Allie sank deeper into the seat. Her right hand found the compass on her left wrist. "Ain't got nothing on my heart needing let off," she said. "What's in there's just stuff worth hanging on to." Then, under her breath, "No matter what other folk think."

"Sure?"

Allie said the one thing she thought would put the matter to rest, at least for this visit: "My stomach hurts."

Marshall glanced down the row of stones and (of course) nodded. "All right, then. I'll leave the truck running. Getting cold out here."

"It's gonna blow."

"We'll take care of it," he promised. "Soon as we get some supper in us. Deal?"

Allie didn't say. Marshall leaned over Sam and pecked her between the pigtails, then gathered the flowers from the seat. Cold wind enveloped the inside of the truck when he opened the door. Allie's eyes bulged. Her hand pressed down over the compass. Marshall offered a quick thumbs-up that made Sam bark and Allie turn her head.

She looked only when her daddy's back was to the side window. Marshall walked hunched over against the increasing weather, past a collection of headstones and marbled crosses that stretched back generations. Here and there, tiny flags flapped—stars and bars for those who'd fallen from Yorktown and Normandy to Khe Sanh and Helmand province, the battle flag of the Confederacy for those who'd succumbed to what many in Mattingly still referred to as the War of Northern Aggression. The banners were faded and their edges frayed, barely clinging to the cold earth.

Midway down the row rested a headstone that had required no righting after the tornado struck on Carnival Day five hundred and forty-three days past. In many ways, that fury had placed the marker there. Fifty-seven similar headstones could be found spread out over the twelve acres of gray grass and rolling hills called Oak Lawn. That's how many souls had been taken that day. And of those fifty-eight, the wind had kept only one.

Allie watched as Marshall set the flowers into a metal vase built into the side of the marker, removing the withering bouquet he'd placed there a week before. Mary Granderson's name was carved into the center of the stone, along with *September 21, 1974*—the day she'd entered the world. The day she'd left stood blank. Allie refused to let her daddy have the date of Carnival Day 2012 carved there, nor any other. And though she believed Marshall Granderson had made a great many poor choices since her momma left, he'd shown right judgment with that. Allie had done more than enough in allowing a funeral service for one pink tennis shoe.

Allie pushed her checkered scarf to the side and eased up the left sleeve of her coat. The plastic bubble over the compass was scratched and dented. A thin layer of fog—likely from washing her hands after that terrible business in the bathroom—partially hid the black needle inside. A thick circle of cardboard lay beneath, curled and moldy. The once-dark letters marking the cardinal points had long faded, but Allie had no need to see them. The compass had never actually worked. Really, an old thing your momma won from some carny game couldn't be held up as a bastion of reliability. The needle had swung free at first but never really pointed anywhere, then had frozen altogether sometime after the tornado hit. It had been stuck ever since, pointing down.

"Pointin' southward, Samwise. I do believe there's a sense of irony to that, don't you?"

Sam whined.

"Daddy's wrong, though, what he said to Miss Howard. Only false hope in our house ain't mine. It's his. That's what he keeps in those bottles hidden in his closet. This here compass, though? Momma put this on me and said that's how I'd find her that day. You remember that?" She looked at Sam. "No, 'course you don't. You were just a little guy on a farm, way away from all that. But she did, Sam. That's what Momma said."

She looked out the window to her father, all slouched over in front of that grave with his hands clasped in front of his work clothes, head down and face straining. His lips moved. Marshall always talked to that tombstone. Sometimes, if the weather was okay and if Allie didn't start leaning on the horn, he'd stand there half an hour or more. Allie could never tell what he said, and he never volunteered. She thought maybe her father was just saying how much he missed her momma and how he had a hurt that wouldn't go away, but maybe that's fine because that hurt at least meant he was still alive. Or that their baby girl was growing up now, and that scared him because he had no idea how to train a baby girl up to be a woman.

In fact it was all of those things and more that Marshall Granderson touched upon while standing all alone in the cold. Mary had always been the only one he could ever really talk to. Her and Grace, at any rate, though Marshall would not dare admit that, not to anyone and especially not standing in front of his wife's grave. He looked to Allie (who looked away) and began speaking to the only thing of Mary Granderson's the wind had left behind, telling the pink tennis shoe buried inside the coffin that Allie hurt just as much as he did, and that was the thing that had crept between them. That pain was wide and tall, and neither of them could see around it to each other. He told the gravestone the reason Allie was so sad and scared was because she was just trying to keep believing. He said their little girl had been cleaved in two, part of Allie believing her momma was gone and the other part believing her momma was not gone forever, and sooner or later one half would grow strong enough to eat the other.

"I don't know what'll come of it," he whispered. "I don't know what to do. What do I do, Mare?"

The plot of ground didn't answer. Allie believed it never would; her momma wasn't in there at all. Yet Marshall remained there for a long while just in case, his feet set against the dead grass and the wind gathering around him. Tears fell hard against his cheeks. Allie watched until her daddy finally turned back. The only thing she said when he climbed back into the truck was to look out the windshield, where the first flakes of snow sailed in the breeze.

5

Supper was never much. Mary Granderson was (*is*, Allie was quick to amend) known to the people of Mattingly as a Good Woman—a vague term that combined many attributes in many ways, but in which knowing how much sugar to put in the iced tea and just when the rolls were baked through played a vital part. That responsibility had been passed to Allie since her mother left. By most accounts, and her own especially, she had failed that task miserably.

Allie and Marshall had been visited by most of Mattingly's residents in the weeks after Carnival Day. Most had arrived bearing the proper offerings for the grieving. Casseroles abounded, along with meat and vegetables and more pies than Marshall could count.

Allie had near starved out of her refusal to eat any of it.

Having all those people stop by just to cry on about how sad and awful Allie's world had become was a horrible thing to endure. The cavalcade of preachers was worse. They rolled in one by one, making sure Allie and Marshall didn't stray from the flock in light of what they termed "the unpleasantness." Marshall showed them the door right away. When they appealed to Allie's sensibilities by asserting there was no graver condition than being fallen away from the Lord, she merely asked them why the Lord had taken her momma away. Five hundred and forty-three days later, Allie had yet to receive a satisfactory answer.

On that night—the night when everything that had ended would begin again—it was mac and cheese from a box with boiled hot dogs mixed in. The entire meal was eaten with the usual silence and in the usual presence of the empty plate, glass, and chair between Marshall and Allie. Marshall pushed away from the table sometime after, deeming the meal a masterpiece. Allie respected her father too much to entertain the thought of that praise being more for her effort than the final product. He never told Miss Howard any of the meals she brought over were masterpieces. Then again, Allie thought her daddy would likely praise Miss Grace's cooking if he bothered to take the fork out of his mouth long enough to say so. The cold from the drive had left him near starved, but as Allie cleared the table, she saw half of her daddy's food scooted to the side of his plate.

"Some masterpiece," she said.

Much of Allie's own meal had gone untouched as well, though for different reasons. Her stomach had started up again when they'd gotten back from town; the business she had to do in the bathroom again had taken care of what appetite she'd had left. She scraped both plates into Sam's bowl. He sniffed and snorted and finally ate, no doubt cursing his dog's life. Marshall excused himself, promising there was still plenty of time to care for the Nativity before company came. If Allie harbored any hope that her father would honor that pledge, it disappeared as soon as she heard his bedroom door close and his closet door open.

The hard wind from outside and the clanging of the dishes in the sink drowned the sound of the arriving truck sometime later. All Allie heard was the front door opening and a slurred voice that called, "Marshall?"

Sam reared up and ran, his long claws clacking as they searched for a grip on the kitchen linoleum. The deep bark he offered came more from the beast he believed himself to be than the pup he mostly was.

Beyond the kitchen wall came a shrill laugh, followed by, "Marshall? You come on out here. Cujo looks hungry."

Allie dried her hands and her compass with a dish towel and poked her head around the corner. Bobby Barnes stood with his back near the front door, rubbing his beard with three soiled fingers. A beer can shook in his other hand. The trucker's cap he always wore sat cocked on his greasy head, the front smeared with so many stains that whatever it advertised had long been erased. Flakes of snow dotted the brim and melted into brown streaks. His jeans were frayed and pocked with holes that teased the two pale, skinny legs beneath. Sam secured his position in the empty place where the living and dining rooms met. His mouth pulled back to reveal rows of sharp, white teeth.

Bobby looked at Allie long enough to say, "Don't you know manners, girl? You're supposed'a keep hold of something like that when you get comp'ny."

Allie draped the dish towel over her shoulder. "It's manners for company to knock instead of barging on in, too, Bobby Barnes."

She walked to Sam and laid a hand to his head. He hid his teeth. The growl remained.

Bobby stayed in his place. "Where's your pa?"

"Back in his room."

"You ain't gonna invite me in?"

"I would," Allie said. "Doubt if Samwise would, though. He's the one you should probably mind. He might be small, but he's brave."

Bobby smiled and rocked back on his heels, knocking himself against the back of the door. He pointed his beer at Allie. "That's funny. You're a funny girl." He looked past them to the table beyond. "Cleanin' up supper, I see. That empty plate 'n' glass for me?"

"It's spoken for. Ain't no food left, neither. Daddy ate it all. Said it was a masterpiece."

"Bet it was. I bet it was just that." Bobby took a step forward. His eyes fell on Allie in that strange way they always did, like he was looking at her but trying to imagine something else. Sam leaned against his back legs and growled louder. Allie loved her dog for that, no matter if she wasn't supposed to love him at all. "You doin' well with what you been given, Allie Granderson. I'll give you that. You'll make a fine woman one day, as your momma was. I ever tell you that?"

He had. And each time Bobby's eyes got that same look in them as Allie's daddy when Miss Howard brought over a roast or a plate of fried chicken. It was a hungry look, the gaze of a man who would gorge himself once he got the chance to eat. Bobby took another step forward and bumped against the Christmas tree.

Allie was about to turn Sam loose, yell out that drunk old pervert probably tasted a lot better than mac and cheese from a box. But as those words came over her mouth, the bedroom door down the hall opened.

There were times when Allie thought her father kept something more powerful than a few bottles hidden in his closet; he kept another him in there as well—someone who looked just like himself on the outside, but was mean and hurtful underneath. That way, when the Marshall Granderson who praised Allie's meals and visited the empty hole at Oak Lawn grew weary of the mark God had left upon his family, he could retreat to that closet and let the other Marshall take his place. When Allie saw the tall shadow moving toward her from down the hall and those deep, glassy eyes, she knew which of him had walked out. A silent argument between two opposing voices broke out in her mind.

Don't think ill of him; that's just Daddy drawing down his curtain after going to Oak Lawn, said one.

Marshall Granderson's got no qualms letting his daughter see that Other in him, but he'd do most anything to keep that away from Miss Grace, said the second.

Allie normally took a keen interest in such inner conversations, paying close attention to which voice turned out the victor. That night she didn't care which won. All that mattered was that someone looking like her daddy was coming and Bobby Barnes was backing away.

"What the world's all that yapping for, Allie?" Daddy asked. "You get hold a'that dog before I get hold a'you."

"Acted like it wanted to kill me, Marshall," Bobby said. "Don't you feed that mutt?"

Marshall moved into the living room past Allie without so much as an *excuse me*. His knee bumped Sam's head, and the dog jumped, confused. Allie reached down and rubbed Sam's side.

"Feed him what we got," Marshall said. "Which ain't as much as we used to have."

Bobby said, "I hear that. You ready? Car ain't gonna fix itself, and I got a cold in me that needs warming."

"Come on, then." Marshall took the flannel coat from the hook by the door. "Allie, you finish up the dishes. Get your homework done before you go to bed."

"Don't have any, Daddy," she said. "It's Christmastime."

"You mind me now." He looked at her and then at the glowing tree in front of the window as though it had sprouted up through the carpet.

Bobby opened the door, letting in the light from the porch.

"Daddy? You said we'd take care of her."

He turned. Those eyes, big and shiny.

"It's gonna blow," Allie said.

"Marshall." Bobby took hold of his sleeve, pulling him. "What the world's she talking about?"

"Never mind," Marshall told him. He turned to Allie. "We'll get it. Bobby and me." He stepped onto the porch as Bobby spoke again. Marshall's answer wasn't one he counted on Allie hearing, but the wind carried the words inside: "Just shut up. It don't matter anyway."

She followed them to the door. Snow fell silent and steady, powdering the dull grass. Marshall and Bobby faded beyond the porch light's arc and brightened again once they fell into the three soft glows coming from the Nativity. Sam pressed his nose against the glass door, watching them go.

Marshall stood there, staring, saying something to Bobby, who leaned back and laughed in his usual way. The sound of that drunken cackle seeped into the living room, turning Allie's cheeks red and stinging the corners of her eyes. Marshall shrugged and shook his head. He accepted the can Bobby pulled from his coat pocket.

Allie believed neither of them would take care of what needed to be done—what her daddy had promised *would* be done—and that stung her eyes even more. She bit down on the soft gum of her cheek, hoping the pain would keep her tears at bay. That tactic had worked often since everything ended. Now it failed her. Of all the horrid things the day had brought to Allie Granderson, the feeling of those tears welling in her eyes frightened her most of all.

It was Bobby who saved her in that final moment, the town drunk who'd taken up with her father because they shared nothing more than a love of drink and a hole in their hearts. Bobby was the one who leaned in and put a hand to the Mary's shoulder, rocking her back and forth. He rested his beer atop her head, nudged Marshall's shoulder, then moved his hand toward the Mary's chest. Allie found the anger that surged through her did what the pain in her mouth could not. Those tears melted away by the heat flooding her cheeks.

She burst from the door and onto the porch. "Bobby Barnes, you get away from there."

Marshall turned and began to speak. Allie cut him off.

"You hear me? You get away. You, too, Daddy. I don't want y'all near—"

(*my momma*, she almost said, and those two words caught in Allie's throat such that she nearly choked)

"—there. I'll do it myself."

Bobby laughed. "Girl, what you saying? Get on back inside afore you catch a cold."

Wind gusted. Allie heard the clacking of the gauge on the porch and felt the snow against her bare feet. Marshall looked as though he wasn't sure what was happening.

"You get away," she said again. "I'll tend to her. You two just go back to goin' to hell."

"Allie," her father yelled.

"Get away."

She wanted nothing more than to go back inside. The snow

stung her toes and the wind was cold and blowing harder, snatching her anger and replacing it with fear. And her stomach hurt, her blessed stomach, and how had she walked around for eleven years with all those woman parts, and why hadn't her momma told her it was going to be this way?

Marshall was the first to go. Bobby trudged off behind him. They fell into the darkness around the side of the house and were gone. Allie remained on the porch, shaking from more than the cold. She found that not even rage could keep her eyes from stinging.

6

Allie went inside long enough to put on her pink Chucks and checkered scarf. She took another scarf from her bedroom as well, this one thicker and striped with orange and blue. That and an extra rock should be enough; there was no sense in going overboard. The neighbors had loved Mary Granderson just as much as everyone else in town had loved her. As such, Allie and her father remained in the street's finest graces. Marshall called them all Good Folk. Allie thought that true enough in the sense that they kept their sins locked up in their houses rather than showing them off in their yards. She vowed to do the same. It wouldn't do well for the neighborhood to look out the next morning and find proof that Little Orphan Allie had officially fallen off her rocker.

Sam appeared to understand the seriousness of his master's undertaking. He waited at the back door and did not so much as wag his tail when Allie came around the corner into the hallway. She considered telling him to stay, then thought better of it when she remembered Bobby Barnes was out there and likely now as drunk as her father. If it came to it, Allie greatly preferred Bobby looking at Sam's bared teeth than at her.

"You gotta be quiet, though," she told him. "That's the only way I'll let you come, Samwise."

Sam offered a short, high whine and laid his ears down.

"All right, then." Allie faced the door. The wind rattled the glass, making her shiver already. "Come on. Sometimes you gotta do for others what pains for yourself. It means more that way. You stay close, Sam. I don't love you, but I don't care to lose you, neither."

She turned the knob. The wind seemed waiting for just that and pushed against the door, wanting to keep Allie there. She pushed back harder and stepped onto the tiny back porch. The snow came heavy now, nearly driven sideways by the gusts. If there was one blessing in all those flakes, it was that they reflected the puny light on the wall beside her. The backyard held the look of fuzzy evening, laying the path to the shed clear.

Sam followed her out. His nose tilted to the wind, catching faraway smells. Allie put a finger to her lips, reminding him of his promise. Not that it mattered. Marshall had raised the shed's bay door enough for the music inside to pour out. It wasn't loud, but it would be plenty to drown out whatever racket the dog had a mind to make.

She eased away from the porch and cut to the shed at an angle, stopping when they reached the edge of the blue tarp Marshall had laid over the woodpile. Beside it in the shape of a cairn were the rocks Allie and her daddy had gathered from the garden the summer before. One near the top felt heavy enough to do the job.

Neither wrenches nor hammers sang out from inside the shed, nor did Allie expect to hear any. There was only the music along with Bobby's muffled voice and the sound of her father saying, "I gotta get that thing outta the front yard, Bobby. Can't let Allie run ever'thing. Dad-blamed house looks like white trash as it is."

Allie heard the *hiss-pop* of another can. Bobby said, "Know what you need? A good woman in the house."

"Don't need no woman."

"Seems t'me you do. Allie's gettin' close to age. She could use another momma, Marshall. I hear Grace Howard calls on you regular. Wouldn't mind takin' a peek under all them pretty dresses she wears."

"You never mind Grace Howard," Marshall said.

"Mary's gone, Marshall. She ain't comin' back. Best you get on with things."

Allie slunk off before she heard anything else. She carried the rock in one hand and the striped scarf in the other, whispering, "To me, Sam" so her dog wouldn't stray. The light on the back porch ended at the side of the house, making for a long walk into darkness that chilled her more than the cold. The Nativity's glow waited on the other side. Snow pecked the side of Allie's face as they reached the driveway. She was well aware of how quick the cups were clicking on the wind gauge and did her best to set aside fear and embrace purpose. Sam must have sensed her unease. He remained close and matched Allie's steps.

She found the orange extension cord leading from the porch and lifted it out of the snow, looking for any frayed spots that could short out the wires inside. There were none, nor did Allie find any in the white plugs jutting from the backs of the plastic holy family. The wind rushed again, hurling tiny balls of ice against her face. Allie knelt behind the Mary and unscrewed the back with a thumbnail. She eased away the light bulb inside and peered through the opening. The rocks in the Mary's base were stacked to the first fold of her painted blue dress.

Normally, that would be fine. Tonight, however, “It’s gonna blow.”

Sam snorted in agreement. Allie slipped the new rock down inside. It fell atop the others with a satisfying *thunk*.

“That oughta do it.”

A cold wet seeped through her jeans and tennis shoes. Allie rose, made a half circle in the snow, and faced the Nativity. The babe lay snuggled in a thick blanket of shining plastic straw. His eyes lay closed, giving the illusion of sleep, though the thin smile that crested Baby Jesus’s lips hinted that he wasn’t. Allie didn’t know by whose hand the Nativity had been made (it had all come in two boxes from the Walmart, years before everything ended), but she thought whoever it was must have been possessed by genius. It would take no less than that to craft such a perfect expression of peace. And though she no longer cared to ponder such things, Allie paused there in the midst of the storm to consider that was likely just how Jesus had looked on that Christmas night long ago—not simply peaceful but happy, and not because He was God in a diaper. No, it was because His momma and daddy had knelt over Him in Bethlehem just as they knelt over him now in Allie’s front yard—arms folded in front of them not in prayer as much as adoration, heads tilted down to their child, forming a kind of heart shape between them.

Allie took a step to her left and crouched down, not wanting to touch the ground and let the snow further soak her jeans. Snow and wind combined to make a plinking sound against the white plastic cloak. The shine from the light bulb inside sparked against the brown of paint of the hair. In all the months the Nativity had sat in the front yard, she had never spoken to the Mary. Doing so would be almost as ridiculous as her daddy talking to a buried shoe. And yet as Sam took his usual place beside her, Allie found the ache in her heart had parted her lips.

Perhaps it was because Christmas was so near, and that was the season when everything seemed twice as sad. Or maybe it was simply that Allie was cold and alone in the dark, and this was the first time she'd crouched in front of the Nativity not as a girl, but as a woman.

"Merry Christmas, Momma," she said. "I don't know where you are or what you're doing, but I hope you're well. I hope you come home soon. If you can't, send word. I'll find you."

She wrapped the striped scarf around the Mary's neck twice and knotted it. The wind played with the edges as it played with Allie's pigtails. Sam whined. Allie agreed. She pulled off her own scarf and knotted that one around Mary's neck too.

"Love you, Momma," she said, knowing those words were safe for a piece of plastic even if they were poison to anyone else. "You stay warm."

Sam growled. It was deep and low as before, signaling trouble rather than sadness. He rose up on all fours and stared out toward the far side of the house. Allie looked that way, biting back a wave of fear. The body that appeared from there looked too small and walked too straight to be Bobby Barnes, and the hat it wore looked much too large to be Bobby's old trucker's cap. She relaxed as Zach's shape morphed in the Nativity's light. He pushed his bike alongside him.

"What're you doin' here?" Allie asked.

He came around to the front of the Nativity and put the kickstand down, stooped to rub Sam's ears. "Good t'see you too."

"You can't be here, Zach. My daddy sees you, he'll throw a conniption."

Zach said, "I ain't scared of your daddy." He tilted his head to the red truck in the driveway, letting the hat shield his face from the snow. "Bobby Barnes, neither. I'll finish whatever trouble they've a mind to start. And that ain't no way to talk to the man who snuck out his house and rode all the way down here in a blizzard to see if you're still livin'. Gonna lose that." He pointed to Allie's wrist.

She looked and pressed down on the clasp of her compass, then snugged her sleeve against it. Zach smiled as though he owned not just the night and the snow, but everything else too. Allie thought it the most stupid thing in the world, him riding all the way out there. Zach would face the wrath of God if his parents found out. He'd face far worse if Marshall caught him. Allie smiled anyway. Zach could have cracked his head open on the two miles he'd pedaled from his house to hers or frozen to death with a hat full of snow, but he'd risked it anyway, and for her alone.

"I been peckin' on your window so long my fingers hurt," he said. "What you doing out here?"

She pointed at the two scarves blowing in the breeze and said, "Tending to things."

Zach looked at the Mary and coughed hard into his sleeve. "What'd you come down with that made you leave school?"

"Nothing. It'll pass in a few days."

"You sure? People were talkin'."

"People always talk."

"Well, you missed it. Tommy got up to sharpen his pencil soon as you left and puked everywhere. Some of it splashed on Lisa Ann. Surprised you didn't hear her bawling. She near knocked the tree over with all her gyratin'."

Allie beamed. Only Zach could make her smile like that, and at such a sad time.

"Momma and Daddy gotta work tomorrow," he said.

"My daddy too."

"Wanna do something?"

"Somebody'll see. They'll tell."

"Ain't nobody gonna see," Zach said. "And who cares if they do? Let'm tell your daddy if they want."

Allie said, "It ain't you he hates, Zach. I'll get in trouble."

Zach didn't ask again. He was brave (Allie thought none were braver, not even Zach's daddy, the sheriff), but he was not reckless.

"All right, then," he said. "Guess I'll head back. Momma thinks the only thing keeping my cold from turning to the plague is her checking on me every fifteen minutes. Glad you're okay."

He rubbed Sam again and mounted his bike. The snow wasn't deep enough to catch in the tires, but Zach popped a wheelie anyway. Again, just for her. Allie watched as he pulled onto the road, hat tight over his ears and body leaning into the wind. He rode slow and easy like a cowboy on his steed, and Allie understood two things.

One was that Zach Barnett was the best person she'd ever known.

The other was that he was the only light left in her life.

7

Allie took Sam inside and dried both him and herself, then changed into a pair of flannel pajamas. Her stomach hurt again. She thought maybe it'd be best to take one last trip to the bathroom and dig out the two boxes of horrible things she'd hidden in the bowels of the cabinet beneath the sink. But no. She'd had enough of womanhood for one day.

She shut her bedroom door and was making her way to bed when she caught sight of herself in the mirror. Allie turned to the side and curled the back of her shirt in a fist, pulling it tight against her body. The two small bumps jutting out from her chest hadn't gone unnoticed; they'd been there for quite some time. Allie had managed to hide them well enough from the people who mattered, namely Zach. That would likely be more difficult now.

"'Cause I got the hormones," she told Sam. "That means all kinds of bumps'll be sprouting up on me, Sam. Not just on my front, neither. My face too. I seen it happen plenty from the eighth graders. Large pepperoni to go, extra cheese. That'll be me."

Sam barked his sympathy. Allie sighed and faced the mirror again. She let go of her shirt and rolled her shoulders forward, hiding her chest. That was better.

The framed picture stared from the dresser. The woman there was dark-haired and smiling, leaning against a fence post. She wore a pair of faded jeans and a white sweater. The trees behind her were thinning; what leaves remained had gone from green to bright yellows and oranges. A gold cross hung from a thin chain around her neck. The woman was smiling and happy and full of joy when that snapshot was taken, and had no idea she'd be gone a year later. That picture was the last thing Allie had seen before sleep every night for the past five hundred and forty-two days, but it was the first time she'd ever paused to notice Mary Granderson's own bumps, and how big they were.

Her stomach rolled again. Sam whined beside her.

"You got that right. Next time the river swells in spring, Sam, you just cling to me. We'll float on out of here together on my natural buoyancy."

Allie crawled into bed. She took one more look out the window to check the wind gauge and the Mary, then settled beneath her covers. Sam lay beside her, his head on Allie's chest. She rubbed his ears.

In a voice so quiet she barely heard it herself, she said, "I can't grow up, Sam. I just can't."

Sleep fell soon and deep. Allie didn't hear her daddy stagger back inside the house an hour later and crawl into a bed far less crowded than it once was. Nor did she see him lying there, remembering the gentle curve of his wife's hip and the way her hair would spill over her pillow, and how he would sometimes wake late in the night and move his hand over the smooth part of her stomach. Just to make sure Mary was okay. Just to make sure she was there. When the sobs began soon after, only Sam raised his head.

Marshall was too drunk and the curtain pulled too tight for him to see Bobby Barnes standing in front of the three soft lights huddled in the front yard, believing it the perfect place to relieve himself of the twelve-pack he'd downed that night. He laughed as he did. He laughed more at the sight of the two scarves around the Mary's plastic neck. When he finally backed his truck out and headed for downtown, Allie's red-and-white checkered scarf hung around his neck.

And no one, not Allie or Marshall or Bobby or Miss Grace Howard or Zach, no one at all, heard the single great roar of wind that came later. It swept down from the mountains violent and sudden, swirling through the deep places in the forests, raking the fragile neighborhoods just beyond town. It poured over Miller's Bridge before racing along the empty streets of Mattingly, pulling wreaths and lights in tow. It gathered even more as it raced across the empty fields and ruined plots of land, swirling into mini funnels. By the time it reached Allie's neighborhood, the roar had become a black train. It slammed against her bedroom window with a shudder that made her jerk and whimper in her sleep, then sheared away the wind gauge outside and swirled the last remnants of snow into a thick white blanket.

The gust was gone as quickly as it had come. The night settled into silence. And in the Grandersons' front yard, two plastic figures glowed where three had once been.

December 20

1

No matter how hardened Allie's world had become since her momma left, she greeted each sunrise with a dare of hope. Night frightened her just as much as everything else; nights with a strong wind frightened her especially. She held her eyes closed and smelled the heavy stench of dog breath close. A wet nose bumped her cheek. There was a smile hidden in Allie's flinch as she pushed Sam away. The nose came back harder and wetter.

"Get away from me, you old dog," she said. "Go brush your canines."

Sam snorted as though offended and buried himself under the blankets. He tickled Allie with his tail, tempting her to peer out from behind her eyelids. She clenched them tighter—not yet.

"You ain't ever in a bad mood, are you, Samwise?" As far as Allie knew, that was the chief difference between them. It was also a point of existential agony. "Maybe that's why Daddy brought you home. Maybe he thought you'd teach me to be how I used to be."

From beneath the blankets, a low yawn.

"You be still now. Gotta see where I stand from where I lay."

There was a time (five hundred and forty-four days ago, in fact, back when it was Mary Granderson's chore to wake Allie every morning rather than a smelly dog's) when the first order of business for any day was prayer. Nothing extravagant or drawn out like the speeches Allie had to endure in church; a simple hello and thank-you was usually enough. Those prayers had continued on in vague fashion after Mary left, though by that point they were expressed more through Allie's mouth than her heart.

And then one morning—this was three days after the funeral and the night after Bobby's first visit to the Grandersons' shed, when he'd looked at Allie in that hungry way and asked what she'd done to anger the Almighty so much, because God had marked her—Allie had merely stared at the ceiling. Hello and thank you seemed the two worst things she could say. To her reckoning, God had gotten mad at everyone in Mattingly. He'd tried to kill them all and had murdered some and had taken her momma away. Allie hadn't known what Bobby meant by a mark (nor did she still, except that it conjured an image of Cain wandering in the land of Nod, always looking back to see who was gaining on him). And yet God had marked her sure enough—Allie could feel it even then, that sensation of always being watched. To her reckoning, no one could be expected to have a thankful heart while in the possession of such information. Saying hello to the Lord on that long-ago morning felt about as smart as a deer abandoning a good hiding spot from the hunter chasing it. And so Allie had just stared at the ceiling with her eyes clenched, too afraid to utter a single word. To her mind, it was the best prayer she'd ever offered. It was also her last.

Yet even the most worldly soul longs for the comfort of ritual, and Allie was no different. What came to replace her morning prayer was a kind of silent inventory covering everything from bodily functions to daily to-dos. Allie gave no thought as to why this small act had grown to contain such great importance, though she was smart enough to understand it was a way of reminding herself she was basically on her own now, and therefore responsible for herself. She still had her daddy, of course. But often the best Marshall Granderson could offer was the weaker half of himself, the one who needed his food cooked and his clothes washed and a stern reminder to put the toilet seat down. Sam at least offered a whole self and did not possess some inner evil twin. But that whole self was still nothing more than a beast incapable of knowing that a world in which he peed upon nearly everything could just as easily pee on him.

That left Zach. Zach was enough.

So Allie finally opened her eyes that morning to the very ceiling that had once caught her prayers and took an account of her life as it was. The date was December 20—five hundred and forty-four days since her momma left and five days until Christmas. Her stomach did not hurt so bad at all—a welcome surprise on a bodily level, even if deep down Allie knew it was never about the pain anyway, at least not really. She peeked under the covers. Thankfully, the only wet thing she felt was Sam's nose. The light oozing through the slats of her blinds looked more yellow than white. That meant the snow was over. Already she could hear the steady drip of water down the gutter. The house was hers until evening. Bobby wouldn't be coming over, nor did Allie expect Miss Howard. All things considered, the day bode well.

"I wouldn't trade it for a ham sammich."

She rolled to her side and turned the rod on the blinds, letting the outside in. Sam crawled from beneath the covers and laid his front paws on the sill. Allie saw his ears perk and his head cock to the right. His tail, which had come preset to speeds of fast or dangerous, hung limp between his legs. He whined.

"What's the matter?"

Allie sat up and nudged him away. The world beyond lay

bathed in a melting layer of white that served as a frame for what sat in the front yard. Allie tried to blink the sight away, certain it wasn't there. It came back even brighter.

A blue tarp had been draped over the place where the Nativity sat, pinned to the ground by a ring of heavy brown rocks. Its plastic skin rippled over a low breeze that sighed through the spaces between the rocks. That wind rose and was trapped, making the topmost part flutter like a banner.

"*Vandals*," Allie said. "Vandals hit."

She bolted from the bed and ran, stopping only to pull on her Chucks. Sam bounded after her and barked, wanting Allie to stop, to explain things. There was not enough time and too much anger. Allie made the turn into the living room too fast and slammed her shoulder into the wall, making the ceiling lights shake. She stumbled toward the door. There she stopped.

Taped at her eye level to the back of the front door was a single sheet of paper bearing the quick, jagged scrawls of her father's handwriting. Allie tore it away, leaving a bit of tape behind. Sam barked once, if not demanding an answer, then protesting the sudden end to their play. As Allie read, his heavy breaths were drowned out by her own:

> Allie, snow got on your Nativity. I covered it up to keep them warm. Please don't bother them, okay? Promise me. We'll take care of them when I get home.
>
> Love,
>
> Daddy
>
> P.S. Don't look, okay? I'll call when I'm on break.

She studied the words again, then lowered the note. Sam moved forward. He sniffed the page, then placed his nose against the door.

"He don't want me to. See here? Daddy says stay away. It weren't no vandals at all, Samwise. They was just cold is all."

Sam whined and scratched at the door. Allie leaned behind the Christmas tree and moved the curtain aside, peering out of the big double windows.

"Guess you gotta take care of your business, though. 'Course you do. Daddy probably figured that." The tarp (the one off the woodpile, Allie guessed) flapped over the Mary, her husband, and their child. It reminded her of a finger extended from a closed fist, beckoning her to come see. "I gotta let you out, right, Sam? Can't have you messing in here."

She laid the note on the television stand. Sam waited until Allie cracked the door and bolted out. Whatever business he had to take care of that morning apparently could wait. He ran straight for the tarp, leaving Allie alone on the porch.

"I didn't know." She looked around, almost expecting someone to accuse her. "How's I supposed to know Sam would do that? Now I gotta go get him."

She moved off the steps, telling herself that was all she was doing, just fetching her dumb old dog and nothing more. It really wouldn't be disobeying if she just did that. Sam moved around the tarp in circles, nose pressed to the ground, tail stiff and still. Allie walked to the front of the Nativity. Gooseflesh broke out on her arms and neck. The cold, she thought. And then she thought no, that wasn't it. Not the cold. Not that at all.

"Something's wrong."

She didn't know what, couldn't pin it to any specific thing. It was more everything. It was how Sam made his laps around the Nativity, sniffing at the rocks her daddy had laid to keep the tarp in place. It was the footprints all over the yard—behind her into the ditch and the road, over to the driveway and the bushes in front of the house, around the back. But it was the wide swath of pressed snow leading from the side of the house to where Allie stood that bothered her most. She didn't know what that could be.

"The rocks," she told Sam. "Bet that's what it was. Daddy had to bring the rocks out and decided to drag them on the tarp instead of carry them. That's smart."

Sam finished his sniffing. He took his place at Allie's side, looked at the cover, then to her. Whatever their next course of action, it would be his master's decision.

"Looks like it's pretty warm underneath there, huh? Bet it's near toasty."

Allie looked up at a clear sky washed in reds and yellows. The sun would peek over the mountains soon.

"Gonna be warm today, Samwise. They say might even hit fifty before it starts snowin' again tonight. Fifty's awful hot for Christmastime. Maybe too hot. If you think about it."

She touched the tarp. Just a brush of the finger, nothing more than that and not really disobeying at all.

"Lotsa snow out here to melt. Oh, you might not think so, you being a simple beast. You might even call it a dusting. But it ain't, Samwise. It's all over the roofs; you see that for yourself. Bet plenty's back there on the shed too. Sun's gonna come up and take all that snow away, and what'll happen then? It'll all melt, that's what. That snow'll turn to water and flow down on our firewood. You can't build a fire outta wet wood, Samwise. That's science. So it wouldn't be disobeyin' at all if I went on and put this here tarp back where it belongs. It'll be serving its function, you see. We're gonna need that wood nice and dry. Snow's coming tonight. It's gonna blow."

It all made perfect sense, and Allie felt a certain pride in piecing it all together. She touched the tarp again. This time her fingers curled around a fold and tugged a bit before they drew back. One of her Chucks settled against a rock. Before she knew it, that rock had slipped off the edge and into the snow practically on its own. Allie frowned upon that bit of unfortunateness.

"Well, it's messed up now. I leave it like that, the wind might kick up again and carry the whole thing off. And where's that gonna leave us, Sam? Right in the middle of downtown Trouble, that's where."

And so Allie did what she must, all in the name of her and her father's warmth. She pulled the tarp away in one motion—quick, before her conscience could tell her no. The rocks anchoring the bottom scattered. The breeze kicked up once more, blowing the cover over her. At once the world became bathed in blue and the smell of old oak and the sound of Sam barking, along with a tumbling sound that had no place there. Allie wrestled the tarp away from her face and looked down. The scowl on her face melted in a succession of twitches. Her lips parted. What words they formed were both partial and silent.

Chunks of firewood lay scattered at Allie's feet. Piled, she now understood, by her father, who'd done his level best to get away with a lie. Emotion flooded her—grief and guilt and loss and rage, all pressed into a fiery iron ball that settled deep in Allie's chest. The plastic Joseph could not look at her. He stared at the ground instead, laying all of his imaginary weight against the imaginary staff painted over his cloak. And the Baby Jesus, whose mouth had once been crafted into a smile of joy and peace by some unknown genius, now looked ready to grimace and cry out.

The Mary was gone.

In her place were the remains of the oak pile Marshall had crafted to conform to her shape. Allie could only look as the Joseph looked, frozen and unblinking. And the Jesus—the child—could only hide behind the shut eyes of one overwhelmed at knowing that he would now have to grow up all alone. Of his mother being exchanged for something fake, something less. Something that could never replace what had been lost.

In a way Allie could not explain but only feel, her mother had just been taken away all over again. The only difference was that God had done it before and her own drunk father had done it now. Marshall had thrown the Mary away, just as he'd told Bobby Barnes he would the night before.

"Can't let Allie run ever'thing. Dad-blamed house looks like white trash as it is."

It was cruel and mean and hurtful and just like the man Marshall Granderson had become—a broken soul who'd long given up hope. Not only of finding Mary again, but of finding himself.

That was when Allie knew she was going to cry and cry finally, right there in the middle of her front yard with Sam sniffing all that spilled wood. Her lips quivered. Her nose turned on like a faucet. Sam looked up as she pushed back her tears.

"I ain't gonna cry. Cryin' means it's over." She sniffed hard. "Can't be over, Samwise."

Sam laid his ears back and lifted a paw against her leg. Far from comforting, that show of solidarity only made Allie want to cry more. So this was it, then. This was where Allie Granderson would finally break down. Not in the middle of the living room with Mary walking through the door, smiling and bursting at the seams to tell her daughter and husband all about her grand adventures over the rainbow. It would be in the front yard instead, on a silent morning just five days before Christmas, half naked and cold. Allie hated her life. She hated the God who had marked her and the father who could never raise her, and she hated them both for taking her momma away.

The tears pooled, ready to spill, and Allie thought, *Let them come* because they were there whether she wanted them or not.

Her hands went to her eyes and stopped when Allie caught a brief movement somewhere near the ground. No—

—not the ground. Her arm. Something was moving on Allie's arm. Her mouth made a series of low squeals that backed Sam away.

It had been nearly two summers since Allie Granderson had held faith in the magic some said had fallen over the town of Mattingly. What had replaced that assurance was the cold and lifeless desire to merely carry on as best she could. But now the very magic she had shunned came upon her in a whisper only she could hear, and despite all of the pain believing could bring, that spark flashed and caught in her once more.

She moved her left arm away from her face and leaned her head back, wanting to be sure. Impossible, yes. Maybe even crazy. But there was no doubt.

Her compass was working.

2

Sam uttered a sound that was equal parts bark and cry and laid his ears against his head. It was a reaction Allie had witnessed plenty of times before, mostly during those awful summer thunderstorms that always seemed borne up in the night and left them both huddled beneath her bed. It was wonder tinged with the fear of something too big to fit in such a tiny world. Allie thought if there was ever a time for that expression, it was now.

"Because this here's a wonder," she whispered. "It's a genuine supernatural experience, Samwise, and if I could feel my legs I'd just about get on my knees right now, snow or not."

She brought her arm closer. Beneath the plastic cap of a compass that hadn't worked since the day her mother left, the thin, black needle now spun in a lazy, unbroken circle. Allie tightened the band and slid the compass around her wrist, reading it like a watch. The needle turned and floated, trying to find north. When it couldn't, it stalled at the brick house across the street.

"No, don't you stop again." Yet even as she spoke those words, a cobwebby place long forgotten in Allie's heart spoke up, telling her to wait. To just hang on.

The needle turned again, slower this time. Past the house across the road to the ranch next door, then to the pile of wood scattered in front of her. There it stopped again, though not completely. The tip jittered no more than a hair's breadth to the right and left, like a second hand gone stuck. Allie lowered her head, studying it. It was almost like

"It's trying to get my attention."

The needle spun again, this time from what Allie called twelve o'clock over to three, where the sun sparked over the mountaintops. Then to six o'clock.

"No," she said. "Not that. To me. It spun to me."

Sam's ears perked. The needle moved away again, back to the empty place at the Nativity.

"Mary?"

The word came out soft and stuttered, as though Allie feared even the small hope of hearing herself utter the name. Seconds passed that felt like hours, more than enough time for her to decide a cheap, old carnival compass didn't have to be stuck to be called worthless. Plenty of things were busted beyond repair but still moved around just fine.

"Like my daddy."

With such thinking, the needle could have done most anything next and still be called busted. But then it moved once more, sweeping back across the driveway to settle back toward the mountains, where the sun looked like a yolk being spilled down over a deep-blue pan. Allie swung her body around and faced the light. The needle held.

"That ain't north," she told Sam. "The sun rises in the east and compasses point north, Samwise. Science."

Sam couldn't argue with that, but the compass could. The needle moved again, faster now, the way clocks sometimes turn in movies to show time passing quick. It spun to Allie's house and to the empty spot and to Allie and then the mountains, over and over, and the morning was so still and Allie so quiet that she could hear the tiny clicks of the compass as it struggled to . . . what? Work?

"No. Talk."

When it stopped at the mountains one last time, it was with such force that her wrist twitched.

She stepped away from what was left of the Nativity, toward the porch. The needle beneath the compass's plastic bubble shook as Allie ran. She cleared the three wooden steps to the porch in one jump and flung the glass door open. Sam barked as the door shut in front of him. He scratched the glass, wanting in, but Allie didn't hear. She ran to her room and tore through the pile of clothes on the floor, finding a pair of jeans and a Yankees sweatshirt with RIVERA 42 on the back. Her Chucks would have to do for shoes; there was no time to dig through the closet for boots. The white sleeve of the parka Allie had gotten the year before poked out from a pile of clothes on the floor. She ignored this and grabbed the jean jacket on top, forcing herself to slow long enough to straighten the sherpa collar, and then rolled both sleeves exactly twice. Just enough of the pink leopard lining inside showed at her wrists. It would be colder, leaving the parka at home. But Allie knew she was going to have to look her best when she went in search of a favor. Showing up like the Pillsbury Doughgirl wouldn't do. She would need wiles of her own. And if Allie knew anything, it was that a wily female could get near anything she wanted with a little pink leopard print.

Her book bag would have to come along. Allie emptied it of papers and pencils and carried it in one hand to the bathroom, where she pulled her hair into pigtails. Sam called from the front porch as she rummaged through the closet under the sink. She brought out both packages Miss Howard had brought over the night before. Two pads were missing from the package on top. Allie couldn't decide if two was a usual amount or not—even if her stomach didn't hurt much, for all she knew what was going on Down There would get worse before it got better. She shoved both packages into the bag. Better safe than sorry.

The kitchen was last. Allie scrounged for all the nourishment for a day of searching, which amounted to little more than four candy bars and two juice boxes. There was more food, of course—a lot more, since Miss Howard had been "happening by" the week before and "just wanted to drop a few things off"—but Allie had given her better judgment over to the excitement bursting inside her. No more than five minutes had passed since she had run into the house. Every choice regarding her clothes and provisions was weighed in haste by an eleven-year-old girl who believed a miracle had just brushed against her. She was too busy looking at the compass, and the compass still held east, but there was no telling how long that would last.

She shouldered her bag and ran back through the living room. Her daddy's note still lay on the television stand, along with the pencil Allie supposed he'd used to write it. She didn't think Marshall Granderson deserved a response, not after what he'd done, but she paused long enough to scrawl four words beneath what he'd written and slap the note back where she'd found it.

Sam backed away as Allie opened the door, easing himself to the edge of the porch.

"Come on, Samwise," she said. "I gotta go somewhere."

Sam didn't move.

"Sam, to me. I ain't got time to wrestle with you. You can stay on my bed till I get back."

She reached through the door and took hold of the dog's collar. Sam shifted his weight back, trying to pull Allie outside as she tried pulling him in. Her free hand reached for his stomach. He growled and nipped at her fingers. Allie cried out and let go, flinging herself back inside. She landed on the living room floor with a thud. The glass door shut between them. Allie lay there, flailing like a turned turtle to right herself against the overstuffed pack beneath her.

"Fine," she huffed.

The back door, then. Sam peered through the door and ambled around the side of the house when he saw Allie disappear. Allie retrieved her bike from the shed, holding her breath as she did. Her daddy's outbuilding once smelled of sawdust and garden dirt. Now it reeked of beer and sadness. When she turned around, her dog was waiting.

"You can't come, Sam," she said. "I'm bound for east, and I don't know how far that is. So you just stay here, okay? You wait for Daddy; then you bite him like you tried to bite me."

She mounted the bike and pedaled past, wanting to put some quick distance between them. The snow wouldn't let her. It bunched in her tires, spinning them against the grass and allowing Sam to keep up. At the edge of the driveway, Allie braked and turned around.

"Go back, Samwise," she said. "I mean it. This here's people work."

Sam sat on the blacktop and perked his ears. The run from the shed to the road was short, but it was long enough to make his brown fur ripple in deep breaths and his tongue hang low.

"See? That's what I mean. You can't keep up, so you be a good dog and stay here."

He lowered his belly to the driveway. Allie nodded and turned right, aiming for the Stop sign at the end of the street. She looked down to make sure the compass still pointed to the sun.

"You just hang on," she whispered. "Allie's comin'."

There was little wind (that would come hours later, and in a world much different from the one Allie pedaled through at the moment), and that silence allowed the sound of panting to come to her once more. Allie looked over her shoulder. Sam was following, not ten feet behind.

She braked again and made a slow half loop back. Sam sat in the middle of the road. The compass had been pointing for fifteen minutes now. That was fifteen minutes Allie should have spent on the road.

"You're a dumb dog."

Sam's tail thumped.

"I don't love you at all."

A bark, low and long, like a moaning.

Allie pedaled to him and bent, lifting the dog into her arms. Sam was heavy, twelve pounds at least, but she managed to settle him against her legs well enough.

"You stay put now," she said, "or you'll wreck us both."

The seat felt strange against her, and Allie realized she'd been so concerned with figuring out how many pads to take along that she'd forgotten to change the one she had. She decided that could wait.

"Ain't got time to grow up today," she told him. "We're off on a quest. And since it's that sorta thing, we'll need help from somebody who won't think I'm crazy. And I know just the one, Samwise."

The compass guided them east. Toward the mountains, toward town.

3

Less than two miles separated the Granderson house from downtown Mattingly. Aside from the big hill just beyond the neighborhood, the going lay straight and easy. Puddles lined the shoulders on either side of the road, releasing tiny rivulets of melted snow across the asphalt. Allie took these head-on and was unbothered by the cold mist that splashed her shoes and jeans. Sam remained on her lap, pinned there by Allie's left arm. Aside from his flapping ears, he did his part in remaining still and shifted his body only when Allie checked the compass. The smattering of houses she passed were quiet and in various stages of disrepair. Some were boarded, some walled but missing roofs, some roofed but missing walls. All empty shells. All victims of what everyone within a dozen miles of town had come to simply call The Storm.

Allie's quick pace lessened as she rode past the iron gates of Oak Lawn. She didn't look toward the base of the knoll beyond. By then her legs were burning from the constant pumping, and her right shoulder ached from having to steer on its own. The sun had cleared the mountains, leaving a layer of sweat beneath her sweatshirt and jean jacket despite the cool air. Allie considered walking the rest of the way but decided that would take too long. Besides, she couldn't push her bike and hold her dog at the same time.

So Allie rode on, past the cemetery and over the train tracks, until she reached downtown—what Mayor Wallis insisted on calling New Mattingly. Few people approved of the name, Allie included. It seemed wrong to let go of the former things just yet, especially when the old was all you'd ever known and the new held everything you ever feared. And there was still plenty of fear downtown. It may have been covered over by the strings of lights suspended over Main Street and the pretty wreaths on the lampposts and the garlands hanging from all the store windows, but it was still there. Buildings could be covered to make them look happier; the sad in people always shone through.

That sadness had been so great the previous year that Christmas had been all but canceled. All the decorations stayed down; there was no caroling in the neighborhoods. Santa still came, albeit quietly. It was a sad time, as all the times had become. The town's preachers and newspaper lamented that the people of Mattingly had become less a family and more strangers trapped in their own despair. That's when the idea of a New Mattingly was born. Big Jim delivered a proclamation sealed by the power of his office a week before Thanksgiving, announcing to all that the time of troubles was officially over.

Allie remembered Marshall reading Big Jim's words in the *Gazette* and shaking his head, saying it was all typical politician talk. Allie didn't know what that meant exactly, but she understood the feeling behind it. Just calling a thing gone wasn't enough to make it go away.

She could still feel that dread as she rode the sidewalks toward the town square. It bubbled just beneath the surface of the people milling about, their eyes drooped to their shoes and the worry lines dark on their faces, passing one another as though they weren't neighbors at all. What few of them bothered to look at Allie did so only as reflex. They smiled through thin lips and their hellos were drenched in a kind of sadness, and Allie imagined their thoughts. *There goes Little Orphan Allie, so good to see her out and about instead of cooped up in that lonely house, too scared to go anywhere because she never knows when another big blow's gonna take away the little she's got left.*

None stopped long enough to ask Allie how she was. Nor would Allie stop to ask them, even if it was mannerly. Because even if the answer she'd receive was "I'm doing just fine, thanks," that sadness would still lie beneath the sentiment—things were not fine for anyone, nor would they be for some time. The people of Mattingly had found it much easier to rebuild their town than themselves.

The compass still pointed. Allie and Sam moved along new sidewalks that fronted empty lots and half buildings. Much of downtown had been reconstructed in the last year—the city hall and the pharmacy, the market, the diner. Many more were near complete. The great elms and maples that had once lined the streets were gone. In their place grew saplings donated by the nearby cities of Stanley and Camden. The Methodist, Presbyterian, and Baptist churches had all been replaced by buildings larger and fancier (at least in Allie's estimation). Their construction had come first, even before many of the homes, and by common accord. Everyone wanted to make it plain that faith took precedence over anything else, especially in the midst of such ruin. Allie's father had said that was only people's shock talking, that soon enough shock would yield to grief and grief to anger.

He was right. Many of Mattingly's faithful had since realized they might have loved the God Who Gave, but it was the God Who Took they'd been bowing down to all those years. Zach said the churches were struggling now. The Methodist one especially because the new preacher was a woman, and everybody knew preachers were supposed to be men. Allie couldn't see how a woman preacher made any difference at all, but she thought all those empty pews constituted the real damage left by The Storm. It had taken homes and businesses and families and her own momma, but it had also taken people's hope, and that was the one thing the heart couldn't bear to be without. In that regard, Allie thought she and Marshall hadn't been the only ones in town who'd gotten marked.

The crowds of last-minute shoppers thinned near the town square. There Allie braked and sat Sam down. He stretched and sniffed at the snow as Allie leaned her bike against a bench. To her left stood the big bronze statue of Barney Moore, whose bravery had saved Allie on Carnival Day and whose love had rebuilt the town after. Just beyond stood the town Christmas tree. Rows of lights ringed the twelve-foot spruce. A wide star sat at its top. Aside from those, the only decorations were the fifty-seven wooden crosses hanging from the branches, each carved with a name to match one of the new tombstones in Oak Lawn. Allie's daddy wanted there to be fifty-eight crosses on that tree. Allie had told him that if he wanted his clothes washed and his macaroni on the table, it'd better stay at fifty-seven.

She looked from the tree to her compass, then to the building across the street. The sigh Allie gave Sam had nothing at all to do with how tired the ride had left her.

"I ain't come to town by myself in a long time, Sam, and I ain't been in there for longer. You with me?"

Sam plopped himself down and put his chin on his front paws.

"Figured. You stay here and keep my bike. Maybe in the meantime you'll lose your bark and start clucking."

She adjusted her pack and got as far as the sidewalk before Sam caught up. Allie carried him across the street and up the stone steps, then stopped with her hand on the knob of the big wooden door. With any luck, the sheriff would be out riding around, and Miss Kate would be with him. Maybe Zach was sitting in there all alone, twiddling his thumbs and wishing his best friend would drop by. That's how it would work in a perfect world.

Allie wasn't surprised at all when she opened the door of the sheriff's office to find the exact opposite of what she wanted.

Zach wasn't there, but Kate Barnett was staring up from behind her desk. The pencil in her hand stopped its twirling and nearly fell atop the *Gazette*'s daily crossword. Allie turned to the glass window on her left. Jake was leaning back in his chair with his boots on the corner of his desk. He had a cup of coffee in his hand and a look of shock on his face.

"Allie?" Kate asked.

She slid her chair back and made her way across the open foyer. Her arms were out before she even cleared the Christmas tree in the middle of the room. When she reached Allie, those arms closed tight. Allie bristled at that touch and didn't know why, other than her awareness that her father would skin her alive if he knew she was there. But those arms felt so warm around her, and Kate's perfume smelled so good, and for one fleeting but precious tick of her life's clock, everything that had happened to Allie in the last year and a half fell away. She had not been hugged by a woman since her momma left. This new thing felt old and good. The two of them settled into a slow rock.

"How are you?"

"I'm fine, Miss Kate."

Sam's tail turned on. He rose and placed his front paws on Kate's leg, hungry for a crumb of attention.

Allie pressed her head deep into the warmth. Her hands slipped between Kate's arms and settled against the back of her sweater, the left rubbing in small circles, the right settling into a series of quiet pats—just as Allie had once hugged her momma. Kate broke the embrace. Allie hung on for a second longer.

"What brings you here?" Kate asked.

"I'm looking for Zach," Allie said. "There's been some unpleasantness, I'm afraid."

Another voice asked, "What unpleasantness is that?"

Allie leaned her head around Kate's shoulder. The sheriff stood leaning against the corner of the wall, quiet and easy in a pair of faded jeans and a brown shirt that matched the scruff on his face. Allie couldn't help but smile at the thought of that being how Zach would look someday, all grown-up and handsome because he'd tried to be neither.

"Hey there, Sheriff Jake," she said.

"Hey yourself, little Allie. Good to see you here. You say something's going on?"

"Yessir. There's been a heist."

Kate turned to her husband, who asked, "What got stolen?"

"My Mary," Allie said. Then she added, "The one that sits in my yard."

She glanced up at Kate, whose mouth had fallen open and whose eyes had grown moist. Allie loved her for it. Jake moved from the wall to the door. He bent and rubbed Sam's ears.

"Who'd want to do something like that?" he asked.

Allie stared at her Chucks. She shrugged. "Wouldn't want to say, really."

"Anything else missing?"

"Nosir."

Jake nodded. "Kate, why don't you fetch Zach. Believe he's still out back studying up on his dinosaurs. I'll sit here and have a little talk with Allie."

Kate tugged at one of Allie's pigtails and smiled. Sam went with her to the door that led out back of the sheriff's office.

Jake waited until his wife was gone before he asked, "Your daddy know you're here?"

"Nosir."

He nodded. "I don't expect he'd like it much."

"Well, right now I don't like him much," Allie said. "Guess that makes us even."

"He doing okay?"

"Well as anyone. Sometimes things are all right; sometimes they ain't." Allie tugged her sleeve down over the compass. "He still thinks you killed my momma."

This time it was the sheriff who looked down. It was only for a blink, but long enough for Allie to know she'd stung him and to feel sorry about it. Her stomach cramped. She didn't know if it was guilt or womanhood.

"Kate and I loved your momma very much, Allie. Everyone did. We all know how you hurt."

"All respect, Sheriff Jake, but you don't. Everybody loved my momma. I still do. Don't think ill—you helped save us. You saved me. And even if sometimes I wish you hadn't and even if my daddy hates you, I don't."

Jake tried to smile. "That's a pretty big thing for such a little girl to say."

"Maybe 'cause I ain't little no more."

The back door opened. Zach and his hat came through first. Sam and Kate followed. Zach's cheeks were red and his eyes looked tired (he'd been reading his book just like Jake said, the one with the mammoth on the cover), but Allie thought the smile on her friend's face was well worth her long ride. She told him most of what had happened, saving the important parts for when his parents weren't around. There was no embellishment to her tale; none was necessary. The only sugar Allie bothered to add was the way she moved her arms when describing the important points of the spilled wood and how the Joseph and Baby Jesus had looked so sad. She knew then the jean jacket had been the way to go.

Zach listened to it all and crossed his arms over his skinny chest. He looked at his mother and said, "I gotta go with her. I'll find it."

"What you need to do is stay here," Kate said. "I don't know about you, but I'd rather Christmas get here without you in bed with a cold."

"Won't take us long if we look together, Miss Kate," Allie said. "And to be honest, I'd rather not go gallivanting around with only Sam at my side." She pursed her lips, trying to decide if she should say more. "Sometimes I tend toward nervousness."

Zach tried his father next: "I can track it, Daddy. Probably just got blown down the street a ways, stuck under somebody's tree. Won't take me long, and our house's right up the road from Allie's."

Allie bobbed her pigtails and added, "We'll be long done before Daddy gets back from the factory, Sheriff Jake. Zach'll be home for supper for sure."

Kate looked at her husband, Jake at the children. In his eyes Allie saw much of what she'd been feeling ever since Kate gobbled her in a hug. It was joy at the remembrance of how things once were between her daddy and Jake and her momma and Kate. It was sadness that those times had slipped by and might never circle around again.

Jake nodded. "I can drive you two and Sam back to your house, Allie."

"No," she said, maybe a little too quick and a little too loud. "I mean, I got my bike outside."

"My old one's still out back," Zach said. "We won't go far, I promise. It'll be fun."

And Allie thought *yes*. It would be fun despite it all. She and Zach would be together for one day, and it would be like it once was. "Like Zach said, Miss Kate. We won't go far. Promise."

Kate still wasn't convinced. In the end she seemed to settle on something close to what Allie was thinking. "Bundle up and be back by supper. And don't go getting into trouble. Santa's watching."

Zach fingered the buttons on his thick green coat before his mother could change her mind. He said, "Just let me get my knife," and ran back outside.

"If it's okay," Allie said, "I'd like to use the facilities before we go. Bike'll go faster on an empty bladder."

"Sure," Jake said. "Just down the hall there, like in the old building."

She told Sam to sit and stay, then moved off slow.

"Allie?" Kate asked. "You can leave your backpack here if you want."

"If it's all the same, ma'am, I'll just take it with me."

Kate nodded a little too late. "Sure."

Allie found the bathroom and twice made sure the door was locked behind her, then wedged a foot against it just in case. The book bag fell from her shoulders.

She finished and scrubbed her hands hard with soap after flushing the evidence. Allie didn't want to leave something like that wrapped up in the trash. Zach waited by the door with Sam as Allie came out. Seeing him there leaning against his old bike, wrapped up in his big hat and a camouflage coat, he looked the picture of gallantry.

"Ready?" he asked.

Allie nodded. She was ready. And for the first time in a long while, she let herself smile.

4

She waited until they were across the street before daring to say, "We ain't going to my house."

"I know," Zach said.

Allie halted at the edge of the square's browned grass. Zach smiled and ambled on. Sam jogged beside him, tail wagging.

"How'd you know that?" she asked.

He shrugged his shoulders cool and manlike and coughed into his sleeve. "Easy. If your Mary really was gone, you'd be freaking out way more than you are. You'd be, like, *bawling*." He stopped and turned, letting Allie catch up. "I don't mean that bad or nothin'. But you wouldn't come all this way to town on your own 'less something else happened. Something *worse*. You're too scared to leave the house on your own, Allie. Ever'body knows it." He paused again. "I don't mean that bad or nothin'."

"She *is* gone," Allie said. "And I did cry almost. Daddy took my Mary. I didn't tell the sheriff because . . . I don't know. Because he's still my daddy. Most times, anyway."

"Your daddy took her?"

Allie nodded and told Zach those parts of the story she'd left out while in the company of his parents: "I heard Daddy tell Bobby Barnes he was gonna get rid of it. I didn't think he would—he's always saying he's gonna box that Nativity up, but he never does." She considered what she said next something like a lie, but not entirely. "I think he dropped her somewhere. Someplace I'd never look."

"So we gotta go somewhere he wouldn't think you'd go," Zach said.

"Yes. And I think I kinda know where. The general direction, anyway."

They'd reached the bench where Allie's bike rested. Sam lingered for a bit, then plodded away to sniff the grass. Allie had not looked at the needle since going inside the sheriff's office, too afraid that it had either gone stuck again or that Jake or Kate would see. The compass was her secret—Allie's magic alone—and she hadn't wanted to share it with anyone until the time came. Now it had.

She and Zach shared a bond far deeper and stronger than either of them knew, but even the deepest and strongest bonds could be stretched to breaking. School was all the two of them had together now. The small moments there were nothing compared to the times they'd once had, back when the Grandersons and Barnetts were so close they were near kin. Back then Zach would take anything she said on faith, no proof required. Just as Allie would for him. And yet life had shown them both (and for that matter, the whole town) that faith could be hard to come by.

"I have to show you something," she said. "You can't tell."

"Okay."

"Siddown."

He did, leaving enough room for her. Sam trotted over from the Christmas tree and nestled himself at their feet. Allie watched for prying eyes. What people lingered were either too far away or too self-involved to notice two children off to themselves. She leaned in close. Zach backed away when her head nearly touched the brim of his hat. His eyes bulged.

Allie punched him in the arm. "I ain't trying to canoodle, you idiot."

"Well, then, what're you doing?"

"I'm trying to show you this." She lifted the left sleeve of her jacket, catching the compass's band before it could slip off. "Look at the needle."

Zach leaned in as sunlight glinted off the plastic bubble. He shook his head, not seeing anything at all at first, and wondered again if Allie really had been trying to kiss him. She shook her wrist. Then he saw.

"Hey, wow." Zach leaned in closer, watching as the needle

floated and then settled into a gentle bob. "When'd that get unstuck?"

"This morning. Right after I found Mary gone."

He looked from the needle to the sky. "It ain't aimin' north."

"I know," Allie said. "But I don't think it's built to aim north. At least, not now."

She told him how the needle had worked that morning, spinning to her and the house and then to where the Mary had sat. How Sam was scared and she had been a little scared, too, but in a way that felt good. Zach reached down and rubbed the dog's head as he listened.

"So now I'm here" is how Allie finished. And when Zach didn't say anything, she waved a bit of the leopard print on her rolled sleeve in front of his gaze.

"I don't get it," Zach said.

Allie shook her head and wondered how someone so handsome and brave could be so stupid. She held her wrist up. "It ain't a *compass*, Zach. Not a regular one, leastways. I think it's more like . . . I don't know. An SOS."

"From who?"

"From her," Allie said. She spoke slowly: "Mary."

"What? Allie . . ." Zach stopped when he realized she wasn't playing a trick. "That's pointing clear to the other side of town. There's plenty of places between your house and mine your daddy coulda dumped her. Or maybe he even took her to work in the back of his truck and dumped her there. Why would he take her east?"

He didn't understand. That stumped her. Allie had considered nearly every possible way Zach could react to what she'd just told him, but she hadn't counted on confusion.

"Because that's where the needle's pointing," she said. "You have to help me, Zach. We gotta get going."

But Zach said nothing. There was no pledge to help and no encouragement given, only a deep silence that bothered Allie more than she could say. She stood and began pacing back and forth in front of the bench, searching for a way to convince him. Her eyes were drawn toward Main Street, past the town hall to where the road curved. A blue Honda crested over Miller's Bridge just beyond. Allie blinked, trying to peer through the sunlight that glinted off the windshield.

"Bless it," she said.

"What?"

"Bless it bless it *bless it*." The car was closer now. "We gotta hide."

Allie bent behind the bench and scrambled to corral Sam, who saw the whole thing as an invitation to wrestle. Zach jumped over the bench instead of moving around it, nearly landing atop Sam's head. He shoved a hand into his coat pocket.

"Who we hiding from?" he asked. "I got my knife."

"We don't need no knife," Allie said. "Just sit here and be still."

They peered through the narrow slats in the back of the bench as the soft whine of the engine neared. The car slowed in front of the town square just long enough to cause panic, then continued on.

"She's gone," Allie said in a long exhale. "That was close."

Zach stood and adjusted his hat. "That was just Miss Howard. What're you doing hiding from her? Ain't no school today." He shook his head. "And you call me an idiot."

"That ain't why I hid."

"Then why did you?"

Allie stood up and said, "It don't matter right now. What does is if you're comin' along. I don't know how long my compass is gonna work." Her book bag leaned to the right. Zach reached out to center it again. She slapped his hand away. "Never mind that, either."

"I was just tryin' to help," he said. "What's wrong with you?"

"What's wrong is I don't know if you believe me or not."

Zach said, "You ain't gotta ask me that," though Allie noticed he couldn't look her in the eye. "'Course I do. We'll find your Mary. And even if we don't, we'll get to spend the day together. Just like we used to."

"So you'll come?"

"Somebody's gotta keep a watch on you. It'll be like a quest." Zach lifted his hat and bowed, sweeping it across his body. "Sir Barnett the Bold, at your service."

Allie rolled her eyes. She said, "You're such a dork," even though Zach Barnett was no such thing, and she said, "I hate you," even though she loved him most of all.

"So where we going?" he asked.

Allie pointed to the mountains. "That way. And we'll go as far as it takes."

5

The few hundred people or so who made up Zach Barnett's world could be divided into two groups: those whom he could trust no matter what, and those whom he would trust not at all. To his credit, the pool consisting of the latter was shallow and for the most part included only those who gave his father trouble. Zach had added Allie's daddy to that list in the past year, and not only because Marshall had come to hate Jake Barnett more than he hated anyone else in the world. The reasons why were simple enough for Zach to state even if difficult to understand. It had been Barney Moore and Zach's father who'd led fifty or so people to safety when The Storm hit on Carnival Day. Allie had been among them. Mary Granderson had not. She had left to look for Allie just before the heavens opened. The tornado took her sometime after, and to a place Zach believed no compass could point. Allie had not been the same since. Nor had her father. Zach's daddy often said he didn't think ill of Marshall for his hatred. He said people needed to blame something for the bad things that happened, and Marshall had just put that blame on him.

Zach, however, felt no such mercy—not because of Marshall's newfound hatred for the Barnetts, but because of stuff Allie had told him. It wasn't much, broken pieces mostly. All of which always seemed to be cut midsentence by either a shrug or the ringing of a school bell. But the little that got through was enough for Zach to believe the Marshall Granderson he'd once known and even loved wasn't around anymore—that maybe he'd died right along with Allie's momma.

The list of people Zach could trust was much longer and included most everyone else in town to varying degrees, each of whom jockeyed up or down on some sliding scale of his own devising. But the names at the top of that list were never altered. In Zach's mind, the whole world would fall away before his parents and Allie ever let him down.

That Allie had largely gone missing from his life since The Storm had no bearing on that trust. Zach still believed in her. That made what he felt now all the more worrisome. There they were, biking through Mattingly's streets with Christmas on one horizon and a full sun rising over another, but Zach felt neither joy nor excitement at the prospects such a day held. What he felt was doubt.

He carried Sam as best he could, pinning the dog to his chest with his left hand. It was awkward and uncomfortable, especially when Sam got it in his head to rear up and nip at the brim of Zach's hat. Already his left shoulder burned from the weight. His right fared no better, aching from the constant adjustments to the handlebars to keep them balanced and moving. The exertion pressed in on his lungs, forcing out a series of thick coughs.

It was enough for him to look at Allie with no small measure of annoyance. Zach didn't think she'd stopped once on the long ride from her house to town. Not only had she carried Sam that whole way, she'd shouldered her backpack as well. Such knowledge would be enough to dent the pride of any man, and a boy who fancied himself one especially. He gritted his teeth and pedaled harder. So far, what they were doing didn't feel like a quest at all. It felt more like work.

Allie rode ahead, her jean jacket fluttering around the edges of her pack. They'd traded the square for the two-lane Main Street that cut at an angle beside the town hall. Traffic in both directions was light—a good thing, considering Allie didn't seem to care what lay behind or around, only ahead. That dented Zach's pride, too, knowing he was being led around by a girl. Yet even that was better than the alternative, which was that he was being led around by the busted compass on the girl's wrist.

He called, "Hey, you wanna slow down? I thought this was a search and rescue, not a race."

Allie looked over her shoulder and smiled. "Ain't my fault you can't keep up with me."

"Well, maybe you can carry your own dog, then. If you ain't heard, I got a cold."

She rode on but slowed enough for him to catch up. Miller's Bridge loomed ahead, marking Mattingly's downtown boundary. The slow churn of the river beneath echoed as they rode over. Past that lay the town's outlying neighborhoods, where the lane widened enough for Zach to come alongside. Allie studied her compass, making sure they were still going the right way.

"Still east," she said. "I think it's stronger now. We might be close."

"I hope so. We're about to run out of town."

What homes they passed stood as fragile monuments to the human will to move on despite it all. Piles of wood and brick remained here and there, covered with remnants of snow from the night before. Much of the wreckage had been cleared and hauled away in the last year and a half, though not all of the houses had returned. The months since The Storm had been a time of hard lessons for everyone in Mattingly. The one that stuck closest to Zach was how quickly lives could be upended, and how long it took to restore them again. In many ways, he supposed that was why a morning he'd thought destined for play around the sheriff's office had turned into riding across town with his best friend. Zach didn't think they were looking for Allie's plastic Mary at all. They were just trying to find a way to fix Allie's life.

They passed the last of the homes at nine thirty that morning. By nine, Marshall Granderson had tried to call his daughter twice. The answering machine had picked up both times. The messages he left were as calm as he could manage, asking Allie again not to bother looking beneath that old tarp, everything under there was fine. He hung up and stared at the clock above his head. Allie was a good girl; she wouldn't look if he told her not to. Still, a growing panic brushed over Marshall as he plugged his ears and ventured back into the clamor of factory machinery. He should have done a better job of covering the Nativity. But looking out the window at first light and seeing Allie's Mary gone had panicked him, and rushing around the neighborhood and not finding it had panicked him more. What else could he have done? He told himself it would all be fine; Allie was probably still in bed.

Actually, she'd just passed the wooden Welcome To Mattingly sign some eight miles from home, and that was when Zach decided it was time to settle on exactly what they were doing.

"Hey, let's rest a minute," he said. "I think Sam needs to go."

He thought she would protest, maybe say they'd stop around the next curve, a man should at least be able make it that far. But Allie eased her bike off the road and onto the shoulder without a word, happy for the break. Zach pulled beside her and sat Sam on the ground, wincing as he flexed his left arm in and out. Sam bounded off just inside the long line of trees at their backs, sniffing for the bathroom. The morning stood clear and bright, the road silent. Allie found a stump that made a serviceable enough chair and sat. She shrugged off her pack and placed it against her leg, then checked her compass again.

"You okay?" Zach asked.

She nodded. "Looks like we're still heading the right way. Making good time too."

"You eat breakfast?"

"Weren't no time. I packed us a lunch, though. Candy bars."

"We could go back if you want. BP's right back down. I ain't got no money, but I bet Andy'd give us some biscuits on loan."

"I ain't hungry," Allie said. "'Sides, that'll mean going the wrong way. It'll take time to get back here, and Daddy'll be home before I know it. He finds me gone, I'll be in trouble."

"We got hours yet," Zach said. "Even if we don't get no food, we should use Andy's phone and call my folks. Tell them where we are."

Allie looked up from her compass. "What exactly is it you're trying to tell me, Zach Barnett?"

"Nothing," he said. "Just that I'm not sure what we're doin' way out here on the other side of town from where we're supposed to be, and you ain't said three words to me since we left the square. I don't mind comin' along with you, Allie, but I care to be more than just a body. I thought we'd . . . you know."

"What?" Allie asked.

"Well, talk for one. We talk more at school than we've talked out here all alone by ourselves. Don't that bother you none?" The trees behind them popped and crunched. Sam sauntered out and sat between them. Zach reached down and stroked the dog's back. "I know we're friends and all, but that don't mean I don't miss you none."

Allie considered how to respond to that. It was something they'd never discussed at length, how far they'd drifted apart. The sweetly awkward moment that followed was filled with the sound of dripping water from the trees and the call of a faraway crow.

"I miss you too," she said. "I'm sorry, Zach. We just have to find her is all. I don't mind talking so long as we're moving at the same time. Promise."

Zach figured that was the best he could manage from her. "Fine, then. We'll go on. Like I said, there's plenty time before we gotta head back. You want me to take Sam again?"

She nodded.

"I could probably fit him in your backpack," he said. "It's big enough, and I'd keep the zipper open for his head to poke through. It'd go easier if he was on my back instead of my lap."

"No. There's other stuff in there that's mine."

"What stuff?"

"Private stuff. Come on."

She rose from the stump and flipped the kickstand up on her bike. Zach lifted Sam and felt the same dull ache in his left arm. Another ache, this one not so dull, crept back into his insides too. Allie had never said anything was private, not to him.

They left the pavement a few miles ahead (at the compass's direction, Zach was quick to learn), and wove their way through the narrow dirt roads that cut into the dense forest between Mattingly and the small villages of the hill country. Zach held his unease in check only because those back ways were still familiar. The peace of the woods soothed him and crept into Allie as well. She was talking now, and not pedaling so hard. And even though she often checked her compass, she was looking at Zach more than her wrist.

"Why'd you hide from Miss Howard?" he asked. "She wouldn't say nothin' if she saw us together. No more'n anyone else would, anyway."

Just like that, all the progress Zach thought they'd made vanished. Allie fell mute and broody, even went so far as to put both hands on her handlebars instead of just the one. She eased to the other side of the road.

"Miss Howard wants to marry my daddy," she said.

"What?"

"She wants to marry my daddy. Been trying to wrangle him ever since Momma left. I think she might even love him."

The words struck Zach as though they were solid, hard in the body. His arm nearly let go of Sam, who took that opportunity to try and wriggle free. It was the first Zach had heard that about his teacher. He didn't know if what he felt was anger over Allie keeping such a secret or jealousy over Miss Howard being in love with someone like Marshall Granderson.

"Miss Howard's been Momma's best friend for, like, ever," Allie said. "Almost as good friends as my momma is with yours. They've known each other since they were just little girls. They used to do all kinds of stuff together. Miss Howard was nice then. She came to the funeral and stood right with me, thinking I was gonna cry, but I wasn't gonna cry over no buried shoe. Wouldn't hold her hand neither, even though she wanted me to. After, she'd come bring us supper and whatnot. She told me she lost her momma when she was young as me. That's when it all started. Her latchin' onto me, I mean. Now she brings us food all the time, even though Daddy says I cook masterpieces. I don't know what he thinks, but I know what *she* thinks. I think she made me be in her class, too, just to keep an eye on me. Miss Howard has wiles."

"She ain't got no wiles," Zach said. "Miss Grace is nice."

Allie said, "A woman knows, Zach Barnett," and Zach decided to leave it at that.

It was just after noon and many miles on when Allie glanced at her compass again. She braked and settled her feet on the road's thin layer of gravel, straddling the bike between her legs.

Zach stopped and asked, "What is it?"

"Needle's moved again."

He leaned over to look. Sam licked him in the face. Zach eased the dog away and studied the compass. The needle had indeed moved, pointing to the right instead of ahead. He looked in that direction. All he saw there were trees.

"Ain't no road that way," he said.

"I know."

"So what do we do?"

Zach realized he was letting Allie decide for the both of them. It didn't seem right, letting her do that. She was the one in need; it was his place to take charge. And yet there they were, miles from the nearest home, searching for a missing Christmas ornament by using a busted old carny compass that had never worked in the first place. Zach may only be eleven, but that didn't take away from his seeing this was the dumbest thing he'd ever done. He hoped Allie would see it too.

She didn't. Yes, maybe coming all that way was dumb if you looked at it a certain way. But if you set it on its side and looked at it another way—if you believed—it wasn't dumb at all. Going in those trees was something Allie didn't want to do with or without Zach, but she'd swallowed her fears so far, and she'd swallow them still.

"Onward ho," Allie said. She chewed on her lip. "That's where it's pointing, so that's where we need to head."

She waited for him to move first. The trees where the compass pointed were tall and mangled, bunched together so thick that the sun penetrated little more than their tops. What snow had fallen to the ground there still remained. And there was no noise from inside, no skittering of squirrels, and no birdsong, only an odd quiet that beckoned as much as warned. Sam's ears perked. He barked once and darted inside the trees, using his nose the same way Allie had used her compass.

"Allie," Zach whispered. "I know you love that Mary, but that Mary ain't your momma. Just like that thing on your wrist ain't something magic—it's just an old compass from a long time gone. Things like that, they're just toys."

Allie looked at him. "You scared, Zach Barnett?"

"I ain't scared of nothin'!" That was not a whisper. Zach said this as loud and strong as the woods allowed. "I'm just saying that thing's took us all the way out here to the middle of nowhere, and if we keep following it, we might end up in Africa and still not find nothing."

"No," Allie managed. "That ain't true."

Somewhere in the trees, Sam barked.

"You wanna go in there?" Zach asked. "You ain't been in the woods since—"

The Storm, he almost said. And he almost added, *Because you say the wind always sounds meaner in the woods, like it's chasing you from behind and eating everything in its path.*

Another bark, followed by the rustling of dead leaves in snow. Allie called Sam to her. He only barked again.

"We'll just go a little ways," Allie told him. "Just to see. We're gonna have to get Sam out of there anyways."

Zach thought that was true enough, and if anyone had to go in there to get Allie's dog, it'd be him. Everyone knew a Barnett wasn't really at home unless he was in the woods. He and Allie would go in there and walk around a bit, no problem. See where the needle's pointing and never lose sight of the road. Allie would get her fill soon. She'd start getting hungry or tired or both, and they'd be back in town by lunch.

He decided to say something manly in an aloof sort of way—*Fine then, I'll take you in there,* maybe, or *You ain't gotta be afraid, Allie, 'cause I'm here.* He never got the chance. Sam's barking went from the sort of yapping pups love to make to something urgent.

"What's he doing in there?" Allie asked.

"I don't know. Maybe he's got a squirrel."

Zach took his bike along, no sense leaving it in the road, and walked into the trees. Ahead of Allie, he reminded himself, and with no small amount of satisfaction. She followed close behind with her bike in tow. The trees thickened more not ten feet from the road, where they tangled with underbrush and made the bikes useless.

"You see him?" Zach asked.

He turned when Allie didn't answer. Her attention was on the compass again. Zach shook his head and called out for Sam. The bark came from only a few more feet away, beneath the corpse of a fallen oak. Zach flipped his kickstand down.

Allie said, "Zach, there's something wrong with the compass."

"Shocking."

He pushed through a maze of thornbushes, wincing as the needles scraped his hands. The tree on the other side rested at a low angle to the ground, propped up by its own splintered stump. Dead branches formed a web over the ground. Sam lay beneath. He whined as Zach approached.

"What you got, boy?" he asked.

"Zach?" Allie called. She sounded far away. "You gotta see this needle. It's really freaking out."

Zach didn't answer. He reached the fallen tree and squatted to where Sam waited, rubbing the dog's ears. "Good boy," he said. "You just take it easy, Samwise. Just let me see what you—"

The last word lodged in Zach's throat, stealing his breath. He heard Allie approaching behind him, felt the sting the thorns had left on the backs of his hands. Smelled the damp freshness of the forest. But all of those things seemed apart from him, inconsequential. It was what Zach saw beneath that rotten old log that consumed him. Because Allie was right. She'd been right all along.

6

Allie's world had shrunk to the space of the tiny, fog-covered bubble over the needle the moment they'd left the road. She never saw Zach move through the thornbush and stoop to that fallen tree. She heard Sam barking and herself calling for Zach, telling him he had to see this, the needle was really freaking out. And it was, Allie could think of no better word. She couldn't tell where the needle pointed now because the needle couldn't make up its mind. It swung in a tight arc between the fallen tree where Zach had gone and a spot to their right. Here, then there, back to here. Slow at first, then faster, and then so fast that the needle blurred. The compass was going to explode. Allie's mind buckled at that certainty. She held her wrist out and away from her body, wanting the compass off, now afraid of the magic that had lain dormant in it for so long.

She wanted Zach. Zach would get the compass off. He would save her, he always had, and Allie believed if she had done one thing right that morning it was to stop at the sheriff's office before heading out all that way alone. She wouldn't have braved the back roads beyond town with only Sam. She never could have strayed into the woods, where even the breeze rushed like thunder through the limbs and leaves. Standing there with her arm outstretched, feeling the needle's vibration against her wrist, Allie Granderson no longer cared what would happen to Zach if God found out she loved him. She only knew she did, and there was no changing it.

Her voice quivered. "Zach? Help me please?"

There was nothing at first, only the trees and the brush and the sound of Sam's whimpers from somewhere under the tree. Allie closed her lips over the scream in her throat. Her eyes tightened at the edges.

The compass made a whirring sound as Zach rose up from the twist of branches, snapping them. The look on his face was not the calm assurance Allie craved. It was instead an expression of shock and shame. When he raised his arm to show Allie what Sam had found, the needle froze with a click so loud it made her flinch.

The scarf had been muddied and browned by a night in the woods, but Allie could still see the blue-and-orange stripes. Sam scurried from the log and wormed his way through the scrub. He reached Allie and rose up, dirtying her jeans with his front paws. Zach followed as best he could, wincing as he passed through the briars. Allie's hand remained outstretched, still calling for help. Zach, thinking Allie's arm was out because she'd known about the scarf before Sam even found it, placed it in Allie's palm. Her fingers closed around the thick wool.

"Sam found it." He bent without taking his eyes away and rubbed the dog's ears, telling him good boy. "It's yours, ain't it?

I seen it last night. You put that scarf and the one you wear t'school around Mary's neck. To keep her warm."

Allie ran the scarf through her fingers. It felt cold and damp and utterly lifeless. This wasn't right, not right at all. She managed a slow, deep nod.

"It's true," Zach said. "It's really true. You were right, Allie. Your compass works. It brought us here. Right *here*."

Her head shook no. It couldn't end this way. This couldn't be all.

"What's the matter with you?" he asked. "We got a ever-lovin' miracle here, Allie. You're standing there like it's the end of the world."

Zach thumped her just to the side of where the strap of her pack met her right shoulder, rocking Allie backward. He chuckled and tensed, waiting for her to retaliate. But when Allie reached out her hand, it wasn't to smack. It was to show. The compass pointed to the fallen tree where Sam had found the scarf, but only because that was the direction where Allie's hand pointed. The needle had frozen again.

"I think maybe it really is the end of the world," she said. "I think it's broke."

Allie left off the *again* her mind wanted to add on, if for no other reason than she still believed the compass was never really broken before. It had been more waiting. And yet standing there just beyond the edge of the road, Allie was reminded once more that nothing ever lasted long in life. The world wasn't built for permanence. Things broke and rusted and faded. Things went away. Sometimes very important things.

Zach said, "Let me see," and took hold of her wrist, easing it to himself. His fingers were dirty and strong. She felt a shiver at his touch. He flicked the plastic dome on top of the compass. The needle didn't budge. "That don't make no sense."

"It does if that's all we were supposed to find," Allie said.

"Why would it just let us find that and nothing else?"

"I don't know. You can't figure magic."

Sam became concerned with this latest development. He raised up on his hind legs and fell into an awkward pirouette, sniffing at the air between them. Zach tapped the dome again. Allie let him. It hadn't worked the first time, and she felt no indication it would work now, but it was better than just standing in the middle of the woods with a dancing beagle.

"Maybe we should pray," Zach said.

"Don't you dare," Allie told him. "I'm marked, Zach Barnett, in case you forgot. You invite Him in on this, things'll end just as bad as they always do. Besides, the Lord ain't the one doing the talking through this."

"Well, right now ain't nobody doing the talking through it. What were you doing when it started working the first time?"

"I was standing in the yard," she said, "looking at that spot where the Mary used to be and tryin' not to cry."

"Maybe you should start cryin'," Zach said. "Or at least get close to it."

Allie shook her head. "Crying means it's done."

They stared at the needle, each of them trying to find another way. Sam gave up his dance and resorted to walking in wide circles around them, sniffing at the snow.

"Maybe we just gotta believe," Zach said.

"How do we do that?"

"I don't know. Believing's not something you do; it's something you are."

So the two of them huddled around Allie's tiny compass in silence, guarded by Samwise and his wide circles. Allie thought maybe Zach was right, they just had to believe. If that was the case, then she hoped Zach could believe enough for the both of them. The Storm had taken no one he loved, and nothing bad had ever happened to him. Faith ran true through such people. They had no cracks inside them for it to fall through and disappear, and they had no walls around them to dam it all up until it turned sour.

"Please," she whispered. "Please work."

Perhaps that word was what unstuck the needle. Or perhaps it was not belief at all, only a need for one more miracle. But something freed the compass just then. It was only a bit, just a tiny twitch of the needle to the side, and if either of them had chosen that moment to blink, they would've missed it. Zach held Allie's wrist and eased his head away, letting what sun leaked through alight on the dome. The needle moved again, this time the other way, like it was a rusty hinge being worked free by some unseen hand. It swung in a slow sweep first to Zach, then to Allie, and finally farther on into the forest. The compass trembled. Allie thought it was going to go stiff again, then realized the shaking was coming from Zach's hand.

"We gotta go," Zach said. "I know it's scary, but I'll be with you. I think we're really going to find her, Allie. I think your Mary's close."

Allie nodded, and the smile she gave Zach was a grin more of conviction than belief. She tied the scarf around her waist like a belt and adjusted her backpack. Sam stopped his circles and joined them. She bent and cradled the dog's head in her hands, kissing him there.

"You're a good boy, Sam. You did real good. You show us the way now."

Twenty miles to the south in the city of Camden, Virginia, Marshall Granderson had spent his half-hour lunch trying to call home. Allie wouldn't answer. Everything was fine. That's what he told himself as he hung up for the last time. Everything was fine and Allie hadn't looked under the tarp, and there would be plenty of time after his shift ended for him to drive to the Walmart and buy another Mary. Craziest thing in the world, how that thing had disappeared. Taken by the storm the night before, most likely. Allie was right: it had been a blow.

He tried thinking of someone he could call, anyone who could stop by the house to make sure the tarp was still there and Allie was okay. But the neighbors were all at work, and he had no real friends except for Bobby, who was likely drunk by now. He thought of Grace next. Grace would go by the house, would probably vacuum the floors and clean the bathrooms and cook supper, too, but Marshall knew Grace would never get the chance because Allie would never answer the door for her. It didn't matter. That's what Marshall thought as he donned his earplugs again. Everything was fine. Everything had to be.

Allie thought so as well as she and Zach left sight of the road and stepped into the deep woods.

Four days would pass until they were seen again.

7

Time slips away in the lonely places of the world. For Allie, Zach, and Sam, the next hours passed with barely a notice as the land of man and machine yielded to the hills and hollows of the forest. The quick pace they'd kept from town slowed to an easy stroll. Gone were the brambles and thick trees that had met them just beyond the road. Here in the deeper woods, sunlight reigned. Only the upper branches of the tall oaks and pines lay between them and the sun, making thin spider webs of shadow upon the ground they trod.

Sam eased out front, guided more by his nose than any sense

of direction. His tail whipped from side to side and froze upon the discovery of some unknown and exotic scent. Zach remained close, fully immersed in what he considered his element, and initiated an extended discourse on everything from how to tell direction by where moss grew on a tree to how to survive a cougar attack. Allie found it all sweet in a way, his going on and on to impress her. Truth be told, it *was* kind of impressive. Not that she'd ever let Zach know.

"Ain't no cougars in these woods no more," she said.

Zach stopped midsentence—it was something about people forgetting how to get along in the woods and what a shame that was—and asked, "What?"

"You said it weren't no use to run or hitch yourself up a tree when a cougar lights on you, but that don't matter since there ain't none no more. They might live on in your dinosaur books, but not in the real world."

"Who told you that?"

Allie shrugged, not recalling. "You ever seen one?"

"No," he said. "But just because you can't see a thing don't mean it ain't real. Or even that it ain't watching us even now. And they ain't dinosaur books, I'll have you know. Not all of them, anyways."

"Only reason you read them things is so you can impress Miss Howard."

"That ain't true," he said. "I like it. Used to be all sorts of creatures in these woods. Mammoths probably. Sabertooths too. And all manner of Indians. There's value in knowing what came before, Allie."

"Well, I don't expect we'll run afoul of a dangerous creature here in the middle of winter," Allie told him. "If we do, we'll just feed it Sam."

"That's awful."

Ten feet in front, Sam paused in his sniffing and raised his head at the sound of his name. He woofed and wagged his tail, as though the idea of being fed to a hungry predator sounded like a fine way to enjoy a sunny afternoon.

Allie smiled and said, "Dumb old dog."

"You ain't gotta worry no way," Zach said. "Something happens, I'll take care of it. Us Barnetts, it's like a ree-zort vacation when we venture to the woods. You see that buck I shot last year? Tracked it three miles. Daddy was along, but he let me take the lead. Gutted it myself too."

"'Course I saw that deer," Allie said. "Everybody saw that deer. You brought it to school after your daddy had the head mounted."

Zach thumped her in the arm. "Hey, that was an eight-pointer. You tell me that weren't the awesomest show-and-tell of the whole year. That was like the hall of *fame* of show-and-tell."

Allie dropped her head to hide a smile. She thumped Zach back. "It was okay, I guess," she said. Which wasn't the truth. If anything, that buck was the most amazing thing Allie had ever seen. Zach was the talk of the school for days. Even the principal had come by to see it.

"We ate it too," Zach said. "Me and Momma and Daddy. Deer meat's about the best there is. Trick is you gotta scare it good before you kill it. Makes it taste better."

Allie thought about that. She said, "That's about the awfulest thing anybody's ever told me."

"All I'm saying's that you ain't gotta worry. You and Sam's in my world now. Things'll be right as rain, you'll see. We'll find her. Compass still working?"

Allie lifted her sleeve. "Still straight on."

Up ahead, Sam stopped long enough to put his nose to the ground and snort. Zach stooped when they caught up. He traced the faint outline of a track in the melting snow.

"That's a deer there," he said. "Pretty fresh too. Good boy, Sam."

Sam lifted his head and licked Zach's nose.

"Maybe you can make a spear outta your pocketknife and rustle us up some lunch," Allie said. "You being the great white hunter and all."

"Could if I wanted," Zach said, and he knew so beyond all doubt. "But you got plenty in your pack. You hungry?"

She was. Allie had left the house without breakfast and figured it was near supper time, at least according to the dull throbbing from the hollow place in her stomach. But aside from that and the patches of snow that kept getting inside her Chucks, Allie felt fine. She shook her head no. Zach might take a yes as reason enough to turn for home, even with his newfound faith in the compass. She couldn't risk that, not with them being so close. If the time after The Storm had taught her anything, it was that what the heart believed was often at odds with what the body wanted. Hunger could be just as powerful as faith. A few candy bars and some juice would only get them so far.

"You hungry?" she asked.

"Not if you ain't. Want me to carry your pack for a while?"

"No," she said. "It ain't heavy."

They moved on. The woods thinned and spread out. Wide spaces opened up between oaks that stood as tall as buildings. Yet here the sun struggled to reach the ground, trapped as it was in the thick canopy of snarled limbs. What little day filtered through drenched the world into a pale twilight. Zach said that part of the forest was old, maybe even ancient. Allie didn't know if that was right (it sounded like something from one of his books, and wouldn't Miss Howard beam at that) but felt it was.

Few words passed between them as they crossed through that place. There seemed no end to it. The only sounds were their shoes crunching against the snow. Even Sam fell silent, choosing to walk beside Allie rather than up front. No wind blew there. Allie thought maybe no wind ever had, not even the one that had taken her momma. She kept her feet moving where the needle pointed, but her head moved everywhere. There was a strange peace to that part of the woods, almost a gentle pulsing, and Allie let the stillness fill the cracks inside her.

And yet there was something else to those woods as well, a shadow only Zach could feel. Lurking somewhere close, flittering among the trees, just out of sight.

"You okay?" he whispered.

"Yes."

"Me too."

But when Allie looked at Zach's face, she saw his eyes darting and his shoulders gone hunched. It was just the way Sam looked right before wailing at one of those summer thunderstorms.

There was no telling how long it took for them to find the borderland where the old forest yielded to the new. It felt much shorter to Allie than to Zach, who nearly sighed with relief when he spotted the jagged line of fallen trees and thornbushes ahead. Just in front of the scrub rested a boulder the size of a small car, and there they rested. Sam made no lap around the rock to sniff and snort, nor did he sit when Allie called him to her side. He only stared back through those ancient trees with his tail sharp and his head twitching, as though his eyes were chasing a fly. Allie ignored this, of course, just as anyone who'd never spent time in the wilderness would, and Zach shook his head as that thought crossed his mind. He himself had taken a keen interest in what Sam was doing. Whatever it was Zach had felt as they'd come through, Allie's dog had felt it too.

"I didn't like that," Zach said.

"Didn't like what?"

"Going through there. It felt funny."

Allie said, "It was just some old woods," though not because it felt exactly true. It did, however, feel simpler.

"Know what going through there reminded me of?"

"What?"

"Going through the Holler."

"Happy Holler?"

He nodded, not wanting to repeat the words. "Ain't too far from where we set out, you know. Maybe like five miles is all."

Allie snorted. "You don't know what the Holler looks like. You ain't never been there."

"But I heard. And what I heard's what that looks like." He pointed back through the trees. "All old and spooky. They say the Holler's all trees and tangles, the worst tangles you ever seen. And spirits."

Allie moved her eyes back to where they'd come. Their footprints had made an S in the broken snow beyond, past where she could see. How far they'd come couldn't be told, nor how long it had taken them to get there. There was nothing other than the ache in Allie's legs, the hunger in her belly, and the thirst in her mouth to gauge their range. Time slips away in the lonely places. Distance as well. Allie and Zach would have been shocked to know that in the hours since they'd left the road, they and Sam had traveled nearly six miles.

Zach climbed the rock and sat. He said, "I'm going there one day when I come of age. To the Holler, I mean. Probably soon."

Allie said, "Daddy took me near there once. He said his name's on the gate. Never understood why anyone'd want to go down there just to do that."

"Carving your name on the rusty gate shows you got spine. Havin' a spine's the most important thing to a man." He rubbed his eyes and coughed again, loud and deep, then cringed when he felt a stinging something in his chest. "You don't understand. Girls ain't brave like boys are. It's science."

"That ain't science," Allie said. "That's just boy talk."

"How far we going?" Zach asked. "Looks like it's getting late. Your daddy'll be home soon, and Momma's expecting me for supper."

Allie studied the compass. "Just a ways more," she said. "It won't be long. Can't be. We'll look a little more and then eat. Guess we gotta go through this scrub."

Zach studied their footprints. Some of them in the distance had disappeared in the last minutes. They'd been there when he'd looked the first time, right after he and Allie found the rock. Barely there, but still visible in the patches of snow. Yet now there were not only no prints, but the snow was gone as well.

"Can I ask you something?" he asked.

"Sure."

"How'd your daddy come all the way out here to drop off that Mary before he went to work? It don't make no sense."

Allie shrugged because nothing came to mind. Zach had a spine, yes, and he was also kind, but he was smart most of all. She'd guessed back at the road it wouldn't be long before he popped that question, and she knew she'd have to be careful how she answered.

"Maybe he didn't go to work at all. He's done that before. Says, 'I'm leaving for work, Allie, and I'll see you this evenin'.' But when his truck pulls back up in the driveway again, it's my other daddy that gets out. I think sometimes he goes down to Bobby Barnes's shop instead and sits there all day, getting liquored up. That's probably what he did."

Of course maybe that's what really had happened that day—it had plenty of times before—and how was Allie supposed to know either way? And if it *could* have happened, then was what she just told Zach a lie? She didn't think so. But even if Allie had known that Marshall Granderson had just left work and was driving to the Walmart for a new Mary with a beer in one hand and his cell phone in the other, trying to call her yet again, trying to tell himself everything was still fine even if something told him it wasn't, trying to comfort himself by saying even if the Mary was gone, he and Allie still had each other, they had each other, and that was all that mattered—even if Allie had known all of that, she would have told Zach the same thing.

"Come on," she said. "Let's go before this needle decides to peter out again."

Zach hopped off the boulder first, happy to be going somewhere away from those old woods, even if it was the wrong way from town. Allie took off her jean jacket and tied it around her waist, just below the scarf Sam had found. The pack was next. She readjusted it over her shoulders and decided if they were out there much longer, she was going to have to find some private time behind a bush.

"To me, Sam," she said.

The dog turned and looked at her, huffed, and looked back through the trees. His tail never moved.

"Sam, let's go."

Still he wouldn't. Allie grabbed his collar and turned him, ushering him off into the brush. The three of them picked their way through a maze of struggling oaks and thistly undergrowth that slowed their pace to a near crawl. Time slipped more. The sun faded as pockets of thick clouds dotted the sky over the distant mountaintops. Here and there, blackbirds called out. A breeze rustled the trees.

"You laughed back there," Zach said. "When I told you about the Holler."

"Just 'cause it was so dumb."

"It was good to hear, though. You don't laugh much anymore."

She kept her pace, picking her way through the tangle, wincing as limbs smacked her in the face. Her feet, which had all that day sent only sporadic messages that they were cold, now reminded Allie of that fact with each step.

"Most times I don't let myself feel nothing to laugh at," she said.

"How do you do that?" he asked. "Decide not to feel?"

"It ain't something I do as much as it was just something that got done to me. Momma left, and a stone got rolled over my heart."

"I know. But sometimes you just gotta roll that stone back away."

"Ain't that easy," Allie told him. "You ain't never lost anybody, Zach. Maybe if you did, you'd understand better. Feeling too much only makes you hurt. There's rare cause to laugh."

"I lost my granddaddy," Zach said.

"Your granddaddy's in the Greenville jail. You can't lose somebody if you know where they are."

"But I still miss him. Not like you miss your momma, but maybe it don't count that he's close and she's far. Neither of them's here, and that's what—"

Zach didn't finish his thought. He pushed through the last of the underbrush they'd spent the last twenty minutes climbing over and through. What lay on the other side was an open space that could have nearly been a meadow in springtime. Now it was only a dead place of gray grass and scattered rocks that not even the last rays of the sun could lighten. In the distance—two miles, maybe five—rose the tip of a distant hill.

A lone oak stood so tall and wide in the middle of the field that no other trees could grow there. The trunk was wide enough that Allie and Zach could stretch their arms around it and still not touch one another's fingers. Not that they would try. Allie had made up her mind already she was going nowhere near that tree. Its bark lay gray and lumpy in the fading sun, like the skin on a man whose long life was near ending. The top was bare but for three giant limbs that grew out and up like tentacles. Two more branches, long and near the middle, stretched out like arms. It was the most frightening thing Zach had ever seen, but that was not what had stolen his voice. It was what lay at the tree's center. Two knots bulged from there like giant, empty eyes. Below those, the wood had been hollowed out by age and disease, leaving behind a long, jagged maw that looked frozen in a scream.

Allie felt Zach searching for her fingers. He did not take her hand but let their skin touch. Sam's ears pointed in the same direction as his tail—back. That didn't seem a bad idea to Allie. In fact, going back seemed the very best thing in the world right then.

"I think we should go," Zach said. It was his whisper voice, the tone he'd used in the olden woods. He hadn't meant to talk that way, but he couldn't help it. "I don't think we should be here no more, Allie."

Allie looked at the compass. The needle pointed on, through the tree's center.

"We can't go back," she said. "We're close, Zach. I think she's just ahead."

Sam took one step forward but went no farther. Allie didn't like that. Samwise had sniffed nearly every tree in the whole woods that day, but he didn't want to go near that one.

"We can come back tomorrow," Zach said. "We know where to come now. Won't take us long at all. Your daddy'll be home soon. I gotta get home for supper." He clamped the hand that wasn't touching Allie's over his mouth, stifling a cough. "I can't get in trouble right at Christmas."

The needle floated, trying to get Allie's attention.

But the tree. That tree.

It scared her, though she gave that feeling little weight. Allie put much more weight to the notion that Zach was afraid as well. He wouldn't admit that—not ever—but she could tell. Worst of all was Sam. He was scared too. Dogs weren't scared of trees. Not regular trees, anyway.

"Okay," Allie said, and she realized that had been a whisper too. "We'll come back tomorrow, though, right?"

"Sure we will."

"Let's go."

Zach turned to leave. Allie lingered, unable to look away from that gnarled oak. How it looked as if it were warning them, screaming to stay right there, to go no farther. Sam left for Zach's side. When Allie finally turned as well, she ran straight into the back of Zach's hat.

"Hey! What's your problem?"

Zach didn't turn, didn't even move against the weight Allie had thrown at him. He only said, "Something's wrong."

"What's wrong?"

The back of his head shook. "I don't know. Everything looks . . . different."

At first Allie didn't understand what he meant—the underbrush was still there, waiting to poke and prod all over again—but then she did. Yes, there was underbrush, but it wasn't the *same*. It all laid scattered in a different way. There were pines instead of oaks. Boulders and small rocks that hadn't been there before.

"It's okay," Zach said. "It is. Really."

But those words sounded small and weak to Allie, as though Zach was trying to convince himself instead of her. Far from comforting, what Zach said released a tiny, horrible thought that bubbled up from the dark place in Allie's heart and whispered that her mother was gone forever, and what had been lost could never be gained again.

A thought that bubbled up in Zach as well. Something far different from Allie's, but one just as terrible.

He didn't know the way.

8

"What do we do?"

Allie looked at Zach, who in the last seconds had gone from a source of great comfort to one of increasing worry. He wouldn't move from his spot at the edge of the meadow and wouldn't say anything other than the same two words—"It's okay, it's okay, it's okay"—as though repetition was the secret to altering circumstance. She thumped him in the arm.

"Zach? What do we do?"

He turned, facing Allie instead of the underbrush. That was enough to pull him from his trance. He blinked twice and opened his mouth wide, like he was trying to pop his ears.

"We gotta not freak out," he said, though the shake in his voice told her he was nearly there. "That's when people screw up. They freak out and then they do something stupid. We just gotta think."

Allie said, "Well, I think that's the way we come," and pointed to the thick tangle of pines in front of them. And of course it was. It could have been no other way. They'd followed a straight line from the brush to the meadow and had gone no farther. Zach turned to see the rotting oak hadn't moved. Its limbs were still raised out and up, warning STOP.

But it didn't *look* like that was the way they'd come, and they both knew it. There'd been oaks, for one, not pines. They'd forced their way through thornbushes—as though reading each other's minds, Zach and Allie looked down at the scratches on their hands that proved it—but now those thornbushes were gone as well, replaced by a mass of rotting branches atop a blanket of pinecones and needles. Zach crouched and called for Sam.

"You take us home, boy?" he asked. "Where's home, Samwise? Huh?"

"That ain't gonna work," Allie said. "Sam's just a pup, Zach. He couldn't find his tail."

Zach paid her no mind. He rubbed Sam's head. "You go on now, boy. Take us back."

Sam made a small circle around them, sniffing at the ground.

"See?"

"He ain't looking for home," Allie said. "Prolly just looking for a place to pee."

But then Sam let out a small bark and lit straight for the trees, trusting his nose over his eyes. He disappeared into the scrub. Allie felt a flash of panic at the thought of her dog getting lost in there and never being seen again. She called for him once and then again, taking a small step toward the trees. A bark returned.

"We should go," Zach said. "You ain't supposed to, you know. When you get lo—" He cut off the word, not wanting to say it. "When you get turned around, you're supposed to hold still. But I think we should go."

Allie looked back into the meadow. She didn't know if people who got turned around were supposed to stay put or not, but she knew she wanted to get away from that tree. She took Zach's hand. He led them into the pines, holding the branches away so they wouldn't clip her face. Allie kept calling for Sam. Zach used the barks that returned as a homing signal to lead them through to the other side. Allie's fingers began to tremble, and not just from the cold that had settled over the woods. Her breaths came fast and shallow. That hollow place in her stomach growled in high, lonely whines.

The pines thinned ahead. Sam continued his barking, though there was no longer need. The white tip of his tail whooshed against the evergreens, and that was the only thing that moved.

"There he is," Zach said.

Allie reached Sam and bent to her knees, kissing him on the nose. She smiled when he licked her face and nearly laughed as his tail slapped her on the leg. True, they were all just as lo—

(turned around)

—as they'd been only minutes before, but Allie realized things were better now. They were together at least, all three of them, and she thought being bewildered wasn't so bad if you weren't the only one.

Zach pointed. "Look."

Not thirty feet to their right sat the most beautiful sight Allie had ever seen. The oaks may have turned to pines and the brambles to fluffy needles, but the boulder they'd rested on remained. Spread out beyond was the same olden wood they'd crossed before. And here and there, where pockets of snow remained, lay a winding trail of footprints.

"It's okay," Zach told her—told himself. This time he needed to say it only once. "All we gotta do is follow the path we made. We should hurry up, though. It's gettin' dark. Colder too."

They moved quickly from one patch of snow to the next, mindful to keep parallel to the footprints in case they found themselves turned around again. It felt good, getting away from that meadow. Zach kept a solid pace in front of Allie and Sam, looking over his shoulder to make sure they weren't falling behind. Allie stopped only once and only so she could shrug off her pack and put her jacket back on. She untied the scarf from her waist and wrapped it around her neck. It was dirty and smelled like the woods, but Allie figured she was both of those things too. Sam went on ahead. Zach tapped the toe of his boot on the ground, waiting. His eyes kept moving.

"You okay?" she asked.

"Just don't like it here is all. You been in the woods as much as me, you get to feeling things other people don't. This place feels bad."

Allie thought that was just about as close to admitting he was scared as Zach could get. It did little to make her own self feel better. She reached for her backpack and said, "I gotta go to the bathroom."

"What?"

"I gotta go, Zach. Just for a minute. It's important."

"Can't you wait till we get back?" he asked. "We're runnin' out of daylight, Allie. You're daddy's probably home by now, and my folks are gonna kill me."

"I gotta go."

Sam paused ahead and turned around, wanting to know which of them was holding up the group.

"Well, can you just wait until we're outta these woods?" Zach asked. "Can you at least do that?"

Allie didn't think she could—it had been forever since she checked Down There, and she thought the longer it went, the worse it would be—but she nodded anyway. Zach made a circling motion with his hand and turned, moving toward Sam. Allie slipped her arms through the straps of her pack and jogged to catch up.

Just as before, that wide wood stole whatever words either of them had a mind to speak. Allie concentrated on the crunching sound of their feet upon the hard earth instead, hoping that would take her mind off the heavy feeling of something being near. The trail was clear enough, which comforted her; the patches of snow were close enough that she could see the next set of tracks before leaving the set they traveled through. She didn't think they were far from the borderland where they'd first entered that part of the wood. After that it wouldn't be long until they found their bikes and the road. That notion made her feel better in one way and worse in another. They'd spent hours searching, and all they'd gotten for their trouble were sore legs and scratched faces.

Zach had promised they'd come back the next day. Allie believed that well enough, at least as far as he was concerned. But tramping through the woods all day had left her best friend looking weary, and his face held a pasty color streaked by long beads of sweat leaking from under his hat. He might have all the intention in the world of coming back the next day, but there was no way his momma would let him. Especially with it being that close to Christmas. And what would Allie do then?

She lifted her sleeve to make sure the needle still pointed. As long as it did, there was at least a chance Allie could come back herself, find the way. She stopped. The compass was still working. It also wasn't. At least not in the way Allie thought it should.

Zach didn't see her and kept walking, his eyes fixed ahead.

"Zach?"

"Shh. When we're out. Then we can talk."

"But—"

"Shh."

He shook his head, not believing how Allie could go on yammering there in the middle of that wood. He fixed his attention ahead, watching for movement. He didn't see any and knew that didn't matter. *Just because you can't see a thing don't mean it ain't real, or even that it ain't watching.* That's what he'd told Allie, and that's what he believed now. Something was hiding among those ancient trees. Whatever it was didn't feel close, at least not in the sense that Allie and Sam were close. But it was watching.

Allie forced her legs to work and caught up. Sam lifted his nose from the ground and made his way with only his eyes, convinced of the way now. Zach matched the dog's steps and glanced around and up. Allie followed his gaze. The trees felt closer, the air thicker, and for a brief moment a primal place deep within her roused, sparking to life some dormant ancestral gene born in a time when the whole world lived in wild places that were big and dark and could swallow you. Nothing around them had changed. The trees were still grand and kingly, the empty spaces still full with welcoming peace. But those things felt false to Allie now. It was almost as if the forest used those things the same way some women used makeup—to hide old scars that would never heal.

"Up there," Zach said. Sam's eyes and nose hadn't failed them. Ahead, the woods ended in the same jagged line of scrub and bush they'd come through early that afternoon. "See that? We're almost through."

Allie looked at the compass again. She shook her head, trying to understand.

"Zach, it ain't right. Something's wrong."

"Not no more. We're good, Allie. Told you I'd keep you safe." He patted Sam on the butt. "Lead on, boy."

The dog weaved his way through the saplings and undergrowth. Zach scrunched down his hat and took Allie's hand again. They picked their way through an old game trail, wincing as the briars scraped them, Allie calling for Sam and Sam answering, Zach homing in on the sound. When they broke through to the empty place beyond, neither of them spoke. Sam's tail fell silent between his legs. Only Allie felt a sense of what had happened, and how.

The needle had pointed through the screaming tree in the meadow. As such, it should have been pointing *behind* them all that time, back from where they'd come. And yet somewhere in that silent and watching forest, something had turned. Them or the needle, Allie didn't know. All she knew was that the compass now pointed ahead, and Sam hadn't led them back to the road. What they'd found instead was a dead meadow of graying grass that surveyed a whitening sky and a rising moon. And in the middle of that meadow stood a tree so bent and grotesque that its wide limbs and rotting mouth did not need to scream STOP for them to do just that.

Zach let go of Allie's hand. "That ain't possible," he said. "How could we end up back here?" Panicking now, freaking out, just what he'd said they shouldn't do because that's when people screwed up. "What's going on, Allie? What'd we do wrong?"

She tried to calm him. Zach's voice came out broken and stumbling. He pushed Allie away when she tried to take hold of his shoulders and screamed into the air—"Help, hey, anybody, help us please"—repeating it, just as *It's okay* had come before. The last call came out more scream than words and ended with three deep coughs that sounded thick with mucus. Only Zach's echo returned, along with a cold breeze that lowered Allie's head to her chest. The three of them stood still and hushed as that echo faded to silence. It was as if they were the only ones left in the world.

9

They took lodging beneath a thick, low-hanging pine in the heart of the undergrowth, away from the wind and cold. The ground there was dry, and that place in the tangle hid them from the screaming tree. Dusk yielded to the kind of dark that can only exist in the wilderness, one so deep and heavy that Allie felt it seeping into her bones. The singing birds and shuffling squirrels that had kept them company through the day fell silent. Sam huddled near sleep in a pillow of needles beside Allie's pack. He looked hungry and thirsty. They all did. The fear over finding themselves back in the meadow rather than closer to the road lingered. Thankfully, Zach had taken charge with a confidence that warmed Allie despite the cold.

"We'll stay here tonight," he'd said. "It's too late to go searchin' for someplace better. Pine'll keep us warm if we bundle and keep Sam close."

Allie looked down at her thin jacket. It had held up okay, as had the sweatshirt beneath. She'd been colder in her short life. But her tennis shoes were soggy from the long walk through the snow, and her feet were tingly.

"We can't freak out," Zach said, more to himself than to her. "We gotta stay calm. It's just one night. Just a few hours, really. It'll be like camping, like Joseph and Mary did. We'll find our way come morning, Allie. The way's always easy to see in the light. My folks and your daddy're prolly looking for us already. Bet the whole town's out hollering."

And that was true. Marshall had returned home hours before, carrying a six-pack that was down to two rather than a new Mary because who knew you had to buy the whole set, the Joseph and Jesus, too, and that was a hundred dollars Marshall didn't have. He'd found the windows dark and the tree unlit and the front door open but still thought everything was fine. The Grandersons had no Mary but they had each other, and it was only when Marshall found his note on the back of the door, with four words scrawled beneath his own, that he knew that notion was a lie and always had been.

She's all I had

Only that. Not even her name beneath or "Daddy" and a comma at the top. But it was enough to send Marshall out the front door, where now his beer-soaked mind cleared enough for him to notice the wood he'd stacked in Mary's place that morning sprawled out on the damp ground. The blue tarp he'd used to cover it lay in a clump nearby.

Allie had found it. He'd left her a note saying not to look but she'd looked anyway, how could she not, that stupid Mary was all Allie had. Screaming his daughter's name across an empty street, he'd raced back inside to find both Sam and Allie's backpack gone, but it was only when he spotted the shed door open and Allie's bike missing that he knew what had happened. Allie had run away. In the days that would follow, Marshall Granderson would come to understand a great many truths about his life. In those first few moments, however, only one truth broke through his panic—he had no one to turn to for help. It took the last bit of strength left in him to stand on Grace Howard's front porch and not cry when she answered the door.

The two words that greeted Grace had come out shouted and slurred, masking the enormity of what Marshall had said for only a moment. Grace stood there with her brow scrunched. Her mouth opened slowly as her mind pieced together what Marshall had just said:

Allie's gone.

He hadn't heard from her all day, had called and called, but it was only when Marshall began repeating that Mary was gone, *gone,* and he wasn't the one who'd taken her at all that Grace had begun to worry. She'd opened the door, inviting him inside. Marshall shook his head no, he had to find Allie. *They* had to find Allie, because Grace was the only person who would help. Grace told Marshall that wasn't true. She'd also told him that Allie hadn't run away at all. And what Grace said next was both the one thing she'd known Marshall most needed to hear and the one thing he didn't.

She'd seen Allie that morning, in the town square. And she'd been with Zach Barnett.

They'd driven to the Barnett home straight away, believing Allie was there. After an argument fueled as much by Marshall's anger as his drunkenness, Jake informed him that Allie wasn't there at all. Nor, Kate said through tears, was Zach. They had instead gone in search of a plastic Mary mysteriously gone from the Grandersons' front yard, and did Marshall know anything about that? Marshall said he didn't, that it was nothing of Jake's business what happened between him and Allie. Jake didn't believe him, not with the stench of beer on Marshall's breath. For his part, Marshall didn't believe Kate's assertion that Allie wasn't there. He would only believe it later and after a long night of looking, when he checked the answering machine at home to find just as many messages from Kate calling her boy home for supper as he himself had left for Allie.

The four of them set aside their differences long enough to begin a search that was more hysterical than methodical. Jake, Kate, and Grace found nothing at all. The only thing Marshall found was the sureness that Allie had finally gotten her fill of him and run off, taking Sam and Zach with her. They scoured the fields and patches of woods between the two homes, rousing what neighbors they could, just as Zach had imagined. The problem Allie saw with that scenario was everyone would be looking in the wrong places. That was all her fault. Hers and the compass's.

10

Zach pointed to Allie's pack. "What food you got in there?"

She unzipped the bag, wary of letting Zach see everything

inside. There was no way he could, not in the darkness of the tree, but woman things were best kept hidden from boys.

"Four candy bars and two juice boxes," she said.

"That's it?"

"I didn't think we'd be out here in no-man's-land for the whole night, Zach."

"Okay. We'll split one of the candy bars and one thing of juice."

"Are you kidding me? I'm starving."

"So'm I," Zach said. "But we better ration, just in case. We gotta be careful, Allie. This is wild country."

"You said we were just camping."

"There's something you gotta understand," Zach said. He inched closer. Allie could see the black outline of his face. "You have to trust me here, Allie. I know what I'm doing. You can handle all the searching and whatever, but when it comes to being safe, you have to let me take the lead. I ain't saying that because you're a girl. I'm saying it because I'm a Barnett. Jesus went for forty days without nothing to eat or drink. He made it okay, even with the devil there. We'll get by fine with half a candy bar and a couple swallows of juice."

Allie frowned. She hadn't stepped foot in church since her momma left (one of the prerequisites of being fallen away, Bobby had told her), but she remembered the stories well enough. Sure, Jesus had made it okay. Mostly because He was God and not a kid, and the angels had been there with Him. Allie peered up through the tangle of branches above. She saw only black mixed with hazy moonlight.

So they ate. Supper that first night was a Snickers bar and two swallows of apple juice, which ended up being divided three ways instead of just two because neither of them could drink in front of Sam. Zach blessed his bites before tossing them in his mouth. Allie didn't. Sam leaned his nose in, smelling.

"You can't eat this, Sam," Allie said. "Chocolate'll ruin your insides."

The dog whimpered. Allie nearly relented. In the end, she turned and swallowed her part nearly whole. The meal was finished in less than ten seconds. It was no masterpiece.

"Fire should be easy enough," Zach told her. "We get a fire, this here'll be like vacation."

"You got any matches?"

Zach smirked and shook his head. He pulled the knife from his pocket. "Don't need none. Come on. You go gather up some wood. Don't matter what it is, just make sure it's plenty small. Then get some bigger chunks too. I'll get the rest."

They crawled out from beneath the pine. Sam raised his head and humphed twice before settling back to sleep. Not far from the pine stood a withering cedar. Zach snapped off the first three good branches he could find and peeled two handfuls of bark from the trunk. Allie returned with an armful of fallen oak and some smaller pine branches.

"That'll do," he said.

"For what?"

"Gonna make a fire Indian-style. Daddy showed me how."

He rubbed the cedar bark into a fluffy pile in his hands, then gathered what Allie had found. They cleared a spot in front of the pine, where Zach arranged the wood into a teepee shape around the cedar bark and a clump of pine needles. He slid a hand down one of the cedar branches, measuring a straight section an inch thick and ten inches long, then broke it against his knee. Allie watched as Zach tapered both ends into a spindle with his knife. He set that aside and split another branch, making sure the length and width would work, then used his blade to flatten both sides and carve a small hole in the middle. It took less time to shape another chunk small enough to fit in his palm, this one carved with a small hole in the center as well. He fished out one of his bootlaces and tied it to both ends of a three-foot section of branch, then wrapped the lace around the spindle. The process took perhaps twenty minutes all told, but Zach was sweating by the end.

"There," he said. "All done. Just gotta drill the sockets."

"Can I help?" Allie asked.

"No, just sit easy. I'll get it."

He rested his right knee on the ground and placed his left foot across the flattened branch. One end of the spindle went into the small hole in the center, the other into the handhold. Zach braced the handhold against his shin and, careful to keep the spindle perpendicular, began drawing the bow forward and back in long, steady strokes. The air filled with the sweet smell of burning cedar. Moonlight trickled through the pines, catching Zach's pale face. Sweat fell from under his hat in thin, tiny streams. He stopped after a few minutes and coughed.

"It's ready," he said. "All I gotta do now's cut the notch."

"Are you okay?"

"Yeah. Just tired's all."

He did look tired, probably just as tired as Allie thought she looked herself. But there was more than that. Zach looked sick too.

"I gotta go to the bathroom." Allie bent her head, couldn't look at him. "I ain't been all day."

"Just don't go far. Fire'll be ready when you get back."

Zach watched but said nothing as Allie ducked back under the pine. Sam perked his head up and wagged his tail.

"You stay here, Samwise," she said.

She grabbed her backpack and wiggled out, wondering where to go. Sticking close to camp wouldn't do, but nor did Allie want to risk losing Zach in the night. The sound of the bow moving the spindle was loud enough, though, and she believed she could use that the same way Zach had used Sam's barks. Allie shouldered her pack and moved slowly, keeping her hands outstretched to ward off any prickly branches. The meadow lay ahead. It was exactly the place Allie didn't want to go, but the moon shone stronger there, and she needed the light. She crouched along the edge of the tree line and bent her head down and away, shielding her eyes from the screaming tree.

Moonlight caught the plastic bubble over the compass. Allie tilted it up to see the needle holding steady at three o'clock, just as she thought it would. She turned to face the tree (still keeping her eyes away) and watched as the needle swept up to twelve. That was where the compass meant them to go. At least there was that. So long as the needle worked, Allie didn't consider them lost. Mislaid, maybe. Turned around, in Zach's words. But people were lost only when they didn't have direction.

The backpack fell. Allie fished out one of the packs Miss Howard had brought and looked around to make sure no one was watching. She unbuttoned her jeans. The cold was like a knife against her skin as she squatted. That chore now complete, another problem presented itself. What was Allie supposed to do with . . . *it*? She couldn't just leave it there in the middle of the field. Zach might spot it the next day, what with his wilderness eyes. Even if he didn't, Allie felt sure Sam's nose would find it. And what would that bring? Enough barks and growls and yips to wake the dead, that's all.

"Dumb old dog'd probably want to carry it around like a chew toy," she whispered.

She bent to the ground and tried to dig a small hole with her fingers. The soil was too hard. In the end, there was no choice but to bury the pad as far as possible beneath the grass and cover it with a nearby rock.

The screeching of Zach's fire maker faded from inside the trees. Allie stood, meaning to head back before she lost the sound, then stopped. She'd forgotten to keep her eyes from the oak, and of course it's always the things we promise to ignore that we end up seeing clearest of all. The tree appeared bigger in the night, if such a thing were possible. Its limbs were bathed in shadows that gave them the illusion of reaching out as far as the meadow was wide. A dark mass leaked through the tentacles in the tree's top—the faraway hill, Allie supposed. She was too preoccupied to be sure. The rotten part in the tree's middle was what concerned her. It had gone hidden. Not because of the darkness, but because of the moonlight streaming down behind. A breeze fluttered through the night, building as it swirled over the meadow's far side before rattling the few dead leaves remaining on the oak. From there that wind became a wave rolling to where Allie stood. It was as if the meadow were infested by a million tiny things, all of them marching for her. A wave of cold rushed over Allie as the breeze reached her, and with it came an awareness that felt as real as anything she had ever known.

She was not alone.

The wind passed, moving from the meadow on into the scrub, but Allie had gone rigid. She stared out past the screaming oak, willing her eyes to penetrate the woods beyond, and in that darkness came a voice that spoke three words:

I See You

Allie swallowed and took a step back. "What?" she asked. The mere sound of her voice made her flinch. Softer, she added, "Hello? Is anyone there?"

Silence again, as though the forest was gathering its breath. The moon shone through the top of the oak, and those long limbs reached out, warning her away. The wind, had to be. Allie wanted to call out again, but the primal part of her spoke up once more and said if she did that, if she made only a peep, something would answer. Something bad.

She crouched to the ground and gathered her backpack, then scurried through the trees. It was thick in there and quiet. No screech of Zach's fire tools, no bark from Sam. No Something in the dark.

"Zach?" she whispered. "Zach."

From just ahead came a faint, "Over here."

Allie followed the voice and realized she'd reached their camp only when she nearly tripped over Zach's foot. She groped for his arm and pulled him beneath the tree. Sam jumped, nearly barked. Allie silenced him. Zach tried to speak. She silenced him too.

"Someone's out there," she whispered.

"Where?"

"In the meadow."

Zach slid himself halfway from under the tree before Allie pulled him back.

"What are you doing?" he asked. "Maybe it's help."

"It ain't help."

"How d'you know?"

"Remember when we walked through the olden woods? What you said about it not feeling right? That's how I felt."

All she could see of Zach were the faint outlines of his eyes. But he didn't try to leave the pine now, and Allie took that as a sign that maybe he believed her. She felt Sam stir and gathered him into her arms, holding him tight.

"You sure you saw something?" he asked.

"I didn't see anything. I heard it."

"Maybe it was just the wind. You know how you are with the wind, Allie. The woods play tricks sometimes." It was his teaching voice again. "That's probably all it was. Maybe it was just a deer or something. Plenty deer around. Remember that track we saw? Lots of critters scurry around in the night, even in winter."

"You sure?" she asked.

"Sure I'm sure."

That made Allie feel some better. Maybe it had all been just a trick, just her mind getting all wonky from having so little to eat and drink and having to pull *that* out of her underwear in the middle of the cold woods. Yes, sure. It would be enough to make anyone hear anything.

"Where's the fire?" she asked.

Zach didn't answer at first. Allie thought he hadn't heard and was about to ask again when he mumbled, "Wouldn't take. Got a coal a couple times, but it fell apart as soon as I tried to get it in the tinder."

He was hurt. Allie knew that, and she knew it wasn't like the scrapes and nicks they'd gotten from the brambles. This was a pain left by something else, and it pricked deeper.

"It's okay," she said. "I ain't cold anyways. It's nice in here."

"We'll gather up some needles," he said. "Make some walls to seal in the empty places around the bottom. I'll get a fire tomorrow. It'll be easier in the daylight."

"I know you will."

"Here." He offered a handful of what looked to Allie like wood from the tree over them. "We had our meal, now it's time for dessert. It's all I was able to gather up. The inside bark on a pine's good enough to eat."

"I ain't eating no wood, Zach Barnett. I ain't no beaver."

"Come on." He put some in his mouth and chewed it, wincing as it went down. "See? It ain't no Snickers bar, but it's passing fair."

Seventeen miles away, Marshall and Grace had returned to the Granderson home and found it empty still. Marshall grabbed for the phone when it rang, thinking it had to be his little girl. It was Jake instead, telling him everyone was meeting downtown. There was no good-bye, no "See you there" or "You keep your chin up, Marshall." Just a click on the line.

Grace asked if there was news. Marshall told her nothing. She was on the couch, one hand over her eyes and the other turning her blond ponytail in quiet circles. She tried talking to him, telling him it would be okay. Wanting to believe that herself. Some part of her had long feared things would lead to this. Allie was such a strong girl, such a broken girl—wounded just as much as her father. As Grace thought on all of those things and felt the agony in the man across from her, the present mixed with the past, and she said it would be okay, Hank; they would be okay.

"Hank?" Marshall asked.

Grace took her hand from her eyes. "What?"

"You just called me Hank, Grace."

"No I didn't."

"You did." He took a step forward and leveled a shaky finger her way. "That what you think, Grace? Huh?"

Grace's voice shook. "No, Marshall, that's—"

"You think I'm gonna turn into your old man? That it? Think I'm gonna go nuts—"

"—Don't you *say* that, Marshall—"

"—and end up like him?"

His cheeks were hot, his lips trembling, but Marshall could not give himself over to the rage inside him, not with Allie gone and Grace holding her hands over her head to hide her tears. He turned, leaving her there, and went to his bedroom. His work clothes smelled of oil and sweat. Marshall pulled a pair of jeans and an old sweatshirt from the closet, along with a mostly full bottle. He'd have to go back to town, look for Allie. And he would. He just needed a drink first.

He didn't know which was worse—that Allie had run away or that she'd gone and gotten herself lost because of that stupid statue. He should have gone out there with her the night before as he'd promised, made sure the Mary was weighted down good. It had been cold and snowing, and the wind had been up. Allie hated the wind. It scared her. But instead he'd gone into the bedroom after dinner to draw that curtain down a little, and by then Bobby was there, and Bobby had enough booze to draw that curtain down as tight as it would go. That was something Allie couldn't understand. He'd had to be strong for the both of them ever since Mary died, and there was only so much strength in a man.

He sat on the bed and turned the bottle up. He had to keep the old nerves calm. Just a couple nips from the bottle. Three at the most.

11

Allie finished her handful of pine bark (which not only tasted like sandpaper but also went down her throat about as well as a doorknob) while Zach did the same. The remaining juice box tempted them. In the end, Zach told Allie to put it back in her bag. What words passed between them were few that night. He huddled close against her. Sam lay between them. For a long while, there was only the sound of the wind through the scrub and the occasional hoot of an owl.

"Zach?" Allie asked.

"What?"

"You sleepin'?"

"Can't be sleepin' if I just asked you what."

"I can't doze, Zach. I got the creepsomnia."

"What's that?"

"You know, when you can't get to sleep because everything's creepy." Allie paused and sent the word over her teeth again, nice and slow. "Creep . . . SOM . . . nia."

"Where'd you hear that word?"

"Just now," she said. "I made it up."

"Can I use it?" Zach asked. "I kinda like that one."

"Sure."

"Allie?"

"Yeah?"

"I got creepSOMnia."

Allie snorted from her place under the pine. That sound gave way to laughter. Zach joined in. It felt good to laugh, even there. Especially there.

Sleep did in fact come to the children that night, a sleep that felt almost bottomless. Allie dreamed she stood in front of a fresh grave at Oak Lawn. A faceless crowd surrounded a small casket. Allie was crying but didn't know why. Her daddy stood beside her. She asked him who had died. When Marshall turned his head, Allie saw it wasn't Marshall at all. Where there should have been a face, there was only a deep, rippling shadow that answered her with three words:

I see you.

December 21

1

Once, back before everything ended, Allie's daddy had convinced her and her momma to go camping in the hill country outside Mattingly. "There's nothing like being out in the middle of nature," Marshall Granderson said, "and you'll never sleep as good as when you're under the stars." Mary had been willing enough. Allie, not so much. Even then, she'd been afraid of what lurked in the mountains. Witches, maybe. Ghosts, probably. Hungry animals, for sure.

The three of them had gone anyway, and it had been a fine time until it got dark. It was the quiet rather than the ghosts that kept Allie awake until morning. It was a stillness so pure that it made the night feel like a big hole she'd been trapped inside. That was when Allie discovered sleeping under the stars was in no way better than sleeping under a roof. The woods had probably been made for some, but certainly not for her.

It was a similar silence that stirred Allie from a thin and restless sleep on this morning. She found herself on her back, looking up through the center of the big pine's bones. Patches of snow clogged the outer limbs. A gray shine oozed through the topmost branches. Allie blinked and exhaled. A cloud of steam rose upward from her mouth. She shivered and rubbed her eyes, trying to decipher the light above her. What she settled on was either a very early morning or a risen sun hidden by clouds.

Her hand found Sam's fur. Allie closed her eyes and sank her body into the pine needles beneath her. Fragments of the previous day flooded her mind—the Mary and the compass, leaving with Zach, the olden forest. The tree.

And there had been dreams, right?

Yes, Allie thought, and she managed to lift her chin and then lower it in agreement. She'd been in Oak Lawn with a crowd of people, and everyone was crying. Her daddy said something to her, something Allie couldn't remember now but had scared her then. Something that had made her scream.

She turned her wrist over and looked at the compass. The needle held strong, pointing to three o'clock. Beyond the meadow.

That Allie was in a strange and frightening place somehow lent her silent inventory a greater importance. She turned toward Zach. A stab of pain greeted her that began in her neck and ended in her teeth. Even moving that little bit felt like cracking ice in a tray. Zach lay huddled against her in a tight ball. At some point in the night, he'd positioned his hat as a pillow. Now it lay crumpled under his head. It was cold under the tree, maybe not as cold as it was outside but still enough to leave Allie shivering. But Zach's face was covered with sweat. His breaths came out in short whistles.

Sam lay between them in his own ball, his tail tucked over his nose. His stomach gurgled, but other than that, he seemed no worse for the wear.

Her companions accounted for, Allie considered her own self last. Aside from creaky limbs, she was pleased that all systems seemed pointed to Go. Her stomach rumbled, but there was no hurt. That was saved for her face and hands. She raised her arms and found her fingers covered with scrapes and cuts. And her feet were cold. That maybe wasn't so big a deal—she was out in the woods in the middle of winter, after all; everything felt cold. She raised her head, wincing again, and tried to straighten her legs. Her Chucks were soggy and crusted with dirt, but otherwise fine. She laid her head down again and breathed deep, trying to summarize the relevant facts.

It was December 21, four days until Christmas and five hundred and forty-five days since her momma left.

She had no idea of the weather, and that was a bother. Facing the day—any day—would be hard enough, but not knowing if the sun would shine or the snow would fall or how hard the wind was supposed to blow would make things harder. Much harder.

She and Zach were still in the woods. Still turned around, according to him. Still just where they needed to be, according to her.

Sam was okay but hungry, and Allie figured she was pretty much the same, all things considered. But Zach still had a cold, and his lungs were whistling. That brought another, more pressing point—they'd have to get home soon.

The compass still worked.

That last point was what stuck in Allie's head and made the day seem brighter.

"Hey."

The word made Allie jerk (which presented another relevant fact—her entire body felt like her neck). She turned her head. Zach's eyes were open.

"Hey," she said.

"Pretty cool, huh? We made it the whole night."

Sam raised his head and grumbled when he saw where he was. There'd be no hiding under the covers that morning.

"We sure did," Allie said. "You feeling okay?"

Zach nodded. He did feel okay. Mostly, anyway. His lungs

felt gunky, and there was a layer of sweat between his upper lip and nose. It had been a long night—a horrible one, actually. He was glad Allie had slept through it all, or else she'd be worried.

"I did a good job on the shelter, huh?" he asked. "Nice and toasty in here. It's the pine needles. I piled them around the bottom to keep the draft out. You probably never even heard the wind, did you?"

Allie shook her head. No, she hadn't heard the wind at all.

"We're gonna go home today," Zach said. "Promise. I'll keep you safe."

"I know you will."

"Bet they're looking for us now. Maybe everyone."

Allie said, "Guess so," and realized she'd somehow left that part out of her personal inventory. Surely her daddy was out looking for her, was probably either worried out of his mind or drunk out of it. She knew she should feel a good deal of remorse for that, but what Allie felt most was a sense that came quite close to happiness. Served Marshall Granderson right for taking her Mary away. For spending so much time in his bedroom with the other Marshall Granderson or out in the shed with that pervert Bobby Barnes.

But there was something else as well. Her father would have to go to town for help. Since The Storm, Marshall had tried to separate himself as much as possible from the people of Mattingly. There was no way he could keep himself separated from them now. Allie wondered how that had gone. She thought not well. Marshall had fallen away just as much as she, in some ways more. To many, his name was now looked down upon even more than Bobby Barnes's. The town would band together to look for Zach, though. In a way that didn't make Allie feel very good at all, she decided that had been another good reason to bring him along.

2

While that may have been true before, that morning Marshall found more friends than he could count. Grace Howard had stayed the night on the couch, wanting to be there if Allie came home but also not wanting to leave Marshall alone. He'd walked from the hallway into the living room little more than a corpse. His hair was jumbled, and his beard had gone an extra shade of gray overnight. His eyes were bloodshot. The smell of whiskey oozed from his pores. It had almost been enough for her to call him Hank once more, this time on purpose.

She'd been on the phone with Kate, explaining that Marshall had taken ill late the night before. It was a lie, of course, one that Kate knew just as much as Grace, but that was neither the place nor the time to say so. Grace hung up the phone and told Marshall everyone was meeting in town, and for him to get himself dressed.

The awkwardness Marshall felt of having to stand all but naked beneath Grace's glare turned to surprise at what he found in the town square an hour later. Word of the missing children had spread overnight. Flyers were posted on telephone poles and in storefront windows, all with Allie's and Zach's likenesses. ("I gave a picture to Jake," Grace said, "since you wouldn't open up your door last night to get one down to him yourself.") Marshall was besieged by well-wishers as soon as he climbed out of Grace's car, everyone wanting to shake his hand and grasp his shoulder, wanting to hug and trying not to cry, telling him he might've left the town but the town had never left him, Allie was one of their own, and they wouldn't rest until she was home safe. It was a moment that touched Grace's heart, if not Marshall's. Allie and Zach had somehow lost their way the day before, but the town itself had lost its way in the past year and a half. The sight of everyone coming to the aid of a neighbor allowed Grace the hope of something good rising from the ashes of such a terrible happening.

The state police arrived at Jake's behest, along with members of the forestry service. Search grids were plotted and distributed. Juliet Creech, pastor of Mattingly's Methodist church, had called everyone to prayer. Heads were bowed and hands were clasped as she spoke of God's goodness and protection. Marshall's head never bent. His eyes remained open. He could not bring himself to ask the favor of the very thing that had led to his daughter's disappearance. When he found one other person who seemed to share those very feelings, Marshall could only smile. It figured. The good pastor had stared at him, wide-eyed and unfeeling, through her entire prayer.

Not long before Allie woke, Jake and a pilot had lifted off in a helicopter from the snow-covered grass of the church softball field, heading east for the hill country. Marshall had balked at that, calling the idea a waste of time, but Jake said he had to do something. It was a simple confession between two former friends, but it had been enough for Marshall to let Jake go. The largest part of Marshall still raged at the man he blamed for Mary's death, but a bit of his old self mourned for the father whose son had disappeared.

Zach lifted his head and blinked, brushing pine needles from his face and arms. He pushed aside the nearest pile and poked his head out from under the tree.

"Hey," he said. "You gotta see this."

Sam rose and shimmied out into the woods. Allie didn't move at first. Her mind had already decided what it was that Zach wanted her to see—something left in the dirt from the night before, a track of a ghost or a witch that had snuck inside her dreams to say something awful. If her eyes beheld something like that, Allie thought she'd go plain mad. But Zach kept telling her to look, and his hand was waving her forward. She crept out and peeked.

The forest outside lay covered in a fresh layer of white. Sam dipped his nose in the snow and shuffled away. When he found nothing of interest, he arched his back and stretched, shaking himself awake.

"Gotta be another two inches," Zach said. He coughed once, short and not that thick. "And we stayed dry the whole time. How awesome am I, anyway?"

Allie smiled. Zach looked at her and smiled back, even if whatever glow shining through the cracks of her dirty face had more to do with the snow than with him. Clean, fresh, unruffled snow. Nothing had come near their tree at all. Whatever she thought had been in the meadow the night before was just her imagination after all, just like Zach had told her.

"I'm gonna start a fire," Zach said. "Snow probably won't last long on the ground, but it'll still be cold today. Then we need to figure out what we're gonna do. We can't stay here, Allie. We ain't got no food or water, and we need both. Sam too. I think we should try goin' back through those olden woods and find our bikes. But fire comes first."

"You do that," Allie said. "I'm gonna go do my business."

He looked at her. "You gotta go again?"

Allie shrugged. "You ain't gotta?"

"No," Zach said. A part of him thought that strange. "Not even a little."

He crawled back under the tree and returned with his bow drill, the wood from the night before, and Allie's backpack. Zach handed the latter to her without a word. She waited for him to ask again what was in there, but Zach only set about clearing a spot for the fire. The silence made her feel better and worse.

"C'mon, Samwise," she said. "Let's get you warmed up with some exercise."

The dog barked once and followed. Allie led them through

the tangle of brush and out the other side. Blades of gray grass poked up from the ground, their bottoms hidden by white. Fog lifted from the top of the hill in the distance. Maybe the sun would shine some and get rid of all that snow. Allie hoped so. The thought of another whole day tromping through the woods in just her Chucks made her feet hurt.

The snow had made the forest look beautiful, but it had done little to prettify the oak standing in the meadow. At least Allie could look at it now. A lot of things didn't look so bad in the light of day, whether a situation or a screaming tree. Even Sam didn't look as scared of it as he had the day before.

The screech of Zach's fire maker wove through the pines behind them. Allie slipped off her pack and moved her scarf away. She unbuttoned her jeans and stopped.

"I'm gonna need you to avert your eyes, Sam."

The dog sat and cocked his head to the side.

"Go on, now. This ain't something I want to see myself, much less you."

Sam turned his head (Allie was pretty sure he could still see her just fine out of the corner of his eye, the nosy old mongrel) and looked across the meadow. She tended to herself and lifted her jacket sleeve, studying the compass.

"I'm coming," she whispered.

The needle pointed on, fluttering under its plastic bubble. She looked past the screaming oak and then to Sam.

"That ain't the way we come, Sam. We didn't cross no hills. But I don't think the way back's how we come either, or we wouldn't have ended up here again."

Sam padded over and rubbed his head against Allie's leg, trying to comfort.

Allie rubbed him and said, "It's okay. Sometimes things are just hard when you love."

Zach was under the pine when they returned. The teepee of firewood he'd stacked in the cleared space out front remained unlit. His face was wet again and looked as pale as the snow.

"Gonna have to find some dry ground," he muttered. "Too wet here to catch a spark."

"I was thinking we should move on," Allie said.

"Me too. Not what you're supposed to do when you're turned around, but I'm hungry for more than another candy bar. Thirsty too."

"We got snow to eat," Allie said.

Zach shook his head. "Can't. You'll get hyperthomola."

"I don't think it's called that," she said.

"Is too. I learned it."

Allie said nothing more. What she had to say next called for diplomacy. She didn't want to risk a fight.

"I don't think we should go back through the olden woods, Zach. We tried that yesterday. It just got us back here."

"We'll be more careful this time," he said. "'Sides, that way'll be better for you. Those trees are thick up top, even in the winter. Ain't as much snow on the ground. You can't walk in the snow with them shoes you got on."

"I don't think it'll work," she said.

"How you know that?"

"Because that's not where my compass is pointing."

There, she'd said it. And even if Allie couldn't look at Zach as those words came out, she felt the better for it.

Zach wasn't much surprised at the reasoning behind Allie's argument, however dim that reasoning was. "It's pointin' the wrong way," he said. "I know the woods, Allie. That ain't the way we come."

"I know it ain't. But maybe it's pointing where we're *supposed* to go. Maybe there's a road nearby, or some old hermit living out here all alone. Maybe we'll be closer to home going ahead than going back."

It was a stretch, Allie knew that, but one she was willing to make. Besides, she could be right. Maybe there really was a road close. One they'd find as soon as they found Mary.

"Guess we do need to find some higher ground," Zach said. "Take a look around, you know. See if we can spot anything."

"Well, there's a hill up that way. You saw it."

"It's a long way, Allie."

"So's goin' back."

He got up, surrendering to her logic. It did make sense in a way, going on ahead. The top of the hill farther on could probably give a good view for miles. Besides, Zach didn't really care to tread back through the olden woods again. But he said, "I really think I should be making the decisions from here on, Allie. Not that you can't, but I'm the man here. I been in the woods plenty. I kept us safe last night."

"I know you did"—anything to keep him moving—"you did real good."

"Okay."

She let Zach store his fire maker in her backpack, along with the tinder. Her only request was that she place them in there herself, and she would be the only one to take them out. Zach didn't mind. He was too anxious to get moving and too tired to care. He cut an opening in the empty juice box and stuffed it with snow, then tucked it beneath his shirt to melt on the way. They set out then, the three of them. Through the pines and into the meadow, past the screaming tree that begged them to turn back. On into a wild land that held neither roads nor hermits.

Sam led them. Allie asked Zach if he felt better and he said yes. It was a lie that would last one more day. He pointed to her wrist. Allie secured the compass midstride and thanked him.

She had once believed in many things before everything ended. Much of that faith left after she'd fallen away. The little left Allie now poured into the tiny plastic bubble on her wrist, believing the needle would lead them to a place of miracles.

Whether that would be true or not, neither Allie nor Zach could say. Nor did either of them pause in that long walk from the meadow to ponder that any compass, magical or not, could only guide Allie from the place they were to the place they wished to arrive. As for what lay in between? That was just as much a mystery to the needle as it was to them. Yet Allie walked on and never considered turning back. Even if ahead lay things far more dangerous and beautiful than two children and one dog could imagine.

3

The way was level and clear but for the bare trees and fluffy evergreens that rose up from the frozen ground. Sam found the woods much too interesting to remain close and wandered farther away. When the silence grew too long and deep, he stabbed it with a bark. Here and there, clumps of snow fell from the limbs above. Sam would hear those hollow thumps and give chase. As far as Allie was concerned, it was the finest day of her dog's life.

Not so for her and Zach. Gone were the brambles and underbrush that had plagued them the previous day. In their place were roots and rocks hidden like traps beneath the thin layer of snow. Sam managed to avoid these with ease enough, but the silence between his yips became filled with painful, aggravated grunts as Allie staggered on. The scarf was knotted around her neck, and her jacket was snapped all the way up, keeping out most of the cold. But her feet felt funny. The numbness in them that morning had gone away. An itch had moved in.

Zach grew more worried the farther they moved away from the meadow. He was coughing again. It wasn't nearly what he'd endured the night before while Allie slept, just enough to aggravate him. He felt okay enough (so he told himself), but he couldn't escape the nagging feeling that the cold he'd left town with was turning into something worse. That wasn't the only thing on his mind. Sam might have been acting fine in his head but he wasn't anywhere else. Burrs dotted brown-and-white fur that looked to have sagged overnight. And then there was the issue of Allie's shoes. Two inches of snow was nothing back in Mattingly, where there were plows and blowers and salt to get it all out of the way. But out there in the deep woods, even a dusting could lead to trouble. Especially when every step Allie took spilled a little of it over her Chucks.

"We ain't making distance like we did yesterday," he said. "Guess we're just tired's all. Snow ain't making it none easier."

"Tired," she said. Yes, Allie was tired. More so than the day before, when the compass had sprung to life, and a piece of her that had gone moldy and stale had sprung with it. There had been a bright sun that day, and an end in sight. Now there was only a low sky and a hill beyond that might be an end or was only another stop. It was the first time Allie considered that the path of adventure she'd set Zach and Sam on had begun to turn to something else. Something maybe more important than finding Mary. Something even like life and death.

She lifted her sleeve and checked the compass. Zach watched but said nothing, only coughed into his sleeve. The needle still held toward the hill. Much of their destination lay hidden by the forest ahead, though its thin top now loomed closer through the tops of the trees.

"Maybe that's all we have to go," she told Zach. "Just to that hill. Maybe we'll find her there, and then the needle'll point us home."

"Yeah," Zach said. "Maybe we'll find a Dairy Queen and a wad of cash along the way too. How about one of them candy bars?"

She turned her pack around and dug inside. "Got another Snickers."

"We had one for supper. Got anything else?"

She dug more. "Baby Ruth?"

"Okay. Split it again, though. Unless you want another handful of pine tree."

She tore the bar free, careful to put the wrapper back inside her bag, and handed half to Zach. He handed a third of his to Sam. The food was good (though at that point, Allie believed any food would have been good), as was the melted snow that washed it down. Allie only wished they'd had more to drink. Food she could do without, but a juice box of water wasn't near enough to quench the thirst in her.

"What would you be doing now?" Zach asked. "If we were home, I mean."

Allie checked the compass again. Up ahead, Sam barked at nothing.

"Not sure," she said. "I don't even know what time it is."

"I'd be with my folks," Zach said. "Probably down at the sheriff's office or out riding with Daddy. We're supposed to get Momma something for Christmas this morning. Then we'd all go to the diner for lunch. Daddy, he'd maybe let me throw his tomahawk some after. I'm gettin' real good, Allie. He's gonna give her to me proper when I come to be a man."

Her. Allie had always thought it funny, the way men named their toys. Her daddy kept a shotgun in the closet (along with the bottles and cans and his other self) that he called Beulah. Likely,

Allie thought, because that was the perfect name for something old and rusty. Jake Barnett didn't have a shotgun, but he did have an old tomahawk named Bessie that Zach had coveted ever since Allie had known him. She almost asked him how that went, becoming a man—if Zach was supposed to get Bessie first, or did that happen after he braved the rusty gate at Happy Hollow and carved his name. Anything to pass the time and keep him talking, keep him with her. She only nodded instead. Zach probably didn't know how boys became men at all. Besides, asking him might lead him to wanting to know how girls became women. The only answer Allie could give him was it was when a girl's body started turning against her.

"What would you be doing?" he asked again.

"I don't know."

"Come on. It'll get your mind off stuff."

Allie checked the compass again. She lowered her head and shrugged her shoulders, shuffling the pack on her back. Sam's nose had carried him nearly fifty feet ahead. He was still now, staring into a place where the trees ended and more scrub began. Almost like he'd spotted something.

"Daddy's off work till first of the year," she said. "He'd likely go down to Bobby's garage all day. If he did, I'd do some cleaning. Tree needs watering, so I'd do that first. Daddy always says the fireplace dries the tree out. If he stayed home and he ain't gone to the bedroom to trade himself in for my other daddy, we might watch some TV. If he gets all drunked up, I'll just sit in my room with Sam. I'll go check on Mary in the front yard later, make sure she's okay. Maybe Miss Howard'll come by in the afternoon. I figure she probably will. It's Christmastime, and that always brings out people's yearnings. Then it's bed. So all things considered, Zach, I'd rather be out here in the deep, dark woods with you than at home."

Zach said nothing. He only stared at Sam and kept moving. Allie felt bad, taking all the fun out of his game; then she realized Zach had probably not heard her at all. He was looking ahead, toward Sam. Toward what was hanging from the tree.

"What's that?" she asked.

"I don't know. Don't look like it belongs, though."

They moved with a slowness that was more fear than caution. Sam was sniffing the base of the tree ahead and whimpering. Zach came to the tree first. He extended a hand to what was there but didn't touch it. The hunk of wood was as thick as Zach's arm and nearly as wide as he was tall, pinned to the trunk by an ancient nail so long and fat he thought it could be a railroad spike. Age and wind had knocked the sign at an angle toward the ground. The wood had faded to a dull gray that could signify brittleness or petrification, he didn't know which. The three words burned into the wood, however, could still be read well enough:

WARE—NO FARTHER

"What's that mean?" Allie asked. *"Ware?"*

"It means beware. It's the way the old people used to talk."

"Why would we have to beware?"

Zach was quiet but for a wheezing sound rising up from his chest. He said, "Maybe this used to be somebody's claim back a long time ago. Looks like it's been here a while."

Sam had finished his sniffing. He crowded into the small space between them and perked his ears. His eyes were no longer on the tree, but to the span of underbrush just beyond. The tangle was tight and dark, nearly a wall. The trees beyond rose up at a steep angle, like the world had gathered into a wave and frozen. Small pines and cedars struggled to find a foothold in the slanted soil.

The rough slope of the hill looked much steeper up close than it had back in the meadow.

"That's some real darkwood, Allie," Zach said. "Could get lost in there. And even if we don't, the branches'll eat us up."

Allie checked the compass—still straight on. The darkwood in front of them didn't hold nearly as much interest to her as what lay on the other side of it. She thought Zach could make it up there well enough, though he'd probably have to stop a few times to cough. Sam would likely have no trouble at all. But Allie didn't think she could make it to the top of that hill, even if that was where Mary waited. Zach had boots and Sam had claws. All she had was the thin tread on the bottoms of her soaked Chucks.

Assuming, of course, they'd even try getting there. Allie followed Sam's gaze into the undergrowth. Zach was right—it was dark. No telling what might be in there. The needle said go but the sign warned WARE. It warned NO FARTHER. Just as the screaming tree back in the meadow had warned them before.

"What's the needle say?" Zach asked.

"It's pointin' on."

"I think we should listen to it."

Allie asked, "You sure?"

"No." He didn't like the look of that darkwood either. "But you said maybe the hill's as far as we gotta go. If this is still somebody's property, that might mean they're close by."

Still, she didn't know. It was Sam who decided for them both. His straining ears finally caught something from the brush. He let out a hard woof and charged.

"Sam," Allie called. "To me, Sam."

The dog disappeared inside. Limbs crunched and snapped. He barked once, high and far away. What followed was a long silence that ended with the sound of splashing.

Zach's eyes widened. "Come on."

The long walk in a hardening cold had left them too tired to run. The closest Allie and Zach managed was a jerky trot. They flung themselves into the darkwood, picking their way through the branches and brambles. What little sunlight leaked through cast shadows around their feet, giving Allie the impression that she was walking through oil. She felt Zach's hand on her pack and turned to push him away, afraid he'd taken that one chance among all the others to finally see what else was in her bag. Instead of fighting her, Zach only stepped aside and carried on. He wasn't nearly as interested in what secrets Allie carried as he was in being first out of the brush. He needed to protect her. To be a man.

They pushed through the last tangle of branches together. What lay beyond was enough to slough off the doom that had crept upon Allie all that morning. A strong creek not six feet wide flowed through the forest there, gurgling its way along a jagged cut in the earth. On the opposite bank stood another narrow strip of brush and the base of the hill.

Sam stood in the middle of the creek, tail swishing and head down. He drank deep. Allie licked her lips and shrugged off her backpack. She moved forward as though in a trance.

Zach took her by the elbow. "No, wait. Ain't supposed to drink water in the woods, even out here. Might be bugs in it."

"We drank the snow."

"That's different. We had to."

"Sam's drinking it."

"Sam's able."

Allie bugged her eyes, not believing what she'd heard. "Ain't no bugs in there, Zach. It's too cold."

Zach said, "Might be some," but his hand had left Allie's elbow, and he'd begun inching forward, toward the water. "Only way to make sure's to boil it."

He looked at the backpack lying in the snow. The tip of the fire drill poked out from the top where the zippers met. Sam looked up as if to ask, *What's taking you stupid humans so long; can't you see what this stuff is?* He bent his head again, gorging himself.

"I'm thirsty now, Zach," Allie said. "We ain't had nothing to drink but some juice and some snow. We need more'n that. Besides, drinking might make your cold better. I heard you coughin' all morning. You ain't managed to start a fire yet, and I know you're trying hard, and I don't mean to say you can't. But if you sit here for an hour rubbing all that wood together while I stare at all that water, I'm gonna go loopy. This creek's probably just snow is all. Probably ain't no water in that cut at all unless it falls from the sky, and it'll be bone dry again in a couple days. Bugs ain't got no time to get in it, Zach. I say we dig in while we got the chance."

"Maybe that sign's warning about the water." Zach licked his lips. They were cracked and looked like hard plastic. He wanted to drink but didn't want to allow himself. Not because there might be bugs in that water, but because Allie was the one doing the deciding again.

Still.

"Just a little bit," he said. "But you gotta let me go first. If it's bad, I don't want you drinking it."

Allie said, "All right." She would've said anything.

Zach walked to a spot along the bank and cupped his hand, dipping it in the water. His fingers came out so shaky that most of the water spilled out. The little that was left went into his mouth. He tried again.

"How is it?" she asked.

Zach nodded and plunged both hands in next. The result was less than a mouthful. He took off his hat and dipped it in all the way past the band, then tilted it into his mouth. Allie joined him. She knelt by the bank and pushed her hands in. The cold was deep and instant and made her forget her itchy feet altogether. She brought a handful to her mouth and swallowed heaven itself.

"Here," Zach said. He handed her a hatful. "Don't put your hands in. Can't get them cold."

Allie drank. The clear water spilled over the brim and down her chin. It mixed with the taste of Zach's sweat, making it almost sweeter.

"That's enough," he said. "Even if it's good, drinking a lot's bad. We've gone too long without."

She handed the hat back before the urge to dip it in the water again grew too great. Zach put the hat on and smiled as the cold met the sweat on his head. He filled the juice box to the rim. Sam had gotten his fill of water and now lay curled in the melting snow, nearly asleep from exhaustion. The gurgling water was soothing, making them more tired. Allie lowered her head and spread her fingers. Pine pitch and dirt entered into every one of the dozen small cuts on her hands. It was because of her that the three of them were out there in the middle of nowhere. Not lost (never that), nor even turned around as Zach liked to say. Searching for Mary. Mary and hope.

Zach asked, "Is this the place?"

She turned her wrist over. Had Allie not been fallen away, she would have used the seconds before her eyes caught sight of the compass to pray for some small act of mercy, some signal that they were to go no farther. And yet the needle hadn't frozen and died, its purpose finally complete. Instead, it had turned sometime since they'd arrived at the slope of the hill. Not pointing straight on to its top, but to the right along the creek. Deeper into the woods. Farther beyond the sign.

4

"This place ain't it."

Zach's eyes fell. He shook his head slow. What now? He figured they'd gone at least a couple miles already that morning. Add that to however far they'd walked the day before (he guessed that distance anywhere from one mile to twenty, the buzz in his head wouldn't let him narrow things further than that). Which meant they were so far in the woods that it would take that whole day to get back to their bikes. His parents would kill him.

"We should stay here for a little bit," he said. "Figure out what to do. It's a good place. I can try climbing that hill after, take a look around. If this's the only water for a ways, might be some squirrels or rabbits nearby. Either'd taste good about now. Go good with the rest of the candy bars."

Allie didn't bother to ask Zach how he planned on killing anything, much less cooking it. The itch in her feet had grown into much the same buzzing as had crawled into Zach's head. All that walking from the meadow hadn't smoothed out the kinks in her muscles. She only wanted to sit down for a while, and the corpse of a fallen oak lying just downstream looked like the perfect spot. Zach followed her there. He wiped away the snow that had accumulated on top with his sleeve, securing her a somewhat dry spot. His body swayed as he sat and closed his eyes. Sam made his way up the bank, lapping the water as he lumbered. Allie patted her leg as he neared. Sam rose up, placing his front paws against the leg of Allie's jeans, but his claws couldn't find a hold on the smooth denim. He made a scratching motion down her knee as he tried to grip and finally surrendered, landing on Allie's foot. She jumped and cried out.

Zach asked, "What's wrong?"

"Nothing." Allie cradled her right foot and tried not to scowl. "Sam just hit me wrong."

Zach pulled his hand from his coat pocket. He took Allie's heel between his thumb and middle finger, touching it as one would coax a butterfly, and stretched her leg toward himself. Allie tried to jerk her foot away. This time the scowl showed through.

"I just wanna see," he said.

Her Chucks had been pink the day before. Now the woods had left them so wet and filthy they'd gone a deep red, almost the color of blood. The laces were frayed to near breaking. Wide patches of the canvas sides had been worn near through.

Zach untied what was left of the lace and lifted her shoe away. Allie felt the cold air against her toes and tensed. Zach pinched her heel again, holding it still. He let go long enough to remove her wet sock.

"Oh man," he whispered.

The skin of her left foot had gone a pale gray. Red and yellow blotches covered the first three toes. Zach raised her heel. Allie didn't know what the skin there looked like. The furrow in his brow told her enough. Zach lifted his coat and shirt. Before Allie could speak, he'd placed her foot against his skin. It was hot there, blessedly hot, and a shiver fell over her.

"You got on the wrong shoes," he said. "You can't walk in those, Allie. Not out here."

"Didn't think we'd end up out here."

She curled her toes against the gentle curve of his stomach, holding them there. Allie wanted nothing more than to take her other shoe off and place that foot there as well. That one buzzed more than the one against Zach's skin. If it buzzed more, maybe that meant it looked worse.

A willow tree stood just inside the edge of the darkwood

behind them. Zach let go of Allie's foot long enough to scrape a handful of bark from the trunk. He whittled away the outer layer and held out half.

"I ain't hungry," she said. "And we got candy bars to eat."

"This ain't for eating. Know where aspirin comes from? Willow bark. Go ahead and chew some. Might help your feet. Aspirin's good for near everything."

"I don't have a stomach for more wood, Zach."

"Don't matter. We gotta do what we gotta do now, Allie. Don't matter if we got a stomach for it or not. Go on. If you can't swallow, just chew and spit."

Allie looked at the fistful of bark in front of her face. Zach shook it.

"Don't watch me," she said.

"Why not?"

"'Cause the last thing I want's you staring at me while I gnaw on some old tree, Zach Barnett. Now you turn away."

Zach shook his head and said fine. He turned his gaze upstream and munched on his own medicine, believing aspirin was good for near everything and a bad cough especially. Allie waited a few seconds to make sure he wouldn't peek before slipping the bark into her jacket pocket. Zach said willow was aspirin, Miss Howard had said aspirin made blood run quicker. Not giving her feet medicine scared Allie, but the prospect of her woman problem getting worse all over again scared her more.

"I'm done," she said.

Sam moved off back toward the stream. He stopped at the edge of the water and lifted his ears, listening. He'd done that so many times in the last day that Allie paid it no mind.

Zach turned back around and spit out a wad of moist bark. "We gotta care for your feet, Allie. We'll need more'n aspirin to do it. I'm gonna get atop that hill and see where we are, get us turned back around right. Then it's straight home. My folks are gonna kill me as it is."

"We ain't turned around wrong, Zach. Needle says the way's on up the creek."

Zach shook his head. "Way's *back*, Allie. We can't stay out here no more. We'll try again later. My daddy'd even come and help us look. I'm just worried about your feet."

"My feet are fine. We gotta fix your insides. You're sick, Zach."

"I got a coat to cover my insides. You got nothing over your toes but town shoes."

Sam barked. They both looked but saw nothing; Allie gave it over to more snow falling from the trees until Zach jerked her foot out from under his shirt and leaped from his seat on the tree. Allie's ankle smacked against the wood. The cry she gave turned Zach just long enough for him to stretch out a hand as an apology. He ran to where Sam stood.

"You hear that?" he asked.

"What?"

"That sound. You hear that sound?"

Allie listened. There was only the gurgle of water over the rocks and the faraway sound of a crow longing for spring. Not even the wind blew there at the base of the hill.

"Zach, I don't he—"

"Shh," he said. "Listen."

She concentrated as much as a hungry girl with two busted feet could. Allie closed her eyes and stopped her breathing. She heard it then. Distant, but getting closer: *thumpthumpthump*.

Allie may have promised herself five hundred and forty-five days ago that she'd never cry again because crying meant it was over, but she'd been okay with fear. Fear had come to rule her life ever since her momma left. She was scared of the wind and scared to love, scared of going on with her life and remaining behind in it. She was scared of the woods. But none of those things frightened her more than that sound coming over the trees and the thought of what Zach would do next.

"Helicopter," he said. Sam barked and swished his tail. "It's a helicopter, Allie. It's Daddy. I know it is."

Allie couldn't order her thoughts fast enough to speak them. Her bare foot hung off the log like a piece of meat.

The thumps turned deeper. Allie looked up, straining her eyes into the thin crescent of sky that had been carved out between the trees.

"They won't see us," Zach said. "Not here. They'll fly right over."

He jumped into the brook and didn't flinch as freezing water covered his knees. Three leaps was all it took him to cross. He bounded up the other side, grabbing hold of what trees and roots he could to help him up the steep slope. Sam barked again, this time at Zach, though he didn't follow.

Allie called out, "Zach, where you going?"

"They'll see us up there," he yelled.

"Don't leave me, Zach. Zach!"

But it was too late. Zach was nearly gone. The trees at the top of the hill grew thinner and shorter than the ones in the forest below, bunched in clumps that rendered a good part of it nearly bare. The helicopter was so close and the thumps so deep that Allie felt its vibration in her bones. She pulled on her sock and shoe and ran past Sam, into the creek.

Cold water rushed over her feet and knees and splashed her jacket, punishing Allie's body with what felt like bolts of electricity. Sam barked and chased her across. The water was shallow, but it nearly swallowed him.

Allie's legs felt numb and heavy as she climbed out on the other side. She forced them to move and grabbed what she could—a hanging branch here, a clump of frozen ground there—to pull herself up the slope. She yelled for Zach, begging him to wait.

The sound of heavy rotors filled the air. Zach reached the top of the hill and disappeared. Sam fell behind, struggling on the slick incline. Allie fought her weariness and the heavy weight of her feet and climbed on. From above came the sound of Zach shouting, "Hey!" and "Over here!"

She reached the top of the hill and followed the sound over her left shoulder. The helicopter wasn't far off (Allie thought maybe it was two miles or two minutes away, but time and distance were things that only existed back in the world), heading straight for them.

Zach stood at the far edge of a small clearing, jumping in the air. He had removed his coat and hat and was now waving them both high over his head. He screamed for help and for his daddy, stopping only long enough to cough. Allie ran as fast as her feet allowed. Zach's voice cracked and gave out, but his arms kept waving. He looked to Allie as she neared.

"We're—" was all Zach managed. Later, he couldn't remember how he'd meant to finish that sentence, whether it was *We're saved* or *We're gonna be okay now* or *We're gonna be home for Christmas*. It didn't matter. Before Zach could say a word more, Allie gathered every bit of strength she had left and dove. She caught Zach in the stomach with her shoulder and hurled him backward into a small stand of cedars. What snow was left on the needles tumbled over them in a short but violent storm. Branches snapped and stuck their skin. Zach's eyes bulged. He heaved, trying to get air.

"What . . . are you *do . . . ing*?" he screamed.

"We can't, Zach," Allie said. "We can't."

Far away, Sam barked. The sound was all but eclipsed by the

whumping noise of the helicopter drawing close. Zach pushed Allie away and tried crawling into the clearing. She leaped on his back, using all of her weight to pin him there. He fought, but the quick climb up the hill and the syrup in his lungs had sapped him. Allie grabbed for Zach's coat and hat. She threw them behind her, farther into the trees.

"We can't go back, Zach," she begged. "We gotta keep looking. We have to find her."

The helicopter, closer. The olive-green body banked toward them. Allie saw two faces peering from the windows. Zach struggled to free himself, couldn't. He screamed, "It's just a stupid statue, Allie."

She screamed back, "We're not looking for a statue. *We're looking for my momma!*"

Allie hadn't planned to tell him the truth that way, but it turned out to be the perfect time. The shock froze him. Zach's body sank into the snow. He struggled no more. The helicopter didn't cross over the hill, but it flew by so close that Zach caught a glimpse of his father's stricken face peering through the glass. He called out once more, though this time the sound of his voice carried no farther than Allie's ear. It was one word:

"Daddy."

The thumping faded quicker than it had come. Allie rolled off Zach's back. He stumbled into the clearing, waving and calling again, but it was too late. A blank look covered his face, as if every emotion a boy could experience had flooded him at once, leaving him numb. Zach's only thought as he stared at the emptying sky was that this was all Allie's fault. Everything—every almost-tear and every word she'd spoken, every bat of her long lashes over two grief-filled eyes. All a trick. Sam finally reached the top of the hill. He sank into the snow, panting. Zach lowered his arms as the helicopter banked again and disappeared.

"Why'd you do that?" His voice was tired and sounded far away.

Allie held her wrist up slow, turning the compass to him. "It ain't pointing to the statue, Zach. It's pointing to my momma."

"You can't think that, Allie."

"It's true." She took a step to him. "I told her to send word, Zach. The night before last, when you came to the house. I told my momma to send word and she did. She's here, Zach. Momma's in these woods."

Zach shook his head, pleading as tears welled in his eyes. "No, Allie. She ain't."

"She's here."

Zach screamed, "She's dead!" Loud and shrieking and full of the hurt that can come only through betrayal, making Sam raise his head. "The Storm took her, Allie. Your momma's *gone*."

He coughed again, this time so hard that it bent him over. He spat a glob of mucus into the snow.

"No, Zach." Allie shook her head. She tried smiling. Zach always liked her smile. "Momma ain't gone; she's just lost. She wants me to find her."

She walked to him, wanting Zach to understand, wanting him to trust. They would make it home, yes. Not all three of them, but all *four*—she and Zach and Sam and Mary. Allie was strong enough to believe that. But that belief wasn't strong enough to convince her she hadn't just murdered something in Zach's heart, some special part of him that would never rise again. And when Allie turned and followed his eyes to where the helicopter had gone, she knew that special part had been Zach's hope. The view from the hill told Allie that she may have just saved her mother, but she had also cost them their best and maybe only chance of rescue. Below them lay a sea of trees and mountains that extended in every direction, stretching on into what looked like forever.

5

Zach couldn't remain there long. Not because the air there was colder (which it was) or because they were once again too far from water (which they were). It wasn't even because the longer he stared at the small dot of white sky into which his father had disappeared, the heavier his body felt. Any of those things would have been enough for him to turn away from Allie and begin the slow and slick descent back to the stream, but none of them was the real reason Zach did just that.

It was what he saw from the hill. That endless forest all around them. The way the trees looked so dead. So bare. Zach tried telling himself it was the season and nothing more, that in December everything in the world looked lifeless and gray. But from their vantage point that gray looked more like ash, as though everything around them was the remains of something once beautiful but now stale. Zach believed he could stand atop that hill in the height of summer and be given that very same view—a grim wood dotted with pockets of green pine and wide clutches of shrubs and fallen trees that he and Allie had come to call darkwood. It was a part of the world where there may have been people once, but the only thing left of them now were signs warning beware. It was a land of long nightmares and slow death.

Had they covered so much ground in the last day that all trace of buildings and roads was gone? Was such a thing even possible? Zach didn't know. He could only go by what his eyes told him, and there on the hill his eyes said they'd gone too far to find their way back. Even if they knew the way, they wouldn't make it. Not with the snow and the cold. Not without fire and proper food.

So he turned away from Allie and climbed down the hill alone. She called out for him, wanting to explain, reciting all the stories she'd read about people who'd gotten whisked away by tornadoes only to later be found alive. Zach raised his hand, telling her no, don't bother, good-bye Allie. Sam whined and raised his head as Zach walked past, hoping for a pat or a rub. Zach offered no affection. He had none to give.

It should have been easier going down than up. It wasn't. Gravity pushed at Zach's tired back, trying to make him tumble forward. His chest felt thick and heavy. The more he struggled against the trees and snow, the harder his heart worked. A spot behind his left eye began to throb. Twice he reached out for handholds—one a pine branch, the other the slender trunk of a dead cedar—that existed only in his mind. The tread on his boots was thick and jagged (*not like Allie's stupid Chucks, guess she didn't think about that before she went and got us lost, huh?*), but they soon became clogged with snow and mud.

Halfway down the hill, his feet slipped. If there was a bright spot to his morning, it was that Zach fell on his back instead of his face. He landed so hard that what little air remained in his lungs burst out in a loud huff. He managed to wrap his arms around what may have been the only healthy tree on the slope and hold tight, trying to catch his breath. The wad of snot he coughed into the snow smelled rotten.

It was ten minutes later when he finally reached the bottom. By then he was soaked and exhausted. He made the trek back through the water and paused to fill his hat before collapsing once more against the fallen oak. The cold water felt good going down. Zach tried to imagine it washing through his body, cleaning him out.

He should have told Allie how bad he felt. It was her fault they were still there, her fault they'd gotten lost in the first place, but Zach understood now that he should've said something. He should have confessed how he'd woken the night before with a pain in his stomach so unbearable that tears had grown in the corners of his eyes. How he'd barely managed to scuffle out from under the pine before suffering through the worst case of diarrhea ever in the history of the world. How he'd vomited twice that morning after Allie had taken her backpack into the woods to do whatever was so secret, and how it had come out watery and tasting like death. He should have confessed that he couldn't get warm no matter how much he sweated.

But Zach had chosen to keep all of this bottled inside because that's what men did. They stayed strong and didn't complain. They were too busy watching over the people they loved to get sick.

There was also this to consider: Would Allie have done what she did atop the hill had she known those things? Would it have made a difference at all? Zach wanted to believe no to the former and yes to the latter. Even after she'd lied, he wanted to believe if Allie had known how bad off he was, she would've been standing right beside him, waving and yelling for that helicopter and thanking the God she hated and feared. She would have done it for him, if nothing else.

He looked up to see Allie making her way down. She held Sam against her chest with one arm and used the other to hold them both steady. Her eyes remained on the ground only long enough to find the next safe step. She looked at Zach and then moved, looked at him again. Town shoes or not, she never stumbled.

It was only when she reached the bottom of the hill that Allie looked worried. Sam struggled, wanting another drink. She couldn't look at Zach from that close distance, knowing how much she'd hurt him. Zach glared and sat the hat back on his head. The freezing water in the band both soothed and punished him. He felt as dead as the land they'd gotten themselves lost in, but he couldn't let Allie cross that creek again. Not with the way her feet looked.

He rose and crossed through the creek. His feet grew colder in the water but stayed dry inside his waterproofed boots. Allie tried looking when she heard the sloshing sound of his approach, but Zach's scowl scared her off. He turned and bent without a word, exposing his back. Allie climbed on. Her only words were to Sam, telling him to be still.

Zach's act of chivalry was nearly all for nothing when his legs gave out midway to the other side. He sank to his knees as the water flowed over his legs and most of his left arm, soaking Allie's sore feet anyway. She let out a cry and gripped Zach's neck, choking him. Sam wriggled himself free and jumped into the water. He waded to the other side on his own and shook himself, releasing a cloud of spray.

The three of them gathered at the fallen log once more. The commotion from the helicopter had long since passed. The quiet of the woods returned. Not a word passed between them. Sam curled at Allie's feet. Zach propped his elbows on his knees and laid his head in his hands.

He was almost asleep when Allie said, "I'm sorry."

"Don't tell me that, Allie. Tell me anything but that, 'cause I know you ain't sorry at all."

Her hand was close to his, and Zach thought he would go mad if Allie touched him just then. He would scream and yell and cuss until his lungs burst, leaving whatever smelly stuff that had grown inside them to leak through his mouth and nose. They sat there shivering, holding themselves because otherwise their bodies might have flown apart, like a child's toy wound too tight. Allie's pigtails hung wet and limp against the sides of her head. Her lips had gone a pale blue.

"You wouldn't have come," she said. "Not if I told you the truth."

A whisper, all Zach was able: "Your momma's dead, Allie.

Storm took her, just like it took all the others. I thought you understood that. You told me you did. You told everybody."

"I always hoped," she said. "You can be fallen away and still hope. Plenty of people're like that. What was I supposed to do? If I'da told anybody, they'da locked me up in the loony bin and taught me how to make birdhouses. It's just a shoe buried at the cemetery, Zach. Momma ain't in there."

"You think she's alive because of that?"

"It's happened. This guy in Missouri, he got taken away by a tornado. Flung him nearly fifteen hundred feet, and all he got was a knock on the head."

"Allie, we're miles from town. Miles. And it's been near two years. You really think your momma'd still be out here walking around after that long?"

She nodded. "My compass started working, Zach. Momma sent word."

"That's crazy," Zach said, and he didn't care what Allie thought of him using that word. He'd been the one to take up for her with their friends in the months after The Storm, telling them sometimes hurt could change a person but Allie would pull through once all that hurt had gone away. Now Zach thought whatever wound lay inside Allie had somehow gotten sunk in her heart and grown there like a vine. Choking her. Turning her crazy. He coughed and thought maybe Allie really should be down at the loony bin. He'd rather have her learning how to build birdhouses than getting them marooned in the cold wilderness.

"It ain't crazy," she said. "Maybe she got hurt or lost. Maybe she ain't come back because she ain't able. That's why she sent word, Zach, like I asked her to. There's no other way."

"And you think she sent word through that compass."

"It ain't worked since the day she left. Then it did, just when I needed it most. Because something important's happened."

"What happened?"

Allie's eyes fell away. "I can't say."

Zach shook his head. "What are we supposed to do now, Allie? That helicopter might not ever come back. Even if it does, it might fly right past us. I seen lots of ravines from up that hill, but the next tall place was whole miles away. Almost to the mountains."

"We keep going. Needle's pointing yonder up the stream. That's where we gotta go."

"No way. I ain't getting us more lost than we are." Zach said it loud enough that Sam stirred and Allie flinched. It was the first time either of them had used that term. Not turned around. Not confused. *Lost.* Sometimes you had to call a thing what it was. "You can't walk, and I'm having trouble enough."

"We *ain't lost,* Zach. That's what I'm telling you. My compass wants us to go on. If we don't, I think we might die. If we go back, I think we'll just end up back here. Like we ended up back at the meadow yesterday. Because we're supposed to *keep going,* Zach. I don't have a choice. You can stay. Sam too. But I can't, because I'm going to find her. We'll come for you when I do."

Her clothes had gone ragged and her face was smeared with the woods, but the steel in Allie's eyes told Zach she meant her words this time, and there was no deceit in them. She would go on because her stupid compass said so, even if it led to a dark place. And Zach would go as well, because it was up to him to keep her safe. He was as sure of that now as he'd been at the beginning. The only difference now was that Zach had believed at the beginning that his purpose was to protect Allie from the world. Now he believed it was to protect Allie from herself.

They split another candy bar and filled up on water. Zach used his pocketknife while they rested, cutting clumps of green needles to stuff inside Allie's shoes and both of their shirts and jeans. They wouldn't last and wouldn't do much, but at least the evergreens would put a dry cushion between their clothes and skin. Zach said they looked like two scarecrows. Allie laughed. That chuckle was another apology more than anything else, Allie's way of trying to bring them together again.

They moved upstream thirty minutes later, where Allie said the needle pointed. Zach was too tired to protest when she walked in front. Time clicked by in steps rather than hours. Zach's cough worsened despite their stops for water, though nothing more came up from his lungs. The gunk seemed to have hardened there instead, making whistling sounds rise from his chest. Allie would stop and turn, asking if he was okay. Zach only waved her on.

He did not know how far they'd gone when he first noticed the compass slipping from her wrist. It wasn't sudden, just a gentle give of the one remaining plastic bump on the band, loosening with each step Allie took. It fell not long after, hitting the soft cushion of melting snow and soggy leaves along the bank with barely a sound.

The words were on Zach's lips even before the compass landed—*Better watch that*. He'd said them so many times before, in class and in the park or in any of those precious hours they stole together along the river in town. Zach kept his pace and stared at the pink band. It had landed with the bubble facing up. He saw the needle floating, pointing them on.

Zach felt his back bending and his arm reaching out, heard himself telling her, *Hey, Allie, here's your compass back. I know how special it is because it's the last thing your dead momma ever gave you.*

That trinket from Carnival Day, that token of an unexpected good-bye.

That cheap piece of plastic won at a cheap game that had taken Zach away from his family for Christmas.

That toy that had gotten them both lost in the woods and had left Zach's daddy looking for him in a helicopter and his momma sitting back in town, crying and wanting her little boy back.

That stupid compass.

Allie never turned around. She was too focused on what lay ahead to worry about what had fallen behind. Zach straightened and stood tall. He reached the compass in three more steps. He used the fourth to kick it into the water.

The pink band bobbed and weaved along a current that washed it away. For those small moments along the riverbank, Zach only felt the sweet release of his anger and frustration. He gave no thought to what he'd done, believed it was nothing wrong. In fact, Zach believed he may have just saved them all. He'd broken the chains that had laid heavy on Allie's heart for a year and a half. He'd freed her. And because of that, perhaps now Allie would listen to reason. Maybe now they could forget about finding her momma and start concentrating on finding their way home. Maybe now they'd be okay.

Only Sam looked at him. The dog's ears drooped low and his tail hung limp and still, as though what he had just witnessed had cost them all something far greater than Zach could know.

He walked on with his head bowed while Marshall, Grace, and thirty volunteers finished combing the riverbank that flowed through downtown Mattingly. The radio clipped to Marshall's belt had chirped often in the last hours as search parties radioed back and forth, relaying news of empty woods and fields. Marshall had answered each of those calls himself with two shaking hands and one hard swallow, each time wishing for a drink and thanking them for their pledges to keep looking. And just as Jake's voice came over the radio to report no sign of the children in the hill country, Allie's mind began to bend.

6

She no longer sees the forest or the stream or how the white sky has gone the dull gray of evening. Sam is no longer padding out front, and his nose has not just led him to a brown glob of something poking up from the snow that he chews and swallows. Even Zach is gone—left somewhere behind to mull and wallow and not understand. She chuckles at the way the straps of her backpack cut into her shoulders, rendering them numb. Numb, yes—everything is numb. Allie cannot even feel the pine needles, stuffed into her shoes and clothes, prickling her skin.

She understands what her mind has done. The woods are too dark and Zach's silence is too awful, and so Allie has fled to a place of her own making. It's no longer muck and snow she trudges through, but the warm grass of summertime. The sun shines bright and hot, turning her skin a deep brown. Fish leap from the creek already cleaned and fried. Their mouths are wedged open with slices of lemon. And there! There's Zach. He's close now, just to Allie's right, wearing a suit of armor that glimmers in the day. He holds a smile and his daddy's tomahawk.

Sam nuzzles against her other side. Allie looks there and laughs at how her dog's legs dangle and his ears flop in the breeze. The laughter turns to a quiet awe as Allie understands they are no longer walking, but flying. Not so high that she is frightened and not so fast that she screams. A few feet off the ground is all, just enough to raise feet and paws to the center of the passing oaks. Just enough to let them rest. They float slow and silent and graceful, three feathers carried by a warm breeze. There is no need to worry about the right way. The woods are Allie's compass now, the wind a needle. All she has to do is let go. All they have to do is ride.

The hill comes like an emerald rising from the earth. Allie feels a pull on her insides as her body is nudged upward. Sam must feel it, too, because he barks once and jitters his leg as though he's being rubbed on the belly. Zach lets out a soft "Ooh." He smiles wider and takes Allie's hand. They glide up the slope of the hill and pause over a crown of green and gold. They land with their fingers entwined and their arms outstretched, as though it is the final step of a beautiful dance.

Mary Granderson waits there.

She is as beautiful now as she was in the picture on Allie's bedroom dresser—hair long and brown, eyes wide almonds. Her dress is made of yellow flowers and ripe vines. A golden cross hangs loose from her bare neck. It shimmers like a living thing.

Allie goes to her. She feels her momma's arms around her and inhales. Mary smells like jasmine and honeysuckle and all things made whole again. Sam rises on his hind legs, mouth yapping and tail wagging. Zach stands close and tips his head to the ground. His hand remains on the tomahawk's shaft, ever guarding against what he says are the bad things in the woods. Allie looks into her mother's eyes and cries. She lets the tears pour forth and feels her body shiver from the power of that release, that final act.

It's over. Now and finally, it is over.

Mary holds her daughter tight and tells her to cry on. She tells them of her adventures in the deep woods and how the bad things wouldn't let her escape, but she found a way to send word through the compass because it was Christmas, and Christmas is when love shines brightest.

And when Mary is done, Allie says let's go home now, Mommy.

She looks up, not breaking their embrace, and finds Mary's eyes have darkened. Her smile fades only some, turning from bright noon to soft morning. She strokes the back of her daughter's head and says we can't go home now, Allie—not ever. Once the forest has you, it won't let go.

Zach's face grows hard. He draws his father's tomahawk

forward as the ground beneath Allie gives way. She sinks to her ankles as

a bolt of lightning raced up Allie's spine, shattering that imaginary place like shards exploding from a mirror. In front of her lay an endless mass of barren trees and melting snow. She shut her eyes, willing the green hill back. Needing her momma with her. But all of that was gone now, a product of cold and hunger and hope, even if it had all been so real that Allie believed she'd just lost her mother for the second time in two days.

She looked down to find her Chucks submerged in icy water. Slivers of pine needles broke free and floated away like castaways from a sinking ship. Allie jumped as the last tendrils of her dream gave way and the cold enveloped her, burning her toes. The ground she landed on was soft and marshy. Zach and Sam stood motionless behind her. The hard caws of two crows echoed from the trees behind them. A third joined them, turning the duo into a trio. There was no sound of rushing water. Allie looked to where the creek should have been and found only a wide pond of melting snow and ice that extended out in a wide oval.

"Where'd it go?" she asked.

Zach said, "It putters out right here," and stared at the tops of his boots. His hat sat low on his forehead, hiding his eyes. "Thought maybe it'd lead to the river eventually, but it don't. You were right, Allie. It weren't no steady stream. It all just gathers in this low spot whenever it storms and flows out."

"Bless it," Allie said. She raised her feet and shook off what water she could. It wasn't much. "Done got my shoes all soggy-wet again."

Dislodged roots and limbs poked up from the surface of the water like hungry fish. It didn't look deep in there, probably just to their ankles. Then again, that water might as well be an ocean because of her town shoes. The crows called again—four of them now.

The temporary pond ended farther to their right. Allie guessed that was where they were supposed to go next. She sighed and turned her arm over, thinking that being told where to go was better than being lost, but not nearly as good as knowing how long it would take to get there.

She found only white skin on her wrist.

Allie stared at that empty spot as her mind listed and sputtered, trying to explain what was wrong. Air gathered inside her mouth, puffing her cheeks. The breath came out in a mad half chuckle that scared her.

Someone was playing a joke, pulling her leg. The fingers of Allie's right hand appeared and curled around her naked wrist, feeling for the faded red band that had to be there, had always been there, ever since way back at the beginning when everything ended, and she had sworn never to take it off because her momma had given it to her on Carnival Day and said the compass would point the way, and that's what it had been doing until now, and now—

"It's gone."

Zach's face was to her now, eyes big and shiny, like he was going to cry. Allie looked down and moved her feet, sure she'd somehow stepped on it. There were only her footprints.

"It's gone," she said again. "My compass is gone, Zach."

He stood motionless until his eyes grew too wide and too wet. Only then did Zach lower his head in a look of defeat. She had crushed him, had murdered his heart on the hilltop that morning. Allie wanted to go to him and beg forgiveness all over again, but that would have to wait. The compass was more important. That had to be reclaimed first, even before their friendship.

She retraced her steps to the edge of the pond and bent to her knees. The water was too murky.

"It must've fallen in here," she said. "Help me look, Zach."

He said, "No."

"Help me look."

Allie hovered her hand over the water's surface and tensed her muscles. It wasn't enough to steel her against the cold when she plunged her fingers in. Crowsong gathered in the deep trees. Allie felt rocks and twigs and mud but no compass.

"Stop it, Allie," Zach said.

Allie's hand was so cold she felt as though it were burning. She jerked it from the water with a gasp and tucked her fingers beneath her sweatshirt. "I must've dropped it along the way. We gotta go back, Zach. Did you see it fall?"

He would not look at her.

"Did you see it fall?"

Sam turned and growled at the noisy birds beyond—crows and now others, mockingbirds and cardinals and sparrows, growing closer. His tail went rigid as Allie felt her body go limp.

The sting returned to the corners of her eyes as she whispered, "Zach? Did you see my compass fall?"

He raised his chin. Lowered it—a nod.

"Where?"

"I don't know. Everything looks the same now."

She moved past him, saying they had to go back. Zach grabbed the sleeve of her jacket and spun her around.

"*No,*" he said. "Ain't no use now, Allie. Compass's gone now. I kicked it into the stream."

Sam barked again. It was loud and sharp and echoed off the trees, but Allie neither heard her dog nor what approached them. She only heard Zach and what he had just said.

"You lost my compass?"

"I had to," he said.

Allie wrenched her arm free. It came loose easy, like prying something from a baby's fingers, and a part of her realized that was all the strength Zach could muster now. A greater part of her didn't care. She screamed, "That was the only way we knew where we were going, Zach," making the birds call louder.

Zach yelled back, "You ain't known where we're going since we left *town*, Allie. We're out here because of a stupid *toy*. Don't you know how dumb that is?"

He shouted that last word with such force that his spittle landed against Allie's cheek. Sam's barks went from singles to doubles to full rage toward the trees behind them. His tail was no longer up but tucked between his legs.

"We're lost without my compass, Zach. We don't know where to go. What're we supposed to do now?"

Zach's eyes fell from Allie's to a place over her shoulder. His mouth fell open. What came out wasn't an answer, but a groan that flattened his face and drained it of all color.

"Run," he said.

"What?"

"Run."

He grabbed Allie's arm and jerked her forward, nearly taking her out of her shoes. He charged back for the pond. Allie tried calling out, but she couldn't find her breath. Zach shouted for Sam, telling him to hurry. Allie turned to see her dog doing just that, and she saw why.

From the trees behind them came a living cloud of wings and feathers moving like a black monster. Allie screamed as Zach pulled her on, veering to the right along the pond's edge, straining to keep them from falling. The cloud enveloped them in a rage of chirps and calls. A crow's wing clipped Allie's head, doubling her over. Her fingers slipped from Zach's hand. He groped for some part of her, any part, as mockingbirds and sparrows bounced off his face and body. Cardinals weaved. Blackbirds dodged. A buzzard the size of a cat barely missed Zach's hat. Sam called out in a bark that was all terror as Zach slapped the birds away, making them squawk, sending them into a frenzy. He grabbed Allie as she grabbed him.

The birds were frantic, screaming to get away. Zach shielded his eyes with his left arm and managed to get them the next few feet. He pushed Allie to the ground first, Sam next, himself last. Allie opened her eyes to a thick section of fallen tree in front of her face. Zach shoved Sam against the brittle trunk. He covered Allie with his own body. The sound was deafening. Like a storm.

The rage blew past. An eerie calm followed. Zach eased his head up over the log. Allie's heart jackhammered in her chest. It beat even harder when Zach said, "Stay down, Allie. Move closer. They're coming."

He covered her again as the ground beneath them began to thrum. Allie heard limbs snap like thunder in front of them and water splashing behind. She turned her head beneath Zach's arm, needing to breathe. A deer jumped over the log, landing only feet beyond. Another followed and then another, large bucks with wide antlers and white tails raised in alarm, joined by their females. Snow and mud pelted Zach's back as the hooves landed and kicked up again. Others came after and between—squirrels and raccoons and possums by the hundreds. Rabbits. Skunks. Foxes. Zach shut his eyes and took off his hat, using it to shield their heads as the entire forest emptied around them.

He raised his head when it was done. His lungs sounded like two clogged holes that allowed only those high, piercing whistles to escape. Allie rose up on two weak legs and gathered Sam in her arms, holding his trembling body tight.

It looked as though an army had passed. Where there had once been melting snow over a blanket of leaves, there now lay only a wide swath of mangled mud. To their left, the pond rippled in tiny waves that lapped against the forest floor. The storm of legs and wings faded in the distance.

None of them made a sound for a long while. Zach bled from cuts to his face and arms. A mockingbird feather hung from the brim of his hat. Allie found her hand still in his. She left it there and realized that fear could do a great many things. It could make you forgive someone who'd hurt you and make you forget about being tired and cold and hungry. It could make you run faster than you'd ever dreamed and scream louder than you ever thought possible. It showed you who you were deep down in places where you'd never looked before.

"I think it's over," Zach said.

Allie's eyes gathered in the silent woods around them. The forest looked darker somehow. Fuller. For the first time, she felt they didn't belong there—that they should have wared and gone no farther, because there were bad things in the deep woods that wouldn't let them go. For the first time, she was truly afraid. Had the fear in Allie let her speak, she would have said maybe it wasn't over at all. She would have said maybe it had all just begun.

7

The decision to stay put was silent and unanimous. Neither of them cared much to go traipsing through the woods so close to night, not with something maybe out there that had scared away every living thing for miles. Zach was too tired, Allie too cold. Taking one step more was impossible.

There was this last, most important point as well: with the compass gone, Allie didn't know which way to go. Ahead through the shallow pond, or back to where they'd come? Should they go left, past where the pond became the stream? Or were they supposed to go to the right and farther into the trees? Allie didn't know. She only knew whichever direction they chose stood a three-in-four chance of being the wrong way, and that would leave them more lost than they'd already gotten.

And that's what they were now, Allie thought. No doubt about it. Lost.

At least they had water, Zach told her, and the rest of the food. Two candy bars were all that was left in her bag, but there was still plenty of tree bark. Zach said people could live a long while without much to eat but only a few days with nothing to drink, so hey, bright side. And the log the three of them had hidden behind made a pretty good place for a shelter. It'd be simple, what with all the pines and deadwood around.

"Like walkin' into an Ace Hardware," he said. Loud and fast, as though he couldn't contain his excitement. Allie knew elation had little to do with it. Zach's teeth were chattering, and his eyes looked like two sunken saucers in his head. He was sick and he was scared. Allie didn't know which of those worried her more.

They built their home for the night together. Zach took care of the big stuff, lugging the thick trunk of another fallen tree and propping it against the highest part of the log. Piles of smaller branches as thick as his arms were next. Allie used his pocketknife to cut away as many pine boughs as she could. These she stacked next to the wood. Zach sent her out on a leaf-hunting expedition next.

"I don't want'em wet," he said, "so don't get any from the ground. There's still plenty on the trees. After that, you can help me get some bark slabs."

The busyness helped settle them. Sam had stopped his shaking and was now sniffing at the ground, growling and huffing at what scents the stampede had left behind. There was no time for Allie and Zach to concern themselves with the cuts on their bodies or her freezing toes or the croup in his lungs. Such things were important, but set aside. What counted was their race against the encroaching dark. Allie thought if they had to sleep out in the open with the woods all silent and waiting, she might start screaming and never stop.

Zach improved the more he took charge, though he often paused in his work to peer into the trees. He would remain that way for a few seconds—body still, eyes squinting—and then resume. Sam did the same, only more often. He'd lift his nose from the ground and perk his ears, turning on some sort of dog radar. Allie watched them both but said nothing. She'd seen them too.

Shadows lurking. Crouched behind the trees and the fallen logs. Not regular shadows either, the sort that are everywhere come the end of day. No, these were darker in a way Allie could not describe—thicker in a way, more *real*. She would see them dancing from the corners of her eyes and turn, only to see that what she was really looking at was an old limb or a rock. But they *weren't*, or at least they hadn't been. They had been something else. Something mean.

The materials were pronounced complete just as night settled. Zach began piecing the shelter together, laying the thinner limbs perpendicular to both sides of the log, then the larger ones. Half of the pine boughs went on next, followed by heavier limbs. The slabs of bark they'd pried from the most rotten trees went on last. The result turned out to be just what Allie hoped—a large green-and-brown hump in the middle of the woods that could easily be overlooked. Zach approved of his handiwork even if the irony of it was thick. He'd spent the entire day trying to get them found. Now all he wanted to do was keep them hidden.

He pulled his coat sleeves down and crawled inside, scooping out what little snow remained. He called for the remaining slabs of bark, then the pile of mostly dry leaves, then finally all but four of the remaining boughs. Sam inched his way toward the entrance. Zach crawled out and took the last of the boughs, twisting them so they interlocked. He held them up to the moonlight.

"Okay," he said. "I think there's room at the inn."

Allie went first. She lowered herself to her knees and shrugged off her pack, pushing it deep inside. Zach told her to crawl in feet first, as the shelter's bottom end would probably be warmer. She shimmied herself in as deep as she could. Sam followed, though he didn't seem sure if it was a good idea. Zach backed in when Allie and Sam were settled. He held the twisted clump of boughs in his hands and plugged the opening once inside.

For the first time since losing the compass, Allie felt safe. The boughs felt soft and dry, the leaves like a mattress over the slabs of bark that kept the cold ground away. Everything felt warm and blessedly close. She thought it was how she must've felt all those years ago, back when she'd been in her momma's belly.

She couldn't see Zach. The roof was so stuffed with branches and limbs that not even moonlight leaked through. But Allie felt him next to her, and that was enough.

"This is amazing, Zach," she whispered.

"Daddy taught me how. Woulda made one for us last night, but we didn't have no time."

"I think it's the greatest thing ever. Even my feet feel better."

"Kick your shoes off if you can," he said. "It'll help get'm dry."

Allie curled into a half ball and reached back, trying to find her feet.

"While you're back there, you can get another candy bar and that last juice box. I'm starving, and we'll need that sugar."

"Okay."

She fished out their supper—a Butterfinger and the last of the apple juice—and brought both back to the front. Sam sniffed and began whimpering. They ate in silence. If Zach blessed his food, he kept it to himself. It wasn't much (and by now, Allie was cursing herself for packing what little food she did that morning at home, which felt like a billion years ago), but it was enough to make her feel better. Zach too.

"I'm sorry I lost your compass," Zach said. "I thought it was right. I was just trying to help."

Allie only lay there on her stomach, chin resting on a pillow of her own filthy hands, prying little bits of chocolate and peanut butter from her teeth. She was still mad. It was the worst sort of mad, too, the kind that had hurt and fear latched onto it. But a good-size part of her knew Zach was still mad at her in much the same way.

"I'm sorry too," she whispered. "You just gotta believe me about Momma, Zach. That's all I want. We weren't lost. Not back on that hill, anyways."

The silence Zach offered didn't mean he doubted her. Then again, it didn't mean he believed her either. He supposed they were even in that respect. In spite of his best efforts, Zach thought much of Allie's trust in him had gone the way of the birds and beasts. Sam lay still between them. Allie felt the long breaths from his side push against her and heard the growling in his stomach. There was no way of knowing what they'd do the next day, but finding something more than a candy bar to eat had to top that list.

"How're you feeling?" she asked.

"Tired. My face hurts from the birds."

It was the first either of them had mentioned what had happened. Allie thought it was kind of like the shadows that had spied on them just before—better not to talk about it, because you didn't know where that talk would lead once you got started.

"Think there's a fire somewheres?" she asked. "Maybe that's why they was all running away."

"We'd smell the smoke."

She heard him move. A hole opened up in the makeshift door.

"What are you doing?"

"Something's out there," Zach said. "Thought I saw something in the trees."

"You think maybe it's who put that sign up?"

"No. I think whoever put up that sign's long gone. Looked like a . . . I don't know."

"A shadow?" she asked. "I seen them too. Thought it was my eyes playing tricks."

"Probably was," Zach said, though he didn't sound too sure of that at all.

"Momma used to say the stuff you see in the woods outta the corners of your eyes are the fairies," Allie said.

Zach shook his head. "Ain't no fairies. Allie, I ain't ever seen animals do that before. Run away like that, all together. Birds too."

Allie lifted her chin from her hands and leaned forward, taking care not to disturb Sam's sleep. She figured they were safe enough there in the shelter, but all that disguising would mean nothing if her dog started barking. Zach used his fingers to make the hole in their front door bigger. Not much, just enough to let them see. The log in front of them blocked most of the view. Zach raised his head higher and straightened his arms, like he was about to do a push-up. Allie did the same. A narrow panorama of the night woods greeted her.

Neither of them saw anything at first, nor was there any sound. It was as if they'd wandered into another world altogether, one with fuzzy edges and deep holes they couldn't crawl out of. Allie felt Zach's hand close around her shoulder. He squeezed and held his fingers there, digging through her jean jacket and sweatshirt, finding the bone. He whispered three words:

"Past the pond."

Allie strained her eyes. Before, when they'd been nearly trampled by the wild things, her heart had thundered. Now she felt it slow. From the midst of the trees far on the other side of the pond was a single ball of light. It seemed to float as it wove its way through the forest, blinking in and out as it slowly danced past limbs and trunks. A mix of reds and whites and yellows, like a miniature setting sun in search of somewhere to rest for the night. To Allie, it was the same sort of glow given by the star atop the tree at home. There was no way for her to know the size of that light or how far they were from it, yet she felt a part of herself—a powerful, unyielding part—longing to race after it. Before she could, the ball winked and faded.

"What was that, Zach?"

"I don't know."

"Was it what chased those animals?"

"I don't think so," he said. "I was scared then, but I wasn't just now. Were you?"

Allie shook her head. When she realized Zach couldn't see her, she said, "No. Not even some."

"Maybe it was an angel."

She shook her head again and rolled her eyes. "Ain't no such thing."

Zach said nothing at first, then: "I seen an angel once. Long time ago, back when I was a kid. Remember when that bad man came to town? The one the newspaper called the devil? It was then. I couldn't sleep one night, and I saw something out in the hallway. I got up to see what it was. I seen one."

"Now ain't the time for story," Allie said.

"Ain't no story. It's the truth."

"What'd it look like?"

"Like a boy," Zach said. "He had blond hair and wore people clothes, but he shined like a light. Like *that* light. That's how I knew he was an angel. Ghosts don't shine. It's science. They don't talk, neither."

Allie looked at him. "It talked to you?"

"He said Momma and Daddy had to go to the Holler. Past the rusty gate. He said it was a bad thing they had to do and it would be hard, and sometimes things were hard and bad because God has sharp edges. I didn't know what that meant, and he didn't say nothing else. I told Momma and Daddy later on. They went to the Holler like that angel said. Daddy, he found that bad man. Killed him with Bessie. Daddy never told me that, but I heard it. Daddy just said it was a hard thing he did. You think that's why we're stuck out here, Allie? Because God's got sharp edges?"

Allie looked out into the woods, thought she saw something, decided she didn't.

"I don't know much about God no more, Zach. I used to, I guess, back before I got Him riled. I don't know what I did or how, but it was bad enough to get Momma taken away. Then whatever I did got leaked all over Daddy, and now he's fallen away too. If that's how God wants it, then that's fine. But I don't guess He's got sharp edges. I think God's more like the moon, just sitting up there in the sky, watching what all's going on. This is all just a TV show to Him. Sometimes the stuff He sees makes Him laugh, and sometimes that stuff makes Him cry, but He can't do nothing about it noways. That's why I don't pray.

Talking to God's like my daddy talking to an old buried shoe in the cemetery or me talking to an old plastic statue that used to be in my front yard. You can yammer on all you want, but what's there ain't never gonna give you an answer. I figure it's best to ignore Him. Maybe then, He'll ignore me. God finds out Momma sent word, He'll do all He can to stop me."

Such was what Allie came to believe after her mother left. She believed it now, even as she searched the woods outside their shelter for a light now gone and felt the smooth plastic band of her compass hugging her wrist like a phantom limb. She would find her momma, and that was no mere thought and no hopeful prayer. Because even if God was just like the moon, things had to end right. They just had to. It would be just like her daydream, finding Mary. She would be waiting for them and Sam would be jumping and Zach would be standing guard, and Allie would run into her momma's arms.

That was Allie's last thought before sleep took her. She dreamed once more of a funeral. Her feet itched and the wind blew cold upon the graveside. Near a mound of fresh dirt stood a small casket atop a sheet of plastic turf. Allie looked for Zach to ask whose grave that was, but Zach wasn't there. Nor was Sam. She wanted to call out, ask the gathered for whom they mourned, but her voice came out a whisper. Only Marshall heard it, standing to Allie's left. And the word she had spoken wasn't *Who,* it was *Why.*

That was much the same question Marshall Granderson asked after slamming the bedroom door an hour later, exhausted from a day spent looking for and not finding his little girl. The only light Marshall turned on that night was the one on the porch. He retreated to his bedroom closet and drank as much as he could, feeling that cold goodness wash over him, succumbing to that sweet nothingness.

He used his cell phone to try Bobby one more time and once again got his voice mail. "Where you at?" is all Marshall could manage, and even those three words came out slurred and jumbled through the thick haze left by the beer. He tossed the phone onto the dresser and lay back in the bed, felt the empty other side with his hand. Felt himself go.

Grace was there and wouldn't go away, said she couldn't leave him the way he was. Marshall's throat had gone sore from screaming at her, telling her to go back home and take all the food the town had brought with her. He refused to eat any of that charity, just as Allie had refused the very same in the days after Mary's funeral. He'd left Grace in tears at the edge of the living room, trying not to hear her screaming back that he didn't understand, she couldn't leave him alone, she'd made a promise and was bound to it.

There was only silence after that; Marshall thought she'd given up and gone home. But then Jake called long after Marshall had drawn his curtain down tight, and the phone had gone silent without the machine picking up. He lifted his head enough to read the tiny screen on the receiver. It read Line In Use.

Like Allie, Sheriff Jake Barnett dreamed. He had done so often in his years, especially in the trying times several years ago, when the bad man came to Mattingly. Yet even those nightmares did not strike Jake with the terror of what he experienced this night. In his sleep he heard Zach's voice calling from a dark so thick and complete it felt like quicksand around him. Jake called back, begging his son to keep talking, to walk toward his voice, but Zach could not hear him. He only kept asking his daddy to help, please help, because he was cold and hungry and tired. He didn't know where he was, and he was scared because there were bad things all around him.

There were monsters.

December 22

1

The voice leaking through Allie's sleep came too deep and too sick to be her mother's. She opened her eyes to a sunlit tangle of branches and boughs inches from her face. Zach's arms stretched through the shelter's opening, shaking her.

She raised her head. "What's wrong?"

"Nothing, just time to get up is all. It's too quiet out here. Driving me crazy. Sun's up. Time to go."

She felt beside her and found only warm leaves and pine needles. "Where's Sam?"

"Out here. Come on."

Her body wasn't as stiff as she'd found it the morning before. All the pain seemed to have settled in her feet instead. It felt as though someone had spent the night ripping the skin open between her heels and toes before stuffing them with hot coals. She groped for her backpack, shoved somewhere in the back of the shelter.

"My feet hurt bad, Zach," she said. "I think something's busted in them."

"Want me to take a look?"

"Maybe. I gotta go first."

The cold just outside was instant and hard, burning Allie's

face. Shafts of golden light cut through the maples and beeches. Tendrils of mist rose from the bitter ground, forcing her to climb onto the log. Sam rushed to her from the edge of the now-solid pond. He wagged and huffed and slobbered on Allie's face, but did not attempt a bark. The quiet over the woods prevented it. It wasn't a holy kind of quiet, she thought, like the silence people fell into at church or a funeral. It was more a vacuum.

Shelter or not, her Chucks had frozen in the night. Putting them on felt like wearing two icy cinder blocks. Allie bit her lip as she pushed her feet inside.

"How'd you sleep?" he asked.

She didn't mention her nightmare, only said, "Not bad. You?"

"Like a vacation." Which Zach felt was true enough, so long as that holiday was spent in the middle of nowhere. His coat smelled like sweat, and his hair had dried into a thick, brown bird's nest. They'd done a good job on the shelter, but Zach knew that wasn't what had kept him so hot all night. The fever had done that.

"You stay with Zach, Samwise," Allie whispered. "I gotta go tend to business."

She shouldered her pack and walked off, fighting the urge to turn and see if Zach was watching.

Because you know he is, she thought. *You know he is because he knows something's up, and sooner or later he's gonna ask. And what are you gonna tell him? Irritable bowel?*

Allie kept her head down and shrugged—*Don't know, don't care.* More concerning were the invisible nails pushing up through her heels, making her stumble. Allie didn't know what was going on down there in her shoes, but she didn't like it. Not at all.

The tree she chose for her necessary was maybe thirty feet tall, healthy and wide enough for her to sneak behind without any chance of being seen. Allie took a final look and saw Zach's eyes dart away, then stepped behind the tree. She'd slipped off her pack and unbuttoned her jeans—had even begun the initial downward movement of what she'd come to call the Squat of Shame—when her eyes drifted to the big oak's trunk. A single cold finger traced a shiver in a line that began at the base of her neck and ended at her tailbone. Allie stood there, half standing and half crouching. Staring.

"Zach?"

She bent her head around the tree. Zach had sat on the log in front of the hut, trying but not quite managing to play with Sam. He looked up.

"C'mere."

"Why?"

"I need to show you something." Whispering. Not so strange, given how much the world had gone still. And yet Allie knew something else had gone wrong overnight, something beyond all the screaming nothing around her. She tried keeping her insides even so she wouldn't drift to worry. Or worse, fear.

"I don't wanna see what you're doing back there, Allie," Zach said, even if that was all he was interested in at the moment. He simply didn't think he could move from his spot on the log.

"Come"—whisper—"*here.*"

He rose from the log, rolling his eyes like boys who think they're men do, a look that says, *Whassa matter, see a bug?* Sam followed, happy to have somewhere to explore with his nose. By the time they reached the tree, Zach was near breathless. He didn't think he'd ever walked so far in his life.

"What?" he asked.

Allie stepped aside. She pointed to the trunk. "What's that?"

Zach bent to look and just stood there. He offered no words, no emotion. It was as though he'd been frozen right along with the ground beneath them and the tree in front of them. His mind tried to sort out what his eyes were seeing. Only static came through.

Scratched into the trunk were five deep gouges that ran in a diagonal from above their heads to just below their knees. Bits of bark hung from the grooves like flaking skin. The insides of the tree were laid bare in the morning light.

"You hear anything last night?" Allie asked.

"No."

"Nothin' at all? Did Sam hear anything?"

Sam's ears perked at the mention of his name. He wagged his tail and pushed his nose against the leg of Allie's soiled jeans. She bent and rubbed him without thought.

"Sam never moved at all," Zach said. "I kept waking up, coughing and stuff, wanting to see if that light came back. It didn't. I didn't hear anything neither. Why?"

Allie reached up and followed the center groove with one hand. She turned her forefinger sideways, trying to judge how deep the cut went. Her nail disappeared almost to the first knuckle, making her shudder.

"We gathered wood right around here last night," she said. "Did you see these marks?"

"No," he said. "Did you?"

She shook her head.

Zach studied the marks again. "That don't mean nothing," he said. "We were tired and you were mad. We had to get something together before it got dark. Sam"—he said only Sam, though in his heart Zach counted Allie and himself as well—"was all shaky because of those animals. How could we have seen this?"

Allie stuffed her hands into the pockets of her jacket, feeling the willow bark she'd hidden there. She shuffled her feet on the ground, trying to stop those needles, and kicked at a rock that didn't budge from the ground.

"We *couldn't,*" Zach said. And so a big chunk of him believed. Because they'd been scared and in a hurry to get under cover, and it was probably near dark when they'd walked over near that tree to gather what they needed, and of course they'd just missed it. Even an experienced woodsman couldn't see everything.

Allie watched him fingering the grooves, sinking his own fingernail in. He shrugged a no-big-deal. Sam growled low and moved away, back toward the shelter.

"You gotta stop being scared of everything, Allie," he said. "That's when people screw up is when they're scared. Those marks probably got made a long time ago by something. A storm maybe, or maybe a hunter."

"Storms and hunters can do that to big old trees?"

"Sure they can. It ain't like we seen no funny-looking trees in the last two days."

"That's right," Allie said. Nodding, wanting with all her heart to believe Zach was right and this was nothing at all, even if that primal place deep inside her, first roused way back in the olden woods, now sparked again. "Lotsa funny stuff around here," she told Zach, just the moment that the voice said, *You know what that means, don't you, Allie?*

"We'd have heard it, something like that. Would've made a racket, especially in all this quiet. And there ain't no tracks nowhere. There'd be tracks for sure."

Another nod, this one so vigorous that Allie's pigtails bobbed in her face. They smelled like wet fur.

Touch it, the voice said.

She moved her hand back to the oak and spread her fingers wide. They covered only a small bit of two scratches out of the five total. The remaining three stretched out to either side—two on the left, one on the right.

"Think it was whatever made that light?" she asked.

"Light don't make marks."

"You sure?"

"'Course I am."

Allie looked at Zach, trying to figure if he was telling the truth. Sam barked. It was low and soft, barely more than a whimper, but in the silence it came like a roar. Only the white tip of his tail was visible behind another tree, this one on the opposite side of their hut. Allie picked up her pack and followed Zach. There were more scratches behind that tree—five of them, deep and wide.

They walked a wide circle around camp, moving from tree to tree. Seven others bore the same scores. One, a tall maple with limbs that stretched over the back of the very place where they'd bedded down, bore only four.

"That one's different," Zach said. "See that? Only four scratches. Don't mean nothing, Allie. Probably just some disease is all. This whole place looks like it's dyin'. 'Sides, ain't no tracks here, neither." And there weren't, Zach had made sure, and that was the only thing that stayed the full-blown panic building inside him. "Don't be scared, Allie. You get like that, the mind starts saying stuff's there that ain't."

Allie nodded one last time, slow and soft. She whispered, "Okay, Zach," even as that small and terrible voice inside her said, *You know why there's only four scratches on that maple, don't you, Allie?*

She shook her head no as Zach left her to call Sam. Shook it no again.

Because that maple's smaller, Voice said. *Why, this here maple probably looked like a pencil to Who made that. This tree's too small to hold all five*

—"Stop it," Allie whispered, not wanting to hear—

CLAWS. Bet he stood right here watching you sleep too. Zach says that's not what happened, but you know, don't you? And you know what? Zach knows too. He's just too scared to say.

Allie stared at the ground, trying to find the path she and Zach had taken around the perimeter of their camp. None of their footprints showed. The earth was too hard. Anything could've come by in the darkness and not left a trace.

Sam sniffed the bottom of the maple and growled. He lifted his head and cocked a hind leg, spraying the tree. Allie rubbed his head once he'd finished. He may have been a dumb old beast, but Allie's dog was no coward.

"Allie." She felt Zach's hand at her back. It was equal parts shaky and calming. "It's like when you said something was back in the meadow. Then you talked to me, and you decided it was nothing. Right?"

"Right," she whispered.

"This here's the same thing is all."

No, it's not, Allie. You thought you could hide out here in the big woods? You can't. Look around you.

She did. From the maple, on around behind her, to the big oak where she'd first gone. The shelter occupied the center like a bull's-eye. All the blood left Allie's face with a speed that made her feel faint.

"It's like we were marked."

"What?" Zach asked.

"Why'd all those birds and critters come running past us, Zach? What was back there?"

He looked at the maple again. This time Zach touched the grooves. One after the other, tracing them from above his head down to his waist. "I was gonna say we could stay a little while," he said. "Got water close, and a good shelter. We could use the rest. But maybe we should move on."

"That's a fine idea," Allie said, "but we don't know where

we are, so we can't know where to go. In case you forgot, my compass is gone."

Zach ignored that. Allie let him. She figured Zach was the only other person in the world who missed that compass as much as she did right then. But Zach was thinking no such thing. He shuddered from the chill in him and coughed into a hand that looked more brown than white. When he wiped his nose, snot streaked his sleeve. He knew exactly where to head to find home, thanks to the clear morning. The trick would be telling it right to Allie.

"Can't go through all that water, not with your tennis shoes. That means north's out. Can't go south, because that's behind us and that's where all them animals came from. I don't know why they were running, Allie, but I figure it's best if we stay away from there. West is out, because we'd have to cross the stream and run into the same problem as north. Guess that leaves east."

"What about my momma?"

"Easy. If that's the only way we can go, then I guess that's where the compass'd be pointing."

Allie nodded. It made sense, but "I don't think I can walk, Zach. My feet ain't so good."

"Let me look at them."

He guided Allie back to the log and removed her shoes and socks. She nearly screamed at what was underneath, quiet woods or not. The skin over her feet looked pasty, almost ashen. Like Salisbury steak minus the gravy.

Zach pressed on her big toe. "You feel that?"

Allie nodded. "They hurt bad when I first woke up. Now I don't feel much. What is it? Do I got the plague?"

"Frostnip," Zach said. He rubbed his chest. "You need a fire soon. We won't go far, only a ways. I'll try a fire again. Think you can walk just a while?"

Allie looked at that perfect circle of scored trunks, imagining the marks behind them. Facing out to the woods rather than in toward them

And why would that be?

"I can walk."

"Let's get on, then. It's gonna be cold today."

They stuffed her Chucks and socks with the pine needles and leaves from inside the shelter. Zach offered to carry the backpack with the promise that he wouldn't look inside. Allie kept it anyway. Not because she didn't trust him, but because she didn't want to have to ask for it when she went to do her business later. She reminded herself she'd have to do that soon.

Sam didn't lead this time. He kept close to Allie instead, looking around and behind but mostly at her, as if making sure she didn't wander off. It was Zach who walked out front. He held his pocketknife in one hand and a straight branch of fallen oak in his other.

She turned to take one last look at the place that had been their temporary home. It had been only one night, and they had both been hungry and tired and sick, but Allie was still struck with a sense of sadness at having to leave. Even with the compass gone, she had felt safe there. Happy, almost. But that was gone now. She'd been found. And because Zach and Sam were with her, they'd been found too. Marked. Zach had not bothered to fasten the door back. Allie almost said something to him about that, then didn't. It felt better, knowing that door was still open. Maybe they could come back someday, show her momma what they did while they were looking for her.

Her eyes went to a place farther back from the hut, where the trees bunched together. Something moved there. Only for a moment, then gone. The breeze shuffling a limb, maybe

(No)

or a trick of light.

(Don't you think like that, Allie. Thinking like that will get you all killed, and it'll be your fault. Just yours.)

She turned, making sure Sam and Zach were still close. From there on, Allie kept her eyes ahead.

2

And so it was east toward the sun where Zach led them, just as a combination of forestry servicemen and state police began mapping the day's search in the cold shade of the Christmas tree in the town square. The crowd that greeted Marshall and Grace that morning was twice the size they'd found the day before. Word of Allie's and Zach's disappearances had spread to the tiny communities of the hill country. Jake in particular welcomed this development. Staties and forestry folks did their jobs well, but no one knew the mountains and hollow surrounding Mattingly better than the hill folk. The cold was near unbearable, and the search thus far had turned up not even a semblance of evidence. Jake allowed himself to believe nonetheless, even as the memory of Zach calling out through the nightmare the night before was still fresh in his mind—a son begging his father to keep the monsters away. The children would be found.

Jake only wished Kate could believe the same. The past days had been harder on her than anyone, even Marshall. She could not sleep, would not eat. Would barely talk. The Barnetts had endured much as a family, had stretched to near breaking the bonds that held them together, but Jake knew Kate's faith was failing. In many ways, she had gone lost right along with Zach.

Strange as it may seem, the one person who truly understood what Kate Barnett felt was the man who had so often cursed the fact that she had survived The Storm while his own wife had not. Marshall would understand Kate's gnawing doubts. He too felt no such compunction for faith. Heartache was the norm now, and Marshall could sense its approach the way birds sensed a coming storm. He and Grace had spoken little that morning. It had taken Marshall a full thirty minutes of stutters and awkward pauses to apologize for all he'd said the night before. Not because he couldn't decide what to say, but because he wanted—needed—Grace to understand.

Grace had accepted that sorry well enough, though the truth was that all she wanted was for Marshall to understand as well. He didn't, of course. Likely couldn't, even if he and everyone else in Mattingly still remembered the sad tale of Henry Louis Howard, the man who had once been "Looey" to his friends, Hank to the many who weren't, and Daddy to his little Gracie before the misery took him.

What hurt feelings existed between Marshall and Grace were put away once they reached town. Now it was more squeezes of Marshall's shoulder and grave tones of faith and hope and Christmas miracles by the throng, all of which Marshall took well. He found those sentiments necessary on a morning when the thermometer in front of the hardware store barely registered seventeen. He thought everyone needed such good words. The town had pulled together again, had bound its fate to Allie and Zach, but Marshall saw that many of the faces greeting him were without the determined looks of the previous day. Dwindling weather didn't have much to do with it. Dwindling hope did.

Zach may have shared that same sense of doom the night before, but he had greeted the new day with a sense of guarded hope that kept his feet moving through the forest. He did not need to see the muted expressions on the townspeople's faces as they dispersed to beat bushes and comb fields, nor did he have to hear the soft pleadings of his mother's voice spoken to a bright, sun-filled sky. He knew their time was low. The deep woods was no place to tarry even in summer, when food was aplenty and the days were drawn in long, warm strokes. Being stranded there in the wintertime was worse and different. Let Allie believe in ghosts and boogeymen. Zach knew what truly stalked them was something that had no need to lurk behind trees or in the cover of night because it hid inside them—deep down in Zach's thickening lungs and in Allie's hard, graying feet. They had more to overcome than the forest now. They had to beat death.

That notion made it easier for Zach to lay aside his guilt over telling Allie east was their only way. The truth was that west had also been an option (the brook had frozen along with everything else overnight, and even if it hadn't, the banks were still narrow enough in some places to jump). North around the pond had been possible as well. Even south had not been beyond the reach of possibility. That would've meant going in the same direction where the stampede had come, but Zach thought it might be worth trying to find the hill again. And they'd stay there this time. He would pray for a helicopter, and Allie would tell him not to bother.

But in the end it was east Zach had settled on. Not because that was where the compass maybe had been pointing or because that was where Mary waited, but because east was Mattingly—if not the town itself, then the farms and roads that surrounded it. The sun had been at their backs when they'd left the town square. It stood to reason that same sun should be at their faces when they returned. So long as the sun shone, they weren't lost at all. And though Zach had been wrong about a great many things in the past two days (and would be proven wrong about a great many more in the days to come), on this point he was exactly right.

"I like the God of the sun," Allie said.

He turned. Allie had fallen perhaps ten steps behind. Sam remained close at her side. Zach had gone to great lengths that morning to tell himself everything was fine, that nothing had happened in the past day to warrant freaking out. That was of course a lie, one Zach acknowledged deep down where only the truths of our lives lay. Much like the other lie, that the stout piece of oak branch currently in his right hand was more an aid to help him walk than a weapon he would perhaps have to use. But the sight of Sam clinging so close rather than wandering out ahead was bothersome, as was the way Allie had been acting all morning. To Zach, it was like something fragile had broken off inside her.

"What'd you say?" he asked.

"The God of the sun. Wouldn't that be nice, Zach? If that were really who He was, I mean? Everything would always be so bright. I wouldn't have to be scared anymore, because I could *see.* I don't think I'd know what to do. That's probably why I'm stuck with the moon."

She smiled then, and in those white teeth and parted lips Zach saw a kind of budding madness that made the hurt in his lungs seem small. Streaks of grime covered Allie's face. Her pigtails hung from the sides of her head like two muddy icicles. Puffs of air oozed from her nose like fog. She squeezed her shoulders, hugging the backpack against her.

"I want the sun," she said, still smiling. "I'm so tired of the moon."

"We're making good time, Allie. Even with the cold. Bet we've already gone a mile or so."

Allie didn't bother with a reply. She only gave Zach a grunting sound that could be taken as something negative just as easily as positive. He waited until she caught up before moving on.

Sam divided his time between them, keeping to Allie's shadow and then Zach's, almost afraid to step into the sunlight. The dog remained watchful, though, and as minutes turned to hours, he became more relaxed, more himself. It was more than Zach could say for Allie, who continued to lag behind. Zach did what he could to coax her along, though he saved much of that effort for himself. His chest felt knotted and his fever burned, bringing with it a pain that sank into his forehead. Flakes of black danced at the corners of his vision. They were chased away only when he blinked hard.

It was the trees back at the camp. He knew that's what bothered Allie, and he understood why. Allie had never spent much time in the woods. That woods was too big and filled with too many stories, and the wind there sounded like something alive. Had her daddy spent more time with her out there than with his whiskey and beer, Allie would have known scratched-up trees were common in the wilderness. Rutting bucks, mostly, though sometimes bears did it too. Cougars—which Allie had said weren't around anymore, but what did she know; she was the one wearing frozen tennis shoes stuffed with pine branches—could nearly tear trees apart sharpening their claws.

Sure, there were big things in the woods. Things bigger and badder than even nearly grown men like Zach Barnett. But most of the truly bad things that once walked those woods were long dead and existed only in the pages of the dinosaur books Miss Howard loved for him to read. What beasts were left wanted little to do with people, especially in the cold winter months. That's what Zach told himself as they wandered a wide expanse of trees taller than any building he'd ever seen. Yet Zach could tell Allie none of this, because doing so would feel almost like a promise. He kept the chunk of oak ready in his trembling right hand.

It wasn't far before the open woods sloped downward, making the way more treacherous. The sunlight ahead met another clench of darkwood and stopped, unable to penetrate the thick tangle of stunted trees and bare thornbushes. Allie's talk of gods in the sun and the moon ended. Sam drew even closer, peeking through Zach's knees. He let out a low growl.

"That's a bad place," Allie said. "Sun don't reach there, Zach. Bad place."

Zach took her words in silence. He only stared ahead, trying to see beyond the first layer of scrub. There was no telling how deep it all was, but he could see how wide. The wall stretched in a wavering line for what Zach guessed was a mile or so in either direction. Avoiding it would mean turning north or south. That would add hours to their walk once they skirted the brush and headed east again, and that was assuming the sun would still be high and not hidden by the thick clouds that always lurked come December in the Virginia mountains.

Sam growled again, low and deep.

There was nothing in there.

Allie: "It's a bad place, Zach. Momma'd never be in a place like that. Bad."

Just some scrub was all. Nothing at all different from all the scrub that had come before, and nothing so bad as some scratched

(trees)

arms and faces from the sharp branches and thorns inside. They could send Sam in first, like before. They could let him find the way to the other side, and Allie could call his name, turning him from dog to beacon. But Sam wouldn't move from behind Zach's knees, and Allie didn't seem much interested in making him, and for as much as Zach told himself nothing at all waited in the darkness just beyond, his hand hurt from gripping the hunk of oak so hard.

"Might not be much at all, Allie. Might be just a couple little steps through to the other side. Lots of times, darkwood like this means a river's near. We find the river, we're saved. Cuts right through town."

"We shouldn't," Allie whispered. "Know which god's in there, Zach? It's the one in the moon. He don't care."

They couldn't turn off, not after coming this far, and as the man it was Zach's decision to make either way. He took a step forward. Another. Slow, so Allie and Sam could keep up and so Zach would not leave the safety of the open woods just yet. He no longer pretended the staff was anything other than a tool to maim and kill. He kept it raised in front of himself, holding it like a baseball bat.

"Bad," Allie said. The sound was far away. Zach didn't have to turn to know she hadn't moved from her spot, nor did he have to look down to know Sam had remained behind as well. Yet far from convincing Zach to turn away, their fear only emboldened him to step forward again—one final time, close enough that the tip of his staff could have touched the first fringes of a struggling old cedar. He opened his mouth to pronounce the way clear. A limb snapped somewhere in the shadows.

Zach flinched. Allie muffled a scream. He backed away slower than he had approached, keeping his back to Allie and Sam and his eyes on the tangle, watching for movement inside. He felt neither chills nor fever, only the thrumming of his heart. A wheezing sound, high and uneven, escaped his chest. The darkwood fell silent again.

He said nothing when he reached Allie's side, only turned and began a slow walk along the northern edge of the scrub. She and Sam followed. *Just a ways,* Zach thought. *Just for a while, then east again.* No use fighting all that brush when there's open woods to travel in. Best to save their energy. His posture began to slouch. His focus shrank to the ground beneath him. Zach offered no more comfort as to what good time they made, nor did he try to coax Allie on. The confidence that had carried him from their place by the pond faded, and there was a heavy pain in feeling it go. For Zach, though in his mind he was still a man of the woods, had been turned from where he knew they should go by the sound of a single snapping branch.

3

The woods were rendering the days as unrecognizable as the children's worn faces. To Allie, there was now only Time to Walk and Time to Rest. They had done plenty of walking since leaving the frozen pond. They would have to do some resting soon. If they didn't, she didn't think Zach would last.

The tip of his staff thumped in rhythm with each step of his right foot. With each step, the hunk of oak in his hand bore more of his weight. His eyes focused on the forest floor, squinting for every leaf and wayward rock, measuring the next pace with a precision that only left him more tired. His fever raged now; he'd already unbuttoned his coat and was now fidgeting with his shirt. Allie walked alongside. Twice she stretched out her hand when Zach began to wobble. Her fingers brushed his sleeve but never managed to grip it. Zach would pull away at the last moment, righting himself and furrowing his brow as if angered. He shook his head and mumbled something Allie couldn't hear.

Sam kept well away and did his best to keep up. He paused often, perking his ears at the tangle beside them. Allie noticed a slight limp in her dog's walk and how his back stood humped. Briars and streaks of mud dotted Sam's coat. His eyes looked swollen and tired. They had to find her momma soon. They had to get home.

The darkwood thinned more. The woods opened again.

"We should stop, Zach," she said. "Take a break."

"Not yet," he wheezed, and thumped his staff on the ground again. The tip caught the edge of a rock poking up from the ground. Zach grunted again as the tip slid off, throwing his weight to the right. He blinked away the flecks floating in his eyes. Cold wormed its way through his clothes, making the skin feel hard and tight. He put on his coat again. "Gotta turn, Allie. East is the way. I know it is."

"You need a break."

"Don't need no break."

"Well, then, *I* need one. And so does Sam. We've been walking a long while. Maybe we should go ahead and eat that last candy bar. Or the juice. Some fruit juice might make you perk up."

"Too cold to stop. Gotta keep moving. We can't get too cold, Allie. We sit down now, we might not be able to get up again."

"Well, we need to try," she said. "My feet hurt, Zach. I can't walk no more."

He lifted his head, and in Zach's red eyes and drawn face Allie saw a flash of anger. "We lost time, Allie. Time's all we got now. It's a race, and we're losing. Don't you see that? We had to turn north to get 'round this tangle. That cost us *time*. We gotta make that time up somehow, and the only way to do that is to *keep moving*."

Those last two words came out loud and sharp, ringing off the trees. Allie ducked, overcome not by Zach's screaming (he'd done that often enough in the last couple days, but it was never as loud as Marshall's yelling when he got in his cups), but by the prospect of that noise bringing Who'd been lurking in the darkwood behind them. She couldn't let that happen. Allie didn't know where they were or where they were heading, but she knew they had to stay hidden. She didn't think He'd let them slink away again.

"Please be quiet," she said.

"Why?"

"Something might hear."

"Who's gonna hear us, Allie?" Zach asked. "Case you ain't been paying attention, we're the only ones out here." He raised his arms high and wide, shaking his head. His hat (which was quickly going from black to dirty brown) bobbed left then right. Zach lowered his hands and straightened the crown, then uttered a phlegmy chuckle. "There's some pines up yonder. We'll stop there and rest for a minute. I wanna get away from this tangle and back on track. We got a long ways ahead."

The cold in the air was no match for the cold in the ground, one that sucked a bit more energy from Allie's legs each time her feet landed. Her jacket was zipped as far as it could go, the scarf was tight around her neck, and the pine branches stuffed between her skin and sweatshirt still held. None of that was enough. She shuddered, thinking how much colder it would get later in the day. And that night, if Zach couldn't get a fire going and they were still looking.

They reached the stand of pines and crawled beneath a full one near the middle. Allie stared at the darkwood, thinking she and Zach would maybe have to add another bit of time to their days from now on—Time to Walk, Time to Rest, and now Time to Hide. A breeze whistled through the forest, making the branches bend and rub. Sam lifted his nose, reading the breeze like a letter.

They ate the last candy bar. It was a PayDay, which suited Zach fine because at least there were peanuts instead of just more chocolate, so Sam could have some too. Allie sipped the water from the pond and let Zach drink all of the apple juice.

Sam ate what both of them had left. The burping contest that followed was brief given their weariness but spirited nonetheless. Allie enjoyed it most of all, even if she came up the loser. Burping all that food up was like eating it twice. She hoped the taste would stay in her mouth a while. Aside from the small amount of water left in the other juice box, that was the last of their food and drink.

Zach looked on beyond the trees. Slivers of the open woods peeked through the branches of the pines. To their left the sun, still rising. East. That was the way, Zach had said. He knew it. But Allie didn't know the way to what.

"We should've gone on in that thicket, Allie. It was the best way."

"Something was in there, Zach. You heard it."

"Weren't nothing in there. It was a branch snapping was all. Listen to this wind. There's stuff snapping everywhere. It's *cold*, Allie. Cold snaps all kinds of stuff in the woods all the time." A pause, then, "Feel like it's snappin' *me*."

"Wind wasn't blowing when that branch snapped, Zach. I told you it was a bad place."

"How do you know that?" he asked. "You think you know more than me now?"

"No. It was just a feeling, I guess."

"Like that compass pointing to your momma was a feeling? Or that we should go deeper and deeper into all these trees was a feeling? Or shoving me out of the way when that helicopter came was a feeling? You mean like that?"

Allie lowered her head. Said, "I already told you I was sorry for that."

"But you weren't."

"No. Just like you weren't sorry for losing my compass. It was protecting us, Zach. But you let it leave and now we're marked."

"What's that supposed to mean?"

"You saw them scratches. You say they were there before but you know they weren't. We'd've seen them, Zach, even if it was going on dark and we were so tired and scared."

"I weren't scared," Zach said.

"We'd've seen them anyways," Allie answered, ignoring him. "You been in the woods long enough. You're the one goin' up to the Holler to carve your name in the rusty gate, show everyone you got a spine. You would've seen those scratches, Zach, but you didn't because they weren't *there*. He came along in the night and made a big circle around the trees to show everything."

"Show everything what?"

"That we been marked," Allie said.

Zach brought his knees to his chest and hugged himself. His body shuddered against the wind. "I don't know which is worse—that I just heard the dumbest thing ever, or that I heard it coming from you."

"Zach?" Allie asked. She reached out for his sleeve, touched it this time. He didn't pull away. "It's okay to be scared."

"I ain't scared of nothing," he growled. "You hear me, Allie? *Nothing.* Because if I get scared, then we're done."

Sam's tail straightened. He barked twice and shot from under the pine. Allie crawled forward and poked her head out, calling him back. Sam had either had his fill of her and Zach arguing or he didn't hear. He didn't quite run toward the open woods on the other side of the brush, but he was no longer walking either.

"What's he doing?" Zach asked.

"I don't know. I think his nose caught something." Then, toward the trees: "Sam, to me."

But Sam didn't—wouldn't—and Allie knew if she let her stupid old dog that she didn't love at all go any farther, she might lose him forever. She pulled herself from under the pine, jerking the backpack free when it caught in the branches. "You stay here and rest," she told Zach. "I'll get him."

Allie rose to her feet (a task she'd probably done thousands of times in her short life, but one that now made her feel old and brittle) and lumbered forward, willing her feet to move quick. The pine shuffled behind her. Zach did not call out, tell her to wait or be careful. To Allie, hearing him follow was enough. It would have to be. Because Allie knew Zach was right—even if they found Mary that day, there was a long path back home. And whether that way was light or it was dark, the only way they would find an end was if they went together.

4

Sam found what was left of the body.

It was east—where Zach had meant to take them—and only a few hundred steps on, past where the deadwood fell away and the open forest took over again. Sam didn't run all that way. Allie thought he would have were it not for the cold that had wormed its way into her dog's bones and the hunger that had stolen his once boundless energy. All he could manage was a lazy trot through the empty spaces between the trees. Even that was more than enough to keep Allie chasing at a distance.

The scent must have swept over him like a wave; Sam had no choice but to let it carry him away. Allie had followed as he sniffed and veered off, called in a voice she hoped was loud enough for Sam to hear but soft enough to go unheard by anything else. Zach followed a few steps behind, grunting and wheezing as his staff click-clacked over the hard ground. And just as Allie slowed, knowing the next three or four hard steps she took would be all her ruined feet would allow, Sam stopped. He stood at the base of a small hillock surrounded by a stand of young maples and cedars. He looked back once and then climbed, disappearing behind the trees.

"He's got something," Zach said from behind.

Allie turned around. Zach leaned his body over the staff and pushed his hat up, revealing a line of sweat beneath. His slick, brown hair made the pallor of his cheeks almost shine. Allie used those last few steps her feet had left to walk back to his side. They watched the white tip of Sam's tail dart in and out of view. He neither barked nor growled.

Don't go in there, Allie. Please don't. It's a bad place.

She didn't want to leave Zach. Nor could Allie stand there and watch her dog walking away. Samwise was a mangy mongrel, and she did not love him at all, but she didn't want him to go wandering off alone.

"Can you make it up there?" she asked. "If he's got something, we should see what it is."

Zach moved only after Allie did and nodded, trying to convince her that making it up there was his idea. They walked shoulder to shoulder, neither of them wanting the other to stray. The sun struggled through the canopy of trees. Rays of light hit the forest floor in jagged lines that looked like wounds that would never heal. The slope wasn't steep, not nearly the slant of the hill Allie had climbed to rescue them from being rescued, but enough for them to struggle.

Zach crept in front as they neared the place where Sam had passed from sight. Allie let him, hoping that by focusing on her steps she could quiet the voice inside her that kept screaming for her to turn away. East, west, south, north, it didn't matter, just so long as it was somewhere else. Zach turned his crutch into a club again. He whispered for Sam.

A scurry from somewhere farther on.

The forest there had spared the maples from the hard winter winds. Dry, shriveled leaves hid the view. Allie tried calling Sam to her once more. Zach moved a branch in their way. He drew his hand back and rubbed his fingers together, studying them with two widening eyes. A tremble traced its way through his shoulders and arms. Allie told herself that was the cold getting into him, nothing more, but the voice inside her said that was wrong. And when Zach stretched out his hand to show Allie what he'd touched, she knew the voice had been right.

There was a brief moment when the trees around her bent and swirled. Her knees gave way. Allie closed her eyes tight, opened them. The stain was still on Zach's fingers.

What she said wasn't a question: "Blood."

Zach's breaths came deep and hard through his mouth. He looked to where Sam had gone, trying to find something else that could be on a dead old leaf. Mud, maybe. Or maybe it was just a little frost turned red by a trick of light, the sun coming down sideways through the trees. Sam barked. He was close.

"Yeah," he told her. "I think it is." He rested the staff under his arm and reached for his knife. There was a soft click as the blade locked open. He offered it to Allie. "Me first," he said. "You stay back, Allie. Stay back and get ready to run."

"I'm coming," she said.

Zach shook his head. "I don't know what's up there."

"I'm coming, Zach. I have to."

Zach moved the branch aside and held it so Allie could pass. She did, bending as far to the right as she could to avoid the blood, only to run into more on the tree beside. Allie shrank back, fluttering her arms like the girly girls she and Zach always made fun of back home. She swiped at the blood on her jacket, trying to get it off. All she accomplished was to smear it more.

Sam barked again from his place higher up—twice this time, hard and quick, like he'd found something incredible. To Allie, the choice was fast becoming either get to Sam or risk him telling the whole forest where they were. A cloud of vapor encircled her head, evidence of how quick her breaths had become. She charged ahead, holding back only long enough for Zach to retake the lead. The leaves shook as the two of them pushed through the branches. Rusty rain fell over their clothes. Allie wiped at her cheek, nearly piercing her eye with Zach's knife.

The noise that came at them was small but sudden enough for Zach to raise his staff. The steel blade bobbed in Allie's hand. But it was only Sam that emerged from the trees. He woofed twice—all he could do, given the size of the leg between his jaws—and turned back into the trees.

"Deer," Zach said. "Maybe it was a hunter. Come on."

Allie followed behind, slowed by the battle between her voice and the voice of her other self:

Hurry up, don't lose sight of Zach.

No, Allie. You have to run away. You have to listen to Me, because I'm the only one here who's gonna save you.

She followed Zach anyway. The trail of blood ended when the trees cleared enough to let in much of the sun.

On the ground in front of them lay a brown lump that looked like a soft, wet blanket. A tuft of white tail lay perhaps twenty feet to their right. To their left, two more legs lay bent and twisted. Allie stepped forward. Her shoe made a sucking sound against the ground. She looked down to see her feet at the edge of a crimson river flowing from the top of the hill.

Zach poked the lump with his staff, rolling it over. The inside was hollow but for a layer of fat on the underside. He walked on, following the blood from the carcass. The maple where he stopped was at the center of the hill and taller than both of them together. The deer's severed head lay in the fork of two branches. Its eyes were the color of honey. Even in death they had held onto a look of fear and shock, as if the animal had carried the image of what killed it to the grave. A gray tongue poked from its open mouth. Drops of blood fell from the neck. They puddled on the ground and oozed down the slope in winding capillaries.

"A doe," was all Zach said.

He did not attach any great meaning to that statement. The time for impressing Allie with his vast collection of wilderness wisdom had long passed, left somewhere miles back with their bikes and the compass. Yet those two words vibrated Allie's very heart. Standing in the shadow of that hanging head, Allie felt that familiar sting in her eyes. This had not simply been an animal that had once stood where they stood now. It had not been only a deer that had met such a violent, awful end.

It had been a doe.

It had been a mate to a strong buck that was now likely miles gone with all the rest of the forest's game, mourning and alone. Perhaps it had even been a mother to a youngling that now filled the wide woods with cries for all that had gone lost.

She turned away, knowing that to look any longer would bring a flood of tears that would not be held back. Sam lay nearby. He'd maneuvered the leg so that it was vertical between his two front paws. Blood and bits of brown fur ringed his mouth. He looked at Allie, woofed once, then resumed gnawing on the meat and marrow. Allie closed the distance between her and Sam before he could move. The bright eyes and thumping tail from seeing his master come close turned sour when he saw the grimace on Allie's face. What followed was the bared teeth and low growl of someone intruding upon what was rightly his. He snapped his jaws as Allie reached him and yelped when the palm of her hand met his backside.

"No," she screamed. "You get, Samwise."

Sam jumped up, teeth gone and ears flat. He tucked his tail between two waning legs and scurried away. The leg remained in his mouth. Allie took hold of his scruff and turned him, wrenching the bone away. She used it to smack Sam again, this time on the nose. He yelped and went for the trees.

"Allie." Zach grabbed her arm, pulling her back. The leg fell from her hand onto the ground in a wet splat. "What in the world are you doing?"

"He can't eat it." Screaming the words, not caring who or what heard. Sam poked his nose out from behind a nearby cedar. "You hear me, you mean old dog?" Her voice cracked, and in those gaps she felt springs of tears ready to overflow. "I hate you and *you can't eat it*."

"*Allie*," again, and this time Zach wheeled her around to face him. He dropped his staff and placed both of his hands on her shoulders. "He's just hungry, Allie. Candy bars ain't good for no dog. Sam doesn't know better. Okay? He don't mean nothing by it."

Allie's shoulder shook beneath the weight of emotions too strong to express. Zach gripped her harder. She clamped her eyes and pursed her lips, pushing the tears back down.

"She was somebody's *momma*," she said. "And now she's dead."

Zach bent his head, putting her face in the shadow of his hat. Sam whined from beneath his tree. Allie stood there, unable to look at either of them. And then Zach did something she could have never expected, something that at any other time in any other place would have nearly burst her heart. He eased her to his chest and wrapped both arms around her tight, holding her there.

They cared for the remains. The head was first. Allie could not bear to watch and so occupied herself with gathering the legs and tail instead. She heard Zach struggling to pull the neck away from the limbs and turned to see him cradling it in his arms like a child. They stacked everything on the blanket of fur. Zach took off his hat and bent over. His stomach convulsed into heaving sounds like fingers rubbing rough sandpaper. Afterward, he said it wasn't because he was grossed out, that it was just his sick. Allie told him it was okay. She remembered what her father had said at the cemetery and told him sometimes people felt better after they got it all up and out of the way.

Sam crawled out from his hiding place. He kept his head low to the ground and crept to Allie's side, tail tucked but wagging. She felt her dog's eyes looking up to her, begging for forgiveness, but she could not bring herself to pet him and say everything was all right. Because nothing was right. Nothing at all. Everything was plain to Allie Granderson now. She'd had her suspicions since that morning at the pond, had gathered more evidence at the thing in the darkwood, but finding the doe had given her all the answers she needed. Zach wouldn't believe it; that's why he couldn't put all the pieces together. Allie knew this as much as she understood the irony in it: Zach wouldn't believe because he wasn't fallen away.

He offered to dig a grave. Allie said it wouldn't do any good trying. All they had was one knife to dig in all that frozen ground.

She bent and stroked the side of the doe's face. Whispered, "I'm sorry, pretty deer. I hope you're where there's no bad things now." It was all she could manage.

They did not remain there long. The sun had reached the tops of the trees, signaling the wane of the day. The voice inside her spoke up again, telling her they had to go. Allie agreed. She decided that was the voice she would listen to from then on.

5

Zach bent his face to the high sun and measured the way. Neither of them had much heart to move east, as he had intended. Not yet, anyway. Allie didn't really think her compass had ever been pointing in that direction in the first place, considering where they'd ended up. And though Zach fought the chill seeping into his bones by telling himself it had been his decision alone to take them off course (temporarily, he vowed), the bigger part of him held on to an image of his head and Allie's hung from the limbs of another tree farther on. Sam's head was at the top, forming the world's most awful Christmas tree.

Had they found the courage to press east only a couple miles more, the woods would have finally yielded to a golden field and a wide, oval stretch of water. They would have seen the wooden pier jutting out from the south end and noticed the single-lane dirt road leading over the soft rise beyond, and they would have known they had just gotten themselves found. Allie and Zach were well acquainted with Boone's Pond. It was where both of their families often went to play and picnic on those summer weekends, years before everything ended. Zach caught his first fish in those calm waters. And on one particularly steamy summer night some twelve years before, Marshall Granderson had lain on that pier with his wife above him and the full moon shining down over her bare shoulders, and they had made a daughter.

Sam would have drunk deep from those still waters, and Allie and Zach would have found a wellspring of energy that only the assurance of continued life could bring. They would have circled the pond and followed the dirt lane to its end, where a sign reading 664 pointed to town along a flat, paved road. They would have met the first home seven miles on, an aging farmhouse owned by Hollis and Edith Devereaux. A long way to walk, no doubt, but on that day it was only a half mile past Boone's Pond where Hollis, Marshall Granderson, Grace Howard, and forty others were searching for the town's two missing children.

Marshall had gone sullen. As had Grace, who was still making good on her promise not to leave his side. His shaking had worsened to the point where he thought she'd noticed. There was every reason to believe she had. Despite his attempts to hide his addiction, everyone in Mattingly knew that Marshall Granderson had turned to drink after Mary's death. Grace understood his need to put up a chaste front, even if most in town did not. It wasn't alcohol that Marshall Granderson was trying to conceal; it was his despair, and Grace knew what would come of it if she abandoned Marshall to himself. The curtain he drew down over his world was the same that her father had once drawn down over his own, long ago now but not much further than yesterday in Grace's mind, back when she was not much older than Allie. Her mother, too, had died early, though not from wind. The cancer had come in a rage and eaten its way through her mother's body. In mere months, she had nearly been hollowed out.

It was a horrible death, but one that at least had the blessing of speed. Not like Hank Howard's, whose death had gone on for years. He tried to sink his loss into the deep waters of drunkenness. Grace stood by him. He fell silent and withdrawn as his pain became a wall between himself and his daughter. Grace stood by him. He succumbed to a despair that neither God nor drink could cure, and still Grace stood by him, had at times even helped her father draw down that curtain, because that at least dulled his hurt. Hank Howard remained that way for years, not wanting Grace there, not wanting her help, his only desire to wallow in what he could not rid himself of. For some, the only thing worse than feeling pain is the embarrassment of bearing it for the world to see. Hurt is weakness, these people think, and the inability to cope with an aching heart a sign that all hope is lost and can never be gained again. In the end, Grace Howard could only say that she had killed her father just as much as the gun he stuck into his mouth three days before her high school graduation. She'd stood by and done nothing.

Marshall knew there wasn't much left in the bedroom closet—three bottles, four at the most. He'd have to lose Grace long enough to go see Bobby, and soon. Their search party combed the area to the pond all that morning but found nothing. Jake radioed back, cautioning Marshall not to take that as bad news. There was no way Allie and Zach would have strayed that far from home, not in the winter. Not in that cold. And as the state police quartered back in Mattingly began planning not a rescue but a recovery, Allie, Zach, and Sam walked on deeper into the wilderness.

The pace Zach set from the hill was as quick and steady as he could manage—a purposeful gait, though he really had no idea where they were going and didn't care. It was still a race, one the stronger part of him was still determined to win. But the stakes were higher now, more immediate. The fever in him, the rot in Allie's feet, the cold. These were things that stalked them, and yes, they were all dangerous. But as menacing as those things were, they could all be controlled, held at bay by a good fire or a warm place to stay or food in their bellies. Zach did not really consider any of those things as *living*. That's what set this new thing apart from the fever and rot and cold.

Because this new thing was alive, and it was hunting them.

It had slunk into their camp the night before. Zach could no longer deny that. If he had any comfort at all just then, it was that he'd done such a good job building their hut that the thing—the *It*—had passed by without seeing them. Zach realized now that instinct had been what led him to build their shelter that way, the sort of inner knowing that could only grow in a man raised to survive in the woods. That same knowing was what had kept him from taking Allie through the underbrush that morning. Something in that notion didn't ring true, but then oftentimes believing in a thing is enough to make it real. So no, it wasn't the fact that Zach had been scared half to death by the sound of a snapping branch (which could have been anything, though now he thought there could have been only one hungry Thing waiting just inside that scrub). Nor was it Allie going on about how that darkwood had been a bad place because some kind of moon god lived there. It was Zach who had saved them. Zach and his smarts. Zach and his courage.

That alone made him stand a little taller, though only for a little while. It was only a few hundred yards from where they'd said good-bye to the doe that Zach realized there would be no going quick and steady that day. Until that moment, Zach believed they both had clung to the idea that their time in the woods had been varnished with an almost holy purpose. Yes, there had been hardships along the way—losing both the helicopter and the compass, their dwindling provisions, their parents worried back home—but didn't every adventure contain struggle? Mustn't every hero leave home a boy in order to come home a man?

But the cold—that deep winter, pressing down around and inside them—and the eyes Zach felt even now, watching from a hidden place . . . He felt trapped in those endless woods. He felt sick. He felt small.

Allie walked hunched over, holding her stomach. Zach's knife rested against her left sleeve. He wanted to tell her to close the blade, at least for now, but tripped over a hidden rock before he could. The ground beneath him gave way. Were it not for the club in his right hand (and that's what it was and would be from now on—not a staff or a crutch or a hunk of old oak, but a club),

Zach would have likely broken his nose against the ground. As it was, he managed to catch himself and stand again. The sound of all that stumbling over rocks and dead leaves bounced off the trees. Allie reached to steady him. Zach cursed.

"I'm sorry," she said. "I was only trying to help."

He shook his head no, wanting to tell her he was only mad at himself, but Zach's mouth wasn't working so well anymore. The cold had separated his lower jaw from the rest of his face. It bobbed and fluttered, and each time his teeth clacked together a new wave of pain raced across his forehead. He wished his fever back, wanting to feel hot again.

"Me," he said. "Mad me, not you. Qw . . ." He stopped, clenching his jaws shut, trying again. The cold. So cold. "Quick and quiet. No noise."

"I'm cold, Zach. I need more branches in my clothes."

"M-moving. That thing was behind us b-back at the pond. It ain't anymore. Could be any-any. Where."

He put an arm around her, hoping that would warm Allie some and steady himself more. That was how they continued on, one small step followed by another, pausing so Zach could cough up a little more of his lungs onto his sleeve and Allie could lean hard on him to raise one foot and then another, giving them a needed rest. Sam kept close. The memory of Allie whacking him had faded; he was again a loving dog with a loving master. He eyed Allie and Zach more than the trees, whimpering as they moved. To Zach, it was as though Sam knew something was wrong with them. He'd read stories about how dogs were like that, how they freaked out just before earthquakes and dialed 911 for their owners and sometimes even smelled death or cancer. It wasn't a good look, what was in Sam's eyes.

The three of them had covered nearly sixteen miles since leaving their bikes along the road two days before, but they had managed barely one in the four hours since leaving the doe. By the time the ground began sloping up once more, their steps had become a crawl. The flecks in Zach's vision had gone to swirls. Above them—it was either a few feet or a few miles, Zach wasn't sure which and believed them both the same—an outcropping of ancient rocks jutted out from a hillside like sentinels guarding a lost kingdom. Allie huddled herself even closer. He felt her shudders and heard her own clattering teeth. Her feet kept listing forward—short, stubby steps that did more to scrape the packed leaves beneath them than move herself along. Her head pressed against Zach's chest and lolled forward.

"I can't walk no more," she whimpered. "My feet hurt, Zach."

The world swirling, the cold reaching through him, scraping his nose and the back of his throat, eating Zach from the inside out. What little remained of Zach's steel and faith came out in one chattering word—"Rocks." He pushed Allie on. She took a step, pulling him forward, and that inertia allowed him to pull her forward again. Step by step, each of them feeding off the other's last reserves as Sam looked on and whined.

They would have stopped to rest right where they were, never to get up again, had the thunder not erupted in the woods behind them. Sam yelped, lowering himself to the ground as he trundled away. Allie recoiled at the crashing sound of snapping trees. Her head swung up and nearly clipped Zach's chin. The world spun as he turned. He heard Allie calling his name. Her voice was hidden in a black-and-gray fog descending over Zach's eyes that reminded him of the birds that had flown past them, seeking an escape. He felt himself falling away *(like Allie haha!)*, and in that moment the world slowed and shrank until it was nothing at all but the trees parting and Allie screaming and the rock racing up from the ground.

A bright light came next. And then came nothing at all.

6

To Allie the world was ending, and it had come in a shout rather than a whisper. The crack of trees, mangled and sheared away, came so loud and felt so close that her eyes shut in reflex. When she forced them open, two competing thoughts vied for her attention: That sound was gunfire. That sound was the wind coming to take her away.

She screamed for Zach. The trees shook far behind them, followed close by the crunching sounds of stumps uprooted and saplings torn away by edges sharper and longer than she ever thought possible. Sam yowled. Allie screamed for Zach again, her eyes pinned to the parting forest and her mind flashing with memories of how Zach was the only one she could talk to about her father's slow descent into someone else and how everyone had turned to God or drink

(*Zach what is that it's* coming *Zach do* something)

after The Storm but Allie had turned to him, always had. Zach was brave and she needed him, because not seeing a thing don't mean it ain't real or that it ain't watching even now.

She reached out, grabbing for his sleeve, but grabbed nothing but air. It was like Zach had become more marionette than boy, and the coming Someone had cut his strings. She tried catching him. He was too heavy. Allie watched him fall, helpless to battle both her fears and gravity, and heard the harsh crunch of his head hitting a rock sunk into the ground.

Sam charged forward from his hiding place farther up the slope, putting himself between Allie and the ruckus. Another tree snapped. Allie could not judge how far away He was, but it sounded closer this time, much closer. Her mind pieced together an invisible line of destruction leading from where they'd laid the doe to rest to where Allie now stood. She bent her knees to the hard ground. The backpack shifted, slipping from her shoulders. Allie cursed and pushed it back, shook Zach, screaming, "Wake up Zach please wake *up*."

He didn't move.

Sam bent low. His tail swished as fast as the needle on Allie's compass when it had wanted to point the way. She rolled Zach over and cried out again as his hat slid away. Blood streaked the entire right side of his face. Allie traced the flow backward from the base of Zach's neck to the side of his chin, up past his cheek and eye, where it gushed from a deep hole above his brow.

Sam's barks grew so loud and fast that they melted into a shuddering howl.

Allie called loud and fast—"Sam, to me."

The dog did not turn. Another crash, the closest yet. Too fast. Everything was too fast for Allie to know what to do. Even the voice inside her had gone quiet, chased away like the deer and birds. Only one word came to her mind then, the last thing Zach had spoken.

Rocks.

Allie whipped her head, trading the swaying trees for rocks that had stood unmoved for eons. They had managed to make it halfway up the slope; she judged only fifty feet or so remained. Not a great distance in the world of Mattingly, only as far from the porch to the Nativity, but in the world of the deep woods it looked infinite. Allie stood and grabbed the legs of Zach's jeans. She pulled once. He didn't budge. Sam took three short steps forward as another tree shook. She pulled on Zach again, budged him some—forty-nine feet instead of fifty. It wouldn't be enough. She jerked again, as hard as she could, using her legs and back for leverage. Pain stabbed her stomach. The coming ruckus from the trees was now close enough to rob Sam of what fight he had. His tail stopped whipping and his ears flattened. He turned and ran back to Allie.

"Help me, Sam," she said. "Please help me. You gotta pull."

Perhaps Sam would have had he understood, but even Zach would have confessed a keen mind was not Samwise the Dog's most shining attribute. What understanding the pup possessed had yielded to the fear of what was about to step forth from the trees. Allie pulled Zach again. Zach's eyes shot open. His body went rigid.

"The trees," he said. "Your momma's waiting by the trees, Allie. They're red."

"What?"

His brown eyes fluttered and turned up, showing only the whites, and his bones turned back to liquid. Allie screamed for Zach to wake. She managed a few more feet. Her feet grew numb and her fingers cramped. The sounds from the trees lessened, as if what had found them had just lost track of them again. Pulling on, grunting against gravity and Zach's weight, her rotting Chucks trying to find traction on the sloping ground. Forty feet. Thirty. Twenty. The rocks grew bigger each time Allie chanced a look behind, changing from a loose collection of boulders to giant chunks of limestone larger than her father's truck. She cried out as her fingers weakened and one final snap echoed through the woods, this time so close that she saw the sapling fall.

She made one final pull and found her heels on level ground. Zach's blood continued to pour. The wound had opened like petals on a flower. Sam disappeared behind the rocks. Allie tried sitting Zach up and lost her grip. He hit the ground again, thudding the back of his head so hard that it bounced. He let out a weak, "Hey . . ."

"Zach?" she asked, and a smile crept across Allie's face in spite of it all. "Keep awake, Zach. Please stay with me."

The sun was at their backs, casting black lines that reached down the slope and into the trees. Allie thought she saw a shadow moving there and dragged Zach faster, aiming for a spot out of sight behind the limestone wall. She turned to find that the back end of the hill formed almost a sheer drop. Sam yapped from a spot to her right. Only his front half was visible. The rest was hidden in the darkness of a large hollow between two of the largest rocks.

Allie pulled Zach's body the rest of the way there and then turned, backing them in. The hole was deep enough to hide from the sun and wide enough to make a small room. The rocks pushed against her backpack, crowding her lungs. Allie felt like she was being swallowed alive. She heard nothing of the forest below, but she *felt* Him.

Close.

He could smell her. He smelled her now, and He knew exactly where they were, and there was nowhere left to run. Sam lowered to the cold floor of the cave and placed his chin on his front paws. He whined once. Allie's hand found the fur of his head. She rubbed him there and told him it would all be okay as a great shadow passed over the mouth of the cave, blocking out the orange of the setting sun. It lingered there like a fog, seeming to reach just inside those hard walls, and then moved on. Zach's hand moved to his head. He flinched from the pain, tried to speak. What came out sounded like gibberish.

"You gotta be quiet," Allie whispered. "He's here, Zach. He's right close."

It was either that Zach understood or that he remembered. He nodded once and shut his eyes, leaning back until he met the slope of the rock behind him.

They remained there, shaking and silent for a long while.

7

She covered Zach's wound with the scarf, cinching it tight enough that it stayed most of the bleeding but not so much that it made his pain worse. He was awake now. Not nearly all the way—he reminded Allie of someone who'd just come out of a long sleep and was unsure if he'd woken to a dream or the real—but enough that he could talk a little. His back rested against the smooth side of the cave's far wall, his neck leaning to the left so the gash on his head tilted up. One of the juice boxes was in his hand. Most of the water had spilled on Allie's jacket when she'd pulled Zach up the hill. Zach coaxed out only a few small sips, but it was enough to strengthen him. Sam placed a paw on the leg of his jeans and licked Zach's hand. Allie shrugged off her backpack and took out the fire maker. Her ears buzzed. She stuck a finger in each one and wiggled them, shook her head. The buzzing was still there. Probably just the adrenaline, she thought. Soldiers and Roman gladiators probably got buzzes in their ears like that all the time. It was near dark inside the cave. The air was cold enough for Allie to see the faint outline of her breath, but it was still better than being outside. She leaned Zach forward just enough to place the pack behind his head.

"It's soft," she said.

He closed his eyes and nestled back. The pads scrunched against his head, making the sound of paper crinkling.

"What else you got in there, anyway?" he mumbled.

"Just some nunya is all," Allie whispered.

"What's that?"

"Nunya business." She smiled through chattering teeth. It was a strange sort of sensation, that bending at the corners of Allie's mouth. It felt good, like finding a favorite thing long misplaced. "I'm really glad you didn't die, Zach. I don't know what I'd do."

He nodded. Already a blotch of dark red had wormed its way through the scarf's thick yarn. At least it wasn't growing any bigger.

"What happened?" he asked.

"I don't know. We were just walking along and then the woods started blowing up. I turned around and started screaming, and you fell. Scared me to death. I thought He was gonna get us for sure."

Zach grimaced from the pain above his eyes. "Where is It?" he asked. "That thing in the woods."

"I don't know. It passed by, Zach. It came right past here. I seen—" Allie stopped there and scrunched her eyebrows, thinking. What *had* she seen? The thing that had chased them all the way up there had near blown up the whole forest trying to do it, but whatever had gone past the door of their cave hadn't made a sound at all. "—Something," she finished. "You said something, Zach, back when you fell. Something about my momma. Do you remember?"

He couldn't remember anything.

"You said momma's waiting where the trees are red."

"I did?"

"Yeah."

"What's that mean?"

"I don't know," she said. "I was hopin' you did."

Zach breathed hard and curled his upper lip at the pain in his chest and head. "How'd we get up here? Did I make it?"

"No. I drug you."

He looked at her. "You drug me all the way up this hill?"

"It was only partway," Allie said. "Sam cheered me on."

She rubbed the dog's ear and got a lick of her own as a thank-you. Allie thought her quarrel with Sam was over now. Funny how nearly being eaten alive could make most everything else seem a trifle.

"Where'd It go?"

Allie shook her head. "I got you on the other side of the rocks and lost Him. I ain't heard nothing in a long while. I think maybe He's gone now. This is a good place, Zach. It was all your idea to get up here. You told me that before you almost died. You said, 'Rocks,' and so that's where I brung you. You saved us again."

She thought that might bring a smile out of him. It did, though barely.

"You really think I did?" he asked.

"Sure. We'd've gotten eaten," she said, "or worse," thinking of that poor momma deer. "What's out there's big, Zach. Bigger than anything should ever be. Did you see?"

"No. I don't remember." Eyes still closed. "I kinda remember the trees snapping, but I don't know. Were you freaking out? You know things seem a lot worse than they are when you're freaking out, Allie. Maybe it was just more deer running off, like back at the pond."

"Do you really think that?"

Zach didn't answer at first. Then he said, "No. I guess I don't."

"Me neither. I know what He is."

"What what is?"

"I know who's chasin' us, Zach."

"Who?"

Allie reconsidered and didn't say.

"If It didn't see you when you and Sam came up here," Zach said, "then we're safe so long as we stay."

He leaned forward, letting the backpack slide down a bit, and put his left hand to his forehead. Zach rubbed the smooth wool of the scarf Allie had wrapped around him and thought, trying to figure out what had happened, what they should do next. That hand kept working when no answers came and eased from his forehead to his hair to the back of his head. It stopped there. Zach's eyes flew open.

"Where's my hat?" he asked.

"What?" she asked.

"What'd you do with my hat, Allie?"

"I don't know. I guess it got left."

Zach bolted upright. The pack thumped to the ground (which only served to further scare an already skittish Sam, who jumped away so fast that he nearly tumbled backward). Allie felt a moment of sheer panic when Zach's head came within an inch of banging the cave's roof. The thought of him slicing his skull all up and lying there looking all dead and ghostly again was more than she could bear. Besides, she was out of scarves.

"You left my hat down there?" he asked. "How could you do that, Allie?"

Allie hoped the buzzing had garbled Zach's words and she hadn't just heard what she thought she had. She pushed her hands down into her Chucks, meaning to itch her feet, but found her fingers could no longer fit inside. Zach kept going on and on about his stupid hat, wanting to know how Allie didn't think of bringing that back up the hill too—it wasn't like it was heavy or anything—but Allie couldn't answer because she was too busy trying to figure out how her feet had gotten so swollen.

"What'd you expect me to do, Zach? Leave you down there but rescue your stupid *hat*? You might not know it, but I didn't know what to *do*. That was *your* job, but you weren't around. I got your knife." Allie dug into her jacket pocket and tossed it to him. It clanged against the rock, making Sam flinch again. "You want your stupid old hat, you go get it. Tell Who's waitin' out there I said hi."

She crossed her arms in front of herself and cinched her collar tight, trying to hug away the cold. Sam sat between them.

He whined and refused to take sides. Zach leaned back against the wall and rubbed the scarf again, which had in the last few moments taken on a deeper shade of crimson. He shook his head.

"A man ain't nothing without his hat, Allie. That's rule number one. Just ask my daddy."

"Maybe I should ask your momma," she mumbled. "Bet she'd say something different."

"You don't understand."

"Don't think I want t'understand something as dumb as that, Zach Barnett." She cocked her ear. "You hear something?"

"No. And it ain't dumb."

It wasn't, not in Zach's eyes. That was the hat his own father had worn while braving the ghosts and spirits of Happy Hollow in pursuit of a madman. Now it lay somewhere in the filth of the forest below them. Left there. By Allie, yes, and Zach was quick to settle on that point in his mind. But his daddy's hat had also been left behind because Zach had decided to clock out of reality at the worst possible time. In the end, that was what made him so angry.

Allie could not understand that.

Marshall Granderson certainly could, standing outside Bobby Barnes's auto shop nearly a dozen miles away, telling Grace he had to take care of just one more thing before putting an end to another day of searching for someone he was coming to believe would never be found again. Bobby had seen him coming across the street from the town square, had seen the drawn look on Marshall's face and the trembling in Marshall's hands, and was ready with a cold one in his hand before Allie's daddy could even knock just above the Closed sign on the door.

Few words passed between them in the next minutes. Marshall had heard enough of "Keep your chin up" and "I'll be praying" and "You just gotta have faith, Marshall; that's all there is now," and he would explode if one more preacher confided that God's ways were so mysterious that He would misplace two children in order to bring a whole town together again. Bobby, ever the realist, couldn't bring himself to offer his only friend in the world such lies. They stood behind a wooden counter that stored an old telephone and two ashtrays and a cash register that hadn't rung in a long while, staring out at a street full of traffic heading out of town. Cars and trucks, SUVs and jalopies. All filled with people going back home. Going back to their families.

Marshall asked Bobby for something a little stronger. Bobby obliged by saying there was a bottle in the glove box of his truck. The good stuff, guaranteed to put Marshall out good. Marshall tipped his head (*If ever there was a finer man than Bobby Barnes,* he thought, *I've never met him*) and walked out the door, careful to make sure Grace or Jake or Kate wasn't approaching.

The bottle was indeed in the glove box, just as Bobby had said. It was resting on the folded scarf Allie always wore to school.

8

What happened to Marshall next was not unlike what had happened to his daughter along the slope leading to the rocks—everything happened too fast. When questioned by Jake later, Marshall could only remember bits and pieces: rushing back inside; screaming as he waved the scarf in Bobby's face; the feel of his knuckles meeting Bobby's gaunt cheeks and chin; Bobby crying out, begging Marshall to stop.

Marshall did only after throwing Bobby through the front window of his auto shop and being tackled by a group of passersby. It was rage of loss and utter failure over not being there when Allie most needed him—not being there to protect her.

That was a feeling Zach would have understood well. He coughed into his sleeve. The sound was deep and hard and echoed off the rocks.

"Any food left?" he asked.

Allie shook her head. "It's all gone. You just drank the last of the water too."

"We need fire," he said. "Sun's warmed these rocks some, even if it ain't warmed nothing else. Won't last, though. We don't do something, we'll freeze to death tonight."

"You wanna go out there?" Allie asked him. "What if He's still out there?"

"You said you ain't heard nothing. We gotta try."

"Not *we*, Zach. You can't move."

"I can move enough."

He sat up again slower this time, easily avoiding their new ceiling. His heartbeat centered just above his right eye. The throbbing felt like an ax to his brain. Zach collected the parts of his bow drill and some of the tinder Allie had taken out.

"Wanna come, Sam?" he asked.

Sam's answer was to lie on the ground. Zach eased forward into what little daylight was left, saw nothing beyond but evening, and crawled out. Allie followed.

"You keep watch," he said. "Make sure ain't nothing coming."

Allie bobbed her head. The buzzing in her ears matched the shaking of her limbs. It felt as though her whole body was nodding, telling Zach *Whatever you say, boss.*

Zach set up his equipment just beyond the cave's opening. Allie collected what wood she could find. Most of the area around the rocks was barren, dotted only by a few scraggly pines. She saw nothing else but Sam, who had emerged from the cave torn between making sure Allie didn't wander off and making sure he kept himself safe.

The woods were quiet, waiting for night. The screeching of Zach's bow was the only noise, and plenty enough to sprout a new crop of fears in both him and Allie. It was an impossible situation—they needed fire to live, they needed the bow to make the fire, and yet the bow may as well have been a bullhorn with all the scratching it made. Allie kept watch as well as she could, using her eyes more than her ears (which were now almost as useful as her feet) as she walked to the edge of the hill. She saw nothing in the trees below. More, she *felt* nothing. Aside from the voice inside her that had gone quiet, feeling was the sense she was coming most to trust.

She circled around, past Zach to the opposite slope, and looked down the sheer drop. Nothing there either. The sky was cloudy, gray. Zach's arm picked up steam. A finger of smoke rose from the fireboard. Sam stared as if beholding a miracle. Allie thought maybe it was.

"Almost got it," he wheezed. "Just a little more, then it'll fall in the tinder pile."

The smoke would have turned to coal had Zach not coughed. Allie saw the grimace on his face first. His lips curled as though he'd just eaten something sour, then he fell over with only a little more control than he'd managed earlier. He landed on his hands and knees, made stiff by the hacks from his chest. Allie ran to him and held his shoulders so he wouldn't fall. The fragrance of burning cedar filled the air. Zach let out a final explosion from his lungs and sprayed the ground with a thick, yellow mist.

"Help me, Allie," he said. "I think I busted something."

She couldn't. The sight of Zach's mouth had frozen her just as the pain in his chest had frozen him. Her mind screamed, *No!* even if her mouth would not. He said it again—"Help me, Allie," the words coming out slurred, almost foreign. And Allie thought they should be, because Zach had never asked her for help with anything, not even homework.

It wasn't the fear and despair in his voice that got her moving, it was the voice that spoke above the buzzing in Allie's ears, telling her to hurry. She helped Zach up and guided him back inside the cave, sat him up against her backpack. She dabbed away the blood on his lips with part of her scarf and fed him the bits of willow bark from her pocket. There was nothing more Allie could do other than sit beside him. And that's exactly what she did.

"I can try it," she said. "I seen how you do that fire maker. Bet I can get one going."

Zach shook his head. "You gotta know what you're doing. You ain't strong enough." He wheezed again. "Maybe I ain't either. I can't move no more. My chest won't let me, and your feet won't let you. I got the fever I think, Allie. And It's out there somewhere. I can feel It. We're stuck here."

"Maybe He's gone now," she said. "Maybe He just got hungry and now He's full."

He shook his head. "It didn't eat."

"What?"

"It didn't eat the doe, Allie. All the meat was still there, far as I could tell. It was just all scattered about. That's what I couldn't understand. Like It weren't hungry at all, It just wanted to kill something. Show us what It can do and what It's gonna do when It finds us. And It will, Allie. We can't run away. Not with me being sick and your feet being shot. We can maybe hide so long as we stay here, but there's no more food and water. We're done. It's no hope."

Allie laid her head against Zach's shoulder, wanting to say something that would prove him wrong. Nothing came to mind. It was always Zach who did the encouraging. Even after everything ended and the only moments they stole together were at school, all Allie had to do was merely think of him. That alone would be enough to make her smile. And yet now the responsibility for offering hope was hers. Allie was the one who had to think of a reason to get them up and going again. But what she found in her heart didn't feel like wisdom. There was no rah-rah and no gung ho that would lead them out of that cave and go charging into the night. What she spoke instead was merely the truth of what she carried.

"My momma's out here somewhere and I believe she sent word. She's waitin' for us where the trees are red, and then this'll all go away. There's gotta be hope, Zach. I've gone so long without it since everything ended. I didn't think I wanted it because it got to be the thing that killed me. But you know what I found out? A body can't live like that. You can't live without hope. All you can do is survive. There's a difference."

"We won't do neither."

"Yes we will," she said. *(No you won't,* said Voice.*)* "I believe it."

"You can't believe, Allie. You're fallen away."

"People who get fallen away can still believe. You're a prayin' man, though. It's hard for you to understand."

"I tried prayin'. It didn't hold."

Allie said, "You can try again if you want."

"Won't do no good. God's got sharp edges. Angel told me that."

"I don't know what that means, Zach."

"Me neither. I wanted to ask, but I didn't think he'd answer."

"He wouldn't've," Allie said. "Angels ain't ever plain. You get to be old as me, you'll learn not to go asking questions of the heavenly things. Even if you get an answer, it likely won't be the one you want."

"You ain't no older than me."

"Maybe not on the outside. But I am on my insides, Zach. On my insides, I'm elderly."

Zach was quiet for a long while. When he spoke again, the words were so hushed that they barely reached Allie's ears.

"Maybe that's what it means," he said. "Maybe the angel said God had sharp edges because He's so hard to understand sometimes. Maybe God's sharp and we're just soft, and no matter how brave or smart we think we are, we just can't figure Him."

The cold set in deeper as the sun sank low. Sam's eyes drooped. He curled into his ball, resigned to another night away from the comfort of his master's bed. Allie heard him shudder against the cold. Zach remained in his position, mostly sitting up and partly lying down. His eyes stared ahead at nothing. Allie had been right in saying even she could still believe in something. She may have fallen away (though not completely and not nearly as far as Bobby Barnes, who at that moment was being bandaged up by Doc March in the Mattingly jail and too busy pleading his innocence to Jake and Marshall to ponder his immortal soul), but Allie knew for a fact now that God had an edge. Everything did—every dream, every love, every person. They all had a slippery place, and if you got too close all you'd get for your trouble was a long fall.

"I think even the world's got an edge," she said. "That ain't science, but it don't matter no more. It's an edge, Zach, and I think maybe we've slid right off it. Do you think so?"

She looked at him when he didn't answer. Zach's eyes lay half open, staring at the front of the cave. Allie's first thought was that he loved her so much that he'd gone on to heaven first, too, just to make sure the lights were on and the gates would be open when she got there. It would have been a terrible notion were it not so lovely, and all the fear and grief Allie knew she should feel gave way to a calm resignation.

This really was it, then: where their noble journey finished and everything ended. Zach's life would go no further. Nor would Allie's. Nor even, she thought, their lives together. She had never thought of Zach in that way—having a future with him. Getting through school and getting married, maybe even having children. Struggling through the hard times that made the good times better. That was the good kind of love. The real kind. It was the sort of love Allie thought of now, watching as Zach slipped off the edge of one world to fly toward the next.

She was too cold and too tired to feel the tears gathering behind her eyes, but she knew they must be there and wiped them anyway. Her hand brushed against the side of Zach's jeans. His arm moved. He grunted once and closed his eyes, settling into sleep. The wet whistle of his lungs soaked the cave.

Fallen away or not, Allie looked through the opening of the cave and said, "Don't You take him away. I don't have a compass no more, you see. Zach'd have no way to send word."

She leaned over and covered him with her arms, hoping that would keep him warm.

The night fell hard.

9

Rest came easy for Zach and Sam. Not so for Allie. She vowed to fight her heavy eyes and slowing breaths, believing that surrendering to either would seal their fates. *Let them sleep,* she'd thought. *I'll keep watch.* They had done for her in the past days (even Sam, who may not have understood the need to help her pull Zach up the hill but who had put himself between the crashing trees and Allie), and now she would do for them. She would stand the watch. She would keep the bad things away.

Her head was still on Zach's chest, arms still tight around him. It made for a good vantage point to the cave's entrance not eight feet beyond. Allie had watched the opening there go from the golden beams of evening to a night the color of oil. A paleness followed not long after—the clouds parting, she thought. The moon would be out.

Every so often her right hand slipped between the snaps of Zach's jacket and under his shirt. His chest was cold and clammy, but Allie wasn't interested in his fever. It was his heart. So long as Allie's fingers could feel that soft undulation just beneath his skin, she thought he would be okay. There was no real reason to do this—she could hear the whistles from his lungs just fine with her head there; his insides sounded like a rusty machine grinding down after running too long. But the heartbeat somehow meant more.

Allie may have tamed her mind (or so she thought), but she was no longer in control of the rest of her body. The itch in her feet had been replaced by a burning sensation sometime since they'd arrived at the cave. Now there were only prickles where the tops of her Chucks pressed into the skin. The buzzing sound was still in her ears. She had almost grown used to that while walking around outside. Trapped in the cave, it dulled and spread into a numbness that flowed over the rest of her. She thought that must be how it felt, freezing to death. She touched Zach's chest again and raised her head when she felt nothing. Blinked, trying to clear her mind. Where was Zach's heart? On the left or the right? Was it up high, near his breastbone? Or lower, near his stomach? Shouldn't she know that?

Her hands moved across him, pressing down. Zach whistled from his mouth. His arm twitched from the dream he'd been trapped inside—something was chasing him through the woods, something huge and hungry, and when he turned he saw nothing but claws and eyes and a black cowboy hat on Its head—as Allie panicked, smacking that twitching arm away and telling Zach to quit his blessed whistling because couldn't he see she was trying to find his heart? Couldn't he stop breathing long enough for Allie to tell if he was dead?

She tried her own chest next. The heartbeat there wasn't difficult to find. By then, it thundered so loud that Allie could feel it everywhere. Her left hand settled in a spot just to the side of one of her bumps. She held her hand there and moved her right hand to the same place on Zach's chest. The beat was there. Barely, but there. Allie looked down, moving the hand on her chest away as the sad dawning of what she'd just been doing fell over her.

It was the cold. The cold and the hunger and the fear. All of them, working together to cut her mind away from its moorings just as the God of the moon and the forest had cut away the moorings of her life.

A hungry growl from her stomach mixed with Zach's tooting chest, forming a kind of death song in Allie's ears. She imagined another cold day some winters on and a hunter stumbling upon a rise in the woods capped by some of the biggest rocks he'd ever seen, thinking there must be something up there worth shooting. She saw him climb up slow and quiet, not wanting to scare anything off, and then standing at the top and looking down over that sharp drop on the other side. He would find a hole in the rocks and think that's just where a critter would make its home, but when he crawled inside all he'd find was bodies—one boy, one girl, and one dog. All the bones would be near each other. The girl's and the boy's would even be mixed up, maybe, because they'd died in a hug. The hunter would cry because it all looked so sad. He'd find his way back to town and go to Sheriff Jake first, and Jake would call Marshall. That's how they would find their lost children, and that's when Allie realized they weren't merely in another shelter, they were in their own grave. That alone was what stirred her. She had to keep moving, keep busy. Had to guard the boy.

Her feet moved well enough, though Allie found she had to concentrate to make them work. She opened her backpack, careful not to snag the zipper on the scarf, and removed one of the pads inside. She curled it in her hand and zipped up the pack, then ran a shaking hand down the back of the dog curled and sleeping beside them. Allie could not remember the dog's name, though she did recall that it was a him rather than a her and that she loved him even if she wasn't supposed to.

She stumbled out of the cave into that pale light. In one final act of defiance, Allie vowed she would not look at the moon. A voice called from somewhere above. Allie followed it, climbing the rocks above the cave as if in a trance. Her body was no longer hers. Her mind listed like a ship being pulled to the depths.

The voice—and it *was* a voice, Allie was sure of that in the sense it wasn't the buzz in her ears or the wind upon the rocks—stopped her in place and died away. Allie lifted her jacket and unbuttoned her jeans. She wobbled and caught herself by lowering into the Crouch of Shame. That's when she saw.

Nearly a day had passed without Allie sneaking away to take care of her woman problem. The pad stuck to the inside of her underwear had gotten too used up (*Just like us*, she thought), and with nowhere left for the blood to go, it had made a blotch on her jeans. The spot wasn't big, no more than the size of a dime, and yet to Allie's fraying mind it appeared as a sea covering the entire lower half of her body. She let out the sort of whimper Sam would understand. It was one last indignity—Allie's final step to her own slippery edge.

Dizziness enveloped her. She stood and looked down at the

forest and the hard ground far below, bathed shadows cast by the faint ruddiness in the air. Beyond lay the expanse of the deep woods, countless miles of slopes and hollows that rose and fell from a land where time became slanted and all hope went to die. There were no red trees. A knowing dawned in Allie at that sight, one that said Mary Granderson could never survive in such a place. There were no red trees. So much time had passed since the tornado snatched her on that Carnival Day. Too much time to wander alone, lost and frightened among the bad things in the woods, her only light a distant sun that rarely shone, a cold moon that offered no comfort, and a glow like now that seemed a mix of the two.

The steep drop in front of her. One more step was all it would take. One lift of a shoe, a single lean forward. Not even that, really—half a step might even do the job, given how wobbly she felt. She could pretend she was flying and spread her arms wide. Feel the wind through her pigtails. It wouldn't hurt when she landed. Zach said he never felt anything when he fell along the slope. All the feeling had come when he woke up, and Allie wouldn't have to worry about that because she wouldn't wake up at all, at least not in this world. *Where* she would wake up was a question she couldn't answer. Would she really even want to be up in heaven, spending all eternity so near those sharp edges?

That meant hell, then. That's where Allie would wake up if she jumped. Not because hell was where you went when you killed yourself, but because she had spent her every hour since everything ended falling away and wanting nothing more to do with God. If He obliged her that right in life, wouldn't He do the same in death? She thought so. God never sent anyone to hell; it's more they sent themselves.

In the end, that was what made Allie step away from the edge of those rocks. The trip down would be fast and painless and would end all of her suffering, but after would come more suffering than she could imagine. And it wouldn't be just her burning flesh (which actually didn't sound all that bad, surrounded by all that cold) or the fact that she would never see Zach again. It would be because Allie would never know where her momma had gone, and they'd be separated forever.

She sighed and closed her eyes, tilting her head up to the light, giving herself over to the moon. And yet when Allie opened them she saw the moon wasn't there at all, at least not the one she'd always known. Much of it had been dulled by a thin wisp of cloud that stretched from beyond the arc of the sky, as though the far mountains had grown a tongue and were trying to devour it. The night should have been black, given that cover. But it wasn't. There was still that strange shine falling over the trees, one so strong it nearly cast Allie's body as a shadow at her feet. And as the dawning of that light's source reached past Allie's fading mind and penetrated her soul, she found herself listing into something more than the dark depths. She found herself immersed in wonder.

It was the stars. All of them. Packed tight from one end of the night to the other like a glittering blanket draped over the world. Trillions of pinpricks crammed into that black dome of sky, more lights than she ever thought possible. Each shone so clear and close that Allie actually raised her hands to touch them. There were planets and suns and the faint blots of ancient galaxies, all scattered to form a pattern beyond her reckoning. And as she stared, her numbed lips parted in a look of awe as each of those lights began pulsing like the hand she'd placed upon Zach's chest. Yes. That's what this was. It was the beating of some deeper heart that ran through all creation, pumping from a single Source that watched over and guided it all. It was mystery and magic.

Though a part of Allie knew none of it may have been real at all, and the sky might be only the last gasps of her fuzzy mind, she bent low in an act of penitence. The night carried the grunts of her prying the Chucks from her swollen feet. She tossed the shoes aside so as not to sully the holy ground she stood upon. Such a sight was too great for human eyes, and yet she could not bear to look away for the feeling it kindled in her—not mere reverence, but the deep comfort of knowing there existed a Something greater than the one in the moon and in the woods, and that the wind she so feared was merely that eternal breath brushing upon the mortal living.

A bright vein of light flew over her head, leading down over the steepest part of the hill—the exact place where she had nearly thrown herself. The silvery tail sparked and faded but never really died, for another star followed close behind and then another, all of them speeding along some heavenly road leading on beyond. And far from the hill where those stars fell, Allie saw the same single, shining light she and Zach had seen the night before along the pond. Calling to her. Showing Allie the way.

In that single tick of time, Allie Granderson understood that their path could be dark and dangerous to the end of their journey, but the end would not come that night. That night, she and Zach and Sam had been covered with a grace that not even the monsters of the wood could penetrate—one that would carry them to where her mother waited. And when Allie climbed from the rocks and returned to the cave, she held her trembling chin high, and there was a feeling of joy in her heart.

10

Allie crawled back into the cave sometime later, guided more by Zach's shallow wheezes than her own eyes. The dog raised his head as she settled against the wall. He thumped his tail once, all he was able. Allie patted Sam's head and bid him good night. She remembered her dog's name again, just as she remembered everything that mattered in the world.

"Are you awake, Zach?"

Nothing.

She shook him. "Zach, wish you'd get up and come out there with me. You wouldn't believe it."

Zach sighed (it was more like a long croak) and ignored her. Allie touched his wrist, feeling for a pulse. When she found one, she lifted Zach's arm over his head and let go. It plopped against his thigh.

"Guess you're too tired for even a miracle. Thought you was stronger than that, Zach Barnett."

Trying to coax a response. None was offered. Zach only remained against the wall of the cave, half sitting and half lying down, and when Allie believed he wouldn't be talking much at all that night, she talked for him: "Don't you know I'm the strongest boy in town, Allie Granderson?"

She giggled, not at the words she'd used but at the way she'd spoken them. It was more John Wayne than Zach Barnett, more how Zach saw himself than how he truly was.

"Well, I'd say you earned a rest. The way you fell out there, Zach, when all that was happening. It scared me.

"Didn't mean to scare you, little lady. Just playin' possum with the scariest thing in the world. Worked, too, didn't it? We're safe in here; he's out there.

"I suppose," she told Zach's face. "But still, I was worried for you, Zach.

"I ain't messed up my pretty face, have I, Allie?" he didn't say. "Wouldn't want anything like that to happen. You know I'm so handsome I can stop time and make rivers run backward."

Allie chuckled again. "Your face is fine. Your head's another matter. Not just that gash in it either. Sometimes it's what we can't see that hurts the most." She stopped there, the smile on her face frozen, then fading. "Can I tell you something, Zach? Just between us?"

Zach's face was still, his eyes shut, and yet Allie imagined him saying, "Won't tell a soul. Cowboy's honor."

"I love you, Zach. I ain't supposed to, because if God found out He'd do something to you like He did to my momma. That's why I'll never tell you right out. It's gotta be heartspoken instead. But I just wanted to say it now. I don't think either of us'll get in trouble, what with you being comatose and all. And you don't have to say nothing back. Okay?"

She laid her head on Zach's chest and wrapped her arms around him. What more Allie whispered that night was for herself rather than him. Zach was not dead, nor would he die. So the voice among the stars had told her. But he was too far lost in his slumber to hear anything Allie said, however wonderful those words might be. And they *were* wonderful, at least to her own ears. They were words that spoke of the hope Zach had lost in the deep woods and the hope she had just found. It was the assurance of an end from which a new beginning would be born.

Allie closed her eyes when she was done (*Just for a minute, gotta stand watch*) and tumbled back into her dream of the funeral. Miss Howard stood on her right, Marshall at her left. Beside him stood Jake and Kate Barnett. Surrounding them were people by the hundreds, their faces masked by a fog Allie realized had been made by warm exhales that came out as whimpers against the frigid air. Dapples of shadow fell over the gray grass, cast there by a weak sun streaming through millions of red trees.

The casket rested just above the broken ground, enclosed by sections of fake grass. Allie began to panic when she remembered it was her in there, that box was for no grown-up but it was perfect for a child, and she'd been marked. She pulled at her father's sleeve, begging Marshall to tell her who was being put into the ground and why everyone was crying. He didn't hear, nor did Grace. Allie looked to her right and left, searching for Zach. She spied all of the faces around her, peered through every bit of that mournful mist. Zach had always been there for Allie and had never left her side, not even after her momma left, but he wasn't there now. Zach wasn't there, and that casket was so small.

Hours later, a shadow darker than the night shifted from the trees below. It crept up the slope with a silence that bordered on the unnatural given the immensity of its size. It moved around the rocks, searching for the cave's opening, and paused there. Not even Sam stirred as that shadow peered inside, drawn by the fear and sickness inside.

Young ones.

It had followed them from the creek. Studying them. Stalking them. Waiting for the right moment. And though that moment seemed now, It turned after filling Its nose and made Its way back, careful not to leave any trace.

Patience. That, more than anything, was the order of the day. There was time enough. In the deep woods, there was all the time in the world.

December 23

1

Zach would have found Allie's morning inventory a strange thing indeed. He may have thought himself a man (and would for a little while longer), but there was still enough boy in him to consider sleep a necessary evil. There was too much to do and too much to see. While Allie would lie in bed weighing her sorrows against the dread of a new day, Zach would spring from his own to devour a little more of the world.

But not on this day. On this day, Zach Barnett understood the value of reserving a few moments to take stock of his condition before daring to open his eyes, because one of them would not open at all.

He was sitting against the rock wall with Allie's pack under his head. Zach didn't know how he'd gotten there, though he seemed to remember his coughs waking him some time in the night and Allie positioning him that way. His chest hurt, of course, though that had been the source of such constant discomfort over the past days that he had grown accustomed to feeling it. His head (and the spot just over the brow of his right eye in particular) hurt worse, like someone was pressing a hot brick against his eye. He moved his hand, trying to pry that eye open. The world beyond lay so fuzzy and off-center that his stomach fluttered.

He thought this must be how people like Bobby Barnes felt every morning, all hungover and wondering what they'd done the night before to deserve such torment. And in fact Bobby was hurting just then, maybe even more than Zach, though that had more to do with how rough the town doctor was handling the bandages. Jake ushered Doc March out of the single jail cell, eager to question Bobby more before the state police arrived. He'd been at it all night, yelling at Bobby, screaming at him, wanting answers. Bobby had only bawled and said there were no answers to give.

By that morning, Bobby Barnes had gone nearly ten hours without a drink. Jake set a cold bottle of beer on the table between them and said it was Bobby's last chance. He could have that bottle and more, so long as he said where Allie and Zach were. The ACLU would have no doubt voiced disapproval over such tactics. Then again, Jake figured no one at the ACLU was missing a son just then.

No one in Mattingly would say a word against such tactics. News of what Marshall found in Bobby's truck had covered the town faster than even the news of Allie's and Zach's disappearance. Days of searching only to return empty-handed had worn on the town, turning most from hope to despair. The fracturing of Mattingly after The Storm had begun to mend after the two children had disappeared. Jake understood tragedy did that. It brought people together and made them see they were a part of something beyond themselves. He also understood that rage could do much the same thing. Bobby Barnes had long been a sore on the people of Mattingly. Allie's scarf was reason enough to justify their hatred. To Jake, what he was doing to Bobby now was more civil than turning him out to the crowd waiting outside his office. And it was downright Christian compared to letting Marshall have his way. To make his point, he popped the cap off the bottle with the long end of his tomahawk's blade.

2

Zach let his hand fall away from his eye before it could do further damage and rested it on the leg of his jeans. The wet, sandpapery feeling of dog tongue ran across his fingers.

"Hullo there, Samwise," he managed.

"Hey there, Zach."

He looked down to see Sam at his side, wondering how it was that Allie's dog had learned to talk (and when that same voice said, "Over here, silly," how Sam had learned to throw his voice). His eyes caught a bit of ruined pink that wiggled just beyond Sam's front paws. Zach followed the line up from there and realized Allie was sitting against the far wall, not three feet away. She held herself tight, which did little to quiet her juddering shoulders. Draped over her shoulders were two raggedy pigtails. A set of white teeth sparkled out from behind lips that had gone a pale white.

"Knew there was nothing wrong with you," she said. "Other'n a bumped head, a clogged chest, and a black eye that would make a coon jealous, a'course. Which is to say nothing too bad when all's considered. I had a dream you died, Zach Barnett. But we made it, and we'll make it still. How're you feeling?"

"Passing fair," Zach said. The words came out well enough, though not so much that he believed them. "Can't see much out my eye. You dreamed I died?"

"You got a shiner."

Allie's smile widened to a beam, like she knew a secret too good to keep to herself. Zach wondered what had happened to her in the night to make her that way, and if that something had been real or not.

"Guess you hit more than just your head on that rock," she told him. "But you'll be okay. We're all going to be okay now."

"How you know that?"

Allie shrugged, though that may have been the chill. "Call it a real good feeling."

"How long you been awake?"

"Most of the night," she said. "I slept some, but I had to stand watch. Sam weren't much trouble since he's all furred, but you shook something fierce. I couldn't make nothing to keep us warm like you did back at the frozen pond, so I just hugged you tight. You coughed a lot. I had to slap you on the back a couple times so you could get your crud up. And you twitched. I think you were dreaming."

Zach tried to nod. All his swollen head managed was a one-way dip of his chin. There had been a dream, though the details had gone fuzzy at the edges. He remembered that the dream had been horrible and he'd wanted to wake up screaming. Sam climbed onto his lap and nuzzled his chest. Zach's fingers traced the line of ribs just under the dog's skin.

"You hungry?" he asked.

Allie shrugged. "Some, I guess. Enough for me to start craving some tree bark."

"Guess that'll have to do for now. But we gotta get us some proper food and water soon, Allie. We won't last."

That look on her face, widening. "I know."

"Why you smilin' so hard?"

"Don't you want me to?" she asked. "You're the one who said I ain't happy no more. Maybe I'm happy now."

"Why?"

She leaned in close, sharing: "I saw somethin' last night, Zach. Up there on the rocks."

"What'd you see?"

"That light. The one we seen back at the pond. It was down there yonder a ways. It called to me."

"What'd it call?"

"Hope."

"Hope?" Zach tried to laugh but found it too much of an exertion. "We're trapped in a cave up on a hill with no water and no food, and there's something chasing us, and you're all giddy because you got some hope? That's stupid, Allie."

Allie smiled anyway. "Hope don't always make sense, Zach, but it always makes things easier. We're gonna be okay now."

"We ain't gonna be okay 'less we can get off this hill without being spotted," Zach said. "And unless there's a McDonald's with a telephone right nearby."

"I think there's something even better'n food, and I think it's close, Zach. I really do. I know it ain't been easy and I know we both screwed up, but things are gonna get better now. I'd lay a wage on it."

"You'd lay a wage on it?"

"Indeed I would," Allie said, and on the back end of that came an actual giggle. "We still ain't lost, Zach. Maybe the whole world thinks we are, but we ain't. We ain't alone, neither." She shivered again.

"You ain't gotta tell me we ain't alone."

"I'm not talking about the Him out there. I'm talking about Something else. I think there's bad things in this wood, Zach. We both know that. But there's good things too."

"What are you talking about?"

Allie shook her head. Her lips pursed into a kind of moving wave against the chill in the cave. She tried to speak, then paused as though reconsidering. Tried again and managed, "It's just" before falling silent. Her eyes sparkled.

"Use your words, Allie."

"That's just *it*," she said. "It's all just too big for me to say right now. I'd probably end up using all my words and not even get close. Besides, we ain't got time. We gotta move, like you said. Food and water, that's the order of the day."

Zach pushed his jaws together, making the skin beneath his ears bulge. He looked out beyond the opening of the cave and saw nothing but the faint light of a day without sun.

"You been out yet?"

"Just for a bit. I had to, you know . . . *go*."

"What's it like?"

"Going?"

"No, dummy. What's the weather?"

"Oh." Allie giggled again.

It sounded like music, really, like Zach had been tuning a radio full of static for a long while trying to find just that song. Now that he had, he almost wished for the static again.

"It's still cold. Ain't no wind, though. You know what wind really is, Zach? I'll tell you later. I found out last night. It ain't nothing bad, neither. It ain't at all what I thought it was."

"Is there sun?"

"Nope. Clouds and fog. It ain't gonna blow, though. I know clouds, and the ones out there ain't the blowing kind. But it'll be cold. I think a front's set in. Like, really cold." Allie shivered as an example. "Is it Christmas yet?"

Zach thought, then counted off his fingers. "I don't think so."

"Then there's still time."

"For what?"

"To get my momma home. That's what I want for Christmas, Zach—this one and all the ones after."

And then another smile, wider than all the others stacked end to end. Zach felt a fear creeping across the small floor of the cave right toward him. Inching up his ankles and into his knees, up through his legs and into his chest, where it mixed with the rottenness in his lungs and made him shiver. Something had happened to Allie in the night, something either wonderful or terrible (Zach couldn't tell which and thought deep down at the center of things, people reacted to both in the same way), and that something had changed her in a way that made the old Allie disappear. Whether this Allie was better or worse than the previous model, he couldn't say. All Zach knew was that her chuckles sounded more like crying than laughing, and he'd begun to believe that the woods had broken them both, only in different ways.

"Can you walk?" she asked. "Because we really should go, Zach. Like I said, cold front's set in. We need to get moving before the way gets too cold."

He thought he could. Zach wiggled the toes inside his boots to make sure and flexed his knees. Everything south of the border had gone solid during the night, but none of the hinges were frozen to the point where a little walking around wouldn't grease them up again. His head worried him more, and his swollen eye. Allie didn't know what to look for in the woods, and sometimes what had to be seen came and went in an instant. Sam might be good for that—dogs had better sight than even a woodsman, not to mention better noses. Zach would have to keep an eye on Allie's dog from now on. He would try to make Sam his eyes.

But that wasn't really the question—not *could* Zach walk, but did he *want* to walk. On that query, he had no answer. Sure, there was neither water nor food (aside from the few scrubby pines atop the hill), but at least the cave offered shelter from the worst of the cold and wind. Allie sat there grinning, waiting for Zach's answer, and the only thing he could think to say was no. He couldn't go. And the more he thought of all the reasons why, the more Zach realized only one of them was near the truth. He'd given up. He could do no more.

"It's east, Allie," he said. "That's where we gotta head. I can't tell where east is without the sun. I won't know the way to go. We're lost."

"We ain't lost, Zach Barnett. How many times I gotta say that?" Still that smile, shaken by the cold and the weariness, but not by his admission of helplessness. "I know the way, Zach. It's straight on. All the way to the end."

3

"Well, then, which way's straight on?"

Allie felt the pinch of her lips widening. Her nose wrinkled. She couldn't stop those smiles, even if she knew Zach found them uncomfortable. Truth be told, Allie had to get used to them as well. It had been so long.

"I'll show you. Come on."

She rose and waddled to the front of the cave, keeping her jacket snug over her hips and the blotch on her jeans hidden. Her feet had stopped their burning, though they were still swollen and sore. Sam followed close. Once he even tried to nip at Allie's heels. She chuckled—and how strange that sound was, and how wonderful!—and jerked her feet away, believing Sam was playing more than he was hungry enough to eat just about anything. Zach shuffled behind, forcing his body to move. It was slow going for him, though not so much that Allie worried. Now there was no worry in her at all.

The day lay frigid and stark. Allie stretched her back and neck as she stood. Sam scurried out and found the nearest tree. He cocked his leg and remained there a long while, hopping a bit to keep his balance. What came out of his bladder was only a dribble that looked more green than yellow. They would have to find water soon. Allie's mood could not be dampened, but she nonetheless felt a pang of hurt for her dog. Not love, but as close as she would allow.

Zach inched his way from the hole and tried to stand. Allie took his arm. He brushed her hand away with his left and then took it with his right, as though it were him minding her. Allie grinned again. That smile reminded her how her daddy used to smile all the time, but then everything ended and that smile had died behind a face as blank and unmoving as a stone unless Miss Howard was around. She thought of how Marshall had fallen into drink and how he would sneak around behind the closed bedroom door and the cracked door of the shed out back, like he was ashamed.

Allie always thought it right that her father would feel that way. Now she thought different. It was her smile and how good it felt—so good that Allie found herself seeking cause to have another and another, however small that cause may be—and how maybe her daddy's bottles had been the same. It was an elegant theory for an eleven-year-old, yet still not to the mark. Marshall Granderson hated his drink, yet he had found it the only thing that could numb him to the world. That's what he wanted most—to draw that curtain down, to not feel anymore.

In that respect, he and Allie were more the same than either of them would care to admit. And so it was a small victory in the grander scheme of things that Marshall had found Allie's scarf in Bobby's truck the night before. Because as he sat with Grace and Kate on the sofa by the glow of the sheriff's office Christmas tree, he didn't want to feel numb. Not anymore. Now Marshall only wanted his little girl back. He calmed the tremors in his hand by taking hold of Grace's. She let her fingers lace with his and thought about how many times Mary had done the same.

Allie and Zach walked hand in hand to the edge of the far rocks. Stretched out before them was the steep drop that had almost been Allie's landing place and the fog over wild country beyond—what Zach could only guess was a maze of ashen hills and rifts hidden by millions of gray trees.

"It's that way," she said.

Zach looked, then looked over his shoulder. The rocks and fog hid what he knew remained there—the wide woods that now lay broken and torn, the doe's grave. The maze of tangle and briar they called darkwood, for lack of a better name. But was that way east? Zach couldn't remember, nor did he have the sun to tell him. He turned back to Allie. Her eyes were straight on and filled with a glow he could only call purpose.

He said, "I don't know if that's east, Allie."

"It don't matter."

"It matters." Whether it was the throbbing in his head or the heaving in his chest or just the end result of giving up, he also told her, "East is town. Any other way we go, all we get is more lost."

And now her smile cracked. It was only a small dip of her mouth, not enough that she suspected Zach saw. And even if he had, Allie thought he would just give it over to the cold seeping into her again. She kept her eyes forward over that unending span of wild land. She saw no tree move but at the wind's hand. She felt nothing of Who chased them, only the pang of hurt that came from knowing Zach had not been leading them to her momma for the past day, but back to town.

"We're not going home without my momma, Zach." Her voice calm and even, wanting to speak truth but not rile. "You made a promise. A man's only as good as how he backs what he says."

For his part, Zach measured his words the same. He had to be careful here, what with Allie being so fragile. One wrong word and she might light out on her own. Might even step over the edge of the rocks, thinking she didn't have to use her frozen feet at all anymore; she could just fly all that way from the hill.

Much of Zach's mind had fogged over, but he understood two things: there would come a time when he and Allie would fight over where they were going, and that time was not now. But when that time came, he would not let Allie go it alone. Zach would drag her back to Mattingly if she gave him cause. A man may only be as good as how he backed his word, but he was also only as good as how safe he kept those he loved.

He followed Allie's eyes, trying to see past the clouds to what lay ahead.

"We need water and food, Allie, and we need to know where we are. River's best for that. Not a brook like the one we found, but the *river.* River leads straight on into town. We'll have water and probably food, too, and we'll have a way home. We find that water, we're saved."

"We'll find it out there." Allie didn't think that a lie; she knew they'd find *something* somewhere beyond that mist. What she had in mind wasn't the river, though. It was red trees. That was where she'd find her momma. It was also the place where Zach might die.

"Okay, we'll go," Zach said. "But you let me go first, and no question. That thing's still out there."

Allie nodded. "You lead, Zach."

She turned and smiled one last time. That glow warmed him despite worries of how it had gotten there and what poison lay beneath it. Yet there was no poison, only truth, and the glow Zach saw came not from Allie's face but from a place deep inside her—one that would spark just a while longer before flickering to the point of death.

"We'll go down where we come," he said. "It's too steep here."

"Let me get my pack. I'll put your fire maker in there."

Allie went quick, giving no thought to how all that fast moving hurt her feet. She gathered the bow drill and cinched the zippers tight. There would be no need for the pads until later. There was no time to change her soiled one now. She'd have to hope pulling her jacket down would be good enough. When she returned, Zach and Sam were waiting at the edge of the hill. In Zach's hand was his knife and a handful of more pine bark. He bent, offering some to the dog, who sniffed and nibbled.

"There's something I gotta get before we go," Zach said. "It's on the way."

"Okay."

She munched and spit the chewy pulp, letting Zach lead them. The woods had taught Allie much in the last days and had much to teach her still, but what wisdom she carried most was how much of a man is his honor, and how easily bruised that honor could become. Sam wedged himself between them, keeping a careful eye on the trees ahead. The three of them managed the slope well enough, though Zach paused once. To make sure nothing lurked, he told Allie. To catch his own breath, he admitted to himself. He found the spot where he'd fallen the day before, marked by a large rock jutting from the ground, stained with his blood. His staff rested nearby. That was all.

"It ain't here," he said. The words turned in him like a key that unlocked his dream from the night before. A part of Zach knew it wouldn't be there even before leaving the rocks—that if he ever saw it again, it would be atop the beast's head. "My hat's gone."

Allie (who'd had no idea why Zach would want to revisit such an awful spot until he'd spoken) tried thinking of something positive to say. She nudged him with her shoulder in their familiar I-love-you way and said, "It's okay. Your daddy'll get you another when we get home. Might even be one waitin' under the tree."

Zach kept his eyes low, afraid that if he looked up he might cry. He shook his head. "That's the one I want. It was important, Allie. You don't understand."

"I know it was important," she said. "You were handsome and rugged and all in it, but that hat was just a thing." She thought of her daddy and his drink again. "You think they have a power, but they really don't. The power comes from something else."

He mumbled something Allie couldn't hear. The words were *Like your compass?*

"Come on," he said. "Day's wasting. Farther we get from here, more likely we won't be followed. We'll have to go quiet."

"As a mouse," Allie said. "You hear that, Sam? You be chary, now."

Sam looked too tired to walk, much less bark. And yet he soldiered on as always, willing to follow his master even into places he knew were black, because if a good dog understands anything at all, it is love. They moved on around the hill, skirting the wood where the beast had been the day before. The sky around them looked like ash, the clouds so thick and overcast that the helicopters would be grounded the entire day.

4

Jake returned from the cell with an empty beer bottle. He told Marshall, Grace, and Kate that Bobby had been in his shop all day when Allie and Zach went missing—had in fact spoken to Andy Sommerville, owner of the town's BP station, who'd brought his old Dodge by for an oil change that afternoon. Jake said he was on his way to Andy's now. He asked Marshall to go with him, fearing what would happen should Marshall be left alone with Bobby. Grace and Kate went as well. For an hour that morning, Big Jim Wallis served as both mayor and sheriff of the town of Mattingly. He kept the state police away when they arrived to form the day's search, and he told Bobby to mind his manners. Bobby promised he would. He sat alone in the cell and finished off the three bottles of beer Jake had left him. A man's only as good as how he backs what he says, after all.

In many ways that was the darkest day for the town. For Allie, it was the brightest. She moved through the woods with a heart as lightened as anything she'd felt since before The Storm. And why not? She'd been privy to a magic bigger than any compass she could strap on her wrist. What that magic had given Allie was a strength she'd forgotten she possessed, and the knowledge that she had not been starving for food the last few days, but for faith the last five hundred. Zach was quiet only until they'd cleared the hill. After, even he felt the difference in the forest that day. The air was still cold and the trees still close, but there was a freshness as well—as though even in the deep winter, spring whispered its promise. The beast had moved on. They spoke of many things in the next two miles. Of home, mostly—how good home had been for Zach, and how good it would now be for Allie—and of Christmas—presents and warm beds and time away from school.

"Miss Howard, she'll be glad to see us again too," Zach said. "She's kind, Allie, even if you don't care for her. And she likes you for you, not for your daddy. Shoot, whole town'll probably throw us a parade."

Even the mention of Miss Grace Howard wasn't enough to fade Allie's smile. Besides, it was true—she was kind. In the end, that was what bothered Allie the most, even more than her teacher's pining for Marshall. But Allie considered for the first time that Miss Grace was probably just lonely and cold and wanted someone to keep her warm. She thought in the end most people were like that, even some who had a body to love. Everyone was lost somehow, turned around in their own darkwood, looking for something that would help them go on. Everyone just wanted to find their way home.

"What do you want, Zach?" she asked. "Most of all."

He measured his steps and looked ahead. Sam wandered out front (another reason for Zach to think they were alone again), though not so far that the mist swallowed him. Zach measured his footfalls with the thump of his staff, trying to ignore the wheeze in his chest and the thumping in his head.

"To go home," he said. "To see my momma and daddy again. I'm tired of adventuring. I guess it's been fun except for the knock on my head and the way my insides feel like they're spilling out, but I'm cold and hungry and dirty, and I really don't want to do this anymore. I want to see you safe, Allie. That's what I want most. What do you want? Besides your momma, I mean."

"For things to be like they were." She looked up at him. Her smile became a fragile thing. "Do you think that's wanting too much?"

"I don't think most people want too much. All they want's just a little more than they have."

Allie thought that true, and it was the ring of those words mixed with the faith in her heart that carried her on through the great wood. The laughter from her mouth became infectious; soon enough, even Sam regained a hint of the spring in his step. And now Zach was laughing too. About how everyone might be so happy to have them home that they might get extra presents under the tree, and how maybe Miss Howard wouldn't give them any homework at all the rest of the year, and how there would finally be someone to sit at the empty place at Allie's kitchen table. They didn't speak of anyone looking for them that day. Zach never craned his neck to peer above the canopy of the big oaks and maples to spot a helicopter, nor did Allie think of her father in tears, searching through the town and wondering why she wouldn't come home. Both of them seemed unbothered by the dawning notion that no one was going to find them and they would have to find themselves. *The river, then,* Zach thought, just as Allie thought, *My momma will know the way.* Each of them knowing that was true, even if neither knew the cold that had stalked them like a thief for three days had finally snuck into their minds, robbing them of their wits.

Such was how they traveled that morning, tracing a winding line on into the woods, a line that looped and doubled back. They traveled north and south before turning westward, toward the mountains. And yet they were both buoyed by a faith that kept them believing even when they shouldn't have believed at all. Isn't that what all faith truly is, the will to push on regardless? And is not every faith judged real or false not by the heart that harbors it but by the world that seeks to break it? Is it not in the end no different from a man's honor or a boy's hat or a little girl's compass, a thing so valuable and precious yet so fragile, so easily lost if laid aside out of fear or worry?

The long stretch of life behind and ahead says yes to each of those questions. Yet for Allie and Zach, the road behind lay too short for them to know otherwise. They were only children, after all. Morning eased into midday when they crested a small ridge to find the fog lifting and the wide woods ending. Before them lay a sea of darkwood wider and longer than Zach believed anything could grow. Sam stilled and would not move, his decision already made by what he smelled somewhere deep in the tangle:

Something waiting. Something ready.

5

No sound came from within (*Not even a snapping branch,* Zach thought), but the silence wasn't enough to convince Allie they were alone. The woods had snatched her hearing and replaced it with that near constant buzzing, had robbed her of her feet and mind, but it had also allowed Allie to reclaim something she'd long been without.

She could feel again, and what she felt from inside the twisted snarl of trees and bushes ahead was Someone waiting.

And yet Allie's first thought wasn't that they were in danger, but that this was what she deserved for daring to hope again. All those good feelings she carried, the memory of the stars and the light and all the calm and comfort of believing they were close, so very close, all fell away at the sight of that tangle of trees and shrubs. What came in its place was a sour reminder that all the treasure one found in life could be taken away in an instant, and so it was better not to find any at all. You could never lose what you never had.

Fog lifted from the ground like fingers. Zach rested the tip of his staff against a jutting rock. He peered through the wall of branches and brambles and tried to remember how they'd gotten there. He couldn't. It was as though he'd slipped into another dream (though a much better one than what he'd endured the night before) and had gone walking in his sleep, only to wake at the edge of that darkwood. He looked at Allie, almost as surprised to find her there as himself.

"It's a bad place, Zach."

He nodded, knowing what Allie would say even before she said it. "This whole wood's a bad place, Allie. You stay here."

Meaning, of course, *Don't move, because I'm the one who's charged with keeping you safe, and so I'm the one who has to take the chances.* But Zach didn't move either, at least not for the first few seconds. Nor did Sam, who had found safe harbor behind Allie's trembling knees.

Zach judged the span between them and the darkwood's first reaches no more than twenty steps. He halved that distance in short order but then slowed to a near crawl, overcome by the sheer enormity of the maze. Allie plunged a thumb into her mouth and bit hard on the nail, ignoring the dried muck that had accumulated there. She wanted to call Zach back before he got too close but dared not, believing—knowing—the sound of her voice would carry. It would make Him come charging out.

The bare limbs forming the scrub's outer wall shuddered. Zach raised his staff and stepped back. His lips tightened when he realized that movement was only the wind sighing through the forest. He turned and cast Allie a long look, hoping she hadn't witnessed his cowardice. She had not. It was Allie's heart, not her eyes, that she looked through now. That made her see deeper and know clearer.

"Zach. He's in there."

Zach took the final steps, even managed to brush the first clump of thornbushes and fallen trees with the edge of his staff. Other than drawing a low woof of warning from Sam, nothing happened. He walked the edge, dipping from his waist with every few steps, trying to peer inside. Allie's head began to swoon. From the cold or the danger, she did not know, though the voice within bid her to think of those things as one and the same, for her good and for Zach's. Her toes itched. She bent and shoved her fingers as far into her shoes as she could manage (which wasn't far at all). When she scratched, all Allie managed was to shift the last remaining bits of pine needles to her ankles.

"Hey," Zach said.

He called slow, but the sound still rocked Allie back into her heels. She wobbled and regained herself, then lifted her head. Zach had moved perhaps a dozen feet to her right. A smile lit his face.

"There's a trail right here," he said. "Come see."

Allie stood well enough, but only because that didn't involve relocating her feet. They stuck to the ground. She didn't think the cold had anything to do with it.

"It's okay," Zach said. "Ain't nothing in here, Allie."

She forced herself forward, telling herself she would get to Zach much like they'd gone all the past days—one foot in front of the other, one step at a time. Allie turned and saw that Sam had not moved. He stood shaking in the very spot Allie had left him, his tail scraping the ground.

"To me, Sam," she whispered.

His ears perked. All else remained still. Allie stood there, penned between Zach and Sam—between her want and her better judgment. Had she not led them this way from the rocks? Had it not been her faith and her belief that had brought them to the edge of that scrub?

She edged her way to Zach, who stood straight again. He pointed his staff through what looked like nothing but one tangled bush among a billion. Yet as Allie drew closer, she saw the empty place beyond it and how it wound and cut through the scrub before disappearing at a left turn some fifty paces away.

"Deer trail," he said. "Gotta be, 'cause it's so wide. Not wide enough for us to walk beside each other, but enough that the brambles won't get us. And it's tall too. See?"

Allie nodded. Whatever animals used that trail had certainly been tall enough to be deer. The young trees growing on either side had yet to be choked dead. They grew almost in a bow, forming a canopy that extended over the slender path. Not only could they walk—should they choose to—without being stuck and prodded by all those sharp branches, they could travel without so much as having to duck their heads.

It looked safe. Fine, even. Had Allie been a believing girl rather than fallen away, she would have seen that trail as a blessing. But it was not.

Was, in fact, "A bad place, Zach."

Zach sighed and rubbed his head, pulling down the scarf that covered his wound before the icy breeze could enter there. That small act only served as a reminder of everything the woods had stolen from him. He had stepped into that forest as sure and strong as any who had ever walked, and all that had happened since had stripped him of every dignity. That land had turned Zach's body against him, forcing him to lie in the darkness shivering against a fever so great he felt near delirium and squat half-naked over a hole he'd dug with his own hands as the diarrhea burned out of him. It had forced him to make his way not under his own power but by leaning on a branch. Zach thought of the confusion he felt over not knowing where to go, how he could not even manage to start a fire to warm them nor find food to feed them. But most of all, he thought of how he'd left his daddy's hat behind and how it had now been traded for a girl's scarf knotted around his head.

They could not skirt that wide spread of darkwood as they had done the day before. The air was too cold and they were too weak. But more than that, Zach understood that he had suffered long enough, and now it was time to show that desolate place he was indeed a man. It was time to show Allie. Most of all, it was time to show himself.

"We go through," he said. "Right here. You spoke the way, Allie. You said we go this way and we'd be good and I said yes. But *how* we go is up to me, and you said I'd lead."

"What about Sam?" she asked.

They looked at the dog, still minding his spot away from the scrub. He did not perk his ears at their attention, nor did he offer another woof. His silence was his warning.

"Can you carry him?" he asked. "You carried him all the way to town on your bike. If he wanders off in there, Allie, we might not find him."

Zach waited as she made her way back. He reached for the knife in his pocket and locked the blade open. Sam did not fight Allie when she lifted him into her arms, though he sank what little weight he had left. Lifting him was like heaving a cinder block. She brushed his face with her hand and cooed in his ear, telling him it would be all right.

"We'll go fast," Zach said.

They set out on the trail in silence, brushing past the few limbs that managed to slow their way. The darkwood pressed in. It was as though what they traveled through was not a clench of old woods at all, but a live thing that meant to have them. What little light the sky offered paled beneath the arching trees, casting the tangle into dull evening. Sam quaked in Allie's arms. She held him tight and stroked his head, but there were no more words of comfort left in her. Zach held the blade with one hand. With the other, he gripped his staff. The bushes were silent and still (not even the wind could penetrate that deep in the clench), but he found his heart fading. Soft whistles filled the air. He tried to silence his chest but could not. Thirty minutes later and a half mile through, he had managed to convince himself he was man enough now and they could go back. But as he turned to glance over his shoulder, Zach saw the way back too far and dark to chance.

"Are you okay?" Allie whispered.

Zach nodded. "Just making sure you're still there."

"How much farther on?"

He didn't know. "Not far now. We're close. Steady Sam."

Sam's ears perked again. His eyes searched the dense wood to their left. Zach decided to move on before the dog could find cause to bark, but his legs were weary now, the knife heavy in his hand. Brush crept over the trail ahead, forcing them around. Zach felt a shiver as he tried to find the way again but only found he could not. Allie did. By then, Zach was too afraid to feel slighted.

On they went. The bush felt never-ending. Zach sparked his courage by singing—softly at first, so only he could hear. The tight space carried his words to Allie, who found the tune comforted her much as her mother's singing once did, back when Mary Granderson would rock Allie to sleep by pressing her daughter's head into her soft bosom.

The words stilted, shaky—"Si-hi-lent night. Ho-oll-y night."

Zach whispering them, using that noise to calm them both. Telling Allie not to fear, that all was calm and all was bright.

"Round yon vir-hir-gin—"

"Zach," came the whisper. He turned. Sam's head was high in Allie's arms, the muscles in his neck stretched tight and his ears raised. The dog's mouth quivered.

Zach nearly apologized, thinking Allie had stopped him before the next lyric wounded her. But Allie in fact had not heard them, nor would even her sorrowed heart object at the mention of "mother and child." It was instead what she knew lay just inside the barrier of trees and tangles to their left, where Sam now looked. Something Allie could not see for the maze of leaning limbs and stunted bushes. Someone who even now called to Allie with a voice she could not hear but feel. Zach felt the pull of that presence as well. As did Sam, who could not decide whether to quiver or bark and so attempted both.

Allie put a hand to her dog's mouth

(Run Allie!)

and bid Sam quiet. The path beneath their feet widened here, almost enough for Allie to go to Zach's side. She turned toward the tangle and took a step there instead, letting her toes leave the trail.

"No," Zach whispered.

(Run Allie run!)

But she could not. Allie's eyes remained on that broken wall of twigs and trees. Listening.

In a voice as timid as it was broken, she asked, "Hello? Is anyone there?"

Silence at first, and long enough for her to think nothing was in there at all. Then from somewhere deep inside the thicket, a single low growl snaked its way through the darkwood.

It was as if Allie's body halved in that moment. Part of it focused on Sam—struggling to free himself from Allie's grip, flashing his tiny, sharp teeth—and Zach, who now shook so much that his knife clattered to the ground. Allie's other half—the half containing both the voice screaming for her to *Run Allie run!* and the shard of faith that remained from the sight of all those stars falling in silvery arrows that pointed the way—could only stare ahead as that growl came once more, swaying her to it like limbs in the breeze. Lower this time. Closer. She felt Zach pulling at her as the trees in front of her began to shake and part, and all Allie could do was scream.

Zach watched the trees part in a straight line that would end in the spot where Allie stood screaming. His mind struggled to know what to do next. Exhaustion and cold—the unrelenting, bone-chattering cold—had turned his thoughts to sludge; all Zach could do was stare ahead and watch for his father's old black hat, bobbing up and down as the Thing in the woods came forth to eat them all.

6

Zach saw more than the darkwood giving way. He watched the thrashing and growling grow ever closer and saw every illusion he'd carried from town give way as well. There in the midst of the end, he could not summon the stout heart he'd always supposed beat inside him. Zach could only react as his truest self commanded. That was well enough, because it was the boy he remained who saved them.

He grabbed Allie's arm and yanked with all his might. She stumbled sideways, away from the crashing brush. The sudden movement of her feet snapped Allie from the spell that growl had cast over her, forcing her back to the world. Sam struggled to free himself in her arms. Allie nearly dropped him. Zach broke into a run. With each step he pulled Allie more, making the gap between her arm and her chest wide enough for the dog to nearly slip through.

Her screams at the splintering wood behind them mixed with exhortations for Zach to move faster and Sam to hold still. The words were like a whip to Zach's ears. He ran faster, pulling Allie along the path as the world behind was devoured. His eyes wanted to look back. His mind screamed no, screamed for Zach to keep his vision to the path, the path would save them. The demon (to him, It could be nothing else) was upon them. It had yet to reach the path but was close, Allie could almost smell His breath, and she and Zach both knew that once what chased them found the trail, they were dead. And yet even a demon had to bow to the power of the darkwood. The more It thrashed and surged through the thick tangle of dead trees and stunted bushes, the more the scrub fought to push It back.

Zach's legs pumped, his lungs heaving. The path snaked ahead. A wayward branch jutting across the trail smacked him just above the wound on his head. Zach screamed out as silvery stars and black flakes covered his one good eye. His hand slipped from Allie's arm.

While Zach was smart enough to know a woodsman never

takes his eyes off the trail, Allie had no such knowledge. The link between her and Zach now broken, she turned her head back to where they'd been. Trees and bushes exploded in the freezing air just past her shoulder. Another grunt, full of rage, reached through the mass of wood between them. It was a wave Allie could not stand against.

Her body pitched forward too fast for her mangled feet to keep up. There came next the feeling of Allie's toes stuttering and then leaving the ground altogether. For the briefest of moments the air caught her, and Allie believed her momma had saved them, was lifting the three of them up with the power of her love, and now she and Zach and Sam would fly to that green and flowered hill with red trees from where Mary Granderson had sent word. Zach felt his grip on Allie gone. He turned to reach for her and saw her flying, saw Allie and Sam arching back toward the ground. There was a cry when her right foot landed and the sickening sight of her ankle rolling under the weight of her body. Her chin slammed against the broken ground of the path. Sam slid forward with a yowl and rose up, turning his body back toward the approaching sound. He let out a bark far greater than his small body, one that convicted Zach of his own cowardice. Even Samwise the Dog had found a well of courage within him.

Zach ran back for Allie. She stretched out her hand for his and pulled Zach down as he tried to pull her up, groping for him as though drowning. The trees still shook, the grunts from within still carried, but were those trees and grunts now farther off? Zach reached for his knife. It wasn't there. Allie spoke in a cracked voice of fear and pain, begging Zach to save her, to save them all, and yet Zach knew he couldn't and perhaps never could have. All the strength in him had gone. The demon changed direction and charged, homing in on Allie's injured voice. A crack like thunder shattered the darkwood as It broke through the last of the tangle and found the path. Zach heard the grunt give way to a roar. The very ground beneath him shook.

In one last yank, he pulled Allie from the ground and shouldered her. He scooped up Sam, who was so frightened by the sudden touch that he whipped around and bit into Zach's sleeve, drawing blood. Zach never felt it and only later would see that mark, wondering what had left it.

He struggled forward down the trail, his face contorted in an expression of agony as his chest and lungs began to fail. His legs refused to heed the sound of approaching death. They buckled under the weight Zach shouldered despite Allie's screams to keep going, to run. Sam twisted in Zach's arm, nipping at what flesh his teeth could find, wanting to be freed, to fight. Past where the path veered ahead came a great rushing sound, and in a fit of panic Zach believed the demon had flanked them. He spun, meaning to go back, and saw the trees behind them bend.

Allie had shut her eyes just as she'd done on that long-ago Carnival Day. She opened them wide when Zach turned and stopped. A whimper escaped him. Allie understood that sound was not a cry of exhaustion, but one of surrender.

"Don't stop," she yelled. "Please, Zach, don't stop now."

And something inside him (the boy, yes, but also the first whispers of the man Zach would become) awoke then, propelling him on. He ran, using the last of his strength to charge toward the rushing sound on the path ahead. He heard the demon charging behind. Forty feet. Twenty-five. Ten. There was no scream upon Zach's lips, only a yell of defiance as he took those final steps into the unknown. The evening into which they'd been plunged became the ashy white of the day they'd left. And when Zach leaped through the last of the darkwood, he found what greeted them was not death at all.

It was a miracle.

7

Marshall, Grace, and the Barnetts returned from the BP with news that Andy Sommerville had indeed stopped by Bobby's shop the day Allie and Zach had gone missing, and the shop had indeed been empty of children. They had no choice but to let Bobby go. He walked out of the sheriff's office and through the waiting crowd, across Main Street beneath a banner that read Jesus Is the Reason for the Season and through the front door of his shop. He never turned the sign from Closed to Open that day.

It would be the last real day of searching, spent looking in places that had already been scoured. Next would come a pall of depression over the town, along with a feeling that in some way, The Storm had claimed yet two more lives.

8

Allie heard the roar and lifted her head just as Zach broke free. Her hands found his hips and squeezed just as Zach's boots slid along the smooth rocks, nearly rolling him forward. He was saved only by Sam, who shifted his weight back at the last moment and added it to Allie's, righting them all. Allie tensed over Zach's right shoulder. An odd embarrassment crept over him and the scrub continued to boom and shake, but all Zach gave himself over to was the sheer joy of being right—of saving them. For that stretch of tangle had grown so thick and endless because it straddled the forest's lifeblood, protecting it like a sheath.

"The river," he said. "Allie, *it's the river.*"

She kept her hands in place and rolled her head, peering from behind Zach's arm. Before them stretched a wide and swirling ribbon of gray, flowing left to right. The noise behind quieted and veered off, as though the water itself had formed a barrier It could not cross. Zach stood so overcome by the beauty that he'd temporarily forgotten what had driven them there. He turned at the sound of one more cracking tree—this one so close he actually saw it being struck—and stumbled on upstream.

"Allie?" he called.

"What?"

"Get your hands off my butt."

"What?"

"Your hands." Heaving against the weight. His lungs searing. "Are on . . . my *butt*."

She released the backside of Zach's jeans as though they were covered with fire.

"Put me down," she said.

"You can't run."

"Neither can you, holding me and Sam. Put me down."

Zach did, grateful to be freed of the burden. Allie's feet landed on the wide bank and nearly slipped on the rocks. Sam found better purchase thanks to his claws and two extra legs. He growled and leaped forward, toward the spot where they'd come out.

"To me, Sam," Allie yelled.

This time he turned, as though not wanting anything at all to do with what had chased them but needing to at least pretend. It was a sentiment Zach understood.

"Is He still there?" she asked.

"Yeah. Probably lost us for a minute, but It's there. We need to move."

"Where?"

Zach's mind still buzzed from the cold (as did his head from the wound and his chest from the sickness), making everything foggy. The darkwood stretched on to their right. It was only a matter of time before It caught their scent again. He thought of the doe again, and the way those honeyed eyes had been frozen in a look of horror.

"Zach," Allie said. "What do we do?"

He looked upstream, where the current bent in a dogleg to the left. The air along the water was even colder than in the forest, pushed on by a constant blowing down from the mountains that went unhindered by trees. Zach shuddered against that feeling, but he welcomed it as well. The river assured them life, and what he now saw ahead assured them safety.

"This way."

They moved faster than either of them believed possible, but then danger sometimes has a magic of its own. Allie could only hobble. Her left foot had feeling enough left to know when to pick itself up, but her right had petered out all together—a blessing, since that was the one she'd twisted along the path. She leaned on Zach and hopped as the rocks crunched beneath them. Sam moved to a spot between them and the end of the riverbank. His eyes kept to the darkwood. Zach had no need to wonder what the dog sensed.

Where the river narrowed and bent rested the rotting carcass of a fallen tree, and that was where Allie thought Zach was leading them. Its bottom had been shorn and blackened by lightning (*The Storm did that, Allie,* Voice said, *just like it's done all of this*), leaving only jagged splinters of wood that lay rotting in front of a lonely stump. A brittle canopy of spiderwebbed branches extended nearly to the other side. The limbs there had been plugged with the river's detritus and a clump of brown foam. Bridging the sides was the trunk—thirty feet of it or so, propped by the canopy in a slow, descending slant to their side. The gap between the trunk and the current ranged from nothing along their side of the bank to nearly three feet where the canopy lay.

"We gotta cross," Zach sputtered. They were close now, and hurried when the bushes in the darkwood rustled. "Trunk's too narrow to walk, so we'll have to go hands and knees. Keep your eyes down and ahead, Allie. And don't fall. You'll be swept away."

Allie nodded. What choice did she have?

They reached the tree as the darkwood fell silent once more. Zach made Allie go first so he could keep her steady. She called Sam and sat him on the trunk, pushed his hind forward. He took a long look to the opposite bank and then back, as if making sure his master wasn't joking.

"Can't carry you this time, Samwise," Allie said. "You gotta go on your own. I'll be behind."

The trunk may have been too narrow and too shaky for even children to walk, but it was plenty wide and solid for a pup. Sam started off slow, one paw at a time. He reached a third of the way and stopped, turning his face in profile. That was as far as Allie's dog would go without her.

"Go," Zach said. He looked into the bush. "Hurry. Don't get wet. It'll freeze us all the way through."

Allie climbed on. The tree felt as cold as an iron railing. She pushed herself an inch at a time, trying to settle her eyes on the wood and not the water. The rounded part of the trunk left room enough for one hand and one knee. She traded rights for lefts as the current smacked against the wood, sending spray into her face. The wind buffeted her, shuffling the backpack. Allie felt Zach right it. Even above the gush of the river, Allie heard Zach's fingers crinkle the pads inside.

She had no need to worry. Zach was more concerned with making sure neither of them rolled off into the water. The tree shook and bucked with each movement they made. The canopy began to shift. How the tree had managed to lie so long against the current was something Zach didn't consider. He only prayed it would stay a few minutes more.

Sam reached the halfway point, Allie and Zach right behind. The current there ran faster, deeper. Much deeper, Allie thought, than she was tall. That knowing stopped her more than the cold. Zach pushed against the backpack, telling Allie to keep moving; they were almost there. She forced her hands and knees to push on and cast a brief look back. In the scrub, a shadow moved.

"He's coming. He's right there, Zach."

"Faster." Not looking, can't look. "Go fast, Allie."

She did. Allie covered the remaining half of the log so fast that Sam was nearly trotting at the end. Zach stopped her there. The water at the canopy was shallow, reaching just to the tops of his boots, but his knees buckled against the undercut. The water felt like ice.

"You can't get wet," he said. "I gotta carry you."

He lifted her onto the bank. Sam didn't wait. He jumped from the tree and splashed in the water, then shook himself dry when he reached soggy ground. Zach waded back in. He found what he judged to be the strongest limb and pushed against it.

"What're you doing?" Allie shouted.

"Gotta move it," he said. "Can't let It cross, Allie. We gotta keep the river between us and Mr. Scary."

"Who?"

"Mr. Scary," he said again. "I figure namin' it might make it less horrible. Help me push."

Allie did. The tree wouldn't budge. "It's too heavy, Zach."

He shook his head and strained as more black snow filled his eyes. The tree barely budged. From the other side of the river came one final crash. Allie ran to the edge of the water and bent forward, grasping the first thin branches. She pulled. Zach pushed. Sam wailed at what he saw peering from the darkwood across the water.

Two children could not possibly move such an object. Even with the rot and wear, the tree lay fifty feet end to end and weighed hundreds of pounds. But something other than a shadow had accompanied Allie, Zach, and Sam through those nearly twenty miles of woods, something beyond the magic Allie believed she had found and lost. There were bad things in that endless forest, and there were good things as well, and perhaps it was more the good and less the children that caused the ruined tree to give way. The trunk slipped only inches, but it was enough for the current to catch it. It swung away from Zach in a series of snaps and crackles. He let go and yelled for Allie to do the same. They watched as the water took the tree in a slow descent downriver, far from sight. Their side of the river looked no different from the place they'd escaped. It was still the same narrow bank flanked by a rising clench of darkwood, but

"We're safe," Zach said.

He staggered out of the water and met a smile on Allie's face that almost felt worth the trouble they'd endured. Yet to Allie, hers was more than a simple grin. It was a look of love for the boy who had saved her and Sam, and of thanks for a hope kindled once more. That beam only faded a little when she saw Zach's shaking body and how his jeans looked. They were soaked from the knees down and dry everywhere else, save for the wide, damp oval at his crotch.

9

Allie's lips went slack and slid down until her teeth disappeared. All that remained was the blank hole of her mouth gaping at him in a look that was equal parts disbelief and mortification. Zach didn't know how such an expression could grow there so quick and looked back across the river, thinking the demon had decided to come into the open and make Itself known. But nothing was there and Sam had gone quiet. Zach turned back to find Allie's mouth had closed, but her face had gone even more pale. Her eyes gaped out swollen and moist.

"What's the matter?" Zach asked.

Allie's jaws clenched. Zach shook his head and grinned (*Girls, they always get so uptight*), and decided it best to get out of the river before his boots went from waterproofed to waterlogged. He looked down, still grinning, even as his heart beat so fast he thought it could very well leap from his chest, and paused before taking the first step. The stain was centered at his zipper, where it flumed out to his thighs. It looked like an evil smile staring up and mocking.

"Look away," he shouted. "Don't look at me, Allie."

Allie spun away with such force that she almost turned herself all the way back around. Her arms shot out to stop the momentum. She landed on her bad foot anyway and buckled. Sam cocked his head, trying to understand, but Allie couldn't see him. She couldn't see anything. She'd shut her eyes again.

Zach stared at his crotch, trying to understand how it had gotten so drenched. No, not *how*. He knew how, at least in the sense of how it had *happened*. What he didn't know was how he had *let himself*. The demon was still somewhere across the river and they were still lost and in trouble and probably dying, but all Zach could concentrate on was hiding his humiliation.

He did the only thing he could and plunged his hands into the water, splashing his legs and waist. Allie clenched her eyes at the sound, trying to deal not only with Zach peeing his pants but with his now soaking himself to hide it. She nearly spoke up, reminding him how much he'd warned against getting wet and frozen all the way through. Allie held her tongue as tight as her eyes instead. To a boy who fancied himself a man, dying of cold would be one thing. Dying of shame was quite another, and far worse.

She peeked when the splashing was over. The legs and waist of Zach's jeans had been soaked in streaks of black that radiated from his zipper. If anything, he had only succeeded in making it look like he'd peed himself more. He walked out of the river, past Allie to where Sam stood, and concentrated on the far side of the river. The demon of the woods could have backflipped out of the brush just then, and Zach wouldn't have noticed. His body shivered, drawing up three deep hacks. He swallowed what his lungs brought up. It was only after the thick wad of something slid down his throat that Zach thought he should have spit it out instead. It would've given Allie something else to look at. He pulled his legs to his chest and hugged them. Sam padded over and pawed at Zach's sleeve.

Allie didn't know what to do. Going over there and pawing at Zach's other sleeve didn't feel right. She kicked at the rock nearest her Chucks. Her right foot throbbed as it took her weight. Normally that would be a good sign, but then Allie realized the hurt wasn't in her toes at all. It was in her ankle. She watched the stone skitter and plop into the water, then took another step, skittering another. Getting closer. The last rock skipped away and she sat. Zach didn't notice her at all. He was too busy thinking what Lisa Ann Campbell and Tommy Robertson would start calling him once they found out what he'd done. It was the first and only time Zach thought never getting out of those woods wouldn't be an altogether bad thing.

"You okay?" she whispered.

Nothing from Zach at first (*Pee-pee Zach,* he was thinking), then a nod that was not convincing.

"It's okay, Zach," she said. Sam nuzzled against him as if conveying that very sentiment. Sam, after all, peed everywhere. "I mean, it was probably water was all. That tree we pushed in, it was real slick. Shoot, got me soaked through too."

In fact it hadn't. Strangely enough, the tree had been dry as a bone the whole way across. But she hoped Zach wouldn't think of that. More, Allie hoped he wouldn't look at her jeans to see for himself. She drew her legs in as well, matching Zach's posture, and tugged her jacket down.

"I won't tell no one," she said. "Not ever, Zach. Even if it wasn't water, I mean. Which I'm sure it was."

A long stretch of quiet followed that only allowed the cold to sink into them more. Zach stroked Sam's head as Allie searched for the more behind Zach's silence. Not that there *had* to be more (in her experience, humiliation was enough to shut anyone up), but it was the *way* Zach had fallen silent. Like he was dealing with more than what he'd done; he was dealing with why it had happened as well.

"Zach? It's okay to be scared sometimes."

Zach's head shot up. Allie saw his pale cheeks turn crimson. His mouth quavered and his lips parted, and what flew out smelled like the death on Marshall Granderson's breath and sounded like the roar of what had chased them down the trail.

"I ain't scared, Allie Granderson. I ain't scared and I never was."

Sam jumped away as Zach stood and stormed off. Allie's eyes prickled at the corners, that dam of sadness pushed to near bursting by his fury. She could do nothing but sit there. Sam made to follow him. She said, "To me, Sam." The dog settled beside her but kept his eyes to where Zach walked.

Zach would have gone far enough to lose sight of Allie and Sam altogether—would, in fact, have followed the river all the way to its beginning—but his body gave way. He stopped at the water's edge and peered in, thankful the current was so quick that he could not see himself staring back. But he could see something. Something so impossible that Zach had to blink to make sure it wasn't his mind playing tricks.

"Allie," he said.

She couldn't hear, not with the noise of wind and water. Zach called again and looked away only long enough to make sure her head had risen. He made a come-here motion with his hand, not wanting to risk too much noise. Allie and Sam limped Zach's way.

"What?" she asked. "You gotta get warm, Zach."

He shook his head and pointed. She followed the finger. There in the shallows rested three bass, each as long as the distance between her elbow and wrist. Monster fish, bigger than anything either of them (not to mention their fathers) had ever pulled out of Boone's Pond. Sitting there just beneath the water, penned in by a ring of smooth stones, as though offering themselves as a sacrifice. What water still lay in the corners of Allie's eyes shot from there to her mouth.

"I'm gonna get 'em," Zach said.

"How?"

He didn't know. Had he still worn his hat, Zach figured he could try scooping the fish out. But the only thing on his head now was a bloody hole and a girl's scarf.

"Gonna grab it," he said.

"You can't. You'll just scare them away."

"No I won't. They're trapped. I'll go slow."

"Zach—"

"Hush," he said, already bending down.

Two of the fish were turned away, toward the middle of the river. Zach's hand came from behind. He dipped his fingers in slow and at an angle so as not to disturb the current. The cold reached from his hand to his shoulder. Sam had come so near that his front paws brushed the water. Allie took hold of his collar and eased him back. Zach's hand, closer. The tail on the first bass swished and the gills flexed, but still the fish did not move. Zach clenched his fingers into a fist at the last instant. The three fish erupted into a fit of spasms, trying to make for deep water. Zach tried to hold on, knowing he couldn't. The water was too cold and his fingers were too weak. Just as the bass was about to slip away, Zach shot his arm up and flung the fish as high and far behind them as he could. It landed with a smack along the rocks and flailed, drowning in the air. The remaining fish whipped at the water. Allie plunged her own hand in, scooping out another, tossing it over her head. Zach retrieved the third.

Sam struggled against Allie's hand, sensing food. She gripped his collar as Zach ran for the fish, scooping them in his hand. He formed them into a pile away from the edge of the bank and found the largest rock he could, bashing their heads. Their flailing stopped.

He picked the first bass up, running his fingers over the slick scales. Allie let go of Sam. He ran to Zach and sat, tail wagging as he yipped. Zach raised the fish to Allie as she approached. It was even bigger on land than it had been in the water, longer than Zach was wide. Ten pounds at least. The other two were smaller, though not by much. Blood leaked from the spots on their heads where the rock had killed them. Their mouths hung open and their eyes bulged. Allie tried not to think of the doe.

"Lunchtime," Zach said.

Allie shrugged off her pack, reaching for Zach's bow drill.

"No," he said. "We can try later with the other two. We'll eat this one as she is."

"Raw?"

"No other way, Allie. We need to eat. I can't get no fire now."

"I can try," she said. "I can do it, Zach. I'll get you warm."

Zach said, "I ain't cold" through two blue lips. "We gotta eat and we gotta move. I'd make us do them both at the same time, but we could use the rest. River's between us and Mr. Scary. Ain't no way to come across since we washed that tree down. Water's too deep, even for a demon. We're okay now."

"He ain't no demon," Allie said.

"Why you say that? Did you see It?"

"No. Not exactly, anyway. I can't eat that, Zach. It's all raw."

"Don't make no difference," Zach said. "Food's food. We gotta. More healthier than all your candy bars."

"I didn't hear you saying nothing about those candy bars while you were scarfing them down."

"That's 'cause it's all we had. Now come on. It ain't so bad."

"Like you eat raw fish all the time," Allie said. "Can you clean it at least? Get all the guts out?"

Zach dipped his head. A fresh wave of shame flowed over him. "I ain't got my knife. Dropped it along the path."

Allie ran a hand through her hair and cursed what devilry lay in a man that could make him go from joy to despair in a mere blink. She said, "That's okay. I'll eat it. Guess I'm hungry too. Still would prefer a candy bar, but at least this is better than having to eat another tree." She looked down and saw the wideness in her dog's eyes. "Sam can sure use something to munch on."

"We'll split it three ways," Zach said. "Even Steven. You go first."

"Why me?"

"'Cause you're a girl and me and Sam are guys. It's proper."

Again, that devilry—one with a hunger on the end that convicted Allie to at least try and eat so Zach and Sam could have their share. He handed her the fish. It felt slimy and heavy in her hands. Allie brought it to her mouth (the smell on it was the river, brackish and almost sour) and closed her eyes. The longer she waited, the worse it would be. She bit midway down the fish's back and felt the crunch of skin and bone. Saliva flooded her mouth at the taste of food. Allie pulled the fish away, tearing the meat. A runner of something—flesh or organ, she didn't know, nor was she much concerned—stretched from her lips to the bite her mouth had left in the bass. She chewed long before swallowing, not wanting one of the bones to lodge in her throat, then opened her mouth again. Her next bite was bigger, nearly severing the fish in half.

"Is it good?" Zach asked.

Allie nodded. Her mouth made an "Mmmm" sound as she chewed. Below her, Sam began to whine. She opened her mouth again, ready for more. Zach stopped her.

"We should pray."

She swallowed part of her bite. The other became caught in her response: "Mm-what?"

"We should pray, Allie. For the food."

Allie swallowed the rest, feeling that warm spot in her throat as the meat slid down, filling her insides.

"Are we back on this, Zach?" she asked. "This is good and all, but it ain't prayer-worthy. Go on if you want. I'm eating."

She finished her third as fast as she could, wanting to rush the food to her stomach and not wanting Zach and Sam to wait. She handed the head to Zach, who took the tail section instead. He was hungry—starved, really—but not to the point where he could eat eyes. He dropped the head to the ground and then lowered his own, offering his thanks to the God who had let them get lost in the woods and the God who had given them just enough to keep going. Sam pounced.

They filled the juice boxes with water and kept their lunch in their bellies, though for a while it was touch and go. Allie found that what went down easy sometimes came up even easier in meaty burps, but she managed to hold the fish in place by drinking deep from the river. It was more food than they'd had in the last five days, and their full bellies mixed with the cold air to make them sluggish. They packed the other two fish in Allie's pack and rested along the riverbank in a silence much different from the one they'd endured before. Zach was no longer imprisoned in his shame (or he was, but at least he could now see daylight between the bars) and set to trying to rub his jeans dry with two dirty hands. Allie no longer fretted about the spot just on her jeans above the hem of her jacket. Sam dozed. They were not happy—not with the memory of being chased still fresh in their minds—but Allie and Zach found in that span a contentment that helped repair the gulf between them. And they were still not lost. They still had a way to go.

The peace between Zach and Allie lasted until he said, "We gotta keep moving, Allie. Mr. Scary's still over there, and he's still gonna look for us. He'll have to go a ways to cross, but who's to say there ain't another tree over another narrow part of the river somewhere?"

"Ain't no Mr. Scary that's chasing us, Zach. And He ain't chasing you and Sam as much as me, though we've all been marked now."

Zach burped and recoiled, more from the taste than how it made his chest hurt. His hands played the legs of his jeans. Everything was cold, but not as cold as it had been. Then again, Zach realized he might just be going numb. "You ain't making no sense, Allie."

"I mean it's God, Zach. God's done found out Momma sent word, and He's done found me coming here to get her. He don't want me and Momma finding each other, why I don't know. But He's out to stop us."

Zach's hands stopped. "What?"

"God's gonna get us, Zach. I'm so sorry."

"That's the dumbest thing I ever heard in my life, Allie Granderson."

"No it ain't." She picked up a stone, tossed it into the water. It made a tiny *blurp* sound. "God marked me when The Storm came. Marked us all, I guess, but me an' Daddy especially. Now He's marked you and Sam too. You seen it, Zach. Back at the pond. God clawed those trees with His sharp edges. He don't want me finding Momma."

"Ain't God that's chasing us, Allie. It's a demon."

"I think they're pretty much the same. And it don't matter anyways. All that matters is we get away. Which way do we go? Upstream or down?"

Zach looked in both directions, trying to decide. He closed his eyes and imagined them standing on Miller's Bridge in town, looking at the water. Trying to remember how the current flowed. Was it up, from the bridge toward downtown? Or was it the other way?

"Water goes through town," he said. "From town, on under the bridge, then on down toward the dump. That means we go upstream."

"What's town got to do with it?" she asked.

"Town's where we're going."

"What about my momma?"

"You're momma ain't out here, Allie. She never was." Cold words, he knew, but words Zach had told Allie before and she needed to hear again. "You ain't thinkin' right anymore. We can't stay out here, and nobody's gonna find us. We're hungry and cold and we're hurt, Allie. We're hurt bad. We gotta save ourselves."

Allie felt her heart drop. Not because they were hungry and cold and hurt bad—she'd known that, and in some ways longer than Zach had—but because she knew he was right.

"I'm here to find my momma," she said again. "That's what she wants, Zach. That's why she made my compass work."

"It never worked, Allie, and we ain't got time to fight over that. Your brain's so cold you think the Lord's over yonder in that bush, tryin' to eat us. Decision's mine to make, and I made it. You can stay here and die, or you can go with me and live. I'm taking Sam, though. You don't love him anyway, and he's a good dog." Those last words hung in Zach's throat like a bit of the fish. He tried to swallow and found he couldn't. "Come with me, Allie. We can go home."

She shook her head and looked out over the water. "You can, maybe. I can't."

Zach would not leave her. Could not. And yet he hoped what he did next was enough to convince Allie he would. He pulled the shoelace from his boot—not the one he had been using to try and start his fires, that one had frayed to near breaking—and found two slender pieces of wood. He tied them around Allie's ankle, bracing them as he could.

"This should hold," he said. "Good luck."

He picked himself up from the rocks and lifted Sam into his arms, then began a long walk up the riverbank. Sam twisted in his arms, turning his head back to Allie, whining at her as tears pooled once more in her eyes.

10

It had been five years since a human had traveled that forgotten land, and that had been the Bad Man of Zach's memory. Others had come in the long stretch of ages before, drawn to that darkwood by a power that only snared them in the end. The old ones (for such was what they called themselves) wandered there first, early in the dawn of time. They knew what lived in the deep places and seldom traveled beyond the olden woods Zach and Allie had passed some five days before.

To the old ones, the world was awash in a spirit that permeated every living thing. The taller one grew from the earth, the more removed from that spirit he became. To them, that was why beasts and children remained so close to God. So they said. Many could pronounce such philosophies as false, and perhaps that is so. Yet that belief had been proven true by Allie and Zach, and most of all by Samwise the Dog, whose tiny paws and short legs bound him closer to the earth than most everything.

Sam had struggled through the last days just as much as his masters. In some ways, he had suffered more. His fur had protected him from the cold and wind, keeping him from sickness. And though his bones ached and his head hung from all the going, he was still able to munch on what grass he could and lap from the nearest cracks of water. Yet Samwise was plagued by this one thing that had for the most part affected neither Allie nor Zach: he knew What chased them. And more than that, Sam knew how long It had followed, and just how close It remained.

That is why he waited for Allie to pick herself up and trod on toward Zach. Only then did Sam move out in front. He was the only one who could spot the danger. In the close times, when It had gotten so near that Sam could smell the stench, he had drawn to Allie's and Zach's sides. Out of fear, Allie thought, and so had Zach. But that wasn't so. Sam understood few words aside from his own name and "To me" and "Allie" and "Zach," but what the dog lacked in the comprehension of words he more than made up for in a comprehension of *feelings*. He knew hurt and fear and sickness, and he felt all of those things in the two people now trailing behind.

His ears were cocked to the far bank, where It had rustled

just after their meal. So long as that sound remained *there* and didn't reach *here,* Sam was prepared to accept it. But now his nose had caught that stench again. Not across the water. Ahead. To where Sam's masters meant to go.

He turned his head and yipped a warning. Allie shushed him. She said, "To me," but Sam turned his back.

The scent grew stronger, charging Sam's body. Nose to the rocks now, ears raised and pointed ahead. His tail went rigid. Zach spoke (it was words the dog didn't know, though he did recognize his own name buried in them) and began to walk faster. Sam's nose found a muddy spot leading to the darkwood on their side of the river. He raised his head and bayed, knowing that would bring his masters quicker than anything else he could do. He turned to see Zach close. Allie was just behind.

Zach knelt, rubbing Sam's head as he studied the spot in the mud.

"What is it?" Allie called.

Zach shook his head. "You better come see."

Allie limped over. The brace on her ankle helped well enough, but not enough to give her any kind of speed. Zach used the seconds before she arrived to try and make sense of what Sam had found—simply shrugging it off, saying it was nothing, wouldn't do much good in restoring the confidence he knew he'd lost in her. Besides, Zach knew it wasn't nothing. It was something, and it was important.

He felt Allie's hand on his back. "What is it?"

"Prints."

Allie looked. Left in the mud were five deep ridges running in perpendicular lines. The marks were long. Allie judged them as nearly ten inches, Zach settled on nearer to a foot. Sam had no idea of measurement and didn't care—it was not the marks that piqued his fear, but the claws that had made them. The space between the ridges was wide, almost the span of the two fingers Zach laid down between them.

"What kinda prints?" Allie asked.

"I don't know. I ain't never seen nothing like that. But it's fresh."

"You mean—" she began, but the words behind wouldn't come out. A fortunate thing, as Zach had decided he couldn't bear to hear them anyway. For his part, Sam didn't need to hear anything at all. He could feel. "See, Zach? Sharp. Sharp like God." She righted herself by pushing her hand off Zach's back and stared into the trees, hollering, "Go away. I never did anything to You. Can't You see we're just kids? You better just leave us alone and go back where You come from. Do You hear me?" Those words were swallowed by the river and darkwood. *"I'm gonna find my momma no matter what You do."*

Zach scanned the river. Allie's ravings bothered him, but not as much as that print. "Can't be," he said. He shook his head and felt the heartbeat in the wound on his head, making him dizzy again. "No way It coulda crossed, Allie. Not up here. Water's too deep. Just no way."

Sam had no inclination toward discussion. The scent stretched from the track on into the darkwood. He nosed his way in, feeling with his senses.

"What else could it be?" Allie asked. "God can do anything, right? That's what you believers think. Us fallen-aways? We think He can do anything, too, but stuff that hurts us."

"Talk sense, Allie. That's an animal mark. Can't be no other thing. Maybe it was a rabbit," Zach said. "Come down here for a drink or something, but slipped on the bank."

"You ever seen a rabbit that'd make a track that big?" Allie asked. When Zach didn't answer (he was too busy studying that mark, trying to decide how big an animal had to be to leave a track like that and if it wore his daddy's cowboy hat), she asked again: "Zach? You ever seen a rabbit that's prolly twenty feet tall?"

"No," he mumbled. "Can't say I have."

Sam couldn't smell anything in all that undergrowth, at least not right away. But his dog ears could still hear just fine, and what they heard was the snapping of a twig. He barked once. Zach and Allie both jumped. Allie silenced him by easing up to the tree line and tugging on Sam's collar, pulling him away.

"We can't go this way," she said. "We gotta turn 'round. Go back where we come."

"Can't do that, Allie. Upstream's the way home. We go down, that just means we get lost."

"We go on, that just means it's our heads up in a tree somewhere and our skin layin' in a pile on the ground. You ain't got your knife no more, Zach. You ain't even got your staff. It's just us. And if we gotta run, I can't."

"Why here?" Zach asked. "If It could cross here, It could'a crossed anywhere. It could'a just come over the way we come, right after we did it. So why up here?"

Allie looked at him. "That's what's on your mind right now, Zach?"

"It's important," Zach said, though he didn't know why.

"Right now all that's important is we go the other way."

"No."

Zach stood up and brushed the knees of his jeans (which did nothing at all other than rub dirt where dirt had already been). He looked into the darkwood ahead and then to the riverbank in front of them.

"What?" Allie asked.

"We ain't turning back, we're going on. I think I know what's happening, Allie. I think I know what It's doing, and we can't let It."

"What? Zach, I don't understand—"

"I gotta know for sure, Allie. Then I'll tell you. We go slow. It'll be okay. You just have to trust me. Do you?"

Allie did. Zach had lost her compass on purpose and had led them toward home without telling her, but she still trusted him as she would trust the only light left in her life. But of course trusting someone doesn't mean what they do is always right, especially when the person you trust is a boy trying to tell himself he's a man. Sam, however, knew better. Allie called, "To me," and Samwise the Dog had no choice but to follow. He shot out ahead and led the way once more. It was only right that he did. Someone had to protect them.

11

Grace found Kate on a bench in the town square—the very bench, in fact, where she'd seen Zach sitting and Allie trying to hide some three days earlier. Three days. The time seemed so small when put in those terms, and yet it felt so long.

The new pastor of the Methodist church had been sitting with her. Juliet Creech had come to Mattingly just after The Storm, rotated there by some church hierarchy Grace didn't understand. It was the sort of decision made by people from Away based on rationality rather than common sense. The former pastor had perished in The Storm, leaving the flock without a shepherd. Juliet's name had come up. Having a woman preacher in a place like Mattingly was bound to fail. It was a horrible thing for Grace to admit, but true. Juliet had been trying well enough to tend to the town's spiritual needs, both after The Storm and especially in the last days, but the way Grace saw the pastor walking away told her Juliet hadn't been able to tend to Kate's. Grace didn't think anyone could. Not now.

The men had gone looking again. Jake had taken a group of volunteers east, into the forests that bordered Happy Hollow. Where Marshall had gone Grace didn't know, nor had he volunteered. To find somewhere private, she thought, to draw down that curtain. Grace had let him go. Though a part of her knew it was the wrong thing, she also felt it was the only right thing after Jake had to let Bobby go. The possibility that the town drunk had taken the children was a horrible one, but it was also the only lead they had left. Now Grace thought what the town was doing wasn't searching at all. It was just wandering, hoping a miracle would turn up.

Kate had her eyes on the town tree as Grace sat. She said nothing, never even moved. Kate was a good woman, a strong woman. She'd given so much to the people in her life, had a passion for the poor, especially the children, though the thick notebook in which she had once used to write the names of those she helped had been long discarded. Now the town Kate loved was trying to love her back, but her grief had built a wall that kept everyone away. Grace would not try to scale that wall. She would instead do as she'd done with Marshall and Allie and stand vigil before it.

"Where are they, Grace?"

The words came out so quiet that Grace believed she'd imagined them at first. Then she saw Kate's face turned nearly to hers.

"They're somewhere," she answered. "I know they are. We'll get them home, Kate. We have to."

"This was all because of that Nativity. All of it. A piece of plastic."

"It wasn't a piece of plastic to Allie."

Kate shook her head, said, "I know. Just as I know Zach had to go with her. He promised me he wouldn't go far, Grace. So did Allie. How's Marshall doing?"

"He's holding up the best he can."

"And how are you, Grace?"

Kate looked at her now, and in that gaze Grace shriveled.

"I'm trying to be strong for him. It isn't easy. I love Allie."

"And him?"

"What?"

Kate looked away, back to the tree. The wooden crosses hanging on the limbs swayed in a frigid breeze.

"I loved Mary, Grace. Everyone did. I know the two of you were always close. I'm glad you were there after her funeral. Marshall shut out everyone in town after that, Jake and me especially. He had to have someone to blame. Things sometimes feel better that way, even if they aren't. I remember your daddy and how things got when the darkness took him. I know you see him in Marshall and yourself in Allie. But people talk, Grace. What's in the past can carry forward. If anyone knows that, it's me."

"I don't . . ." was all Grace could manage.

"Don't think wrong of me, Grace," Kate said. "I mean no ill. I just want my son back, and I want Allie back, and I've been struggling for days between praying to God and cursing Him. Things don't always work out the way we want, the way we know things *should*. If they don't, Marshall will need you more. He'll go back into his hole and have nothing but his sadness, and you know how that ends."

It was Grace's turn to fall silent. She did know how that ended. She knew well.

12

It was the wrong way. Allie knew this with a sureness that opposed her every step, slow and clumsy as those steps were. She thought Sam knew it as well. He was still ahead of Zach, though not by much, and his steps had slowed to an almost imperceptible padding of his paws. Only Zach seemed ignorant. His eyes were set straight upstream, doing his best to help support Allie's weight. It was a task made a bit simpler by the chunk of driftwood he'd found and broken in half across his knee. He held one section in his left hand. The other rested in Allie's right. There was no talk of staffs or weapons. These were crutches, and both of them knew it.

In fact Zach knew he had made an unwise choice in continuing upstream. Not in the sense that the direction was wrong (he was sure it was not, Zach had stopped at Miller's Bridge only a million times in his life to watch that water and knew just how it flowed), but in the sense that the air itself was heavier and laden with a stench of a rotting something that wasn't the fish in Allie's pack. But what choice did he have in the end? They were hurt, sick, and exhausted, and the only hope they had lay in the fact that Zach knew the way home. Upstream was the only way.

What continued to vex him most was why the beast had crossed so far up the bank. For that matter, why It had not snatched them back in the darkwood. The path had been their only way through, so why not lie in wait there, just inside the tangle? Yet It had chosen to hide deeper in the trees, and Zach had begun to piece together why. Unfortunately, the only way to finish that puzzle was for him to lead Allie and Sam where they all knew they shouldn't go.

They moved in silence for the next mile, which took so long that the sun had reached the top of the sky and was now beginning a slow descent. The smell of rotting leaves and spoiled water wafted up from the river. They had come to a shallow part, where the current washed over an assembly of smooth stones and debris, narrowing the bank. The rushing noise muffled the stones clacking beneath their feet. They could hear nothing, not even a growl.

Twice Sam stopped ahead to peer deeper into the darkwood to their left. The low growls he uttered shook his jowls. Zach and Allie stopped each time, and each time her grip strangled his shoulder. Neither of them realized Sam's snarls had driven them closer to the water's edge. Zach had made no plan of what to do if—when—they were attacked again. He didn't think he needed one. If

(It) (the demon) (Mr. Scary)

the beast came for them there along the banks, all they could do was jump in the river. It would mean death, but getting to heaven soaked and shivering felt much better than getting there without a head.

Allie whispered, "To me, Sam. Don't you tarry."

Sam remained in his place not a dozen feet ahead. His tiny, razored teeth lay bared against the cold. He gave a bark that ended in a low growl toward the scrub.

Allie called louder, "Sam?" Her voice trembled. The water churned beside them while just to their left—close enough that Allie could nearly reach out and grab it—lay darkwood so deep it held night inside. Her feet had died again, buried in a layer of soggy pine needles and worn canvas, and she was cold. So very cold. "To me, Sam. Please to me."

Sam refused. He only stared at what he saw crouched and waiting just inside the crooked wood. The dog's next step was toward the clench rather than his master. The darkwood was quiet and still. Allie wanted to go to him, grab him by the scruff, but she was too afraid to move. She squeezed Zach's shoulder and felt the tremor there.

"Sam?" Zach asked. "Please come on."

Sam tore into the brush with a sound Allie had never heard

before, one long woof of rage and fear. Zach let go of her and ran for the spot where the dog had disappeared. Allie screamed, begging for Zach to come back and Sam to come back and please don't leave me here all alone. The darkwood exploded in volleys of shaking trees and snapping limbs, followed by a roar that stopped Zach's heart and sent him scurrying back. Allie grabbed him. She pressed her face hard against his back, keeping Zach between her and the God she feared, screaming for Sam, for help. That scream was cut off as the sounds of Sam's thrashes and barks ended in one final yelp that gave way to silence.

13

Zach felt the mud and rocks rise up over his boots, sealing them to the riverbank. There was no sudden surge of adrenaline to force him into choosing between the foolishness to fight or the hopelessness to flee. His very spirit abandoned him, unwilling to remain behind and suffer the same fate as the doe and now Allie's poor pup. All that remained of Zach Barnett was a trembling shell hollowed out but for the fever in his bones and the poison in his lungs.

Allie stepped out from behind him and took his hand. Her pigtails dangled limp and filthy and smelled of rotting leaves. Streaks of drying dirt ran from her cheeks. Her bottom lip quivered.

"Sam?"

She took a single step away—enough to stretch Zach's arm out as far as it was able. The next step Allie took broke their hold. She looked at him, wanting him to follow, but Zach couldn't. *It's the rocks,* he wanted to say. *See all the rocks, Allie? They won't let me move no more.*

Allie asked again, "Sam?" Louder this time and with a hitch in her voice. She took another step and then another, pausing to let her crutch come alongside, and then she didn't stop at all.

"No," Zach said. "Don't go in there, Allie."

She turned and gave him the only three words she needed to say—"He's my dog."

Zach tried to move. He managed only to wiggle the first three toes of his right foot. Allie peered into the darkwood, calling for Sam again. There was no answer from inside, no noise at all. She ducked beneath a fallen trunk and disappeared through a jumble of dead branches and what looked like dry, decaying vines. What came next was a shuffling noise and the sound of limbs cracking, and at last a pained, almost tearful cry of, "Zach, please help me."

He did not know how the riverbank released him then, though a part of Zach understood that it had nothing at all to do with his own strength. He was simply stuck there one moment and in the darkwood the next, pushing through the branches as they struck his face and neck. He called out for Allie, asking if she was okay. Her answer was neither yes nor no, only that same plea for help. Zach shoved through and glimpsed a sliver of blue backpack. Allie knelt in a tangle of bare bushes, her back to him. Her eyes watered as she turned. She bit down on her cheek, sucking back the tears from her eyes.

Sam lay on his side in front of her. His hindquarters had been flayed open to reveal the snarl of bone and muscle beneath. Blood poured from the wound. His back legs lay limp and dead, his head still. Two small, brown eyes gazed up at them.

"Sam?" Allie pled. "Samwise?"

The dog thumped his tail once, barely raising it off the ground. Allie stroked his head and bent to kiss the side of Sam's face. Zach knelt beside them and turned his head. Not at the sight (which was bad enough to force up a fishy *urp* from his belly), but the smell. Sam had messed himself sometime during the attack; the waste mixed with the gore to swoon him and Allie both. But there was another, more putrid stink. The demon, Zach thought. Had to be. And if the smell was that strong, It was close. He set that aside long enough to study Sam's damage. The wound was deep, made by the same sharp edges that matched the ones they'd found along the riverbank. Even if Sam lived, Zach doubted Allie's dog would ever walk again.

He untied Allie's scarf from around his head and laid it over Sam's back legs, trying to stop the blood and cover the exposed bone. Sam yelped when the wool touched his wound. He nipped at Zach with what strength remained. Zach shushed him, saying it would all be okay, though the look on his face betrayed his doubt. He slipped the scarf under the dog and then around, diapering him. He ended with a slow but tight knot.

Allie thought she heard movement from behind. She looked and was met only by a great wall of mangled wood.

"He can't walk," Zach whispered. "We gotta carry him. We have to leave here, Allie."

Allie picked Sam up and tucked him inside her jacket, cradling him like a babe. Zach handed her staff over. They pecked their way through the darkwood at a creeping pace that was both necessary and terrifying, careful to choose their steps with care and yet knowing care no longer mattered. He or It was still in there, could see them, and both Allie and Zach knew it.

Zach followed the sound of rushing water and looked back more than ahead. Sam lay shivering and whining in Allie's arms. His tiny eyes were shut. Blood leaked through the scarf, staining the pink leopard print of Allie's jacket. They reached the riverbank and kept walking. Downstream now, away from home and as fast as they could, which wasn't fast at all anymore. Allie's feet landed hard on the rocks, almost like a stomp, lifting her feet by will and letting gravity slam them down. She tripped when the brace on her foot clipped her left calf. Sam woke long enough to squeal. Zach reached out, trying to steady Allie and keep her moving at the same time. He turned to see if anything followed.

"Can you walk alone?" he asked.

Allie looked at him as though he'd gone mad. "What do you mean?"

"I need to try something." She stopped. Zach pushed her on. "Keep walking. I'll be right back."

"No. Zach—"

He spun and raced the other way as mud and spray kicked from his heels. Allie cried out again. Zach heard her but only dug his boots in more, pumping his legs as fast as they could carry him and ignoring the stabbing in his chest. He reached nearly ten feet past where they'd found Sam when thunder vented from the trees again. Zach stopped and turned back, yelling for Allie to run. She couldn't, not with the bottom half of her body dying ahead of the top, but the small act of trying was good enough. The scrub quieted again.

Nothing about their last days in the woods had gone right. The grand adventure, the noble quest, their high calling—all of these things had been proven false. Zach had enough food and water to survive, but no fire to warm them. Allie's feet were rotting, her ankle likely dislocated. Zach could not bear to ponder what ravaged his lungs. Sam was near death. And though they had wandered those wide woods for days, now they were truly and finally lost. Zach's final gift to his parents would be for them to gather what sparkly packages lay waiting to go under the tree and hide them away forever. But there was a sense of calm in his heart now, despite all of those things. Zach didn't know how much longer the demon in the darkwood would let them live, but at least now, finally, he knew what It was doing.

Allie stumbled ahead, pitching her crutch and nearly pitching Sam. The look she gave Zach was one of pure horror that melted to confusion at his slowing pace. He walked to Allie and rubbed Sam's ears. The dog did not stir.

"It's okay," he told her. "We ain't gotta run anymore. All we need to do's go straight downriver. We'll have to stop soon and make camp. That'll be okay too. We won't be bothered."

Allie shook her head and looked over Zach's shoulder. He didn't have to turn to know nothing was there, that the trees had gone silent again.

"It's gone, Allie. For now, anyway."

"How you know that?"

"It chased us away from east so we could find the doe," Zach said. "Just like It chased us from the darkwood to the river, and from upstream to here. Don't you see, Allie? All this time, I thought we were being hunted. We ain't. We're being herded."

14

It wasn't what happened with Bobby Barnes that became Marshall's undoing, it was the trip down the hallway that evening to gaze once more into his daughter's empty room. He stood there recalling all those times he'd found her staring out of the window to check their wind gauge or to make sure the Mary was still in the front yard where she belonged. All those times Marshall would watch as she played with Sam and pretended not to. Yet not even the stillness struck him as much as the smell—a growing staleness seeping into the comforter on the bed and the paint on the walls, as though no one had lived in Allie's room for a long while. That was what finally cracked Marshall open. That long scent was what nudged him over his own sharp edge.

He had spent the last days wandering through a darkwood of his own, one crafted not by the slow decay of nature but the slow decay of his life. It was a place of shadow and despair, a thick and unending tangle of dead faith and dying hope, and shrouding it all was the haze of a future planned no further ahead than the end of a work shift or the start of a weekend. In that scrub Marshall had found all but two of grief's stages. He had denied and grown angry, had fallen into a depression so thick he had ceased struggling against it. Still Allie had not come home. Would not, because Marshall had been nothing to her and the Mary had been *All I Had*, and now even the memory of her presence in his life had gone musty.

Allie was gone, just as her mother before, and there was nothing Marshall could do about it. This weighed upon him more than anything else. There is no greater fear than that of a parent for his child. That wrinkled lump of screaming flesh you are handed is more than person and soul, it is a part of yourself, and what you discover as the years wind on is that the tiny boy or girl is the very *best* part—the You that you could never quite be. The world does not shrink when you have children, it expands, and with it comes a beauty you never knew was there and monsters you never knew existed. They lurk in a loosely wrapped crib blanket or an exposed electrical outlet, a tub too full of water. Those monsters are there at every busy intersection and every day of school, and you can pray and instruct but you know deep down that sooner or later one of those monsters will slip through your guard and strike. That was Marshall's weight—the hopelessness of it all, and the knowledge that in the end, the monster who had driven his child away had not been God or the wind—it had been himself.

He could no longer look in the mirror. What Marshall found

looking back was a gaunt and old face cracked with lines and black circles orbiting two bloodshot eyes. Nor could he bear to look at the world and see those sorrowful stares given by the townspeople on their way back from the day's search. Marshall could not even close his eyes without seeing Allie cooking her macaroni and hot dogs or decorating the tree with a smile on her face that did not cover the pain and sadness in her heart.

Having nowhere else to cast his gaze, Marshall Granderson finally looked up. Then came the bargaining.

It was his fault, he told Grace, and his alone. It was the way he'd lived his life since Mary's passing and how he'd given himself to anger and doubt. How he'd never hurt Allie with his fists but often had with his words, and those bruises went deeper. How he'd turned away from the God of heaven and embraced the god of the bottle. And as he wept and cursed his very life, Marshall thanked Grace for always being there and never giving up on him, even when he himself had. And so it was that Grace Howard found herself on the Grandersons' back porch that evening, watching with a mixture of pity and awe as Marshall brought out what was left of his beer and whiskey.

He emptied them all beneath the same cold and moonless sky that Allie and Zach now traveled. They followed the flow of the river beside them, heads bowed rather than forward, willing their bodies to keep moving. Zach had crept out front as the wind began to gather and blow. It whistled over the water and swirled in his face, where it buried itself into his lungs and the wound on his head. He would have given anything for his hat just then, or even Allie's scarf.

Allie crept along behind. The wind played with her pigtails, making them flutter. She'd abandoned her crutch so she could cradle Sam tight. Zach hung on to his own. It didn't feel right, knowing Allie was just as hurt as himself but could hobble on anyway. He considered tossing his crooked branch aside as well, then thought better of it. The wind stole his breath as much as it stole his strength. The going was made harder with one of his shoelaces now wrapped around Allie's ankle and the other nearly frayed in half on his boot. He needed the driftwood to lean on if they were to keep moving; the time for pride had long passed.

He paused every dozen or so steps to turn his head farther around from the breeze, making sure Allie was still there. Little more than her shadow could be seen in the waning evening. Zach slowed his already sluggish gait, letting her catch up. She never did. She remained behind, choosing to be alone. It was for the best. Finding them real food and discovering the truth of their situation had buoyed Zach's spirits, but not enough for him to forget peeing himself. As for Allie, she had nothing to concentrate on but her swelling feet and ankle, which guided her body in tiny, almost shuffling steps.

Allie had decided in the last mile that the farther she kept from Zach, the safer he would be. She whispered as she tried to walk, telling Sam to hang on and please stay with her. The dog felt heavy in her arms. *Because I'm so tired,* she thought. The voice in her spoke again, saying Sam felt so heavy because he had so little life left in him.

Ahead the riverbank narrowed again into a sprawl of larger rocks. The darkwood rose in a steep slope to a ridge to their right. Farther up, black outlines of trees reached across the bank to the water's edge. Their limbs bent out and down to the water, as though thirsty. Zach lowered his head and walked on, stopping at what he judged was a safe distance from the trees. The river would protect them to their left, the ridge to their right. It was a good place—as good as they could expect. Besides, he could walk no more.

He turned and called, "We'll camp here," waiting for Allie's reply. She stopped and spoke something, but the wind swallowed it. Her body tilted to the left as she drew near. There were many things Zach would have to do to keep them alive that night. He added fixing Allie's brace to the list.

She arrived and sat on the rocks, so thankful to finally rest her feet that she paid no mind to their screams and protests on the way down. Zach set about gathering the largest rocks he could and stacked them in a semicircle against the wind. That cover would have to do. It didn't matter to Zach if the demon would leave them alone or not; he wasn't about to venture into the darkwood for shelter. He heaved the rocks into place one by one, trying to use his legs and not his back, trying to gather himself with deep breaths. He managed to find only a small amount of air. The rest he coughed out in thick, loud gasps.

Allie stroked Sam's head and kept whispering. She reminded him of home and her bed and how warm the covers would be when they got back, how she'd gotten him a new tennis ball for Christmas, anything to keep him in the world. The scarf around him had gone from orange and blue to a sticky red. Allie put her hand beneath, careful to stay clear of the wound. She felt Sam's chest just as she'd felt Zach's back in the cave.

Zach layered another rock and asked, "He okay?"

"He's breathing," Allie said. "There's so much blood, Zach."

"I know. Keep the scarf on'm. He'll be okay, Allie."

But Sam didn't look okay, not with those eyes that had almost gone shut and the pink tongue lolling from his mouth. His breaths came shallow, barely moving the scarf against her chest, and his tongue came alive just enough to lick the space below her neck. She shrugged off her backpack. Zach finished the windbreak (which wasn't much of a break at all, what with all the gaps between the stones) and crouched down, coughing more.

He said, "I need the bow drill from your pack. We'll need fire tonight, Allie. I don't get this to work, the cold'll take us. I'm still freezin' from the river. We ain't got no cave or hut, and I won't dare that darkwood."

She nodded, barely registering that Zach was unzipping her backpack and reaching inside. He pushed aside the two remaining fish and brought out the bow, then brushed his fingers against the packages inside as he groped for the clumps of tinder. He placed the parts in the middle of the semicircle and then strayed far enough from the camp to scavenge what wood he could find. When Zach returned minutes later, he carried only an armful. Allie began rocking Sam in her arms just as her momma had once rocked her, humming a tune she did not know. She watched Zach set the pieces in place. He drew out his remaining shoelace and tied it around the bow, wrapping the spindle inside. He placed his foot on the fireboard and rested the handhold against his shin. Then came the familiar music of wood scraping wood as he drew the bow back and forth.

"Zach?"

He coughed again.

"What did you mean when you said we were being herded?"

"Mr. Scary don't want us leaving, Allie." Looking at the bow and not her, trying to push the handhold down just enough so the spindle sparked the hole in the board. "It wants to keep us here, wear us down." And as tendrils of sweet-smelling smoke began to lift from the bowels of all that screeching wood, he thought, *Because if you scare it good before you kill it, the meat tastes better.* "It gets us wore out; It knows we won't fight."

"Sam fought." Allie nuzzled him closer. The dog didn't move. Sleeping, she thought. Sleeping was all. "He was brave."

Zach bore down harder. His shoulders and back began to burn and his breaths came faster, threatening to choke him. "It won't come. Back. Not so long as we go the wrong. Way. We're lost now, Allie. For sure. Hafta stay strong."

Two more minutes, he thought. Maybe less than that. Then the wood would spark. Then they could be safe for the night.

"I ain't strong," Allie said. "God's gonna get me, Zach. I'm marked. He got Sam because Sam got marked too. You're gonna be next. I can't stop it."

It was not what she'd said but how she'd said it—low and soft and full of longing—that pulled Zach's eyes from the bow. His hands stopped long enough to lower the smoke. He looked down and cursed himself, then drew the bow faster.

He wheezed, "That ain't true," but Allie didn't hear. The wind had taken those words away just as it had taken Mary, leaving Allie to mourn the fact that so much of life seemed a bargaining of one thing for another. Of watching one thing fall from the vine so something less beautiful could grow.

"So long as I stayed sad, everybody'd be okay. They'd be *safe*. That's why I shoulda stayed sad, Zach. But I believed instead, and now we're lost."

On that particular point, Zach couldn't argue. Nothing helped a person so much as faith, but nothing could cause so much harm as that faith being placed anywhere other than where it rightly belonged. He didn't bother telling Allie this and wouldn't have, even if his total attention weren't centered upon the smoke rising from his bow drill. Thick smoke, with a color as black as the night around them. And at the bottom of the spindle, a single frail ember.

"Get ready," he said.

Allie leaned forward just as Zach did the same. Yet while she shifted Sam to her left hand and waved the smoke away with her right, Zach had no hands left. The smoke enveloped his head, seizing his nose and throat and flinging him into coughs Allie had never heard before, barks so deep and violent it was as if Zach had gone possessed. Reflex overtook his mind as his hands let go of the bow and spindle to cover his face. He wheeled away as his body convulsed, expelling warm liquid from his mouth. Allie skirted the smoldering wood and crawled to him on two knees and one hand. She rubbed his back, asking Zach if he was okay. She mourned the love she felt for him.

Zach looked at the dying remains of the fire and shut his eyes, not bearing the sight. One last cough erupted from the furthest place in him, leaving a coppery taste in his mouth. Allie lifted his head. Even in the night, Zach could see on her face an expression that stopped him, one worse than fear or worry. It was a look of hopelessness.

Two of her fingers grazed his lips. Allie drew them away and rubbed what was there with her thumb, telling herself it wasn't that at all in much the same way as she'd told herself Sam was only sleeping. She held them up to Zach.

"Is that blood?" he asked.

A nod was all.

Zach's voice bent under the sight of those few drops, followed by his courage and the last of his heart. His eyes cracked last, healing themselves with the tears that flooded there.

"I coughed up blood?" Asking, begging Allie to say no, it wasn't blood, it was just mud maybe or a little frost turned red by a trick of light. They'd endured so much in the past days. They'd fought the cold and the hunger and the thirst and the loneliness, even the demon that followed them. But Zach knew he couldn't endure this. And as the first tear spilled from the corner of his swollen left eye, he knew the only person in the world who could make it better wasn't Allie or God, it was his momma.

That tear frightened Allie even more than the blood on Zach's mouth. She shifted Sam's body to her left hand again and held out her right, wanting to wrap it around Zach's neck. He jerked away instead and got to his feet, telling her no. He had to cry, had to empty himself of his pain, but he was still too proud to do it in front of Allie. He walked away as she called, pleading for him to come back. Zach shook his head and cursed his weakness as Marshall cursed his own miles away on the back porch, weeping on his hands and knees as he lapped up the alcohol he'd poured out.

And just as in that moment Allie loved Zach more than her heart could bear, so Grace Howard held Marshall tight and believed she held her own father. Her tears rushed out, mingling with Marshall's own, two hearts wrung dry by the hard turns of life. She had loved Mary Granderson like a sister. Mary had been there after Hank Howard died, had listened to Grace as she mourned not only that loss but what she felt was her part in it. Now there, in the darkness of that backyard and the crumbling of Marshall's own self, Grace understood for the first time that she loved this man who had buried what had been found of her best friend after The Storm. It was a love far deeper than Allie or Grace ever believed they could feel, one kindled not by the ugly sight of Zach and Marshall being brought down, but by the beauty of what they would become if they found the courage to rise up again.

Zach could not dry his face. Fresh tears fell in the places where he wiped the old tears away. They mixed with the blood seeping from his mouth, making his cheeks slick and sticky. Allie still called. Her voice faded in the wind as Zach walked on, stopping only when the great trees that grew onto the bank would let him go no farther. There he slumped and shut his eyes. He cried out to both heaven and home, hoping someone would hear.

When Zach opened his eyes again, two lights shone among

the branches not ten feet away. Hovering there, unmoved by the wind and creaking trees. One red, one white. Beholding him. Zach reached out, believing those lights could be taken in his hand like two swollen lightning bugs. They disappeared at his movement, only for an instant, then emerged again. And with them came a grunt.

Zach's arm went lifeless. It slapped the front of his jeans, scaring him. He took two steps back as his tears continued to flow and wiped his mouth again, feeling the blood.

The blood.

A new horror now, one larger than even the eyes staring back at him. The demon was here, yes—and It smelled Zach's blood.

The eyes shifted again, this time rising instead of blinking out. Climbing into the limbs of the trees, up and up, so high that Zach had to stretch his neck to see them. And then it was as if the trees themselves gave birth to a moving trunk that began to push its way out onto the riverbank, a breathing mass larger than anything Zach had ever seen, grunting and growling and coming toward him.

The scream that flooded the riverbank was nearly inhuman in its pitch and carry, and Zach didn't even cough when he was done. He only yelled, "*Run,*" yelled it long and loud behind him as that shadow advanced, and then he ran himself. Not back to Allie, but toward the rise on his right. Into the darkwood.

15

Allie had been watching all this time, though from that distance all she saw was the patch of night into which Zach had disappeared. Yet the night could not swallow the scream that came from downriver. Allie's every sense came alive at the terror behind that wailing, and of the boy who'd made it. She stood. Her arms squeezed Sam so tight that he woke long enough to give a tired yelp.

She screamed into the darkness, "Zach?" but no sound returned. There was only the wind and the current rushing past. "Zach. Are you okay?"

Allie took a step forward. The toes of her Chucks met the widest part of Zach's windbreak. Sam drifted back to unconsciousness. He hung limp and heavy in Allie's arms.

"Zach can you hear me what happened?"

She had to go to him, if for no other reason than Allie knew Zach would have gone to her. She should go toward that scream. Brave the dark. And yet her feet wouldn't move at all.

She called once more—"*Zach?*" Praying he would answer. Praying, even, for the moon. Not even the trees farther on could be seen. The clouds overhead lay like a blanket over the stars, holding the night close. Allie took a step back and to the right, feeling for the edge of the stone wall. Telling herself she had to save Zach. Her eyes strained forward, trying to peel away the gloom, then widened in wonder.

Two lights shone ahead. One red, one white. Tiny, glowing holes that swayed from left to right in a slow rhythm that bewitched her. Allie smiled as joy flowed over her. They were beautiful, those lights. They were the most beautiful things she'd ever seen.

"Zach? Is that you?"

Closer now. Zach must have found them. They were not lost at all. Zach had meant to lead them to town but they had found the light instead—the one from the pond; the light she'd seen from the rocks. A kind of magic maybe, like her compass. Her momma sending word once more.

That's not magic, said Voice. *At least, none you've ever imagined.*

But it was, had to be. And yet as those lights moved toward her, Allie remembered what she had seen at the pond and upon the rocks was not two lights but one. Maybe Zach had managed to spark a fire and what he carried was not one ember but two, a red one from the fire inside and a white one because that was the color of the hottest fire and that was science, and now they would be warm and not die. Allie waited for her Voice to speak up again. It didn't have to. She looked away long enough to see Zach's fire bow at her feet, along with the spindle and board and wood.

Closer.

No longer pinpricks but firefly glows. Bending in the night as though pulled by their own breeze. Here Allie's grin faded. Surely Zach was far enough along the bank to be able to see her, or at least the solid outline of the rocks she stood behind. Yet he did not call out, telling Allie to look at what he'd found. Sam squirmed in her arms. It was as if a part of him had awakened just then, perhaps a voice speaking up like the voice that had spoken up in her.

She called into the wind, "Zach?"

The voice that returned was not Zach's, nor was it human at all. It was instead a roar that made Sam squirm again despite being nearly dead, that made the hair on Allie's arms and neck uncurl. She stumbled forward as the lights grew nearer and ducked behind the pile of stones. Sam struggled and fell silent again. Along the riverbank, rocks scattered and rolled as God crept closer. Allie clenched her eyes and bit her tongue nearly in half, trying to swallow a scream. Had He seen her? She felt sure He had. God could see anything, as could eyes that glowed in the dark. And even if the night had rendered Him just as blind as it had rendered her, Allie knew her screams had carried. They had carried far.

She eased her head up and over the lip of the wall. The eyes were larger, heading straight on. There was no time. Even there, all alone on the riverbank except for a dying dog and a hungry God, Allie understood the irony of that. They had wandered through a place where time held as much meaning as the rocks beneath their feet, and yet she had run out of it. There was only enough to understand she must save Sam and Zach because she loved them both, and that's what people who loved did.

She laid Sam against the rocks and kissed him, fighting the sting in her eyes as she told him to lie still and quiet. The rocks beyond the windbreak scattered and rolled. Not far, Allie thought. Now or never. She leaped over the wall and ran, wailing as she forced her feet and ankle to move even as she had no idea where to go. Ahead was no option—the eyes had stopped moving, as had the hulking shadow behind them, but running ahead would mean running right into Him. Nor would running upriver help, as that would lead Him right past where Sam lay. The river flowed to Allie's left. That meant only the darkwood remained. She moved there, hopping on her one good ankle. Screaming for God to follow.

The eyes swung her way. Allie cleared the riverbank in ten short hops and vaulted herself into the brush. She began climbing the slope, straining her every muscle against what roots and branches she would find to boost herself up. Yelling for Zach to come, to help. Bushes shook, limbs snapped. Behind, to her left. Allie turned to see if she had put any distance between them. Roars turned to grunts and then growls. The eyes were nearly at her heels.

Allie screamed again and felt a tear in her lungs. Her Chucks slipped in the slope's mud. Something swung out and slapped at her heels, nearly knocking her off balance. Allie reached up, searching for something to pull her onward, and grasped only air. Her shoes dug in as she stood, convinced her only escape was to run, but the dying feet that Allie had willed forward for four days finally failed her. Gravity flung her backward. Her head lolled back as she fell free of the earth and tumbled. In her mind, Allie saw herself flying away with Sam and Zach beside her and a green hill not far ahead.

That image remained until she struck the rocks and trees below. A pain like being run through with a hot poker jolted her neck. The world spun as she fell end over end down the thirty feet of the slope she'd scaled. She hit the riverbank on her shoulders and rolled twice, coming up on her feet only long enough for them to pitch her toward the sound of hissing water. There was darkness and a final, pleading scream. Then came a drowning cold that stole Allie's breath.

16

The current gripped her like the hands of a hungry giant, towing her from the shallows. What she felt wasn't the frigid water nor even those hands pressing down upon her lungs, but the soft tingling of her body shutting itself down one cell at a time.

She could not lift her head and so floated facedown, arms stretched out from her sides in a position that could only be described as submission. The water drew in her fingers and toes, turning them to claws. Her body folded in on itself. She thought of Zach's screams and how he must have spent the last breaths from his tired lungs trying to keep her safe. She thought of poor Sam, lying alone behind the rock wall on the bank.

The river pulled her deeper into its maw, promising an easy passage to better lands. And those lands would be better, would they not? Allie's jumbled mind thought yes. She had been through enough in her short life. There would be no hell on the other side. Hell was what Allie was about to leave behind.

Breathe, spoke the voice in her. Her eyes were open to black, and in that space grew stars that glittered and shot like those Allie had seen in the sky that night upon the rocks. The water would wash through her lungs, paralyzing her. It would be a proper death. Paralyzed was how she'd lived.

But it was Allie's heart that spoke louder as she began to sink under the roil. What it offered was more picture than words. Not the dream that had plagued her nights ever since she'd entered the woods, but something that felt like a promise—the gates of Oak Lawn swinging open on some faraway day as townspeople follow Marshall Granderson through. He leads them up the slender lane to the foot of the knoll and then on, midway down a long line of the honored dead. There, two stone markers sit where only one had been before. And while a pink tennis shoe still lies in Mary Granderson's grave, there is only Allie's empty box beside it. Allie sees her daddy wailing and Miss Grace standing beside him, offering what comfort she can. She sees her mother's eyes in the way Grace looks at him, and her mother's heart in how Grace longs to give Marshall peace. But that peace will never come to Marshall Granderson now, not when the short years of his life are spent under a shadow of knowing that he has been marked by the same God who has taken his wife and child. His hand shakes. The scruff on his face has gone all gray. He looks to the small casket with the same dulled brown eyes, but Allie knows another person looks out from them. Not the Marshall Granderson who once ate mac and cheese and called it a masterpiece. That Marshall is gone now and forever. Locked in the bedroom closet, perhaps. What looks out now is the Other.

It was her heart's picture rather than the swirl of the current that lowered Allie's head to her chest. She could murder herself, had almost done so above the rocks only the night before, but Allie Granderson would never dare kill what goodness remained in her father. She used what strength remained to tuck her chin and roll her right shoulder. That was enough to turn her face from the icy water to a moonless sky. Allie forced the air from her lungs like jump-starting a dead battery. The heave she took in sounded like one of Zach's.

She lowered her legs. Next came a flash of confusion as she found purchase. Not with her feet, but with her hands. Allie curled her fingers in the muck at the river's bottom and pushed herself up. The current overcame her, flooding her mouth and nose and threatening to wash her away. The struggle ended when she rose to her knees. And as she looked, the air filled with the sound of her laughter. The river had not swept her away at all. The bank lay only steps ahead, the windbreak only steps beyond that.

Something—the laughter or the cold, Allie couldn't decide—kept her from standing. She crawled instead, bracing a hand against the current so it would not sweep her away. Her pigtails had knotted themselves behind her head, forming a rudder that pulled her eyes away from shore. That too was funny, as were the bold outlines of the darkwood across the way and the thought of Zach's head hanging in one of those trees.

She reached the bank and stood. Her body convulsed from the cold, but Allie's skin felt hot and sweaty, like she'd spent an entire July day fishing with her parents and the Barnetts at Boone's Pond. She unbuttoned her jacket and let it fall, pulled at the neck of her sweatshirt to force it over her head. Tore at her shoes and socks. Her jeans came loose next. Allie left her clothes in a long line stretching from the river to the windbreak, and she made the last steps on feet so bare and blistered that they were no more than two hunks of frozen meat. Laughter turned to muffled cries of "Muh . . . muh," over and over, speaking a language she could not understand.

It was Sam who brought her back to her senses. He stood waiting in the center of the windbreak, whole and unbothered by the darkness around him. There was a smile upon the dog's face, though his tail had gone sharp and still. His ears perked, leaving the floppy tips to dangle in the wind.

He said, "You have to start the fire, Allie."

She laughed again. Not because her dog had both healed himself and learned to speak in the last thirty minutes, but because starting a fire now would be like running from the cold by hiding in a freezer.

"Start the fire, Allie. You know how."

Allie staggered forward, then stopped feet away from the rocks.

"Do you love me, Allie?" Sam asked.

She said, "Muh."

"Then come start the fire. You have to. I can't. I don't have any hands."

Sam tilted his head and lifted a front paw, showing her. Allie nodded (though it may have been just to whisk the sweat from her forehead) and stumbled forward. Sam stepped aside as she fell to her knees, searching in the dark for Zach's drill.

"Put the bow in your right hand, Allie," Sam said. "I have no hands, but I have a brain. You have no brain, but you have hands. Do as I say, and don't be afraid. He's gone for now."

She nodded again

("Muh")

and put the bow in her hand. Kept the spindle tight around Zach's bootlace and a rotten foot on the fireboard. She placed the spindle in the socket, just as Sam instructed.

"The tinder won't work," he said. "It doesn't go under the

board, Allie. That's why Zach hasn't gotten a fire. But I know just the trick."

The wind whipped again—God's breath about to push Allie over the edge of the world. She looked up to find one of her pads stuck in Sam's mouth. She reached out and took it, placing it beneath the fireboard under her foot. She looked at Sam, wondering when he'd learned to talk.

"I can't talk, silly," he said. "None of this is real. You've gone crazy, you see. But you still have to saw. Saw away, pretty girl."

She didn't think her hands would allow it, not with that wind (which had now somehow gone from hot to cold) pushing against her face. Sam told her to move so that the gusts hit her back. She did and began sawing again, pressing down on the handhold as the spindle churned in the socket.

"Faster," Sam said.

He rose up on his hind legs and waved his paws in the air, cheering on the thin wisps of smoke rising from the board. Allie rocked the bow back and forth as smoldering dust filled the pad beneath. She stopped only when Sam said, "Now the tinder, Allie. Hurry now, but don't rush."

Her body cramped. Allie lifted the bow and fireboard away and thanked Sam as he handed her the tinder in a paw. She held the pile in one hand and lost half of it from her spasms, then tilted the pad so the coal dropped inside.

"Lift it, Allie," he said. "To your face. Lightly now." And when she had, "Now blow. Right to the center. Steady and hard."

The breaths came out jerky through her chattering teeth. Allie's arms wavered in the cold.

"That's my girl," Sam said. "Almost now."

The smoke gathered, wrapping Allie's hands and face in a tight hug that nearly choked her. And with a final breath that coal sparked to flame against the tinder, covering her with warmth.

"Down now, Allie. On the rocks will have to do. Find the sticks and twigs. Feed it well, as you'd feed yourself."

She laid the flame down and gathered what Zach had collected—the smaller wood first and then the pieces as thick as her wrists. The flame grew, coloring the gray rocks of the windbreak orange and yellow. Allie began laughing again. She looked at Sam and found he had grown too tired to celebrate, had lain down and found a sleep so deep it looked near death. Allie's bloody scarf covered him. She thanked her dog and fed the fire more. It blazed against the wind and water and all the evil lurking in the wood. Her naked legs and feet began to tickle with life. And when Allie stood to face the darkness, it was that same life and defiance that gave voice to her shouts.

I ain't afraid of you no more, was what her mind said. *Do you hear me? I ain't afraid.*

What echoed along the riverbank was nothing more than a series of moans and grunting sounds. And yet the Hollow tested those words just as it had tested Allie all that time, stripping away the fear and sadness so only the heart of her remained. Bringing her down, so she might finally learn how to rise again. For from the darkness where she looked, on past where Zach's final screams had been uttered, there came a flicker of light yet again.

17

The terror that gripped Zach had taken him no more than a football field's length from Allie. Just before she'd gone tumbling, that distance had shrunk to eighty feet. Had Zach the presence to turn around, he would have seen her land like a rag doll in the river. But of course Zach didn't turn around, and for the simple reason that his mind was no longer his own. The forest had taken it, just as it had taken his dignity and his lungs and his holy quest, and what it had given him in return was all the awareness of a wounded animal.

It was that wounded animal inside him that heard every huff of his clogged lungs as another growl at his heels and every branch he cracked as teeth snapping just out of reach. Wind swirled the darkwood, making shadows leap and dart. He ran. To where didn't matter, only how far.

But no matter how far Zach's fading legs took him, he could not escape the sounds of Allie's cries carried by the breeze. Begging Zach to come, to save her.

His course had taken him from the trees along the riverbank to midway up the slope. There his sense of direction failed him. Zach had run back toward Allie rather than away, and then looped, returning in the direction he'd come. He would have kept running had it not been for the coughs that doubled him over, reducing his sprint to a stumble. And when Zach finally reached the bottom of the slope and discovered the trees in front of him once more, he thought of how Sam had tried to lead them home through the olden woods only to find the meadow and the screaming tree again.

He crouched there in the trees along the bank, whimpering as his lungs filled with blood and muck. Zach felt as if he were drowning on land.

The wind fell on him like a hammer, but aside from that there was only silence. He could not hear the demon and realized that didn't improve things at all; It could be hiding right in front of him and he'd never know. But neither could Zach *see* anything, and unless what chased him was walking around with Its eyes closed, he'd see those horrid bright eyes. His chest seized again. Zach threw a sleeve over his mouth and coughed hard.

More blood. He couldn't see to know for sure, but his lips felt sticky and his tongue tasted like pennies.

The quiet allowed his body to relax. It tensed once more at the realization that not only had the demon grown still, but Allie was no longer screaming. To Zach's battered thoughts, that could mean only one thing.

Allie would have been too scared to run at the sight of those red and white lights.

Not like me, Zach thought. *At least I didn't go limp standing out there. I ran.*

True enough. Then again, Zach hadn't run to where he *should* have, had he? He hadn't run to Allie at all. He'd shot up the slope instead, meaning to put as much space between him and those glowing eyes as he could, and it didn't matter who had been caught in the middle. And now Allie was dead because she was too afraid to run.

No, Allie was dead because she *couldn't* run. Not with a busted ankle and two busted feet, and not with Sam lying there all tore up and bleeding.

A shiver fell over Zach that had nothing at all to do with the wind wriggling its way through the trees. He was no man at all. He'd never make it to the rusty gate, never carve his name in the shadow of that cursed and haunted wood known as Happy Hollow. He'd be too chicken to get close.

The tears fell freely this time. No one was there to see. No one but God. That only made Zach shiver more. If the Almighty did indeed have sharp edges as the angel told him long ago, He would want nothing to do with a boy who was a coward. That's what Zach was—chicken. Nothing more than a fraidy-cat who peed his pants. And hadn't a part of him always known so? Wasn't that why Zach wore his father's big hat? To hide the little boy beneath? Now Allie was dead and so was Sam, and Zach was all alone and bleeding in the darkwood. He would have wet his pants again, had there been water enough in him.

This must be what it's like, he thought, to fall away. Strangely enough, it didn't really feel like falling at all. What Zach felt instead was a feeling of being stuck, of being so frightened and despairing that going back or going on was no longer an option, and so all you could do is stand right where you are and sink. That must have been how Allie felt after her momma died. It had been a stone rolled over her heart, and the only light she'd found lay in a broken compass that had led her to die along the river. Zach's only wish was that he could have died with her. At least he would have had the satisfaction of leaving this world brave. Instead, Zach Barnett's last thought would be that he had all the spine of a jellyfish. His end would come huddled at the edge of the darkwood, and only weeds would grow in the place his bones rotted.

He rested his head on his knees and rocked. He thought of his own mother and father and of Christmas, and how every Christmas for them from then on would be a time for mourning rather than joy.

When the echo of Allie's call carried along the bank, Zach thought it only a dream. The sound came again—not a scream, something other. Something *strong*. Zach lifted his face to the trees. Far beyond the twisted limbs he saw a light against the darkness. And from that very place, he heard Allie's voice once more.

This time Zach did not waver. He charged through the trees without care of how hard his lungs and legs protested, calling out to Allie that he was coming. And as Zach ran he prayed that he didn't have to wear a hat to be a man, that instead it meant doing for others even what you most feared. Not because he was strong and brave, but because he loved. Because in the end, love is the most powerful magic of all.

18

The call came late, long after Marshall had retreated behind his locked bedroom door. Grace didn't recognize the number and wasn't surprised. Everyone in the world had called in the last days, from TV newspeople wanting a sound bite to psychics offering their services.

She let the phone finish its first ring. A map of Mattingly and the surrounding wilderness lay sprawled on her lap. Grace had spent the last half hour circling with a yellow highlighter the areas that had been searched—the town proper, the neighborhoods, the farms and fields, and nearly all of the back roads leading into the mountains. Many miles had been scoured. Many more had not.

Grace jumped when the phone rang again, her thoughts too scattered and her mind so tired that she'd forgotten someone was calling. Her hands came together and would have made a clap had she not been holding the highlighter. The tip slid across her opposite thumb in a long yellow scrawl and then slipped off, leaving another scrawl on the cream-colored pillow under her arm. Grace picked up the phone and offered a numb "Hello?" as she stared at the mark on the pillow. Wonderful. Mary would've killed her for that.

Juliet Creech apologized for the hour but said it couldn't be helped. It took Grace a few seconds to place the new pastor ("new" being a relative term; Grace was three when her parents moved to Mattingly, and even though that was thirty-seven years ago, many in town still considered her "new" as well) before saying there was no need for a sorry, she was still awake.

"I had to make sure there was enough support before calling." The preacher's voice dropped to a mumble. "Sometimes the idea itself isn't nearly as important as who comes up with it."

"What idea's that?"

"I'm organizing a midnight vigil for tomorrow," Juliet said. "Mayor Wallis gave me the okay. After he was on board, everyone else was. And I mean everyone, Miss Howard. The church won't hold everyone, so we're having it in the Square. I've already spoken with Jake and Kate. They said they'd come but only after the day's search. Jake said they were going farther into the mountains tomorrow morning. On foot this time. They'll bring the helicopter, too, if the weather's right."

Grace cradled the phone at her neck and looked at the map. No marks were upon the wide swaths of light green representing hills and hollows around Mattingly. Her eyes followed the blue curve of the river as it wound through town and on into places that were familiar—Boone's Pond, George Washington National Forest, the small communities of Riverwood and Three Peaks. But much of that land was foreign to Grace, as unknown and exotic as the moon. It had generally been agreed upon that the outer forests of the hill country were simply too far away for two children to lose themselves in, even with bicycles. Besides, everyone knew Allie would never dare the woods. The wind sounded closer in all those trees. Meaner. But now Jake had decided to go there anyway. Desperate times, yes? She didn't know how much of that land could be covered by searchers and so didn't know how much of it to circle. She pushed the highlighter into her thumb again, coloring in a bit more of the skin from white to jaundice.

"—needs it," Juliet said.

"I'm sorry, what?"

"It'll be Christmas Eve. I think the town needs it. I'd very much like Marshall to come. And you, of course."

Grace kept coloring. Her thumb was now as yellow as the flashing star atop the Grandersons' tree. "I think it's a fine idea," she said. "But there's something you should know about Marshall, Pastor Creech."

"Please, it's Juliet."

"Juliet," Grace said. "Marshall's what some here call 'fallen away.' Allie too. I know it might be difficult for you to understand, but ever since The Storm and Mary—"

"He's blamed God," Juliet finished. "Trust me, Grace. I understand. That's a feeling I know well."

Grace blinked. The line went quiet with an awkward pause she couldn't understand. She adjusted the receiver against her neck. Was Juliet waiting for her to say something, or was it that the pastor had just shamed herself by admitting something she shouldn't? Grace couldn't decide which, couldn't understand, just as she couldn't understand why her hand refused to lay down that highlighter. Her entire thumb was as yellow as the sun now, the ink so wet it shimmered in the tree lights, and her thought was that it would take a gallon of soap to get it all off.

Juliet cleared her throat and said, "Doubt is the most natural thing in the world. Do you know what religion is, Grace? It's the worship of mystery. It's getting close to Something we can never comprehend, because that Something is so much bigger and so fundamentally different from us. It's like the world's just a piece of paper, Grace, and we're all just squiggles on the page drawn by some unseen hand. How can we understand the Being behind that hand? Someone with dimensions we cannot fathom? Someone who exists so far outside of us? Come tomorrow night, Grace. Please. Tell Marshall it'll be good for him."

A noise worked its way up the hall, something like crying. Grace wanted to go there. She wanted to knock on that closed bedroom door and tell Marshall to open it, tell Marshall he didn't have to suffer alone, but in the end Grace didn't because that wasn't her door. It was Mary's, and even if it wasn't she was too afraid she would once more say the name Hank instead. Yes, going would be good for Marshall. Grace thought it would be good for her too.

"I'll try," she said.

Juliet said she would pray. Grace set the phone down and studied the map across her legs. Those streets crisscrossing in red lines. The river winding its way from the mountains. Those squiggles that represented her entire world. Grace was somewhere on that page, along with Marshall and Jake and Kate. Along with Allie and Zach. That was their life, laid out in two dimensions. Their everything. Maybe Marshall and Juliet were right. How could anyone know beyond doubt there was some unseen hand beyond it all, looking down even now? How could faith be had in a God so separate, so different from themselves?

Her left hand crept over the map. Grace watched with a passive detachment, vaguely aware that some part of her mind must be telling those muscles and tendons to move, yet convinced it wasn't her mind at all. Her palm moved from left to right, over the very neighborhood where she currently sat, over the town, on past roads and fields searched and searched again. When it reached the green oblongs of forest and wood (*Miles,* Grace thought, *out there are just miles and endless miles*), her fingers curled inward as her thumb remained out. And in a spot high in the hill country where the river flowed and a frightened little girl now stood, that thumb pressed down onto the page. When Grace moved her finger back, she found a perfect print of yellowed squiggles. An image of her three-dimensional self, shrunk down to fit into a world of only length and width.

It was that answer Grace Howard settled on, that hope by which she finally found sleep. Wherever Allie and Zach were, they could not go to God. God would have to come to them.

19

The wind swirled, whipping the flames into a dance that beat back the darkness. Night thickened in the heart of the far trees—from where the light was coming. Allie reached into the fire and pulled one of the logs free. The heat against her arm was so intense it felt cold. Everything felt cold. Had she the sense to try and understand why, Allie would have noticed she was nearly naked from top to bottom. Only her underwear and T-shirt covered her, and those were nothing more than thin layers of sopping cotton.

The light no longer flickered but held a steady glow, telling her it had weaved its way through the trees and was now upon the bank itself. Growing as it came for her once more. The fire's arc stretched out front, casting moving shadows of the windbreak and Allie's thin body. The river shimmered like uncountable millions of gray snakes that hissed and lunged. The darkwood stood to her right—a single, impenetrable wall. Allie would not run this time, could not, and so held the flaming log up and out with both hands like a sword.

"Wish you'd wake from your nap, Samwise," she said.

The words came out in a stuttering jumble that sounded coherent only in Allie's mind. Sam remained still and lifeless under Allie's scarf, warmed by the heat of the flames reflecting off the wall of stones at his back.

The light eased its way closer.

The flames ate their way down the wood toward her knuckles. Allie strengthened her grip on the log. She didn't know how much longer she could hold it, thought about heaving it out as far as she could toward the light, then reconsidered. Not because heaving it would do any good (even in her short-circuiting mind, Allie knew God wouldn't be afraid of fire), but because she realized that glow was not the same as what had driven her into the darkwood. What approached was only one light, not two. And it was neither white nor red, but golden.

It was as if that understanding alone made the light ahead brighten. What came over Allie was a peace so pure and deep that she felt herself drowning all over again. The night ceded enough for her to see that the pulsing came from the center of a shadow that held a different shape from what had marked her. Allie stepped out from behind the windbreak. The log fell from her hands, nearly singeing her bare legs. She let it drop back into the fire as the figure approached. The glow throbbed again, this time as fast as a bolt of lightning, revealing a pair of faded jeans and a white sweater.

A wave of pain rushed through Allie that was not her heart breaking but swelling, pushing against her lungs so that her breaths came in quick gulps. Gooseflesh broke out on her arms and behind her neck. Her knees buckled. And as that figure approached, everything that had happened to Allie, not just in the last three days but in the last five hundred and forty-seven, came gushing forth in a feeling that was purer than love and stronger than joy. That emotion fit inside the single word she spoke:

"Momma?"

The glow grew to a sun that covered the entire riverbank, bathing the slope of darkwood to Allie's right in the clear light of a summer's day that turned the gray waters to crystal. Mary Granderson took the last steps to her daughter from the center of a shine that poured as a fountain from the gold cross around her neck. She stopped when that light was enough to nearly drown Allie in ecstasy. In her smile Allie saw Christmas and home and all of their tomorrows, stretched out in a far line to an endless horizon.

"Is it you, Momma?" she asked, so overcome that her body felt floating.

That smile again, like a blanket. "Look at you, Allie. You've grown so."

Allie rocked forward on her heels. So many questions flooded her. So many thoughts. So much feeling. She thought this must be what it felt like to be born. "You sent word."

Mary grinned and dipped her eyes, nodding her head. "I did. And you were brave enough to follow. And now we're almost done, Allie. You're almost to the end."

"Can we go home?" Allie asked. "I'm so tired, Momma. We came all this way, me and Zach and Sam. Sam's my dog and I said I didn't love him but I do, and now he's hurt. He helped me build a fire, but he's *hurt*. There's so much blood on his blanket. And Zach's dead, Momma." A tear threaded its way into Allie's eyes. Her smile dulled. If Allie ever doubted that there could be no happiness in this world that was still not tinged with ache, those doubts were now settled. Even there, standing in front of her lost mother, Allie found cause to mourn. "There's something in the woods."

"I know there is, Allie, but He's gone. He's gone, but Zach isn't. Zach has something to find yet, something wonderful and true."

Allie stepped forward. The light around her mother grew from a sun to something like heaven. "Can we go home?" she asked again. "Daddy's waiting, Momma. He's awful sad."

"Soon," Mary said. "We'll all go home soon, Allie—you and me and Sam and Zach. We're almost there. There's just a little more, and then we'll all go home together."

Allie said, "I don't know what to do" as a voice called somewhere close, shouting her name. "I don't understand, Momma."

"You're not supposed to understand, sweetheart. There's so much you can know and so much more you can't, and that's why God has sharp edges. Hug Him anyway. A life with pain means more than a life without it. Will you do that for me?"

Allie nodded, telling her momma she would do that, would do anything. "I haven't cried," she said, and the voice behind Mary called again. "Not once, even though I was close some. Because I believed, Momma. I wouldn't let it be over."

"Because it isn't," Mary said. "It isn't the end. I'm waiting where the trees are red. You aren't lost, Allie, but you must be brave now. Be brave always. Do you understand?"

"I will." That tear held in place and would have spilled had Allie nodded again. She held her chin high instead, keeping that single drop there even if everything in her wanted it to fall, because it wasn't over. The end was close but it wasn't there, not yet. "I do."

Mary opened her arms. The glow of her necklace called Allie forward. Allie stumbled there with her hands outstretched, saying, "I love you so much."

"I love you, too, Allie. More than you'll ever know."

Allie closed her eyes as radiance enveloped her. That small bubble felt like a world hidden just beyond the woods and town—just beyond everything—another place where every hope is fulfilled and every pain is kissed away and every wrong is made forever and irrevocably right. The embrace came like a wall that knocked her backward before holding her tight.

She opened her eyes to find the light gone. Night had returned to the riverbank just as thick and suffocating as before. The arms around Allie were not her momma's. There was only the smell of mud and wood and blood against a filthy canvas sleeve, and the soft voice of Zach saying, "I love you too."

20

Zach felt Allie's body go rigid in his arms. She pried herself away and leaned back, looking over his shoulder. Only the night lay behind him. Afterimages of swirling gold filled her vision. And in the middle, a blackened figure with her arms still outstretched.

"No," she said.

Her eyes wide, trying to breach the darkness, Allie backed off and nearly stumbled into the fire. Zach reached and pulled her back. She pried herself away again, as though she couldn't bear to touch him. Zach understood. Why would Allie even want to, after what he'd done?

"I'm sorry, Allie. I'm so sor—"

Allie screamed, "Momma" into the wind. She turned on her ankles, one of which had swollen to at least twice its size now that her brace had gone missing, and screamed in the other direction. "Momma, where are you?" She turned back, facing him, and asked, "Where'd my momma go, Zach?"

That question was Zach's first clue that something sad and awful had happened (the second, now that he'd noticed it, was the fact that Allie was as close to bare as he'd ever seen a girl). Her skin was dry, yet in the firelight he saw wet patches covering the neck and left side of her T-shirt, fed by the drops of water falling from her pigtails. He looked away and found Sam huddled by the rocks. A trail of Allie's clothes led from there to the river's edge.

"*Momma!*" she screamed into the night, but there was only the wind and the water and the cracking fire. "She was here, Zach. My momma was right here."

"No one was here, Allie," Zach said. He kept his voice soft and his boots quiet, even if all he wanted was to go to her and hold her again. "I was back in the trees, and I heard you call. I saw the light. That's when I ran."

"My *momma* was the light."

"No, Allie. It was the fire. No one was here."

No, Allie thought. No, it couldn't be. That just wasn't true.

"What happened, Allie? Did It come after you? I saw It. The eyes. The eyes came after me, Allie, and I"—*yelled out to save you*, he wanted to say, but Zach knew that was wrong and couldn't lie by saying otherwise, not anymore—"I ran off. Did It see you? Didja fall in the river?" He looked around, searching the bank.

Once more—"Momma." So low and soft that Zach knew the word wasn't meant for him. "She was here, Zach. My momma came. I heard you call out and I saw the eyes. I saw God, Zach. He came for me and I didn't know what to do, so I laid Sam down and ran. I just wanted to save Sam and I thought you were dead."

He coughed, not bothering to cover his mouth with a sleeve, and said, "I thought I was too."

"I was in the river," she said. "I climbed out. I got all wet."

Allie looked down and found horror staring up. She pulled her shirt down to cover as much of herself as she could and told Zach not to look. He hadn't (not much, anyway, and wouldn't dare more), but jerked his eyes away just to be sure. He unzipped his coat and handed it to her, keeping his eyes on the flames.

"How'd you build a fire?" he asked.

Allie pulled the coat over her. "Sam told me."

They looked at the dog together. Sam had not moved from his place by the rocks, nor did it appear as though he'd be moving anytime soon. The tip of his tongue poked from his mouth, landing on the brown-and-white stones that had become his pillow. Blood still covered the scarf. Most of it had gone brittle, like dried paint.

"Sam told you?" Zach asked.

"He talked to me," Allie said. "He showed me how to make it. You had the tinder wrong, Zach. You're not supposed to put the fireboard in the tinder, you're supposed to use something else first. That's what he said. And it worked. But then I saw the light again, and I got scared because I thought God was coming and Sam went to sleep again because I guess he was so tired but it wasn't the same light, Zach; this one was different because this one was my momma. The light was coming from her cross."

For his part, Zach understood none of this. Allie was shaking like a leaf in a gale and was talking so fast without saying anything that he couldn't separate what had happened in her mind from what had happened in reality, so he tossed it all into a bin in his mind that read *Crazy*. Crazy from shock and fear and cold. Crazy because Zach hadn't been there for her. He'd run away because he didn't want Allie to see him cry and think him a coward, and then he'd run away again because he'd been a coward all along.

"We gotta get warm," he said. "It won't bother us no more, not with a fire. We just gotta hunker down, Allie. We gotta get you better."

He gathered Allie's clothes and laid them by the fire to dry. The flames were strong enough for Zach to gather wood from the scrub. He saw no eyes. Allie remained close to Sam, crouched between the windbreak and the fire. Zach's coat lay wrapped around her. Only once did Allie's words betray her thoughts, and that was when Zach left to claim one last armful of wood to see them to the last sunrise they would meet in the woods.

"Can you say more stuff, Sam?" she asked.

Sam never did.

They huddled close, keeping themselves between the rocks and the fire. Zach said something about the rocks maybe exploding if they got too hot because of all the water in them. Allie paid that warning no mind. She was going to be brave now. She'd promised it.

"I'll stay awake," Zach told her. "You sleep. Someone's gotta feed the fire in case It comes back."

"He's gone now," Allie stuttered, "least for a while. Momma said. And it ain't an It, it's a He."

"That weren't God," Zach said.

"Yes it was. He's just playin' with us like two toys, Zach. That's all we are to Him. All everybody is. And when God finally breaks His toys, He just throws them away."

"What happens if It comes again?"

"We have to be brave is all," Allie said.

Zach watched the flames. "I got no spine, Allie. I'm too scared to be brave."

"I don't think brave means not being afraid. I think it just means being afraid of doing a thing but going ahead and doing it anyway."

Allie hoped so, at any rate. She looked down at Sam and wondered if he had really shown her how to make the fire. Her mind had yet to thaw and her heart lay as tangled as the darkwood just beyond their light, but she wanted to believe yes, however impossible it was. She had to. Because if her dog hadn't really spoken, then maybe her momma had never been there at all.

December 24

1

She dreamed not of the funeral but of flying, high above the river where God's sharp edges couldn't reach, and when she landed it was on top of a narrow, jagged cliff. Sam waited there. The scarf around him had become a noose that he struggled against, yelping for aid. Allie called for Zach. Only the wind replied. It was cold there and hard and the wind blew in her face, as though trying to silence her. She yelled for Zach again. Panic built at the back of her throat. And when Allie turned to where the cliffs ended, she saw a tiny coffin standing upright between two stunted pines. The river churned far below. With it came a grunt followed by a growl. Darkwood exploded behind her.

Allie jerked her eyes open and saw the world on its side. Her body had formed a tight ball beneath Zach's coat. Sometime during the night, she (or had it been he?) had pulled the coat down to cover her feet, leaving her arms exposed. The skin there wasn't cold, not with the fire still blazing mere feet away and the piled rocks warm behind her. The windbreak hadn't exploded in the night, as Zach feared it maybe would. Allie knew it wouldn't. She had closed her eyes to the same promise that had greeted her come that next morning.

We're almost done, Allie. You're almost to the end. We'll all go home together.

A smell filled her nose that brought Allie all the way alive. Not the loamy scent of the forest or the brackish odor rising from the river. This was *fragrance*. Her neck creaked as she lifted her head. Sam lay still and had not moved all night except to put his tongue back in his mouth. Only the tip showed now, leaking out between the gaps in his white teeth. His breaths came shallow but faint against her scarf.

"He's okay."

Allie lifted her head and peered around the backside of the flames. Zach sat hunched over the fire, poking at the wood with a long stick. The flames rose to lick at a makeshift stove-top fashioned of small saplings. On top lay hunks of fish. They sizzled and popped in the fire. The breeze carried the smoke to her.

"Breakfast time, Allie." He smiled through the dirt and blood on his face. It was a tired grin, the look of a man made weary by a long journey with no end. "Sure does smell good, huh? Better'n Milky Ways and such, I'd say. Surely better'n some old pine bark."

He speared three big pieces on the end of a stick and handed it to her. Allie sat up and, making sure she was still covered, took the stick in her hand. The meat was hot and sweet. She'd never tasted anything so delicious.

"Better eat slow," Zach said. "Couldn't gut them proper without a knife, but I found a sharp enough rock to pretend. Still got some bones in there, probably."

Allie didn't care. She'd eat the bones, too, would eat anything. She gobbled her first helping and then asked for a second. Zach obliged.

"This is awesome, Zach. I mean it."

Zach settled in with his own portion. He blessed his before

taking the first bite. "Plenty here," he said. "I tried feeding Sam. He's too far gone right now, but we'll be full today, Allie. Full and ready."

In the rocks to his left stood a cedar sapling no more than two feet high. A black ball of dirt and roots rested beneath a pile of river rock. Smaller stones had been laid in the branches, along with dollops of moss and grass. An acorn was lodged into the topmost branch.

"What's that?" she asked.

"Figured we'd might as well celebrate," Zach said. "I done some thinking. We spent one night under the pine, the next at the pond. The rocks were after. Now the riverbank. If I figured right, it's Christmas Eve." Another grin. So tired, so beaten down. "Merry Christmas, Allie."

She studied the tree and then Zach. There was a warmth in his smile that reached places the fire never could.

Allie had no idea they had been gone that many days. She wondered how her daddy was and if he still searched for her. In a way she hoped he had given up, hoped everyone had. The pain of looking for something you've lost was tall and wide, but the pain of looking without knowing you'll ever find that something again was deep. Tall and wide could be overcome well enough, even if it made you into someone else in the end. But what ran deep in a person could loosen him from his moorings and set him adrift in the dead space between yesterday and tomorrow. That was a feeling Little Orphan Allie knew well. Should things come to that, she would rather her father give up than hang on.

What pain she felt over Marshall doing just that—giving up—was assuaged by the hope he would never have to, and for this one reason: it was Christmas Eve. The part of Allie still hardened under a cold far more dangerous and lasting than any in the woods balked at that notion. But this was different now.

She would still not allow herself to believe all the way, but if they were almost to the end, she believed that end should come at Christmastime. That's when most miracles happened.

It was a sentiment much of the town believed as well. Jake and Kate Barnett continued organizing the day's search, fanning volunteers out into the forests that lay at the foot of the mountains and passing word of the midnight vigil downtown. Marshall woke that morning to the notion that the stale, empty room next door had become a new normal. He thought the old normal had hurt enough, even if it had gone dull around the edges thanks to the fog he walked through much of the time. And though his eyes still burned from the tears he'd shed the night before (and though he could feel the soggy spots still on the knees of his jeans from bending down to lap back up the old life he'd tried to pour away), Marshall vowed to at least face the loss of his little girl straight on. This time, he would not bow to his lower self. He would not become Bobby Barnes. That kindled a hope in him, however small, much as the one that kindled in Allie even now. He found Grace asleep on the couch and felt that familiar heat of hell and longing, a heat Grace now felt as well.

2

"Merry Christmas, Zach. I think your tree is beautiful."

"Sam's okay," he said again. "He even stirred some in the night. He can move his front legs, I think. Least he did well enough jittering in his sleep. I think he was having bad dreams."

"Did you have any?"

"No," he said. "I never got that far. You?"

She remembered the cliffs and the coffin and the sound of God coming behind her. "No."

"Good," Zach said. "I stayed awake all night standin' guard."

"You didn't have to do that."

He answered, "Yes I did," and the look of his eyes—stone-set and determined—told Allie not to say otherwise.

"Thank you. That must be why I slept so good."

Zach nodded. The dip of his chin lasted a bit longer than its coming back up, giving Allie a clear view of the gash on his head. He coughed and spat onto the rocks—more blood. He said, "Your clothes are dry. Even your shoes. I made sure. You can get yourself dressed, I won't look. And I made something. Besides the tree, I mean. It's for Sam."

He pointed to a spot between the rocks and the darkwood, perhaps seven feet away. A clump of wood sat there in the shape of a rough triangle. Two gnarled limbs as long as Allie was tall had been tied into the shape of an upside-down V. Midway to where the limbs were farthest apart, three smaller branches had been lashed horizontally like steps on a ladder.

"What is it?"

"A travois. Figured we couldn't carry Sam no more, not with us maybe having a ways to go yet. We can put him on that and drag him, though. Had to take your shoelaces to make it, and one from my boot. I saved the other one for the fire bow, in case you can start another one."

There was a poison in Zach's voice he couldn't help. He hoped it wouldn't show.

Allie stroked Sam's head and said, "That's very kind of you, Zach."

She rose up and gathered her clothes, careful not to let too much of her legs show. Zach stared at the fire as she dressed.

"Don't matter, I guess," he said. "We won't take Sam nowhere till I know where to go, and I don't." The words came out tasting bitter, but Zach felt he had to say it. He had to be honest. He'd sat up all night feeding the fire and watching Allie and

Sam—protecting them, if that could be called protecting at all. Zach had used that time to do more than fix breakfast and decorate a sickly tree and fashion a misshapen barrow. He had thought long on just what to say to Allie when the night finally yielded to daybreak. After running through so many lies and omissions, he'd settled on the plain truth, as hard as it was. "I don't know what to do anymore, Allie. I don't think I ever did. All I've done is get us into more trouble. I couldn't even start the fire."

"That don't matter—"

"Yes it does," he said, and a little too loud. "And don't say it don't. I peed my pants, Allie. I peed'em because I was *scared* and I started bawling when I coughed up that blood because I was *scared* and I ran away because I was *scared*. And then I"—those pennies in his mouth, so awful—"and then I saw those eyes when It came up on me and I ran again. I ran away from you." Zach bit his bottom lip to keep it from shaking. "Because I was scared."

He looked down at a pair of hands covered with slits and cuts from all the miles they'd covered. The fire cracked and sparked in the silence between them. Allie breathed in the sweet smell of the smoke and thought of home. She thought of her father and how hard he'd tried to make things good for the two of them. How the more he'd tried, the more he'd hurt, and yet he'd tried anyway.

"But you came back," she said. "That's what matters, Zach. Not that you left, but that you came back."

That wasn't what mattered at all, at least to Zach Barnett. He knew the courage he'd always thought he had was a fleeting thing. It was something as easily lost as his daddy's hat. And even if he found it again, there was no way to hold it so tight that it wouldn't blow away once more.

"I ain't leaving you again, Allie. No matter what."

"I know you won't." She took his hand in hers and squeezed. And though that one small act felt more intimate than even the kiss they'd shared the week before Carnival Day nearly two years gone, they both let that touch linger. "I saw my momma, Zach. She was right here."

Zach fed the fire and picked at another hunk of bass. He didn't know what to tell her and settled on plain truth again.

"I didn't see no one here when I came up on you, Allie. You were just standin' there with your arms out."

"It was the light, Zach. It was the same light we saw at the pond."

"I don't know what that light was at the pond."

"She was here. I don't know what you didn't see, but I know what I did. She told me we're all goin' home soon—you and me and Sam and her. She's waiting at the red trees, Zach. Just like you said. She said all we gotta do's be brave."

"Ain't no brave left in me," he mumbled.

"She said there is. She said you're gonna find something wonderful."

"A road'd be wonderful," he said. "Or some demon repellent. Can you walk? Your feet look bad."

An understatement if there ever had been. Allie's feet looked as though they'd been dipped in the fire to roast sometime overnight. The skin was still waxy-white, but not much of it could be seen for the blackened blisters that covered them.

"Ain't got much choice, do we?" she asked. "We can't stay here. I can't feel them noways. Just fix me up a brace for my ankle, and I'll be good to go. How's your sick?"

He shrugged. "Ain't got much choice, do we? But I don't know where to go."

"I do." She turned and looked over her shoulder, to the trees along the riverbank. "Through there, Zach. On downstream. That's where Momma came from, so that's where we need to go."

"That's where *It* wants us to go."

"I know," she said. "But I know something He don't. I know where God's gonna be, Zach. So long as we know that, we can keep away. Let Him sit there waitin', we'll be long gone."

"Where's It at?"

She pointed on past the trees. "Somewhere down there's cliffs. That's where He is."

"How do you know?"

"I dreamed it. Those cliffs are a bad place, Zach, maybe the worst place of all. We can't go near there, no matter what. We stay far away, we'll be good."

Zach wavered. Going by dreams seemed just as silly as going by visions conjured by fear and freezing water. He asked himself if he didn't want to walk on past those trees because that's where those glowing eyes and sharp claws wanted them to go, or because that was where he was *afraid* to go.

Allie sighed. "Zach Barnett, it's time for me to take my morning inventory. It's a thing I always do but always kept private, but today I'm gonna say it out loud because it's something you need to hear." She looked at the sky. "Cold today. Still cloudy. Looks like we got a pressure system stalled right over our heads. But those clouds look a little thinner than they did yesterday, and that leads me to believe there might be some sun before it's all over with. Today is Christmas Eve. We're worse for the wear. Cold but not hungry, 'cause our bellies are full to bursting. We got water so long as we got river, however disgusting that water is. Sam's alive. We're alive. Something is out here close, watchin' us. That's okay too. For now, anyways. And do you know why, Zach? Because God or demon or beast don't want me finding Mary, but it don't matter. It's the fourth day we been in these here woods and the five hundred and forty-eighth since everything ended, but this here's gonna be the first day that all gets put to rest, because this is the day we bring Momma home."

She finished her speech and looked at Zach. He took a bite of fish. He wasn't hungry (in fact, Zach was so full at the moment he didn't think he'd ever be hungry again), it was just that he felt he had to do something or there would be nothing to do but answer everything Allie had just said. And he couldn't.

"I'll douse the fire," he said. "Then I'll help you with Sam."

Allie smiled. It was a thing so pretty to Zach that he felt it almost awful. They would go on, yes. He did not know to where, not with the sun hidden above the thick clouds again. He did not know to what end. Nor, he suspected, did Allie, regardless of what pretty speeches she made and what visions she thought she'd seen. And yet the reason she smiled on while Zach lowered his head was because Allie had found what he had lost.

Hope.

One that said the moorings of her life may have come loose, but what was loosed could be tied back again.

3

The morning stood gray and cold but windless. Zach packed what possessions they had, which amounted to little more than the bow drill, the travois, and what was left of the fish.

Zach considered bringing their Christmas tree as well. The sapling wasn't big and could probably fit just fine in Allie's backpack, and leaving something so pretty alone in all that ugly felt wrong, like an abandonment. But in the end he decided the tree should stay where it was, just beyond the lip of that surging gray water. He stacked more rocks around its base of dirt and old leaves and packed it down as well as he could. It wouldn't be long before the river swelled and carried that tree away, or the wind turned the green branches brown and brittle. Let some beauty be planted here, he thought, no matter how short it lasts or if no one else sees it.

Sam rested on a pillow of pine and cedar branches in the middle of the travois. The scarf still covered him and he was still breathing, had even opened his eyes and lapped the water Zach had carried from the river in his hand. Still, Zach thought the demon had taken more than hide from Allie's dog. He was but a pup. Long and full years had lain ahead of him when they'd first stepped into the woods. Now those years had become days. Hours, if Zach could not find them a way out.

In order to do that, they would need to push on soon. Zach didn't see this as a problem, even when he coughed and spit a wad of bloody phlegm. They were warm and fed and at least had a direction. No, the problem lay in the patch of darkwood where Allie had disappeared nearly ten minutes ago. So much of a man's life was spent waiting for the one he loved.

He was about to call for her when the scrub parted. Allie returned with her backpack slung over her left shoulder. Her eyes were down. Watching her feet, Zach thought, though in fact it was because Allie could not bear that questioning, hurry-up look she'd seen on his face. That expression became more questioning and less hurry-up as she padded her way toward him. Her pigtails were gone. The two bands of elastic fabric that had kept them in place were now around her left wrist. Her hair—*Just like her momma's,* Zach thought—had been pushed back in the front. Long curls hung from either side of her face. They bobbed like springs with each step Allie took.

She reached Zach and said, "What?"

He shook his head. "Nothing."

"Well, close your mouth before a fly lays eggs on your tongue. You're freaking me out."

"Sorry," he said. "Everything okay? Thought you got lost in there. Or worse."

Allie laid her backpack down long enough to tuck the fire bow inside. She was careful not to crush her lunch, which she'd wrapped in a section of Zach's coat the darkwood had left torn and dangling.

"Only thing in there's the forward march of time, Zach Barnett." She slung her arms through the loops, centering their provisions on her back. "That's a ride we can get off only once."

"What's that mean?"

"Nothing," she said. "Sam okay?"

"He drank some."

"You sure that thing'll carry him?"

"Should," he said. "We'll go slow. Might be some bumpy 'cause of the rocks, but it's best we go along the bank as long as we can. Darkwood might get close on down, but I don't want to go in there unless we have to. We'll have to carry him then. You sure we should go on ahead, Allie? If that Thing's on some cliffs ahead, the way upstream's clear. That's where town is."

"We ain't goin' to town, we're goin' to my momma. She said she's waitin' at the red trees, Zach. That's the very same thing you said after you conked out on me and Sam."

"I don't remember saying that, Allie."

"Which means what?" she asked. "I'm makin' that up just like I made up seeing Momma?"

Zach didn't say. Honesty didn't seem the best thing just then.

"You go on if you want," Allie said. "Me an' Sam's going this way. I love you, Zach, but this ain't about you no more, or even me. We keep going, even if it kills us."

Zach would have argued that point had Allie not already grasped the two handles on Sam's travois and begun pulling away. He followed only long enough to realize he wasn't leading, then caught up. Sam's body hopped up and down as the poles skipped over the rocks, but not enough to wake him. Nor did he appear to be in any pain.

That was more than Allie could say for herself. Her body hurt from sleeping on a pile of rocks all night. Her pride hurt maybe even more, having to endure that look from Zach when she came back from the scrub. Her ankle throbbed even with the new brace Zach had tied on, making her steps along the rocks sluggish and jerky. At least there were no pine branches shoved into her shoes. Allie had told Zach not to bother, she couldn't feel her feet anyway. Zach was more worried than Allie about that, and had been ever since checking her blisters before she'd walked into the scrub. He'd run a finger down the bottom of Allie's feet from her toes to her heels to make sure she wasn't fibbing. She'd felt nothing at all.

"Want me t'carry Sam some?" he asked.

"It's okay, I can manage. Least till we get to the trees."

She let Zach take over there. The trees at the water's edge were too thick to pull Sam through, and so Allie held him while Zach maneuvered the travois through to the other side. He looked for any prints that might have been left in the soft mud the night before. He found only his own.

Allie followed as Zach pulled Sam's cart through on its side, weaving among the willows and oaks. Zach turned his head before finding the bank once more. The windbreak looked small from that distance, like a stack of his Legos. The top of his Christmas tree poked up from the center.

Allie placed Sam back in his bed and took hold of the handles. She began pulling again. "He ain't there," she said.

"So you say. What's to say you're wrong?"

Allie shrugged. Or maybe it wasn't a shrug at all, just her struggling under the weight of pulling all that dog and wood. Zach couldn't tell.

"He can smell me."

"Cannot," he said. "Besides, I stink just as much as you do. If anything, it's Sam's blood that'll draw It."

"Not Sam's. Not yours, neither. It's me He smells, Zach. Me he's after."

"Well, Sam's wound's covered and mine's all dried up. And you ain't bleeding at all."

"You cain't see everything."

She tilted her head up and was met by that look again, that wanting to know.

"You remember back in the fall when the guidance counselors came and split the class up?" she asked. "Girls stayed with her, boys went with—"

"Mr. Matthews," Zach finished. He cringed at that particular memory. "What about it?"

"What'd y'all talk about?"

"I don't know. Stuff."

Stuff, yes. Hilarious stuff. Stuff Zach and everyone else joked and guffawed over in that typical boy way that was all tough on the outside but utter fear down deep. How their bodies were about to change like the caterpillar in the film Mr. Matthews had shown them. How they were all going to start growing hair in strange places and their voices were about to change. Zach remembered thinking that didn't sound like caterpillars at all. To him, it sounded like a monster had been living quiet down inside him all that while, and what was going to waken it was something so little as an extra candle on the cake. It had all been nearly enough to make him sick. Thankfully, Touchdown Tommy Robertson had beaten him to it.

"Why?" he asked. "What'd y'all talk about?"

"I didn't go," Allie said. "I never gave Daddy the paper to sign. It felt gross somehow, letting him read that. Kind of mean too. I got sent to the library until it was done."

She kept her eyes forward, on past where the riverbank bent to the right. The handles on Sam's stretcher vibrated each time the bottom poles thunked over the rocks, pinching her fingers. Allie didn't want to tell Zach more, hadn't wanted to tell him even the little she had, but in a way she felt she owed him that much. It was something she had to do even if it scared her, much the same way as she saw their trek down the riverbank. And just like that trek, the only way Allie found to deal with that fear was to put one foot in front of another and slog on.

"Turns out I coulda used a seat in there, though."

"Why? It was gross."

"You don't know gross, Zach Barnett. Pain, neither. You're just a man. That day I ran outta class? I was sick. I know you heard stuff. Probably from that old Lisa Ann Campbell, I don't doubt it."

"She told us you were cryin' and screamin' in the bathroom," Zach said. "One of the kids in the class down the hall told her, 'cause they'd heard it. I didn't believe her. Then I heard some teachers talking about it after school's over. That's when I decided I'd come see you that night, check on you."

"I'm glad you did. Lisa Ann was right. I really did cry and scream. Something fierce too. And right there on the *toilet*. I won't tell you what happened, and you won't ask if you care about me at all. But I ain't a little girl no more, Zach. I'm a woman now."

"How you know you're a woman?" he asked.

"Because I'm doing woman things."

Her eyes drifted up, fully expecting to be met with that quizzical look again. It wasn't there this time. What Allie saw on Zach's face was instead a gentle acceptance, as though what she'd just said had been plain for a long while, and to all but herself. Zach couldn't for the life of him understand how a girl became a woman just by going into the bathroom, but he didn't think that mattered. He thought Allie had stopped being a little girl a long time ago. Being hurt made you grow up, and sometimes it made you grow up before you were ready. Allie had been doing woman things ever since her momma died, cooking meals and washing clothes and tending house. She'd kept her daddy from turning into someone worse than Zach figured he could ever imagine. Of course Allie was a woman. Not because she wanted to be one, but because she had to. She'd never had a choice.

"Why you saying all this?" he asked.

"Because we're almost there."

"Almost where?"

"To the end of things," she said. "I don't know what that means exactly. I don't know if it's when we find my momma or when we just give out. Maybe it'll come when we see those eyes again. And we'll see 'em, Zach, because God chases everybody. I tried running from Him all this time, but He found me anyway. I can feel it the same way an animal feels its time's near up and just goes off to die on its own. I think you can feel it too."

Zach said nothing to this. It was either speak a lie and say no, or speak the truth and make it real. He crept alongside and took one of the handles. Allie let him, thankful her load had been halved.

"Either way," she said, "I just wanted you to know."

"That why you been going off in the woods all alone?" he asked. "To use the bathroom and see if you're still a woman?"

"No. Once you're a woman, you stay. Ain't no going back to being a kid, no matter how much you wish it. Trust me, I've wished it plenty."

"Bein' a man's the best thing ever," Zach said. His voice was quiet and full of longing as he remembered he'd never be one now. "Prolly the same to a boy as bein' a woman is to a girl."

"Not for me. All it means is that I'm moving on and leaving stuff behind. It's an end, just like this riverbank's gonna end somewhere. Only thing is I'm moving on alone. Least you got your daddy to show you how to be a man. He'd probably drive you on up to the Hollow to carve your name himself, if you'd ask. I ain't got nobody to do that. That's why Momma sent word through my compass. She knows she's gotta come back, because I can't grow up on my own."

Zach said nothing to this as well, and for much the same reason as he'd held his tongue about an end being near. He only did what he thought he should and matched his stride with Allie's, keeping beside her. On they walked over the smooth stones and muddy patches of the riverbank. Herded. Downstream, farther into the wilderness. Toward the end of things.

They kept in lockstep, heads down against the cold, their feet trundling forward in rhythm with the clattering sounds of Sam's travois. The hours wore on without a sound from the darkwood to their right. Not one snapping branch, not a single low growl. It was as though they'd become the only ones in the world again, and all that was left for Allie and Zach to battle were the pains and wants inside them. The riverbank widened farther on, making their way the easiest it had been since leaving the road some four days before. Zach, ever the optimist, saw this as a sign of blessing. Allie considered it a mark of trouble.

She knew she was right when they rounded that last small bend and saw what lay just to the horizon. In what Allie could only call one horrible and cruel act, the sun peered out from the thick clouds that very moment and shined itself there, to what lay between them and the spire of a great hill in the distance, as though God Himself wanted to make sure they saw it. The sight stopped them both. The river churned and flowed in a deep gurgle to their left. In the wind was pine and cedar and the hint of spring deep down. But neither of them could sense any of this. Their eyes were too full of the cliffs rising up ahead.

4

Allie said, "We need to turn around."

Zach shook his head no but could not answer, could only stare. A mile on, perhaps less, the water had cut its way through an entire mountain. Eons ago was his best guess, clear back to the dinosaur times, and the swift understanding of this—of just how ancient that land was, and how time could stretch so far back and yet be so clearly seen—silenced him even more than the two jagged cliffs towering over the wood. The sun appeared through a thin spot in the clouds, just as Allie had said it would. Its light winked upon those hardscrabble crags, turning the face of the cliffs from brown to yellow to the color of blood. Small, leafless bushes dotted the contours of the rock. The tops were barren but for clumps of struggling pines and cedars that sprouted like tufts of green hair atop an otherwise bald pate. Shoulders and arms of thick darkwood extended down to the river's edge. Zach shuddered at what might lie in all that tangle.

"Zach? I changed my mind. We need to turn around. For real. That's a bad place."

"Don't look bad," he answered. "What that looks like to me's the tallest thing in these whole woods. We get up there, Allie, we might be able to see the way home. Least we'll be able to take a good look at that hill further on."

"No." Allie let go of her end of the travois, threatening to spill an unconscious Sam. She caught it with one hand. The other grabbed the front of Zach's coat like a bully demanding

milk money. "Something bad's gonna happen if you go up there, Zach. Something terrible."

"How you know that?"

"I dreamed it."

"Allie—"

"God's up on those cliffs, Zach. He's waitin'. I thought we could skirt on past but we can't. Those cliffs go straight above the river and there's darkwood all around. Don't you see?"

Zach moved her fist away with two fingers and one roll of his eyes. "Don't be so stupid," he said, even if a part of him wondered if Allie was right. She'd been right about a great many things, had even started a fire. The idea of that fire being nothing but blind luck offered Zach little comfort. Allie had worked the bow drill while frozen and wet and near naked just after being attacked by a demon. She'd been so delirious that she'd even believed Sam had talked and her momma had appeared, but she'd still done it.

There was this too—if Allie was convinced that *It* was atop those cliffs, that meant the way behind them really was clear.

"We could turn around," he said. "We could go back the way we come, Allie. Upstream's town. I know it."

Allie believed that could be so, but upstream was definitely not the way to her mother. Mary hadn't come strolling *down* the riverbank, she'd come *up* it. They were close now, and they'd all go home together. All she had to do was be brave.

"Allie?" Zach asked. "We can go back. I think back's best."

"Momma's on this way."

"Allie." Soft now, and with a kindness that hid Zach's frustration. "You said something bad's gonna happen if we go this way. I don't know if your momma's there or not. I don't think you do either, deep down. So I'm askin' if you wanna risk us for something that might not be. I'm askin' if one small chance is worth your life and mine."

She thought, *Almost done, almost to the end* and she thought of that boy-size casket in her dreams, propped on its end between two scrubby pines on the cliffs ahead. In that moment, Allie found she could do nothing. The weight of her choice was too great and too awful. She was a woman trapped in the body of a tired and cold little girl, but Allie knew well the pain of living. It is the things we want most of all that require the greatest sacrifice, and in that regard Allie believed she had suffered enough for her reward. She had given her body to the woods, had surrendered her doubts and most of her fears, hoping that would prove her worthy of finding Mary again. Now the God she'd grown to loathe asked for one thing more. He wanted Zach. And though the thought of losing him frightened her, what scared Allie more was that she still faced those cliffs, and hadn't turned back.

Zach turned for her. He nudged the travois toward the river and on around, pointing it upstream as gently as he could so as not to upset Allie or Sam. And just as he lifted his boot to take that first step back, a tree cracked not a hundred yards away.

Neither of them moved. There was no further sound from the darkwood. None was needed. They had been in the forest for five days, and in many ways had come to understand that world better than the one they'd left. Zach merely steered the travois back around and pointed it to the cliffs. He began a slow stumble forward. Allie took hold of her handle and walked with him, because that's what animals did when they were herded.

"Something bad's gonna happen if we go up there, Zach."

"We ain't goin' up there. I got a plan."

"You do?"

"Yeah."

A lie (maybe the biggest Zach had ever told in his life), but one that was at least partly embedded in the truth. He at least had the first steps of a plan, and that was not to make the demon angry again. It didn't matter to him if they were going the wrong way. Sooner or later the woods had to end *somewhere*, and maybe there they would find help. Maybe they could even escape. But not now. Not with Sam near death and Allie's feet not working. Not with Zach's own clogged chest and fading courage.

They reached halfway to the cliffs when Allie asked, "What's your plan?"

"Let's sit down and rest. We can do that. It'll understand."

Staying put was better than going on ahead. Allie let go of her side of the travois and shrugged off her pack. Her shoulders hurt from pulling Sam all that way, and her fingers buzzed from the tremors of the wood bouncing over the rocks. Her ankle ached but her feet felt fine, at least in the sense that Allie couldn't feel them at all. She thought as long as they were numb they hadn't gone any worse, though she didn't have a mind to take off her shoes and socks to look. Allie had come to the conclusion that what was left of her Chucks was all that was keeping her feet whole. If she took them off, those blisters on her feet would pop and millions of black spiders could come spewing out. It was an impossible thought, utterly childish. Then again, the most frightening things often were.

Zach walked to the water's edge and gathered a handful of water for Sam. The dog's eyes fluttered from closed to the thick look of someone unsure if what he's seeing is real or not. Allie didn't ask Zach whether he thought Samwise would live. She was too afraid of the answer. Besides, she didn't think it would matter as long as they were moving toward those cliffs. Zach sat, happy to get off his feet. Allie looked at the serpentine shape of the river behind them, that wide bank leading back to their old camp. Zach only looked ahead, his thoughts plain.

"You can't go on those cliffs, Zach," she whispered. "Please promise you won't."

"It ain't up there, Allie, It's behind. I get up there, I can find a way out."

"I saw what's gonna happen if you get up there. I dreamed it. I been dreaming it a long while. Started the night we slept under the pine, next to the meadow with the tree. I dreamed I was at a funeral. Everybody was there and everybody was crying, and there was a casket."

"Whose was it?"

"It wasn't like the big ones they buried everyone in after The Storm. It was small. Like what they'd put a kid in." Allie couldn't look at him, only her shoes. Her hands appeared from somewhere. They weren't a child's hands, more an old woman's. "Dreamed it again the next night. That time I wanted to ask you who was getting buried, because I couldn't see the name on the stone. But you weren't there, Zach. Everybody was there but you and Sam, and now Sam's . . ."

She couldn't finish. The world beyond Allie's shoes was covered by the long strands of her hair. She was glad for that. It meant Zach couldn't see the tears that had welled in her eyes. Allie tried shooing them away and then thought better of it. Crying might mean it was done (and it wasn't, she thought, at least not yet), but Allie would let those tears fall if that was what convinced Zach to listen. To trust.

"The next night was the night when I figured out it was you," she said. "That was the night you bumped your head. It scared me, Zach. I ain't never been so scared, not even when those eyes were chasing me. Then last night, I had it again. Only this time there wasn't no funeral. It was just the casket. It was sitting up on its end, up on those cliffs."

"Just a dream," Zach said not long after, though with a tone Allie believed had a few tears in it as well. "Don't mean nothin', Allie. It's your fear's all. These woods ain't been kind. We both been beaten up, along with poor old Sam. You get cold and scared and beaten up, your mind starts playing tricks. You took your clothes off in all that freezing wind. That ain't what no normal person would do. You said Sam talked you through how to make that fire and you talked to your momma. You know those ain't right, Allie. In your heart, you know."

Allie brushed half of her hair behind her right ear. She looked up at him. Zach's words may have been full of doubt, but his face had gone pasty with fear. "You just have to believe," she said.

"Kinda funny, being told to believe by a girl who's fallen away."

"I got more faith than you think, Zach Barnett. Faith's all you got when all else gets taken away. Maybe Sam never talked to me at all and maybe that was never my momma, but I believe it because I'm here. I didn't die from falling in that water, and God never ate me in that darkwood. Maybe what I saw was just her sending word, like she did with my compass. That's my faith either way, and I believe it no matter what. Maybe that's the truest kind of believing there is. And that's why I need you to believe me now."

She kept her eyes on Zach, needing his answer. And though Zach's pride had remained just enough for him to make the wavering he showed seemed real enough, in truth he'd made up his mind the moment Allie had told him of her last dream.

"Are you scared?" she asked.

"Yes," he said. "Are you?"

She nodded slow. "Momma said I gotta be brave, though, so I will. I don't think it matters much whether you think she told me that or not, it holds true. You know that. Right?"

Zach did. But knowing a thing was right wasn't near the same as believing it, and believing it was a far cry from doing it.

"All I wanna do's go home," he said. "Why'd this have to happen, Allie?"

Allie panned across the darkwood and over the water, all the way to the looming cliffs, hoping something'd catch her eye that would answer his question. She saw how in some places the river swirled in tight whirlpools that unwound themselves and disappeared into the current, gone in a breath. Vast and cramped trees stretched away from the darkwood. Their limbs reached high into that thick, gray sky as though trying to rupture the bottom of heaven itself. It was the cold breeze that swept down through her hair and the way the river rocks lay dappled with every color Allie had ever seen and others she never had. She realized then that even in the deep woods, there was beauty. It was hidden and ragged, but there. It moved like a hidden river that wound its way around the hills and scrub and entwined itself around every splintery limb. It was everywhere, that beauty, and it had no need to return to itself because the fount from which it flowed never dried. And though she felt death lurking all around them, Allie Granderson found herself thankful for it. She had found a peace that only the brevity of life could bring.

"I still see that twister bearing down," she said. "I feel the wind trying to pick us all up and the rain smacking my legs like little pieces of glass. I can smell Mr. Barney's basement, all soggy and sour with fear. I can still hear me screaming for my momma because she wasn't there. But you know what, Zach? I still believed. Even then, I did. I kept my faith because I thought that was what would make everything all right again. I kept it when all that wind was gone and we all climbed out and seen everything gone. 'It's still all right, Allie,' I told myself. When me and Mr. Barney went running to look for Momma, I believed. When I hollered her name until I was hoarse, I believed. It was only when we stood there looking down at the place where Momma got taken from and seeing her pink shoe that I didn't believe no more. That's the worst part of any storm, Zach. It ain't the during. It's the after."

"But you still made it," Zach said. "We made it."

Allie shook her head. She curled a bit of hair behind her ear and looked away, toward the river. "You made it. I didn't. It was easy for you. You had your momma and Sheriff Jake. I only had my daddy, and by then he was broken. I was broken too. Or am. The days pull on me, Zach. They try to get me to carry on. But I can't and I don't want to, because carrying on means leaving my momma behind. I won't do that. I'm gonna find Momma. We're gonna take her home. She said so. Then we can all move on together. Me and her and Daddy, like it should be.

"We ain't all the way out here just to find my momma, Zach. I'm looking to find my faith and lose my fear too. Here we sit all cold and sick and beaten up, but I believe again. Almost, anyway. But I can't move on. Momma said I had to be brave. I don't think I can. I've been scared ever since she left. I didn't want to love nobody anymore, because it's the ones you love that you always lose. But we're coming to an end now one way or the other, so I'll just be bold and say I love my daddy. I love Sam. I might even love Miss Grace a little, for all she's tried to do. But I love you most of all, Zach Barnett, and I just thought you should know."

Zach sat there for a long while, peering first at Allie and then the river. The cliffs followed next. The darkwood behind them came last. It didn't seem right, going through all of what they had just so Allie could find her happiness again. He loved her and still wanted to save her, but all things considered, he'd rather she'd stayed sad back at home.

"Don't you wish everyone could just have everything they thought would make them happy?" he asked. "No one'd have to go out looking for any of it at all."

"I used to, but no more. I think it'd make a horrible world."

"Why you say that?"

Allie stroked Sam's muzzle. His eyes opened some. She

looked at Zach and offered him a tired smile. "Because then there'd be no place for love."

5

That Zach hadn't bothered to share any particulars of the plan he'd designed was enough for Allie to wonder if he'd ever had a plan at all. If he did, they'd surely be doing something besides sitting there talking about secrets and feelings.

"What're we gonna do?" she asked.

"We go on. I don't know if It's still in the scrub or up on those cliffs or nowhere at all, but we ain't in no condition to poke It. We try goin' back, I think that's what'll happen. We stay here too long, I think that'll do it too. So that means straight on."

"What about the cliffs?"

"We go under as quiet as we can. River's making such noise that if It's up all that way, It won't hear us. Problem's gonna be if It sees us. Up there, I figure a body can see for miles."

That thought kindled another in Zach, one that burned only briefly but long enough to make him wonder. He picked up a stone and tossed it into the darkwood behind them. It crashed and settled. Silence followed. The demon had either moved on or was sitting quiet.

"Maybe It really is up there, Allie. If It is, I bet that's where It's gonna stay. It's lyin' in wait, thinking that's where we'll head. That's where I meant to go before you told me about your dream. That's where anyone who knew about the woods would go."

"God," Allie corrected. "Where *God* is, Zach."

"Whatever, it don't matter. What I'm sayin's maybe It ain't up there to spy on us, but to make sure we don't climb up and take a look. We stay along the bank, maybe we'll be left alone."

"You sure about that?"

He shook his head. "But right now that's all I got."

They set out as smartly as they could, just in case either of them changed their mind. Sam was already loaded in his cart. Allie took the left handle and began pulling, Zach the right. He eased toward the tree line just long enough to pry a thick limb from among the scrub. Part of him lied and said he wouldn't need a club. Another part said a hunk of branch would prove no more worthy a weapon than the one he'd carried before. It felt good in his hand nonetheless.

No noise could be heard other than the hiss of the water and the rat-a-tat of the travois over the rocks. The stone face of the cliffs had looked smooth far back. Now it appeared more layered, checkered by bushes and trees that somehow hung on by their roots, defying gravity. Zach thought he caught a flutter of movement at the top. Sam's eyes opened again, his nose catching a scent. He offered a weak but rebellious growl.

"Can you go faster?" Zach asked.

"Yes."

Allie pulled with all her might, willing her legs to move. She stared at the ground, not wanting her dead feet to misstep and not daring to look up, to find those eyes looking down at her. Zach guided the travois closer to the river's edge, meaning to keep as far from the side of the cliff as possible. His chest began to seize. He coughed and spit onto the rocks. Shadows danced in front of his eyes.

As they neared, Zach saw a mound of rocks stacked along the bank on the other side of the cliffs. Hundreds of them, as big around as he was wide, forming a barrier between the darkwood and the bank in a long parallel line. In all their time in the woods, Zach had only seen one thing crafted by human hands. Now there were two. There was something about that pile of stones he found familiar—something he felt he should know—but the only thing Zach could settle upon was that the mound was no more natural than the sign they'd found reading WARE, NO FARTHER. A thought so quick and unlikely that he believed it could be true sprouted in his mind—*Allie's momma made that to warn us away.*

Their pace had grown to a near jog, bringing them into the cliff's shadow. Twenty more steps and they'd be on its other side. Fifteen, if they hurried more. And then what? Keep running, he thought. Run until they could run no more, and then find a place to hide. Survive. That's all living was, anyway. The woods had taught Zach that. He parted his lips to let the cold air in. The pain in his chest was unbearable, as was the nail hammering into Allie's ankle each time her right shoe slapped the ground.

In ten feet, they met the cliffs. In twenty, the cliffs were behind them. Allie tried steering them close to the mound, using it to hide them. Her right foot caught against her left ankle. She stumbled into the wall of rocks, knocking three of them free and onto the travois. Zach's pole was yanked from his hand, spinning him around. Allie's yelp as she fell was drowned by Sam's howl as he was thrown onto the bank.

Allie tried to stand as Sam crawled to her. Only his two front legs worked, and those only barely. She took him in her arms.

"I'm sorry," she said. "I slipped, Zach."

Sam trembled against Allie's chest. Zach waved his staff like a bat, moving it in wide circles. He searched the darkwood for any movement and saw none. Allie's side of the travois lay tilted, its back pole sunk beneath a layer of the mound's rocks.

"It's stuck," he said.

He ran to the back of the travois and tried pulling the pole away. It wouldn't give. Allie remained in a position that was half sitting and half lying down. Something stirred in the darkwood ahead, turning all three of their heads.

"Help me, Allie." Zach's voice sounded cracked and near frantic. "Help me get these rocks off. Do it quick."

She laid Sam down and scurried to where Zach knelt. The stones were big, larger than basketballs, but thicker and much heavier. Moving them felt like moving small mountains. Allie managed to roll one free, Zach another, but the last was too heavy and something was moving in the trees, something big and hungry, and when that something growled it frightened Allie so purely that she rose to scream, her broken mind wanting to ask God to please give them *Just one blessed minute,* and the words came out a sob as she watched what made its way onto the riverbank a few hundred feet in front of them. Moving from the darkwood over the rocks like a brown mist. One that gathered and grew into a shape more towering than Allie could grasp.

From that body grew two eyes, one white and one red, that burned as bright in the day as they had in the night.

It wasn't a demon, as Zach had thought. Nor even Allie's God.

It was something worse.

6

Allie thought it was a bear until she realized no bear could grow that size. It stood as motionless as the rocks beside them on a wide part of the riverbank that shrank to a narrow strip on either side of its massive body. Its coat was a dense layer of matted brown broken by a patch of white that ran from four long legs as thick and strong as a horse's thighs to the center of a chest that was higher than Allie could reach on tiptoes. Meaty shoulders twice the size of the rocks she and Zach had just tried to move rose above that chest, leading to a thick neck crowned by a domed head. The bear's snout was short and cropped, with black nostrils that flared in the wind. A cloud of fog gathered in the air as he sniffed. His eyes, not forward of his head but almost to the side, glowed.

Even from that distance, Allie could see the long black knives at the end of the bear's paws, and how they almost curled downward into the rock and mud. Talons more than claws, and able to cleave flesh and bone with even less effort than they had the oaks and maples back at the pond.

The bear took a single step forward. Muscle churned beneath rippling fur.

"Don't look at him, Allie," Zach whispered. "Look down."

Allie did as he said. She slowly bent and scooped Sam into her arms, telling him not to move, not to make a sound. Sam obeyed the latter well enough, but nothing Allie did could settle the shivers that had fallen over him. The dog's eyes were wide with fear. The bear remained where it was, staring at them. Smelling them. Tasting them already.

She felt those eyes pulling at her. Wanting her to look.

"What do we do, Zach?"

Zach didn't hear. He'd told Allie to look away but couldn't do so himself, overcome by the impossibility of a living thing so large. A bear, he'd thought at first. Zach still believed that true, even if the thing watching them was unlike any bear he'd ever known. A bear would be a terrible thing, yet it would almost be a relief given what his mind had conjured living behind the eyes that had chased him. But this bear stood well over six feet on his four legs, taller than Zach's father. And when it moved three steps closer, it was with the quiet grace of a wolf.

"We can't run," he said. "That's what it's waiting for us to do, Allie. That's when he'll charge."

"What do we do?" she asked again. Allie would not look up. Had she, her eyes would have filled with what Zach saw next—the bear dropping to a low crouch, his left legs a short distance ahead of his right, taking the position of a sprinter ready to explode from the blocks. Neither of them expressed it, but both longed for their fathers in that moment. Mothers promise their children comfort from hurt and fathers promise protection from the bad things in the world, and what Allie and Zach saw in that bear was all the bad in the world. Yet as the bear took another step forward, Jake Barnett was miles away, knocking on doors to tell the people who opened them of the midnight service. Marshall Granderson was farther still, standing with Grace Howard at the foot of a grave that held a single pink shoe and mourning the knowledge that what would go into the grave beside it was the scarf he'd found in Bobby Barnes's truck.

"The rocks," Zach finally said. He gripped the staff in his hands. "We gotta go up the rocks, Allie. We have to do it slow."

"It can get up on the rocks, Zach. It's bigger than the rocks." Her head still down, yet Allie felt the bear's eyes upon her, that unwavering stare wanting to lift her chin.

"The water, then. I'll take Sam. We'll jump in and swim to the middle. The current will take us."

"We'll die."

"We'll die here too."

The pull on her was stronger now, as though Allie was being hypnotized from far off. The buzzing sound returned to her ears, followed by a throbbing in the center of her stomach. She shook her head no, even as the rest of her said yes. The small voice inside her that had spoken often in the woods now spoke for a final time:

There's nothing you can do, Allie. Do you understand now? There's nothing you could have ever done about anything.

Allie lifted her chin. The bear's eyes blinked, the red one first and the white one second, like a ripple. And with a roar like a wind she had heard only once before, it charged.

7

The bear covered half the distance between them before Zach understood what was happening. Even then, he could not move. The link between his eyes and his mind had been muddied by the spell of such power and speed. The muscles beneath the bear's thick hide pulsed as he raced forward. Claws longer than the fingers Allie used to cover her eyes clacked against the river rock. Each paw landed in the precise spot where the ground would not give way, propelling him forward. Huffs of breath streamed from his nostrils like steam from an engine. The red and white eyes narrowed into slits that only magnified their light. To run seemed less than fruitless. Seemed, almost, an irreverence. They were in the presence of something so far beyond themselves that it could not exist even in their dreams, and so Zach could only do what he'd done on Carnival Day as that dark funnel bore down—he lowered his head and waited for the end.

It was Allie's scream that saved them, one filled not only with terror but despair and anger as well, lifted from her very depths. The sound crashed into Zach. He lifted his head to the sight of the bear slowing—only for a moment—and its eyes widening in surprise. Zach took hold of Allie's arm and pulled her up the rock pile's slope, gripping her as she gripped Sam. Their legs became pistons struggling to find traction on the boulders. When no traction could be found, they fell to their hands and knees and scrambled. Zach's chest tightened. His breaths came in shallow spurts as he crested the pile. He scurried to the other side just as the bear reached the edge of the mound and yelled for Allie to move faster. He grabbed her shoulder and jerked her over the side as the bear began to climb, caring not what part of her or Sam he damaged in the process. Allie wrenched herself free long enough to collect one small rock. She threw it at the beast, striking him in the neck. The stone bounced away like a swatted bug, making him roar again.

Allie stumbled down, crying out again as she landed on her sprained ankle. The riverbank ended there and the darkwood began. There was no deliberating this time, no pondering dangers and what-ifs. They ran headlong into the tangle and wormed their way through the thickets and brambles. Moving as fast as they could without regard for the clamor they made. Wanting only to get away.

Zach used his best judgment to navigate. The darkwood rose in a shallow climb over a rise. The cliffs stood to their left, the bear to their right. Escape could only come straight on and only through speed. He gripped Allie's free hand. Branches whipped at their faces, scraping Allie's brow and the wound on Zach's head, bringing tears to his eyes and small cries that escaped his lips.

They heard nothing. The bear had either lost them or had decided to take another way. Allie stumbled. Her hand slipped from Zach's and she fell hard, first to her knees and then her stomach, rolling at the last moment so as not to crush Sam beneath her. Zach picked her up and dragged her on as the ground sloped upward. The crowded shrubs and trees smelled dank and earthy, like something rotting. Nothing beyond the reach of their arms could be seen.

Something snapped to their left, halting them. Allie's eyes were wide and searching. She managed a single sound:

"Hide."

Zach shook his head. To stay put was to invite their end. He held a single wobbly finger to his mouth, needing only one more sound, a single step on a single limb. That sound came seconds later, ahead and to the right.

He moved his finger from his lips and mouthed *quiet*, then pointed left and led Allie on. She covered Sam's mouth. They stepped slow and soft, minding the snarls of limbs and leaves at their feet, taking care to move the branches around their legs and chests just enough to let them pass. The darkwood fell silent again as Zach led them up, bearing left more, to where the bear had already passed.

Allie let him lead and kept a cautious eye behind. Zach held the branches back for her to pass. She did so, keeping her body as far from their tips as she could. Her numbed feet and swollen ankle seemed intent on steering Allie straight into them, rubbing her scent on every limb and shriveled leaf, leaving behind a smell that might as well have been a neon sign pointing the bear their way. She heard another crunch, this one more distant and farther behind. Sam squirmed in her arms. Allie hugged him closer, pressing the scarf over his wound against her jacket.

They were guided more by the day's fading light than Zach's senses. Pockets of early evening oozed through the scrub, and these open spaces became their map. Allie's legs burned for rest. Zach had given himself over to long gasps through his mouth that came back out in whistles, as though his breaths were mired in their own darkwood. They found the trail the bear had blazed, a wide strip of broken scrub that allowed them to move in relative silence. Zach kept them left, from where the beast had come. They spotted a break in the trees. Zach took her hand again and led Allie there, using his staff to ease away the few limbs the bear had missed.

Ahead the darkwood ended in what appeared to be another

meadow. The soggy stink of the scrub turned sweeter in the open air, mixing with the scents of cedar and pine. A marbled gray sky stretched before them. To their left, past a line of sickly evergreens struggling in the rocky earth, glimmered a sunset Zach would have taken a particular interest in had he stopped to notice it. But Zach didn't see that sunset at all. His eyes were ahead instead, and full of terror.

There was no open land in front of them, only a tapered channel that faded and disappeared fifty feet ahead, where the sound of rushing water rose from far below. From their place atop the cliff, the river appeared as a thin artery winding its way through a body of a dying giant. Zach spun and faced the darkwood. The only thought in his mind was if where he stood now was where his coffin had stood in Allie's dream.

He found her standing to his left, holding Sam tight.

"We have to leave, Allie," he said. "We gotta go right now."

Allie heard his warning but couldn't move. Her eyes had been drawn to the left, where she'd turned to the small, withering pines that lined the very edge of the cliff. Some part of her mind understood that Zach had led them to the cliffs even if it was the one place both of them had sworn not to go. It was where the bear would be. Where the coffin had been. But that tiny bit of comprehension had been overridden by the trees in front of her. A sliver of sun setting over the hill beyond struck there and lit the thin spaces between the limbs, making the branches and needles glow from dull green to light brown and finally—

"—Red," she whispered. "Zach, the trees are red."

"What?"

Zach stared not at the trees but back to where they'd come from, watching as the darkwood began to part. To his mind, the bear appeared not to come out of the brush but *grow* from it—as though it were more trees and plants and forest than flesh and blood and teeth.

It crept onto the cliff top. Zach placed Allie behind himself and backed them both farther onto the cliff as she screamed, "Momma, I'm here Momma!" and the red and white eyes bore down. Zach backed them away more, trying to keep himself upright.

"Momma, Momma, where are you?" Shouting it as she scanned the narrow bluff—behind the few trees; down the sheer stone side beside her; into the darkwood itself, seeing nothing but emptiness and the bear moving toward them. Sam bucked in Allie's arms. He wailed at the pain in his crushed body and growled through his cries.

Those eyes bore in on Sam. The bear growled back. There was thunder in that call, the noise of wind and crumbling stone. Close now, that moving mountain taller than many of the pines they had passed and wider than every place they'd sought shelter. Coming for her.

"Momma," Allie tried once more, and in a voice so low the bear's huffs swept it away, she added, "please help us."

And yet even then, Mary Granderson would not answer. Allie backpedaled on one bad ankle and two blackened feet as the bear crouched, digging his claws into the dirt. His eyes pulsed and shimmered. No help would come. Allie knew this with the same certainty with which she knew the bear would cleave her in half, but it wouldn't be the claws and teeth that ended her. Hope would do that—hope dashed. That was what had killed Allie time and again ever since The Storm. At least this death would come only once.

Zach moved Allie back as far as he could. A clump of withered pines stood just behind them. Beyond was only sky. He stopped as the bear slowly closed in. Its head lay low and forward, body crouched—just as it had on the riverbank before sprinting for them. Its mouth moved but it did not growl. To Zach, the beast seemed to be smiling, mocking its prey.

All their time in the woods, he believed he served little more purpose than to be the well from which Allie drew her strength. Now at the end, he found Allie was the source of his. Zach no longer saw the bear. He saw only Allie screaming for a mother who wasn't there and her world crumbling before her very eyes, and he knew that would be her final memory of this world. All the thoughts of all his failings fell away in that single moment. What replaced them was a burning to fight, to protect the one he loved even if it meant his own end. There is a kind of bravery born from understanding that what lies in front of you is merely the end result of every choice you've ever made, and there is nothing left but to follow that path to its end. And if death should indeed sling its arrows, Zach swore they would pierce his chest and not his heels.

The hunk of wood in his hand shot forward even before Zach willed it. He took one step and raised his arms high, and when he screamed it was a call of both war and defiance that echoed over the cliffs and the bear into the very darkwood that had haunted him for days. He stood forward this once and final time. For himself. For Allie.

Zach Barnett would run no more.

8

The bear stopped as Zach's cry of war washed over it. Its front left paw hung in the air. That wide, compact head swung away from Allie and to him. The eyes became flaming slits. A long string of drool fell in a wet line from its bottom jaw onto the dust and rocks. Canine teeth the color of chalk grew from the bear's jowls, each longer than Zach's index finger and twice as wide.

That look did little to strengthen Zach's conviction, but the bear's pause did. The branch of oak in his hands appeared as a toothpick against the hulk of fur and muscle now turning to him. His father's words came back to him about what to do should Zach ever find himself in the path of a bear—don't run, don't look it in the eye, make yourself as big as possible, slowly back away. Zach had declared the first no longer an option. Nor the last—he could back up only to Allie, who had retreated to the scrawny pines behind them, screaming for Mary to come. He could not back away more, had to keep as much distance between the bear and Allie as he could. Besides, moving back would mean Zach would have to look away from the bear, and he couldn't seem to do that. Those lights held him. They were horrible. They were beautiful.

The bear landed his left paw. A low growl worked up from its chest. Zach did all he could of making himself big, arching his back and puffing his shoulders, waving the staff in wide half circles.

"Turn off," Zach yelled. "Get on, beast. Go back to the hell you come from."

He jabbed the air—"Back!"—moving the bear away as Allie stooped to lay Sam in a ball upon the ground, "Back!" as the bear began a slow retreat away from the cliff an inch at a time, "Back!" as he realized too late that the bear was not backing away at all, but only crouching for a pounce.

Zach let out another scream and charged before the bear could do the same. He brought the staff down at an angle from his right shoulder to his left foot, aiming for the snout. A paw larger than Zach's own head shot out and up. The bear's claws sheared the chunk of wood in half before it came near, peppering the air with splinters that struck Zach's face and eyes, blinding him. The blow came so fast that his hands didn't have time to let go of the wood. Zach felt a tearing sensation in his shoulders and flew sideways, rolling headlong into the rough trunk of a cedar. He looked up, blinking away the fog falling over his eyes, that same black-and-gray mist that had fallen over Zach when the woods emptied at the pond and when he fell away near the rocks, shadows that fell over his eyes. He couldn't see. The fog consumed him. He curled into a ball as the fog was pierced by the lights of two blinding eyes.

The bear rose on its hind legs, eclipsing the darkening sky. Its jaws opened. And though Zach had vowed to stand firm, he had made no such vow to do so quietly. His scream was different this time, full of fear rather than courage. It came nearly as loud as the bear's roar.

The first rock came then, clipping the beast where Zach's staff had missed, square on the snout. The bear rocked sideways and landed its front paws mere feet from Zach's head. Another rock followed, finding its ribs, angering it even more. Zach turned his head to see Allie making a slow march forward. Her left arm lay folded in front of her body. In the space where Sam had been were now three stones the size of her fist. She drew back and fired the next, letting out a sharp "*Momma!*" as she did, the way pitchers sometimes *oomphed* when trying to sneak a fastball by a ready batter.

The rock thudded against the hump on the bear's back. She watched its eyes shrink, as though the bear were staring down the sights of a loaded gun. It wheeled in Allie's direction. She began to shake as she backed toward the place where she'd laid Sam. She tripped over her pack and called for Mary again. The bear took three quick steps forward. Allie picked herself up and backed away more. The first branches of the lonely pines near the cliff's edge brushed the edge of her jacket.

Two rocks. Two rocks left. She aimed the first and threw it as hard as she could, willing it toward the eye that glowed white. The stone caught nothing but air and sailed past, skittering into the darkwood. Sam crawled toward the bear on his two good legs, lips drawn back in a snarl. Allie called for him to attack, but Sam could do little more than drag her bloodstained scarf behind him. Allie's last rock flew no better than the one before. By now she was shaking so hard and breathing so fast that her body had left her control. That last pitch fell short. The bear kicked it away and lowered its head once. She took one last step back and tripped again, tumbling beneath the bottom branches of the pine. She pushed her feet against the ground, trying to move her body farther in, but the tree was too small. The beast bared his teeth. Smiled.

She heard the river roil below and felt the cold breeze against her face, saw a faint curve of moon peering from an otherwise blank sky. Allie had been so afraid of life ever since her momma left, could not bear the thought of carrying on. But there at the cusp of death, to carry on was all she wanted. One second longer, one breath more. It was the final lesson of their long journey, one as bitter as it was sweet.

She cried out. It was Zach who answered. Allie had drawn the bear's attention away long enough for him to gather himself up and make a final charge. He ran across the narrow strip of earth full bore, ignoring the swelling in his lungs and the weight in his legs, and just as the bear leaned back, Zach yelled and leaped. He landed hard on the bear's hump. All Allie heard was that scream, and all she saw were two skinny arms searching for a place to grab in all that hide and might.

His arms barely reached past the sides of the bear's neck, but it was enough for the bear to be caught in surprise. Zach beat his fists on the bear's head and ears, and though that pummeling would have stopped any child and even most men, it did nothing to slow what Allie had come to view as the inevitable. The bear reared back again and then flung his weight forward, dipping his head to the ground. Zach spilled forward in a writhing heap of arms and legs, landing hard on his back just to Allie's side. His eyes were open but blank. He tried sitting up, wanting to keep himself between the bear and Allie. He couldn't. The world spun too fast. It held too much pain.

Allie felt beneath the pines behind her for anything, everything. She threw pinecones and handfuls of needles and what rocks her hands could find. Still the bear inched forward, eyes shining, mouth open in a grin. Her fingers closed on a smoothed section of branch. Allie sat up, putting herself between the bear and Zach. The bear drew his paw back, aiming at the place where her pigtails once were. She raised the branch high over her head and tried to scream. Nothing came from her throat but a tired squeak.

The cliff grew still for what felt to Allie like eternities. Only the wind moved along the cliff top, and only enough to gather in the fringes of her hair. The bear's eyes dimmed like two falling stars as its paw eased back upon the ground. Its ears, perked straight as Sam had once perked his tail, flattened behind his head. Allie saw that one of them had been bloodied by Zach's flailing. It backed away slowly and turned when it got farther on, easing toward the darkwood with a gait that reminded Allie of something far old and fading.

Zach struggled to his elbows and then his knees. The first fingers of night crept over the wood, making the beast appear as a waving brown blob in his cluttered eyesight. His breaths were throttled with fear and gunk.

"What happened, Allie?" he asked.

Her voice shook—"I chased him."

But that didn't sound right, couldn't be. Nothing like that could be chased.

Allie lowered her arm as the last shadows of evening settled over what rested in her hand. She moved her fingers across the branch, feeling the chips and cracks. And then the hairs on Allie's arms straightened as she realized it wasn't a piece of wood at all.

It was a bone.

9

Allie dropped what she held in her hand. It made a clinking sound as it landed in the dirt, as though hollow inside. The tip bounced and landed against her left leg. Zach's head swooned as he crawled forward from the pine and stood. He felt as able to walk as Sam, but he wouldn't let the dog be so far away. Right then, he felt they all needed to be as close to one another as possible.

The sight of him scooping Sam into his arms and stumbling back was something Allie saw only peripherally. Her attention centered upon the splintered and dulled piece of ivory against her thigh, barely aware that her stomach was fluttering in a way that meant neither nausea nor a woman's labors. Zach sat beside her and faced the tangle. He didn't think the bear was done, at least not yet, though the manner in which it had left at least signaled that *something* had changed. Evening was near gone. On its heels was a dark he no longer feared. Zach knew now what monsters lurked in that wood—the Bad Things, as Allie had said once.

His hand searched for her knee and settled on something hard. A quiver settled over him when he looked down.

"What's that?"

Allie lifted her head and then the bone. It tingled in her hand.

"Where'd you find that?"

"I don't know," she said. "I was just grabbing for stuff to throw and grabbed this."

She turned around and felt beneath the first sagging pine. Zach laid Sam down. Neither of them spoke as they rooted; both were too afraid of what words the shaking inside them would form. Sunk just beneath a thin layer of browned needles were more bones, scattered in a rough line extending perhaps five feet behind the tree. Zach found part of a rib and half a pelvis. Allie, a hand and the mate to the bone that had chased the bear. A lump lay buried beside a rotting pinecone. She brushed the needles off and pried it away.

Allie had gone so long without taking a breath that she'd begun to think she'd forgotten how. As she took in the dark outline of the skull in her hands, she remembered once more. The cold air of the woods entered into her lungs in a short, stuttering gasp and was held there, trapped. She tilted the skull to the sky. Cracks spider-webbed down from the crown to the two empty holes that had once held eyes.

The tip of a lower jaw rested in the depression. Allie handed the skull to Zach and dug it free. She saw a thin, glimmering strand beneath and pulled it from the earth like a loose thread.

The chain had dulled to a muddy brown from so many seasons, but the gold cross still shone. It was not as bright as Allie had seen it along the riverbank, but enough to illuminate the fingers that held it.

"Allie," Zach whispered. He looked from the necklace to the skull in his hands (it had become heavier these last seconds, almost too much for him to hold) and laid it on the ground with a gentle reverence. He wanted to brush his hands against his coat and cursed himself at the thought. "It can't be, Allie. It just can't."

She rubbed the cross, smearing it with blood that leaked from a slit on her thumb. Allie shook her head. She had cut herself at some point, scrambling up the rocks or through the brush or along the cliff top or all three, it didn't matter because her whole body felt cut just then, felt bleeding, and it also didn't matter because Allie did not care about any of those pricks now, no more than she cared about the blisters on her feet or her swollen ankle. There was only that pressing at the backs of her eyes and the burn in her nose, and how the world had blurred like she'd gone underwater.

The first tear gathered in the corner of her left eye. It waited to be beaten back with a bite of the lip or a shake of the head, but Allie only sat there. The drop swelled. It freed itself in a single bead that raced down her cheek past the corner of her mouth, settling at the top of her chin. There it dangled before falling with a faint slapping sound to the ground, one that Allie barely heard and Zach heard not at all. All those miles in the wilderness, the unending cold and gnawing hunger, even the bear that surely stalked them still, none of these entered Zach's thinking. He could only stare at the bones of Mary Granderson.

Allie's mouth twisted into a grimace. She bent forward, overcome by the dam bursting inside her that surged from her eyes and nose, a deluge she felt leaking from her very pores. All the hope she'd found and lost. All the days she'd refused to let pass by. Cards she'd bought and signed and tucked into a living room drawer. Hours spent mopping and dusting and keeping a clean house for her momma to come home to.

All of that mourning. Poured out.

There upon that lonely crag of rock, the air filled with wounded howls muffled not by the wind but by the blanket of needles pressed against Allie's face as she covered the bones with her own broken body. She tried to gather them all into her arms, wanting one last embrace. Zach laid his body over hers. He did not tell Allie everything would be all right; such notions had long passed. He did not offer counsel; none could be given. Zach only shut his eyes as the stone over Allie's heart rolled away. He let her tears come, because crying meant it was over.

Allie sniffed, tried to push herself up. Zach moved away as she rose to her feet. She felt him following her across the cliff. He veered off to their left, saying something. Allie kept walking. She stopped at the edge of the darkwood, at the place where the bear had gone. No sound came from inside, but Allie said, "Thank you." Then she lifted her head to the sky, on past where the moon shone down over breaking clouds, above the stars themselves. The tears stung her eyes as she spoke again: "Thank you."

"Allie?" Zach said. "Come here."

She wiped her eyes and turned. Zach had drifted to the far edge of the cliffs, facing the direction they'd come. The breeze fluttered his coat in quiet snapping sounds, yet his body had gone rigid. Allie looked to make sure Sam was still safe and went to him. Zach took her hand in his right and pointed with his left. He spoke one word.

"Look."

At first, Allie believed she would cry again. She bit her lip and sucked it back instead, thinking there would be time enough for that. Her hand squeezed Zach's. His squeezed back.

Far below lay the river and the bank upon which they'd trod nearly two whole days. Ahead and to their left, trees and hills and deadwood stretched on into forever, growing to blue mountains.

But it was to the right Zach's finger pointed. To the sliver of land where hills and deadwood yielded to the flat squares of fields and the town lights beyond.

10

They gathered what bones they could. There was no telling if the ground had returned them all, not with so many pieces and so little light. Zach said they could wait for morning to be sure, but Allie found she could not do that to him. Not after Zach had come so far and done so much. Not after seeing the pain on his face and that longing for home. They remained atop the cliff a while longer, feeling through the needles and dirt for any hard thing, laying it all together under Sam's drowsing eyes. Allie took care not to let the bones form a pile, feeling that somehow wrong. She left a small space between each instead. When the time to leave had come, Zach retrieved Allie's backpack and brought it to her. Even now, he did not look inside.

She unzipped it and set aside the fire maker and what was left of the fish, then packed the bones inside. The skull went in last. Allie could not look at it without crying. She held the pack horizontal in her arms like an offering as Zach led them back into the darkwood. He carried Sam at his chest. The dog wavered between sleep and wakefulness. He lifted his head over Zach's shoulder and peered at Allie. She smiled and called him a good boy.

Finding the river was easy enough. The sound of rushing water was the only thing they heard, and Zach figured all they really had to do was keep heading downhill. He stepped soft through the tangle of branches and burrs, easing them aside for Allie before taking his place ahead of her again. They did not speak. Zach kept his eyes to the crowding night. Allie said not to worry, the bear would leave them alone now. She did not know how she understood this and gave it over to the God of sharp edges. He'd brought Allie to her mother, and her mother would keep them safe.

They found the mound of rocks. The remaining stone that had pinned the travois had been moved away. Next to the place it now rested, Zach found a single print of five long claws. He laid Sam on top and snugged the scarf around him. Allie removed the bones from her pack and arranged them between Sam and the front of the travois as best she could. It felt better now, having Mary lie under the open sky just a while longer. Allie draped her backpack over the bones so none of them would spill. Sam perked a bit at the responsibility of not only keeping his master safe but his master's treasure as well.

"It's gonna be a long way," Zach said. "We ain't never walked here at night before."

"I'm able so long as you can craft another splint for my ankle. How's your breathin'?"

His breathing didn't sound good at all, but Zach's grin looked fine. "Home for Christmas," he said. "We hurry, we might even beat Santa."

He set her ankle between two sections of oak he broke across his knee and tied with the bootlace from the fire bow. They set out for the tall hill ahead. Zach took one end of the travois and Allie the other. Before long, the sound of *thunk-thunk* joined with the wind and the water and the gentle clapping of the bones, making an orchestra that sounded to Allie like the angels who once told shepherds the future had been saved.

The darkwood stirred once not too far on—one snapping branch that bent just enough to catch their attention. Zach nearly screamed loud enough to soil himself, believing it to be an ambush. Allie showed no such fear. She stopped and peered into the deep trees as though pondering the mysteries of the world, then pulled her side of the travois away from the bank.

Zach gripped his side hard and asked, "What're you doing?"

"It's this way," she said. "Come on."

"It's in there, Allie."

She looked at him and smiled. "I know. This way, Zach."

He had no choice but to follow. Zach looked back, meaning to grab one of the bones. Mary's bones had been what had driven the bear away, her bones and nothing more, and he believed waving a leg or arm or even a bit of shoulder in front of the beast's face would be like wielding a cross in front of a vampire or shooting a werewolf with a silver bullet. Yet there was no need for talismans, real or imagined. The darkwood in that place was only a small patch; after a dozen steps the scrub ended at an expanse of olden woods much like what had greeted them that first day so long ago. The land here was flat and open, covered with a carpet of leaves that did not so much as bob the ends of the travois. Moonlight leaked down through the canopy, making the world bright. Another crack echoed ahead. Allie put the sound in front of her and turned the travois there. By then Zach was too tired to argue.

The woods ceded to a wide meadow farther on, one populated not by screaming trees but giant stones. To their left the ancient forest stood tall and silent, so tightly packed that it appeared as one tree rather than thousands. Past the meadow the bear called again, leading them over a small rise with another cracking branch. They followed a trail blazed by sound rather than sight through the deep woods, skirting steep ravines and places Allie believed had been darkened by more than the night—places where she thought the bad things truly were. They walked long through that twisty land, slowed by burdens carried within and without. Then, as though the night's events had finally tired him, the bear let out a single growl from the shadows.

This time it was Zach who altered course first, and it was he who received the first glimpse of their journey's end. There, only a few hundred steps more (which seemed miles to both of them; a sorry thought, given they both knew there would be miles more ahead), moonlight fell through the bare branches of oak and maple to reveal their end. It glimmered off the iron bars of a rusty gate. And on the other side, a flat blankness that could only mean a road.

"Allie," he said.

"I see it."

"I never knew."

"Me neither."

The forest fell silent once more as they neared the rusty bars of the gate that guarded the entrance to Happy Hollow. Zach twisted and leaned the travois around the last of the trees and finally crossed to the other side, stepping onto a mix of clay and stone that made the most beautiful road he'd ever seen. Allie paused there and turned for a final look. She spied a flicker of two lights, one red and one white, in a patch of darkwood. There for only a moment, and then gone. For good, she believed, at least as far as Allie Granderson was concerned. She swore never to return to that wood. And yet Allie would do just that once more years later, this time to lose something rather than find. The God of sharp edges does not mock the promises we stake to our futures, though at times He does chuckle.

Zach let go of his hold on the travois long enough to stoop for a sharp rock at his feet. He walked back to the gate and regarded it, then slowly carved two names into the crossbar at his face.

ZACH BARNETT read one.

ALLIE GRANDERSON the other.

11

The road would have made walking a delight to anyone not plagued by hardened feet, sprained ankles, and worn joints. It was not town but may as well have been; Zach knew exactly where they were. More, he knew the way. That narrow road led to a wider one of gravel not far on and then to pavement, and that pavement brought them three hours later to the old wooden road sign reading Welcome to Mattingly. By then, the mere act of placing one foot in front of the other had become an act of torture. The cold felt like a wall pressing against them from the top and front, hunching them over. Sam had fallen silent and would not even perk when Allie waved the last bites of fish in front of his nose. Whether it was sleep or death, Allie thought her dog had done all he could; his fate now rested in how soon they could get help.

Andy Sommerville's BP station was long shuttered for the night. The houses beyond (including the very neighborhoods Allie and Zach had passed in a former time as their former selves) stood dark and empty. Only a spattering of electric candles and wooden reindeer bore witness to their return. They stopped at the first few homes and beat on the windows and doors, crying for someone to please help. No one answered. To Allie, it was as if the town had emptied. Or—and this was far worse—that the townspeople had grown so callous as to let the cries of two lost and broken children and their equally broken dog go unheeded.

"We'll stop at the sheriff's office," Zach said. "Daddy always leaves the back door unlocked. We'll call from there. Least we'll be warm."

Past the neighborhood stood Miller's Bridge and the glow of Main Street. At the sight of that, their slow pace quickened. Allie eased the burden of her ankle by leaning on Zach's shoulder. They'd reached the midway point of the bridge when he came to a sudden stop against the railing and looked down at the water. Zach shook his head slowly. When he looked at Allie, she saw wonder and regret on his face.

"I was wrong," he said.

"About what?"

"Water's goin' the wrong way. I thought town was upriver.

It ain't. It's down, Allie. Downriver. If we'd've gone the way I wanted when we found the river, we'd still be out there."

Allie looked at him and shrugged. When that didn't work, she smiled and pulled at the travois, hoping Zach would put the bad behind him and move on. Really, that's all anyone could ever do in life.

"He was only meaning to help," she said. "The bear, I mean. That wood's a bad place, Zach. It's the Holler, and we found out all those stories our parents scare us with about the Holler are true. There's bad things there, bad things like all those shadows we thought we didn't see and whatever thing killed that poor doe. But the bear wasn't one of them. It marked us back at the pond, just like I said—like I was scared of. It was only after we started walking home that I thought about how those marks were."

"What do you mean?"

"Those claw marks were on the *backs* of the trees, Zach. Why'd that be? If it really wanted to scare us, that bear would've marked those trees so we'd see them plain. As it was, the only way we found them was because I had to go make sure I was still a woman. Even then, we had to go looking for the rest. Don't you see? That bear clawed the trees that way not so *we'd* see we was marked, but so the bad things would—so they'd know the bear was protecting us."

"He still hurt Sam."

Allie turned to check on her dog. Sam lay curled in a ball, his eyes barely open but staring at the backpack. "I guess he had to do whatever he needed to keep us going the wrong way." She fell quiet. "I thought he was God, but he was just my compass."

Zach kept his eyes on that water, watching as it flowed down past them. Thankfulness flooded his heart, along with a sadness so deep it could not even draw tears. "I think it's the same thing."

The sight beyond the bridge was as familiar as slipping into old clothes and as alien as any world could be. The glow of downtown lights nearly blinded them after so many dark nights in the wilderness, but what caught Allie's eye was the dome of light oozing up from between the buildings. As they neared the corner, the sound of singing rose into the night. Trucks and cars were parked in a wide circle around the town square, their headlights gleaming against the broken shapes of a crowd unlike any she had ever seen in Mattingly, not even for Carnival Day. Hundreds of them, maybe thousands, all clustered around the town tree. Raising their voices in praise and grief not as many, but as one.

Among them were Marshall Granderson and Grace Howard, as well as Jake and Kate Barnett. The four of them had formed the center of that night's vigil. Gathered around them in a tight circle that kept away the dark and the cold were friends and neighbors both current and forgotten, all but Bobby Barnes, who stood at the window of his shop with a beer in his hand and tears on his cheeks, whispering those old carols to himself. The trembling that had overtaken Marshall's body was not made better by all that good Christian charity, though it calmed a bit when Grace's hand stroked his back.

As the last verses were sung of neither sins nor sorrow grown and the wonders of His love, the crowd fell to silent prayer. Marshall heard his own whimpers and those of others. He heard Kate's and Jake's, and knew their sorrow as his own. He heard the wind as it rustled the wooden crosses on the tree and a steady clacking along the road beyond.

He and Grace looked up at that last sound, unsure what it was. What Marshall beheld seemed more miracle than he deserved. There at the corner of Main Street where the new town hall had been built came the figures of a boy and girl bearing a load behind them. And though Marshall felt far too much fear to believe, he stepped away from Grace and called into the darkness.

"Allie?"

The gathered turned, their prayers suspended. The children had just passed beneath the first street lamp. The girl's head looked up as they passed back into the faint shadow, struggling on closer for the square. Marshall called out her name again. This time, even in the darkness, he saw the girl lift her hand.

Marshall ran. He ran as he had never run before, not even when news of The Storm had reached him at work some five hundred and forty-eight days before. He ran such that his legs felt free of the ground altogether, making him float the rest of the way. He felt Grace running beside him and reached out for her hand. The others chased after them. Jake and Kate called for their boy, asking if it was really him.

There was nothing left in Allie but to smile. She labored on as Zach labored for them both, their eyes filled with the sight of home. Unspoken between them was the sudden knowledge of what they'd just done and how much they'd given in their search. Every ache in Allie's body flamed and burned, just as Zach felt in each step the thick weariness of all the steps that had come before it, and they both understood that it all could not have happened another way. Allie did not use what small breath she had left to call out for her father, who was now so close that she could see the love mixed with horror in his eyes. She looked to Zach instead, all muddied with blotches of dirt and filth that looked like liver spots. They'd gone old in the woods, and yet in the seconds it took for Marshall and Jake to reach them, Allie realized the town would still see them as the boy and girl who'd gone lost and not the man and woman who'd gotten themselves found. If that was the case, there was something she needed to say now, before it was too late.

"You're very brave, Zach Barnett."

He smiled. "So are you, Allie Granderson."

Marshall reached them first. He swept Allie into his arms and squeezed her, mourning the sunken look in her eyes and every rib poking out of her shriveled frame. He covered her dirty face and shambled hair with his kisses and then did the same with Zach. Grace wrapped her arms around father and daughter, pressing them into one another as though molding not a memory, but a bridge to span what had been broken and what was now healed. The sheriff and his wife followed. Kate could not speak through her tears. All she could manage was an unbroken melody of "I love you" to Zach sung over and over. She covered her son, holding him tight. Allie watched as Zach's momma looked far into the sky, past the moon and stars, to the very place where Allie had offered her thank-you hours before. The crowd rushed over them with tears of their own, washing them with cries of shock and praises to Jesus.

No one noticed what lay upon the travois. None would have were it not for Sam's tired bark. Grace was first to kneel by the dog. She patted Sam's head and turned the scarf around him over, revealing a wide wound that made someone scream. Grace then lifted Allie's knapsack, revealing what lay beneath.

A silence fell over the crowd. To Allie, it was as if they had all turned their backs and walked on, leaving only her and her father. Marshall looked at the bones as a paleness swept over his face. Allie told herself she would not cry, not there in the midst of all that happiness. She instead kept her voice even as the tears flowed down her cheeks. She held out her hand and opened it, showing the cross inside.

"We found her, Daddy," Allie said. "We brought Momma home."

Epilogue

It took weeks for the Commonwealth of Virginia to declare what the people of Mattingly had known all along. The bones Allie and Zach had found far in the wilderness of Happy Hollow were those of Mary Louise Granderson, missing and presumed dead since The Storm of 2012. Authorities were puzzled at how even such a powerful tornado could deposit her remains so many miles from town. Allie accepted their doubts with a shrug. She had come to think most anything was possible. All a body had to do was believe enough.

That the identification took so long was just as well. Allie and Zach spent that Christmas and New Year's as guests of the Stanley hospital, where a team of doctors, nurses, and motherly townsfolk tended their wounds. Both of them had suffered varying degrees of dehydration and hypothermia. Allie's injuries—the physical ones, at any rate—reached no deeper than one sprained ankle, two frostbitten feet, and enough pulled muscles that the doctors joked her body was basically a piece of taffy. More cuts and bruises than anyone could count littered her hands and face. It took a week's worth of hot showers to free her from a grime so concentrated it had formed a second skin. Her woman problem was gone, however, at least for the next thirty days. Based on that alone, Allie thought she'd gotten off easy.

Zach's injuries—the physical ones, at any rate—were far

worse. The cut on his head had begun to heal before they'd reached town, making stitches impossible. He would wear a jagged scar above his brow for the rest of his life. The blow itself had resulted in a severe concussion. Doctors expressed astonishment that he'd woken at all. Zach told them he was a Barnett. To him, no further explanation was necessary. The cold he'd left town with had bloomed into pneumonia. Those same doctors wanted him moved to a private room. Zach refused. Even there, far from the bear and the woods, he would not leave Allie's side. A man's only as good as how he backs up what he says, after all.

Allie honored that sentiment by refusing to leave the hospital until Zach could go home as well. By then, the nurses had begun whispering that a rental truck would have to be brought in to haul away all the gifts—stuffed animals and balloons and flowers and enough cowboy hats to last Zach until the Rapture. Get well cards from townsfolk and teachers and classmates were piled on the small tables by their beds. Even Lisa Ann Campbell and Touchdown Tommy Robertson made contributions. One stuffed animal in particular had become Allie's favorite. The large, brown teddy bear with two dark, glassy eyes had come holding a card with only her name on the front. The inside had gone unsigned. Allie had no way of knowing for sure, but the smell of oil and the smudge of grease on the envelope made her believe it had come from Bobby Barnes.

Among the townspeople who had greeted the children's return that Christmas Eve night was Mattingly's doctor, who had seen enough in his long years not to be surprised at all that a boy and girl could survive in such hostile conditions. Doc March was the one who had scooped up the unmoving ball of fur from the travois as Allie and Zach were rushed away. While everyone else celebrated, he carried his patient to his office and did what he could. Some would say the human anatomy is far different from that of an animal. Doc March would say that is true enough, though many of the parts are the same.

With the help of a veterinarian from the nearby city of Camden, Samwise the Dog was waiting when Marshall and Grace brought Allie home. He'd been fixed with a chew guard that left him looking like a furry radar dish. Doc warned Allie that her dog would always walk with a limp. Allie didn't mind; all three of them had left something of themselves in the Hollow. Sam licked her face for most of that day and all the days after. Allie spent much of that time telling her dog how much spine he had and how she loved him in his brokenness.

Jake delivered the news that Mary's remains had been returned. He and Marshall stood on the Grandersons' front porch a long while that day. Much was shared between them. Had Zach been there, he would have discovered grown males can indeed cry and still be called men. They parted with a vow to mend what had been torn between them.

The funeral was held that Friday. Mary's grave was re-dug, the casket containing the pink tennis shoe removed. Resting atop two chromed rails and a rug of artificial grass was a smaller casket of bones. It was a sad moment, as all burials are. It was also a hopeful one, as all burials should be.

Allie scanned the gathered for Zach. She couldn't see him but felt his hand rest upon her shoulder. She heard him whisper in her ear, "You never turned 'round in your dream, did you?" Through her tears, Allie shook her head and smiled. No, she'd never turned around in her dream at all. That's why she'd never seen Zach. He'd been too close the whole time.

Marshall donned his best suit for the ceremony. He'd placed his daughter between himself and Grace that whole day, too weary to battle the guilt and warmth he felt for Allie's teacher.

Grace wiped her eyes as the last song was sung through sniffles and tears. Allie slipped a hand into hers.

The next day—Saturday this was, one so cold that Allie's toes itched as though remembering—she asked Marshall to drive her and Sam to town. They parked near the square and walked to the sheriff's office, where Jake and Kate had coffee waiting. Talk was pleasant and warm. Marshall even laughed. Allie thought there would be more of that now, and for the both of them. She thought something always begins when everything else ends, and often what begins is better.

She found Zach out back, sitting on a bench with his daddy's old tomahawk in his hand. Beside him rested the same dinosaur book he'd been trying to impress Miss Grace with back in school. He patted the empty part of the bench seat like an old man welcoming his old wife. Allie sat and placed Sam in his lap.

"Need to show you something," he said. "You can't freak out, though."

"Okay."

He picked up the book (*Walking with Prehistoric Animals* read the cover) and settled it on his lap, then settled on one dog-eared page.

One look at the picture convinced Allie it was a good thing she had agreed not to freak out. Had Zach not warned her, she would have screamed loud enough to send the whole town running to the back of the sheriff's office. The artist hadn't gotten everything right—he'd been good, but not as good as whoever had made her Nativity—but it was close enough for Allie to both smile and mourn. The beast in the picture was on its hind legs. Beside it was a rendering of an adult man. Drawn, Allie believed, for the sole purpose of communicating just how huge the animal was. The man barely reached the bear's midsection. Allie thought that right.

It was the same short snout, the same ears. The same massive shoulders and long horse legs, even the same patch of white on the belly. The only thing missing were the red-and-white eyes.

"*Arctodus simus*," Zach told her, and with a confidence that convinced Allie he'd been practicing saying that all morning. "It's a giant short-faced bear. Used to be all over the country. Grew up to thirteen feet long, ran almost forty miles an hour, and could weigh a ton."

Allie read the words as Zach spoke them, trying to follow along.

"They died out over ten thousand years ago, Allie," he whispered. "Ain't supposed to be here no more."

"Guess there's one left."

"How?"

Allie shrugged. "I don't know, Zach. Maybe whatever light came through its eyes kept it going all this while."

Zach closed the book. Allie petted her dog. On the other side of the door, she heard her daddy laugh again. It sounded good, hearing that. It sounded fine.

"I gotta go do something," she said. "Won't take long."

"I'll come."

"No, I'll be okay. You stay here with Sam."

"You sure?" he asked.

Allie nodded.

Sam whined as she went. Allie took the narrow path between the sheriff's office and the hardware store, pausing before stepping onto the sidewalk. To say she and Zach had become celebrities in the past weeks would be like saying The Storm had been a quick shower. Allie herself was convinced sooner or later someone would get the idea of bronzing Sam's likeness and erecting it right beside Mr. Barney Moore's, marking the beginning of some sad Mattingly Hall of Fame. She appreciated the attention (and in fact enjoyed it), but that morning she wanted time alone. Downtown was busy, the air clear and buoyant with calls of hello and good morning. It seemed to Allie the true beginning of New Mattingly. That wasn't so bad. It felt so much like the old.

She dodged cars and trucks as she crossed the street. Head down, hands shoved into coat pockets. Allie remained that way until she met the shadow of the town tree, still decorated for Christmas. From her pocket she pulled a simple wooden cross. MARY GRANDERSON was carved along the crossbar. A piece of the scarf that had accompanied them through the woods had been threaded through a small hole in the top. Allie looped the string around an empty branch in the tree's center. Her eyes stung as she stepped back.

A God with sharp edges still troubled her, and yet Allie knew her mother had died believing that very thing. Had maybe even spent her last moments reaching for Him as she fell from that green-black sky. Allie believed God had caught Mary Granderson at the very end, or at least the part of Mary Granderson that mattered most. The eternal part. Of that, Allie had no doubt. Nor did she doubt that what had fallen away in her own heart could be gathered up again.

"I love you, Momma." She felt for the gold cross around her neck. "I'll find you again someday. I promise. Daddy'll find you too. You don't have to send word. We know where you are."

Marshall found her sometime later. The two of them stood arm in arm, staring at that small cross. Many in town paused in their coming and going to look. They smiled as their hearts broke and knew that mix of joy and sadness was perhaps the purest thing a person can feel. They let the Grandersons be. There is a great amount of healing that can come from others, but much of it can come only from yourself—and only when allowed.

They turned back for the sheriff's office when Marshall said he needed to leave for Stanley soon. It was the one thing Allie would let take them from that spot. Womanhood was teaching her many new things, and among these was that a person could never stop learning so long as he didn't want to. Grown-ups had schooling for near anything imaginable, including how not to drink. Marshall made the drive from Mattingly to Stanley three nights a week to study just that very thing. Though he often returned red-eyed and sobbing, he told Allie it was the best thing he'd ever done. Often on those nights, Grace Howard would come by and sit with Allie. Miss Grace would often get red-eyed as well. Allie understood.

Sam sat on her lap as Marshall drove them home. Allie rolled the window down despite the chill, letting her dog sniff the air. The wind swirled in Sam's collar, making a whumping sound that reminded Allie of helicopter blades. She shuddered both at the memory and the feel of hard winter blowing through her hair. Marshall flipped the switch on the truck's dash, turning the heat higher. He did not tell Allie to roll the window up before she caught cold, did not ask what she was thinking. Marshall knew. In the weeks since everything had ended and everything else had begun, he had come to believe once more that life could be a wondrous thing. There was pain in it, yes, and often more hurt than one could ever endure on his own. But there was a hidden beauty to it as well, one that ran like a river through the brambles and snares and dark places, and to keep to those smooth banks and follow that current wherever it led was enough to keep him going—to keep him found and never fallen away. Love would carry them through.

It was such moments that Marshall Granderson longed for, now and always. Tiny bits of time like this one with his daughter, driving home after a trip to town so Allie could say something that felt more like See You Again than Good-bye, stealing glances to marvel at how the sunlight painted the contours of her face to an angel's glow. It was a good ride that day. Marshall counted it among the three best ever, behind only the drive from church after his wedding and the drive home with his new baby girl.

They met the neighborhood and their street. Sam woofed and wagged as Marshall waved back to those brave enough to dare the frigid January day. He pulled into the driveway and slipped the gear into park. The truck shuddered and wheezed before settling into a silence like death.

They both sat quiet, knowing that sometimes there is so much to be said and shared that silence becomes the only proper thing. Allie stroked Sam's neck and studied the scabs on her fingers and hand. She felt her father's gaze and turned her head to him. Marshall met her with a smile.

"Know what I'd like right now just about more than anything in the world?" he asked.

"What's that?"

"Some of your special mac and cheese."

"Hot dogs?"

"You know it."

Allie grinned back at him. "It'll be a masterpiece."

They took the steps up the porch with a slow ease. Allie still favored her ankle and leaned on her father's shoulder to help her along. Marshall held himself strong and smiled once more. He kissed the side of his daughter's head where a pigtail once was, blinking his eyes as he did. There were times when it still hurt, looking at Allie only to find Mary looking back. It hurt more to deny himself that dark curtain to draw down over his pain. And yet, as they reached the door, Marshall gazed at her nonetheless, and with a pride that humbled him. Allie had taught him much in the weeks since she'd returned, both in the bits of story she shared and the long silences in between. She and Zach had walked through the darkness and found light at the end. Marshall would do the same. He would walk and not stumble. Baby steps, soft and sure, just as they'd climbed onto the porch. Only time can repair the heart. Only time and love.

He went to his bedroom to put away his coat and boots (leaving the door open as he did; he hadn't shut himself away in his room once since Allie had come home) while Allie carried Sam to hers. Girl and dog sat side by side in the center of a warm square of sunlight on the bed. Sam pressed his nose against the window. Allie leaned her cheek against the right side of the pane. In the distance, blue mountains climbed and fell in a gentle line that reminded her of a beating heart. Somewhere in that lost land, a bear so ancient it had no business living in this world curled to sleep in a cave that had once sheltered two children and a dog.

Allie slid the side of her fist over the glass, wiping the fog left by her breath. Sam nuzzled against her. A smile worked its way to her lips—not full, but there just the same. Two plastic figures remained in the front yard. The babe lay in profile atop a bed of painted straw. Only a shock of false hair and the faint ridge of his nose could be seen. The father's back was to the window. Both of his arms disappeared at the elbows, bent so his hands could join on bended knee. His right shoulder slouched a bit, mimicking the dip of his head. Two effigies pondering their blessings, one looking down in thanks, the other staring up in hope. Allie could not see their faces from where she sat, but she wanted to believe they would remain that way forever. She wanted to believe they were smiling.

Reading Group Guide

1. Much of *In the Heart of the Dark Wood* revolves around the search for a lasting happiness to sustain us in life. Allie in particular is intent upon leaving all the hurt she's felt behind in the hope of embracing a future without emotional pain. And yet the book makes the point that "a life with pain means more than a life without it." Do you agree? What do you think this means?
2. What do you think Allie meant when she told Zach, "Believing's not something you do, it's something you are"?
3. The struggle between doubt and faith is an important one in the book, especially with Allie. She's known as someone who's "fallen away" from her faith in God, a fact with which she readily agrees. And yet in many ways, she displays more faith than Zach through the darkwood. Do you agree with her notion that "people who get fallen away" can still believe? In what was Allie's faith placed?
4. What changes did Zach undergo to lead him from the beginning of the story, where he thinks it's his job to protect Allie in the wild, to him carving both his name and hers onto the gate at the end?
5. Do you fault Marshall for his feelings toward Grace?
6. Have you ever felt God's "sharp edges"? Did it lead you away from God or toward Him?
7. Allie's view of God is inextricably linked to the tragedy that befell her town in general and her mother in particular, so much so that she sees Him at the beginning as "like the moon, just sitting up there in the sky, watching all that's going on." The disadvantages of this way of believing might be obvious, but are there also advantages to believing this?
8. How is Allie's compass a metaphor for the faith we are all called to have?

Acknowledgments

It feels a little strange that I first said hello to Allie, Zach, and Samwise the Dog while mired in the deep winter of the Virginia mountains, and I say good-bye while overlooking the Atlantic on a hot June morning half a year later. Truth be told, I still think about them. I think about them a lot. If I've done my job right, you'll be thinking about them for a while too.

This story couldn't have been written without the help of a talented group of people I've been honored to be a part of. Amanda Bostic and LB Norton are the finest editors a writer could have. Kathy Richards provided her usual welcomed guidance, as did my agent, Rachelle Gardner. Jodi Hughes did a masterful job of putting the manuscript to print. And thank you, Elizabeth Hudson, for the daily chore of getting a bumpkin like me out into the world.

My most heartfelt thanks goes out to you, Dear Readers—for your dedication and your passion, for your e-mails and letters. I'm often asked what will happen next to that little town in Virginia, or what ever happened to Leah Norcross and her Rainbow Man, or what is it about the Hole in Happy Hollow. Honestly? I have no idea. Here's a secret you might not know: the characters a writer sifts out from the sludge of his or her mind aren't characters at all. They're as real as anyone else, built of the same flesh and bone. They might not inhabit our own world, but they are surely part of a world just past our vision. Just next door. Somewhere out there, Allie Granderson and Zach Barnett are continuing on as best they can. Sam is a bit gimpy but otherwise no worse for the wear. The town of Mattingly still stands. The bear of the darkwood still keeps watch. And somewhere close, you can bet something is lurking. Something dark. And somewhere in all that darkness, you can bet there shines a light. There's always a light, isn't there? I think so. Let's go find it together, shall we?

Emerald Isle, North Carolina
June 2014

About the Author

Photograph by Joanne Coffey

Billy Coffey's critically acclaimed books combine rural Southern charm with a vision far beyond the ordinary. He is a regular contributor to several publications, where he writes about faith and life. Billy lives with his wife and two children in Virginia's Blue Ridge Mountains. Visit him at www.billycoffey.com.